Tempt Me
at Twilight

St. Martin's Paperbacks Titles by
LISA KLEYPAS

Tempt Me at Twilight

Seduce Me at Sunrise

Mine Till Midnight

Blue-Eyed Devil

Sugar Daddy

Tempt Me at Twilight

LISA KLEYPAS

St. Martin's Paperbacks

This is a work of fiction. All of the characters, organizations and events portrayed in this novel are either products of the author's imagination or are used fictitiously.

TEMPT ME AT TWILIGHT

Copyright © 2009 by Lisa Kleypas.

For information address St. Martin's Press, 175 Fifth Avenue, New York, NY 10010.

ISBN: 978-1-61523-478-3

Printed in the United States of America

St. Martin's Paperbacks are published by St. Martin's Press, 175 Fifth Avenue, New York, NY 10010.

To Teresa Medeiros—
In the road of life, you steer me past the detours, potholes, and red lights.

The world is a better place because you're in it.

Love always,

L.K.

Chapter One

LONDON

The Rutledge Hotel
May 1852

Her chances of a decent marriage were about to be dashed—and all because of a ferret.

Unfortunately Poppy Hathaway had pursued Dodger halfway through the Rutledge Hotel before she recalled an important fact: to a ferret, a straight line included six zigs and seven zags.

"Dodger," Poppy said desperately. "Come back. I'll give you a biscuit, any of my hair ribbons, *anything!* Oh, I'm going to make a *scarf* out of you . . ."

As soon as she caught her sister's pet, Poppy swore she was going to alert the management of the Rutledge that Beatrix was harboring wild creatures in their family suite, which was definitely against hotel policy. Of course, that might cause the entire Hathaway clan to be forcibly removed from the premises.

At the moment, Poppy didn't care.

Dodger had stolen a love letter that had been sent to her from Michael Bayning, and nothing in the world mattered except retrieving it. All the situation needed was for Dodger to hide the blasted thing in some public place where it would be discovered.

And then Poppy's chances of marrying a respectable and perfectly wonderful young man would be forever lost.

Dodger hurried through the luxurious hallways of the Rutledge Hotel in a sinuous lope, staying just out of reach. The letter was clamped in his long front teeth.

As she dashed after him, Poppy prayed that she would not be seen. No matter how reputable the hotel, a respectable young woman should never have left her suite unescorted. However, Miss Marks, her companion, was still abed. And Beatrix had gone for an early morning ride with their sister, Amelia.

"You're going to pay for this, Dodger!"

The mischievous creature thought everything in the world was for his own amusement. No basket or container could go without being overturned or investigated, no stocking or comb or handkerchief could be left alone. Dodger stole personal items and left them in heaps beneath chairs and sofas, and he took naps in drawers of clean clothes, and worst of all, he was so entertaining in his naughtiness that the entire Hathaway family was inclined to overlook his behavior.

Whenever Poppy objected to the ferret's outrageous antics, Beatrix was always apologetic and promised that Dodger would never do it again, and she seemed genuinely surprised when Dodger didn't heed her earnest lectures. And because Poppy loved her younger sister, she had tried to endure living with the obnoxious pet.

This time, however, Dodger had gone too far.

The ferret paused at a corner, checked to make certain he was still being chased, and in his happy excitement, he did a little war dance, a series of sideways hops that expressed pure delight. Even now, when Poppy wanted to murder him, she couldn't help but acknowledge that he was adorable. "You're still going to die," she told him, approaching him in as unthreatening a manner as possible. "Give me the letter, Dodger."

The ferret streaked past a colonnaded lightwell that admitted sunshine from overhead and sent it down three floors to the mezzanine level. Grimly, Poppy wondered how far she was going to have to chase him. He could cover quite a lot of territory, and the Rutledge was massive, occupying five full blocks in the theater district.

"This," she muttered beneath her breath, "is what happens when you're a Hathaway. Misadventures . . . wild animals . . . house fires . . . curses . . . scandals . . ."

Poppy loved her family dearly, but she longed for the kind of quiet, normal life that didn't seem possible for a Hathaway. She wanted peace. Predictability.

Dodger ran through the doorway of the third-floor steward's offices, which belonged to Mr. Brimbley. The steward was an elderly man with a full white mustache, the ends neatly waxed into points. As the Hathaways had stayed at the Rutledge many times in the past, Poppy knew that Brimbley reported every detail of what occurred on his floor to his superiors. If the steward found out what she was after, the letter would be confiscated, and Poppy's relationship with Michael would be exposed. And Michael's father, Lord Andover, would never approve of the match if there were even one whiff of impropriety attached to it.

Poppy caught her breath and backed up against the wall as Brimbley exited his offices with two of the Rutledge staff. ". . . go to the front office at once, Harkins," the steward was saying. "I want you to investigate the matter of Mr. W's room charges. He has a history of claiming that charges are incorrect when they are, in fact, accurate. From now on, I think it best to have him sign a receipt whenever a charge is made."

"Yes, Mr. Brimbley." The three men proceeded along the hallway, away from Poppy.

Cautiously, she crept to the doorway of the offices and peeked around the jamb. The two connected rooms appeared to be unoccupied. *"Dodger,"* she whispered urgently, and saw him scurry beneath a chair. "Dodger, do come here!"

Which, of course, produced more excited hopping and dancing.

Biting her lower lip, Poppy went across the threshold. The main office room was generously sized, furnished with a massive desk piled high with ledgers and papers. An armchair upholstered in burgundy leather had been pushed up against the desk, while another was positioned near an empty fireplace with a marble mantel.

Dodger waited beside the desk, regarding Poppy with bright eyes. His whiskers twitched above the coveted letter. He held very still, holding Poppy's gaze as she inched toward him.

"That's right," she soothed, extending her hand slowly. "What a good boy, a lovely boy . . . wait right there, and I'll take the letter and carry you back to our suite, and give you—*Drat!*"

Just before she could grasp the letter, Dodger had slithered beneath the desk with it.

Red with fury, Poppy glanced around the room in search of something, *anything,* she could use to poke

Dodger from his hiding place. Spying a candlestick in a silver holder on the mantel, she tried to pull it down. But the candle wouldn't budge. The silver holder had been affixed to the mantel.

Before Poppy's astonished eyes, the entire back of the fireplace rotated noiselessly. She gasped at the mechanical wizardry of the door as it revolved with a smooth automated motion. What had appeared to be solid brick was nothing but a textured façade.

Gleefully, Dodger darted from the desk and went through the opening.

"Bother," Poppy said breathlessly. "Dodger, don't you dare!"

But the ferret paid no heed. And to make matters worse, she could hear the rumble of Mr. Brimbley's voice as he returned to the room. ". . . of course Mr. Rutledge must be informed. Put it in the report. And by all means don't forget—"

With no time to consider her options or the consequences, Poppy dashed through the fireplace, and the door closed behind her.

She was engulfed in near darkness as she waited, straining to hear what was happening inside the office. Apparently she had not been detected. Mr. Brimbley continued his conversation, something about reports and housekeeping concerns.

It occurred to Poppy that she might have to wait for a long time before the steward left the office again. Or she would have to find another way out. Of course, she could simply go back through the fireplace and announce her presence to Mr. Brimbley. However, she couldn't begin to imagine how much explaining she would have to do, and how embarrassing it would be.

Turning, Poppy discerned that she was in a long

passageway, with a source of diffused light coming from somewhere overhead. She looked upward. The passage was illuminated by a daylight shaft, similar to the ones that ancient Egyptians had used to determine the positioning of stars and planets.

She could hear the ferret creeping somewhere nearby. "Well, Dodger," she muttered, "you got us into this. Why don't you help me find a door?"

Obligingly Dodger advanced along the passageway and disappeared into the shadows. Poppy heaved a sigh and followed. She refused to panic, having learned during the Hathaways' many brushes with calamity that losing one's head never helped a situation.

As Poppy made her way through the darkness, she kept her fingertips against the wall to maintain her bearings. She had gone only a few yards when she heard a scraping noise. Freezing in place, Poppy waited and listened intently.

All was quiet.

But her nerves prickled with awareness and her heart began to drum as she saw the glow of yellow lamplight ahead. And then it was extinguished.

She was not alone in the passageway.

The footsteps came closer, closer, with the swift purpose of a predator. Someone was heading right for her.

Now, Poppy decided, was the appropriate time to panic. Whirling around in full-scale alarm, she dashed back the way she had come. Being chased by unknown people in dark corridors was a novel experience even for a Hathaway. She cursed her heavy skirts, grabbing them up in frantic handfuls as she tried to run. But the person who chased her was much too fast to be eluded.

A cry escaped her as she was caught up in a brutal, expert grip. It was a man—a large one—and he seized her in a way that arched her back against his chest. One of his hands pressed her head sharply to the side.

"You should know," came a low, chilling voice close to her ear, "that with just a bit more pressure than this, I could snap your neck. Tell me your name, and what you're doing in here."

Chapter Two

Poppy could scarcely think above the blood rushing in her ears and the pain of his tight grasp. The stranger's chest was very hard behind her. "This is a mistake," she managed to say. "Please—"

He forced her head farther to the side until she felt a cruel pinch of the nerves in the joint between her neck and shoulder. "Your name," he insisted gently.

"Poppy Hathaway," she gasped. "I'm so sorry. I didn't mean to—"

"Poppy?" His hold loosened.

"Yes." Why had he said her name as if he knew her? "Are you . . . you must be one of the hotel staff?"

He ignored the question. One of his hands coasted lightly over her arms and her front as if he were searching for something. Her heart threshed like the wing beats of a small bird.

"Don't," she gasped between fragmented breaths, arching away from his touch.

"Why are you in here?" He turned her to face

him. No one of Poppy's acquaintance had ever handled her so familiarly. They were close enough to the overhead lightwell that Poppy could see the outline of hard, lean features and the glitter of deep-set eyes.

Fighting to catch her breath, Poppy winced at the sharp ache in her neck. She reached for it and tried to soothe the pain as she spoke. "I was . . . I was chasing a ferret, and the fireplace in Mr. Brimbley's office opened, and we went through it and then I tried to find another way out."

Nonsensical as the explanation was, the stranger sorted through it efficiently. "A ferret? One of your sister's pets?"

"Yes," she said, bewildered. She rubbed her neck and winced. "But how did you know . . . have we met before? No, please don't touch me, I . . . *ouch!*"

He had turned her around and had put his hand on the side of her neck. "Be still." His touch was deft and sure as he massaged the tender nerve. "If you try to run from me, I'll only catch you again."

Quivering, Poppy endured his kneading, probing fingers and wondered if she were at the mercy of a madman. He pressed harder, exacting a sensation that was neither pleasure nor pain but some unfamiliar mingling of the two. She made a sound of distress, writhing helplessly. To her surprise, the burn of the pinched nerve eased, and her rigid muscles went lax with relief. She went still and let out a long breath, her head dropping.

"Better?" he asked, using both hands now, his thumbs stroking the back of her neck, slipping beneath the soft lace that trimmed the high-throated bodice of her dress.

Thoroughly unnerved, Poppy tried to step away from him, but his hands clamped on her shoulders instantly. She cleared her throat and attempted a dignified tone. "Sir, I—I should like you to guide me out of here. My family will reward you. No questions will be—"

"Of course." He released her slowly. "No one ever uses this passageway without my permission. I assumed that anyone in here was up to no good."

The comments bore a resemblance to an apology, although his tone wasn't regretful in the least.

"I assure you, I had no intention of doing anything other than retrieving this atrocious animal." She felt Dodger rustling near the hem of her skirts.

The stranger bent and scooped up the ferret. Holding Dodger by the scruff of his neck, he handed him to Poppy.

"Thank you." The ferret's supple body went limp and compliant in Poppy's grasp. As she might have expected, the letter was gone. "Dodger, you blasted thief—where is it? What have you done with it?"

"What are you looking for?"

"A letter," Poppy said tensely. "Dodger stole it and carried it in here . . . it must be somewhere nearby."

"It will be found later."

"But it's important."

"Obviously, if you've gone to such trouble to recover it. Come with me."

Reluctantly Poppy murmured her assent and allowed him to take her elbow. "Where are we going?"

There was no reply.

"I would prefer that no one knew about this," Poppy ventured.

"I'm sure you would."

"May I rely on your discretion, sir? I must avoid scandal at all costs."

"Young women who wish to avoid scandal should probably stay in their hotel suites," he pointed out unhelpfully.

"I was perfectly content to stay in my room," Poppy protested. "It was only because of Dodger that I had to leave. I must have my letter back. And I'm certain my family will compensate you for your trouble, if you would—"

"Quiet."

He found his way through the shadow-tricked passageway with no difficulty at all, his grip on Poppy's elbow gentle but inexorable. They did not go toward Mr. Brimbley's office but instead went the opposite direction, for what seemed an interminable distance.

Finally the stranger stopped and turned to a place in the wall, and pushed a door open. "Go in."

Hesitantly Poppy preceded him into a well-lit room, a sort of parlor, with a row of Palladian windows overlooking the street. A heavy oak drafting table occupied one side of the room, and bookshelves lined nearly every inch of wall space. There was a pleasant and oddly familiar mixture of scents in the air—candle wax and vellum and ink and book dust—it smelled like her father's old study.

Poppy turned toward the stranger, who had come into the room and closed the concealed door.

It was difficult to ascertain his age—he appeared to be on the early side of his thirties, but there was an air of hard-bitten worldliness about him, a sense that he had seen enough of life to cease being surprised by anything. He had heavy, well-cut hair, black as midnight, and a fair complexion in which his dark brows stood out in striking contrast. And he was as handsome as Lucifer, his brows strong, the nose straight and defined, the mouth brooding. The angle of his jaw was sharp, tenacious, anchoring the grave features of a man who perhaps took everything— including himself—a bit too seriously.

Poppy felt herself flush as she stared into a pair of remarkable eyes . . . intense cool green with dark rims, shadowed by bristly black lashes. His gaze seemed to take her in, consuming every detail. She noticed faint shadows beneath his eyes, but they did nothing to impair his hard-faced good looks.

A gentleman would have uttered some pleasantry, something reassuring, but the stranger remained silent.

Why did he stare at her like that? Who was he, and what authority did he wield in this place?

She had to say something, anything, to break the tension. "The smell of books and candle wax," she remarked inanely, ". . . it reminds me of my father's study."

The man stepped toward her, and Poppy shrank back reflexively. They both went still. It seemed that questions filled the air between them as if they had been written in invisible ink.

"Your father passed away some time ago, I believe." His voice matched the rest of him, polished, dark, inflexible. He had an interesting accent, not fully British, the vowels flat and open, the *r*'s heavy.

Poppy gave a bewildered nod.

"And your mother soon after," he added.

"How . . . how do you know that?"

"It's my business to know as much about the hotel guests as possible."

Dodger wriggled in her grasp. Poppy bent to set him down. The ferret pranced to an oversized chair near a small hearth, and settled deep into the velvet upholstery.

Poppy brought herself to look at the stranger again. He was dressed in beautiful dark clothes, tailored with sophisticated looseness. Fine garments, but he wore a simple black cravat with no pins, and there were no gold buttons on his shirt, or any other ornamentation that would proclaim him as a gentleman of means. Only a plain watch chain at the front of his gray waistcoat.

"You sound like an American," she said.

"Buffalo, New York," he replied. "But I've lived here for a while."

"Are you employed by Mr. Rutledge?" she asked cautiously.

A single nod was her answer.

"You are one of his managers, I suppose?"

His face was inscrutable. "Something like that."

She began to inch toward the door. "Then I will leave you to your labors, Mister . . ."

"You'll need a proper companion to walk back with you."

Poppy considered that. Should she ask him to send for her companion? No . . . Miss Marks was probably still sleeping. It had been a difficult night for her. Miss Marks was sometimes prone to nightmares that left her shaky and exhausted the next day. It didn't happen often, but when it did, Poppy and Beatrix tried to let her rest as much as possible afterward.

The stranger contemplated her for a moment. "Shall I send for a housemaid to accompany you?"

Poppy's first inclination was to agree. But she didn't want to wait here with him, even for a few minutes. She didn't trust him in the least.

As he saw her indecision, his mouth twisted sardonically. "If I were going to molest you," he pointed out, "I would have done so by now."

Her flush deepened at his bluntness. "So you say. But for all I know, you could be a very *slow* molester."

He looked away for a moment, and when he glanced back at her, his eyes were bright with amusement. "You're safe, Miss Hathaway." His voice was rich with unspent laughter. "Really. Let me send for a maid."

The glow of humor changed his face, imparting such warmth and charm that Poppy was almost startled. She felt her heart begin to pump some new and agreeable feeling through her body.

As she watched him go to the bellpull, Poppy recalled the problem of the missing letter. "Sir, while we wait, would you be so kind as to look for the letter that was lost in the passageway? I must have it back."

"Why?" he asked, returning to her.

"Personal reasons," Poppy said shortly.

"Is it from a man?"

She did her best to deliver the kind of withering glance she had seen Miss Marks give to importunate gentlemen. "That is none of your concern."

"Everything that occurs in this hotel is my concern." He paused, studying her. "It is from a man, or you would have said otherwise."

Frowning, Poppy turned her back to him. She

went to look more closely at one of the many shelves lined with peculiar objects.

She discovered a gilded, enameled samovar, a large knife in a beaded sheath, collections of primitive stone carvings and pottery vessels, an Egyptian headrest, exotic coins, boxes made of every conceivable material, what looked like an iron sword with a rusted blade, and a Venetian glass reading stone.

"What room is this?" Poppy couldn't help asking.

"Mr. Rutledge's curiosities room. He collected many of the objects, others are gifts from foreign visitors. Have a look if you like."

Poppy was intrigued, reflecting on the large contingent of foreigners among the hotel guests, including European royalty, nobility, and members of the *corps diplomatique*. No doubt some unusual gifts had been presented to Mr. Rutledge.

Browsing among the shelves, Poppy paused to examine a jeweled silver figurine of a horse, its hooves extended in mid-gallop. "How lovely."

"A gift from the Crown Prince Yizhu of China," the man behind her said. "A Celestial horse."

Fascinated, Poppy ran a fingertip along the figure's back. "Now the prince has been crowned as the Emperor Xianfeng," she said. "A rather ironic ruling name, isn't it?"

Coming to stand beside her, the stranger glanced at her alertly. "Why do you say that?"

"Because it means 'universal prosperity.' And that is certainly not the case, considering the internal rebellions he is facing."

"I'd say the challenges from Europe are an even greater danger to him, at present."

"Yes," Poppy said ruefully, nudging the figurine

back into place. "One wonders how long Chinese sovereignty can last against such an onslaught."

Her companion was standing close enough that she could detect the scents of pressed linen and shaving soap. He stared at her intently. "I know very few women who are able to discuss Far East politics."

She felt color rise in her cheeks. "My family has rather unusual conversations around the supper table. At least, they're unusual in that my sisters and I always take part. My companion says it's perfectly all right to do that at home, but she has advised me not to appear too learned when I'm out in society. It tends to drive away suitors."

"You'll have to be careful, then," he said softly, smiling. "It would be a shame for some intelligent comment to slip out at the wrong moment."

Poppy was relieved when she heard a discreet tap at the door. The maid had come sooner than she had expected. The stranger went to answer. Opening the door a crack, he murmured something to the maid, who bobbed a curtsey and disappeared.

"Where is she going?" Poppy asked, nonplussed. "She was supposed to escort me to my suite."

"I sent her to fetch a tea tray."

Poppy was momentarily speechless. "Sir, I can't have tea with you."

"It won't take long. They'll send it up on one of the food lifts."

"That doesn't matter. Because even if I did have the time, I *can't*! I'm sure you are well aware of how improper it would be."

"Nearly as improper as sneaking through the hotel unescorted," he agreed smoothly, and she scowled.

"I was not sneaking, I was chasing a ferret." Hearing herself make such a ridiculous statement, she felt her color rise. She attempted a dignified tone. "The situation was not at all of my making. And I will be in *very . . . serious . . . trouble . . .* if I am not returned to my room soon. If we wait much longer, you may find yourself involved in a scandal, which I am certain Mr. Rutledge would not approve of."

"True."

"Then please call the maid back."

"Too late. We'll have to wait until she comes with the tea."

Poppy heaved a sigh. "This has been a *most* difficult morning." Glancing at the ferret, she saw bits of fluff and clumps of horsehair being tossed in the air, and she blanched. "*No,* Dodger!"

"What is it?" the man asked, following as Poppy raced toward the busy ferret.

"He's eating your chair," she said miserably, scooping up the ferret. "Or rather, Mr. Rutledge's chair. He's trying to make a nest for himself. I'm so sorry." She stared at the gaping hole in the thick, luxurious velvet upholstery. "I promise you, my family will pay for the damage."

"It's all right," the man said. "There's a monthly allotment in the hotel budget for repairs."

Lowering to her haunches—not an easy feat when one was wearing stay laces and stiffened petticoats—Poppy grabbed bits of fluff and tried to stuff them back into the hole. "If necessary, I will provide a written statement to explain how this happened."

"What about your reputation?" the stranger asked gently, reaching down to pull her to a standing position.

"My reputation is nothing compared to a man's

livelihood. You might be sacked for this. You undoubtedly have a family to support—a wife and children—and whereas I could survive the disgrace, you might not be able to secure a new position."

"That is very kind of you," he said, taking the ferret from Poppy's grasp and depositing him back on the chair. "But I have no family. And I can't be sacked."

"Dodger," Poppy said anxiously, as bits of fluff went flying again. Clearly the ferret was having a grand time.

"The chair is already ruined. Let him have at it."

Poppy was bemused by the stranger's easy consignment of an expensive piece of hotel furniture to a ferret's mischief. "You," she said distinctly, "are not like the other managers here."

"You're not like other young women."

That elicited a wry smile from her. "So I've been told."

The sky had turned the color of pewter. A heavy drizzle fell to the gravel-covered paving blocks of the street, tamping down the pungent dust that had been stirred by passing vehicles.

Taking care not to be seen from the street, Poppy went to the side of one window and watched pedestrians scatter. Some methodically unfolded umbrellas and continued walking.

Costermongers crowded the thoroughfare, hawking their wares with impatient cries. They sold everything imaginable: ropes of onions and braces of dead game, teapots, flowers, matches, and caged larks and nightingales. This last presented frequent problems to the Hathaways, as Beatrix was determined to rescue every living creature she saw. Many a bird had been reluctantly purchased by their brother-in-law, Mr.

Rohan, and set free at their country estate. Rohan swore that by now he had purchased half the avian population in Hampshire.

Turning from the window, Poppy saw that the stranger had settled his shoulder against one of the bookshelves and folded his arms across his chest. He was watching her as if puzzling what to make of her. Despite his relaxed posture, Poppy had the unnerving sense that if she tried to bolt, he would catch her in an instant.

"Why aren't you betrothed to anyone?" he asked with startling directness. "You've been out in society for two, three years?"

"Three," Poppy said, feeling more than a little defensive.

"Your family is one of means—one would assume you have a generous dowry on the table. Your brother is a viscount—another advantage. Why haven't you married?"

"Do you always ask such personal questions of people you've just met?" Poppy asked in amazement.

"Not always. But I find you . . . interesting."

She considered the question he had put to her, and shrugged. "I wouldn't want any of the gentlemen I've met during the past three years. None of them are remotely appealing."

"What kind of man appeals to you?"

"Someone with whom I could share a quiet, ordinary life."

"Most young women dream of excitement and romance."

She smiled wryly. "I suppose I have a great appreciation for the mundane."

"Has it occurred to you that London is the wrong place to seek a quiet, ordinary life?"

"Of course. But I'm not in a position to look in the right places." She should have stopped there. There was no need to explain more. But it was one of Poppy's failings that she loved conversation, and like Dodger facing a drawer full of garters, she couldn't resist indulging. "The problem began when my brother, Lord Ramsay, inherited the title."

The stranger's brows lifted. "That was a problem?"

"Oh, yes," Poppy said earnestly. "You see, none of the Hathaways were prepared for it. We were distant cousins of the previous Lord Ramsay. The title only came to Leo because of a series of untimely deaths. The Hathaways had no knowledge of etiquette—we knew nothing of the ways of the upper classes. We were happy in Primrose Place."

She paused to sort through the comforting memories of her childhood: the cheerful cottage with its thatched roof, the flower garden where her father had tended his prized Apothecary's Roses, the pair of lop-eared Belgian rabbits who had lived in a hutch near the back doorstep, the piles of books in every corner. Now the abandoned cottage was in ruins and the garden lay fallow.

"But there's never any going back, is there," she said rather than asked. She bent to regard an object on a lower shelf. "What is this? Oh. An astrolabe." She picked up an intricate brass disk that contained engraved plates, the rim notched with degrees of arc.

"You know what an astrolabe is?" the stranger asked, following her.

"Yes, of course. A tool used by astronomers and navigators. Also astrologers." Poppy inspected the tiny star chart etched in one of the disks. "This is

Persian. I would estimate it to be about five hundred years old."

"Five hundred and twelve," he said slowly.

Poppy couldn't repress a satisfied grin. "My father was a medieval scholar. He had a collection of these. He even taught me how to make one out of wood, string, and a nail." She dialed the disks carefully. "What is the date of your birth?"

The stranger hesitated before replying, as if he disliked having to give information about himself. "November the first."

"Then you were born under Scorpius's reign," she said, turning the astrolabe over in her hands.

"You believe in astrology?" he asked, his tone edged with derision.

"Why shouldn't I?"

"It has no scientific basis."

"My father always encouraged me to be open-minded about such matters." She played a fingertip across the star chart, and looked up at him with a sly smile. "Scorpions are quite ruthless, you know. That is why Artemis bid one of them to kill her foe Orion. And as a reward, she set the scorpion up in the sky."

"I'm not ruthless. I merely do whatever it takes to achieve my goals."

"That's not ruthless?" Poppy asked, laughing.

"The word implies cruelty."

"And you're not cruel?"

"Only when necessary."

Poppy's amusement dissolved. "Cruelty is never necessary."

"You haven't seen much of the world, if you can say that."

Deciding not to pursue the subject, Poppy stood

on her toes to view the contents of another shelf. It featured an intriguing collection of what looked like tinplate toys. "What are these?"

"Automata."

"What are they for?"

He reached up, lifted one of the painted metal objects, and gave it to her.

Holding the machine by its circular base, Poppy examined it carefully. There were a group of tiny racehorses, each on its own track. Seeing the end of a pull cord on the side of the base, Poppy tugged it gently. That set off a series of inner mechanisms, including a flywheel, which sent the little horses spinning around the track as if they were racing.

Poppy laughed in delight. "How clever! I wish my sister Beatrix could see this. Where did it come from?"

"Mr. Rutledge fashions them in his spare time, as a means of relaxing."

"May I see another?" Poppy was enchanted by the objects, which were not toys so much as miniature feats of engineering. There was Admiral Nelson on a little tossing ship, a monkey climbing a banana tree, a cat playing with mice, and a lion tamer who cracked his whip while the lion shook his head repeatedly.

Seeming to enjoy Poppy's interest, the stranger showed her a picture on the wall, a tableau of couples waltzing at a ball. Before her wide eyes, the picture seemed to come to life, gentlemen guiding their partners smoothly across the floor. "Good heavens," Poppy said in wonder. "How is it done?"

"A clockwork mechanism." He removed the picture from the wall and displayed the open back. "There it is, attached to a flywheel by that drive band. And the pins work these wire levers . . . here . . . which in turn activate the other levers."

"Remarkable!" In her enthusiasm, Poppy forgot to be guarded or cautious. "Obviously Mr. Rutledge is mechanically gifted. This brings to mind a biography I read recently, about Roger Bacon, a Franciscan friar of the Middle Ages. My father was a great admirer of his work. Friar Bacon did a great deal of mechanical experimentation, which of course led some people to accuse him of sorcery. It was said that he once built a mechanical bronze head, which—" Poppy stopped abruptly, realizing she had been chattering. "There, you see? *This* is what I do at balls and soirées. It's one of the reasons I'm not sought after."

He had begun to smile. "I thought talking was encouraged at such affairs."

"Not my sort of talking."

Tap. Tap. Tap.

They both turned at the sound. The maid had arrived.

"I must go," Poppy said uneasily. "My companion will be very distressed if she wakes to find me missing."

The dark-haired stranger contemplated her for what seemed a very long time. "I'm not finished with you yet," he said with stunning casualness. As if no one ever refused him anything. As if he planned to keep her with him for as long as he wished.

Poppy took a deep breath. "Nevertheless, I am leaving," she said calmly, and went to the door.

He reached it at the same time she did, one hand flattening against the door panel.

Alarm jolted through her, and she turned to face him. A swift, frantic throbbing awakened in her throat and wrists and the backs of her knees. He was standing much too close, his long, hard body nearly touching hers. She shrank against the wall.

"Before you leave," he said softly, "I have some advice for you. It's not safe for a young woman to wander alone through the hotel. Don't take such a foolish risk again."

Poppy stiffened. "It's a reputable hotel," she said. "I have nothing to fear."

"Of course you do," he murmured. "You're looking right at it."

And before she could think, or move, or breathe, he bent his head and took her mouth with his.

Stunned, Poppy went motionless beneath the soft, burning kiss, so subtle in its demand that she wasn't aware of the moment her own lips parted. His hands came to her jaw, cradling, angling her face upward.

One arm slid around her, bringing her body fully against his, and the feel of him was hard and richly stimulating. With every breath, she drew in an enticing scent, an incense of amber and musk, starched linen and male skin. She should have struggled in his arms . . . but his mouth was so tenderly persuasive, erotic, imparting messages of peril and promise. His lips slid to her throat and he hunted for her pulse, working his way downward, layering sensations like silken gauze until she shivered and arched away from him.

"No," she said weakly.

The stranger gripped her chin carefully, forcing her to look at him. They both went still. As Poppy met his searching gaze, she saw a flash of baffled animosity, as if he had just made some unwelcome discovery.

He let go of her with great care and opened the door. "Bring it in," he told the maid, who waited at the threshold with a large silver tea tray.

The servant obeyed quickly, too well trained to evince curiosity about Poppy's presence in the room.

The man went to retrieve Dodger, who had fallen asleep in his chair. Returning with the drowsy ferret, he gave it to Poppy. She took Dodger with an inarticulate murmur, cradling him against her midriff. The ferret's eyes remained closed, lids completely concealed in the black mask that crossed his face. She felt the tapping of his tiny heartbeat beneath her fingertips, the silkiness of the white undercoat beneath the overlying guard hairs.

"Will there be anything else, sir?" the maid asked.

"Yes. I want you to accompany this lady to her suite. And come back to inform me when she is safely returned."

"Yes, Mr. Rutledge."

Mr. Rutledge?

Poppy felt her heart stop. She looked back at the stranger. Deviltry glittered in his green eyes. He seemed to relish her open astonishment.

Harry Rutledge . . . the mysterious and reclusive owner of the hotel. Who was nothing at all as she had imagined him to be.

Bewildered and mortified, Poppy turned from him. She crossed the threshold and heard the door close, the latch clicking smoothly shut. How wicked he was, to have amused himself at her expense! She consoled herself with the knowledge that she would never see him again.

And she went down the hallway with the housemaid . . . never suspecting that the course of her entire life had just changed.

Chapter Three

Harry went to stare at the fire in the hearth.

"Poppy Hathaway," he whispered as if it were a magical incantation.

He had seen her from a distance on two occasions, once when she had been entering a carriage at the front of the hotel, and once at a ball held at the Rutledge. Harry hadn't attended the event, but he had watched for a few minutes from a vantage point at an upper floor balcony. Despite her fine-spun beauty and mahogany hair, he hadn't spared her a second thought.

Meeting her in person, however, had been a revelation.

Harry began to lower himself into a chair and noted the shredded velvet and clumps of stuffing left by the ferret.

A reluctant smile curved his lips as he moved to take the other chair.

Poppy. How artless she had been, chatting casually about astrolabes and Franciscan monks as she had browsed among his treasures. She had thrown out words in bright clusters, as if she were scattering confetti. She had radiated a kind of cheery astuteness that should have been annoying, but instead it had given him unexpected pleasure. There was something about her, something . . . it was what the French called *esprit,* a liveliness of mind and spirit. And that face . . . innocent and knowing, and open.

He wanted her.

Usually Jay Harry Rutledge was given something before it ever occurred to him to want it. In his busy, well-regulated life, meals arrived before he was hungry, cravats were replaced before they had shown any signs of wear, reports were placed on his desk before he asked for them. And women were everywhere, and always available, and every last one of them told him what she assumed he wanted to hear.

Harry was aware that it was high time to marry. At least, most of his acquaintances assured him that it was high time, although he suspected it was because they had all put that particular noose around their own necks and wanted him to do the same. He had considered it without enthusiasm. But Poppy Hathaway was too compelling to resist.

Reaching into his left coat sleeve, Harry tugged out Poppy's letter. It was addressed to her from the Honourable Michael Bayning. He considered what he knew of the young man. Bayning had attended Winchester, where his studious nature had acquitted him well. Unlike other young men at university, Bayning had never gotten into debt, and there had been no scandals. More than a few women were attracted by his good looks and even more by the title and fortune he would inherit someday.

Frowning, Harry began to read.

Dearest love,

As I reflected on our last conversation, I kissed the place on my wrist where your tears fell. How can you not believe that I weep the same tears every day and night that we're apart? You have made it impossible for me to think of anyone or anything but you. I am mad with ardor for you, don't doubt it in the least.

If you will be patient only a bit longer, I will soon find the opportunity to approach my father. Once he understands how utterly and completely I adore you, I know he will give his approval to our union. We have a close bond, Father and I, and he has indicated that he wishes to see me as happy in my marriage as he was with my mother, God rest her soul. How she would have enjoyed you, Poppy . . . your sensible, happy nature, your love of family and home. If only she were here to help persuade my father that there could be no better wife for me than you.

Wait for me, Poppy, as I am waiting for you.

I am, as always, forever under your spell,

—M

A quiet, scoffing breath escaped him. Harry stared into the hearth, his face still, his mind busy with schemes. A log broke, part of it falling from the grate with a plush *pop,* sending out fresh heat and white sparks. Bayning wanted Poppy to wait? Unfathomable, when every cell in Harry's body was charged with impatient desire.

Closing the note with the care of a man handling valuable currency, Harry slipped it into his coat pocket.

* * *

Once Poppy was safely inside the family suite, she settled Dodger into his favorite sleeping place, a basket that her sister Beatrix had lined with soft cloth. The ferret remained asleep, as limp as a rag.

Standing, Poppy leaned back against the wall and closed her eyes. A sigh slid upward from her lungs.

Why had he done it?

More importantly, why had she allowed it?

It was not the way a man should have kissed an innocent girl. Poppy was mortified that she had landed herself in such a position, and even more that she had behaved in a way she would have judged harshly in someone else. She felt very certain of her feelings for Michael.

Why, then, had she responded to Harry Rutledge in such a way?

Poppy wished she could ask someone, but her instincts warned that it was a matter best forgotten.

Clearing the worried grimace from her face, Poppy tapped at her companion's door. "Miss Marks?"

"I'm awake," came a wan voice.

Poppy entered the small bedroom and found Miss Marks in her nightgown, standing at the washstand.

Miss Marks looked dreadful, her complexion ashen, her quiet blue eyes shadowed the color of bruises. Her light brown hair, usually braided and pinned in a scrupulous knot, was loose and tangled. After tilting a paper of medicinal powder to the back of her tongue, she took an unsteady gulp of water.

"Oh, dear," Poppy said softly. "What can I do?"

Miss Marks shook her head and then winced. "Nothing, Poppy. Thank you, you're very kind to ask."

"More nightmares?" Poppy watched in concern

as she went to a dresser and rummaged for stockings and garters and undergarments.

"Yes. I shouldn't have slept so late. Forgive me."

"There's nothing to forgive. I only wish your dreams were more pleasant."

"They are, most of the time." Miss Marks smiled faintly. "My best dreams are of being back at Ramsay House, with the elders in bloom and the nuthatches nesting in the hedgerow. Everything peaceful and safe. How I miss it all."

Poppy missed Ramsay House, too. London, with all its sophisticated delights and entertainments, could not hold a candle to Hampshire. And she was eager to see her older sister Win, whose husband Merripen was managing the Ramsay estate. "The season's almost over," Poppy said. "We'll be back there soon."

"If I live that long," Miss Marks muttered.

Poppy smiled sympathetically. "Why don't you return to bed? I'll fetch a cool cloth for your head."

"No, I can't give in to it. I'm going to dress and have a cup of strong tea."

"That's what I thought you'd say," Poppy commented wryly.

Miss Marks had been steeped in the classic British temperament, possessing a deep suspicion of all things sentimental or carnal. She was a young woman, barely older than Poppy, with a preternatural composure that would have allowed her to face any disaster, whether divine or man-made, without blinking an eye. The only time Poppy had ever seen her ruffled was when she was in the company of Leo, the Hathaways' brother, whose sarcastic wit seemed to annoy Miss Marks beyond endurance.

Two years earlier, Miss Marks had been hired as a governess, not to supplement the girls' academic

learning, but to teach them the infinite variety of
rules for young ladies who wished to navigate the
hazards of upper society. Now her position was that
of paid companion and chaperone.

In the beginning, Poppy and Beatrix had been
daunted by the challenge of learning so many social
rules. "We'll make a game of it," Miss Marks had
declared, and she had written a series of poems for
the girls to memorize.

For example:

If a lady you wish to be,
Behave with all formality.
At supper when you sit to eat,
Don't refer to beef as "meat."
Never gesture with your spoon,
Or use your fork as a harpoon.
Please don't play with your food,
And try to keep your voice subdued.

When it came to taking public walks:

Don't go running in the street,
And if a stranger you should meet,
Do not acknowledge him or her,
But to your chaperone defer.
When crossing mud, I beg,
Don't raise your skirts and show your leg.
Instead draw them slightly up and to the right,
Keeping ankles out of sight.

For Beatrix, there were also special codas:

When paying calls, wear gloves and hat,
And never bring a squirrel, or rat,

Or any four-legged creatures who
Do not belong indoors with you.

The unconventional approach had worked, giving Poppy and Beatrix enough confidence to participate in the season without disgracing themselves. The family had praised Miss Mark for her cleverness. All except for Leo, who had told her sardonically that Elizabeth Barrett Browning had nothing to fear. And Miss Marks had replied that she doubted Leo had sufficient mental aptitude to judge the merits of any kind of poetry at all.

Poppy had no idea why her brother and Miss Marks displayed such antagonism toward each other.

"I think they secretly like each other," Beatrix had said mildly.

Poppy had been so astonished by the idea, she had laughed. "They *war* with each other whenever they're in the same room, which, thank heavens, isn't often. Why would you suggest such a thing?"

"Well, if you consider the mating habits of certain animals—ferrets, for example—it can be quite a rough-and-tumble business—"

"Bea, please don't talk about mating habits," Poppy said, trying to suppress a grin. Her nineteen-year-old sister had a perpetual and cheerful disregard for propriety. "I'm sure it's vulgar, and . . . how do you know about mating habits?"

"Veterinary books, mostly. But also from occasional glimpses. Animals aren't very discreet, are they?"

"I suppose not. But do keep such thoughts to yourself, Bea. If Miss Marks heard you, she would write another poem for us to memorize."

Bea looked at her for a moment, her blue eyes

innocent. "Young ladies never contemplate . . . the ways that creatures procreate . . ."

"Or their companion will be irate," Poppy finished for her.

Beatrix had grinned. "Well, I don't see why they shouldn't be attracted to each other. Leo is a viscount, and he's quite handsome, and Miss Marks is intelligent and pretty."

"I've never heard Leo aspire to marry an intelligent woman," Poppy had said. "But I agree—Miss Marks is very pretty. Especially of late. She used to be so dreadfully thin and white, I didn't think much of her looks. But now she's filled out a bit."

"At least a stone," Beatrix had confirmed. "And she seems much happier. When we first met her, I think she had been through some dreadful experience."

"I thought so, too. I wonder if we'll ever find out what it was?"

Poppy hadn't been certain of the answer. But as she glanced at Miss Marks's weary face this morning, she thought there was a good chance that her recurrent nightmares had something to do with her mysterious past.

Going to the wardrobe, Poppy viewed the row of tidy, neatly pressed dresses made up with quiet colors and prim white collars and cuffs. "Which dress shall I find for you?" she asked softly.

"Any of them. It doesn't matter."

Poppy chose a dark blue wool twill, and laid the dress out on the rumpled bed. Tactfully she looked away as her companion removed her nightgown and donned a chemise and drawers and stockings.

The last thing Poppy wanted to do was trouble Miss Marks when her head was aching. However, the events of the morning had to be confessed. If any hint of her misadventure involving Harry Rutledge ever got out, it was far better for her companion to be prepared.

"Miss Marks," she said carefully, "I don't wish to make your headache worse but I have something to tell you . . ." Her voice trailed away as Miss Marks shot her a brief, pained glance.

"What is it, Poppy?"

Now was not a good time, Poppy decided. In fact . . . was there any obligation to say anything ever? In all likelihood, she would never see Harry Rutledge again. He certainly didn't attend the same social events the Hathaways did. And really, why would he bother causing trouble for a girl who was so far beneath his notice? He had nothing to do with her world, nor she with his.

"I dropped a bit of something-or-other on the bodice of my pink muslin frock the other evening at supper," Poppy improvised. "And now there's a grease stain on it."

"Oh, dear." Miss Marks paused in the middle of hooking up the front of her corset. "We'll mix a solution of hartshorn powder and water and sponge the stain. Hopefully that will take it out."

"I think that's an excellent idea."

Feeling only the tiniest bit guilty, Poppy picked up Miss Marks's discarded nightgown and folded it.

Chapter Four

Jake Valentine had been born a *filius nullius,* the Latin term for "son of nobody." His mother Edith had been a maidservant for a well-to-do barrister in Oxford, and his father the selfsame barrister. Contriving to rid himself of mother and son in one fell swoop, the barrister had bribed a loutish farmer to marry Edith. At the age of ten, having had enough of the farmer's bullying and beatings, Jake had left home for good and struck out for London.

He had labored in a blacksmith's forge for ten years, gaining significant size and strength, as well as a reputation for hard work and trustworthiness. It had never occurred to Jake to want more for himself. He had been employed, and his belly had been full, and the world outside London held no interest for him.

One day, however, a dark-haired man came to the blacksmith's shop and asked to speak to Jake. Intimidated by the gentleman's fine clothes and sophisticated bearing, Jake mumbled answers to a multitude of questions about his personal history and his work experience. And then the man astonished Jake by offering employment as his own valet, with many times the wages he was now getting.

Suspiciously, Jake had asked why the man would hire a novice, largely uneducated and roughcast in nature and appearance. "You could have your pick of the finest valets in London," Jake had pointed out. "Why someone like me?"

"Because those valets are notorious gossips, and they're acquainted with the servants of leading families across England and the continent. You have a reputation for keeping your mouth shut, which I value far more than experience. Also, you look as though you could give a good account of yourself in a dustup."

Jake's eyes had narrowed. "Why would a valet need to fight?"

The man had smiled. "You'll be doing errands for me. Some of them will be easy, some of them less so. Come, are you in or not?"

And that was how Jake had come to work for Jay Harry Rutledge, first as a valet, and then as an assistant.

Jake had never known anyone like Rutledge—eccentric, driven, manipulative, demanding. Rutledge had a shrewder understanding of human nature than anyone Jake had ever met. Within a few minutes of meeting someone, he sized them up with complete accuracy. He knew how to make people do what he wanted, and he nearly always got his way.

It seemed to Jake that Rutledge's brain never shut off, not even for the necessary act of sleeping. He was constantly active. Jake had seen him work out some problem in his head while simultaneously writing a letter and carrying on a fully coherent conversation. His appetite for information was voracious, and he possessed a singular gift for recall. Once Rutledge saw or read or heard something, it was in his brain forever. People could never lie to him, and if they were foolish enough to try, he decimated them.

Rutledge was not above gestures of kindness or consideration, and he rarely lost his temper. But Jake had never been certain how much, if at all, Rutledge cared for his fellow men. At his core, he was cold as a glacier. And as many things as Jake knew about Harry Rutledge, they were still essentially strangers.

No matter. Jake would have died for the man. The hotelier had secured the loyalty of all his servants, who were made to work hard but were given fair treatment and generous salaries. In return, they safeguarded his privacy zealously. Rutledge was acquainted with a great many people, but these friendships were rarely discussed. And he was highly selective about whom he admitted into his inner circle.

Rutledge was besieged by women, of course— his rampaging energy often found outlet in the arms of some beauty or another. But at the first indication that a woman felt the merest flicker of affection, Jake was dispatched to her residence to deliver a letter that broke off all future communications. In other words, Jake was required to endure the tears, anger, or other messy emotions that Rutledge could not tolerate. And Jake would have felt sorry for the women, except that along with each letter, Rutledge usually included some monstrously expensive piece of jewelry that served to mollify any hurt feelings.

There were certain areas of Rutledge's life where women were never allowed. He did not allow them to stay in his private apartments, nor did he let any of them into his curiosities room. It was there that Rutledge went to dwell on his most difficult problems. And on the many nights when Rutledge was unable to sleep, he would go to the drafting table to occupy himself with automata, working with watch parts and bits of paper and wire until he had settled his overactive brain.

So when Jake was discreetly told by a housemaid that a young woman had been with Rutledge in the curiosities room, he knew something significant had occurred.

Jake finished his breakfast in the hotel kitchens with dispatch, hurrying over a plate of creamed eggs scattered with crisp curls of fried bacon. Ordinarily, he would have taken the time to savor the fare. However, he couldn't be late for his morning meeting with Rutledge.

"Not so fast," said Andre Broussard, a chef whom Rutledge had lured away from the French ambassador two years earlier. Broussard was the only employee in the hotel who possibly slept less than Rutledge. The young chef had been known to rise at three in the morning to begin preparing for a day's work, going to the morning markets to personally select the best produce. He was fair-haired and slight of build, but he possessed the discipline and will of an army commander.

Pausing in the act of whisking a sauce, Broussard regarded Jake with amusement. "You might try chewing, Valentine."

"I don't have time to chew," Jake replied, setting aside his napkin. "I'm due to get the morning list from Mr. Rutledge in—" he paused to consult his pocket watch, "—two and a half minutes."

"Ah, yes, the morning list." The chef proceeded to mimic his employer. " 'Valentine, I want you to arrange for a soirée in honor of the Portuguese ambassador to be held here on Tuesday with a pyrotechnic display at the conclusion. Afterward, run to the patent office with the drawings for my latest invention. And on the way back, stop by Regent Street and purchase six French cambric handkerchiefs, plain not patterned, and God help me no lace—' "

"Enough, Broussard," Jake said, trying not to smile.

The chef returned his attention to the sauce. "By the way, Valentine . . . when you find out who the girl was, come back and tell me. And in return I'll let you have your pick of the pastry tray before I send it to the dining room."

Jake shot him a sharp look, his brown eyes narrowing. "What girl?"

"You know very well what girl. The one Mr. Rutledge was seen with this morning."

Jake frowned. "Who told you about that?"

"At least three people mentioned it to me in the past half hour. Everyone's talking about it."

"The Rutledge employees are forbidden to gossip," Jake said sternly.

Broussard rolled his eyes. "To outsiders, yes. But

Mr. Rutledge never said we couldn't gossip amongst ourselves."

"I don't know why the presence of a girl in the curiosities room should be so interesting."

"Hmmm . . . could it be because Rutledge *never* allows anyone in there? Could it be because everyone who works here is praying that Rutledge will soon find a wife to distract him from his constant meddling?"

Jake shook his head ruefully. "I doubt he'll ever marry. The hotel is his mistress."

The chef gave him a patronizing glance. "That's how much you know. Mr. Rutledge will marry, once he finds the right woman. As my countrymen say, 'A wife and a melon are hard to choose.'" He watched as Jake buttoned his coat and straightened his cravat. "Bring back information, *mon ami*."

"You know I would never reveal one detail of Rutledge's private affairs."

Broussard sighed. "Loyal to a fault. I suppose if Rutledge told you to murder someone, you'd do it?"

Although the question was asked in a light vein, the chef's gray eyes were alert. Because no one, not even Jake, was entirely certain what Harry Rutledge was capable of, or how far Jake's allegiance would go.

"He hasn't asked that of me," Jake replied, and paused to add with a flash of humor, "yet."

As Jake hurried to the private suite of unnumbered rooms on the third floor, he passed many employees on the back stairs. These stairs, and the entrances at the back of the hotel, were used by servants and deliverymen as they went about their daily tasks. A few people tried to stop Jake with questions or concerns, but he shook his head and quickened his pace. Jake took care never to be late for his morning meetings with Rutledge. These consultations were usually brief, no more than a quarter hour, but Rutledge demanded punctuality.

Jake paused before the entrance of the suite, tucked at the back of a small private lobby lined with marble and priceless artwork. A secure inner hallway led to a discreet staircase and side door of the hotel, so that Rutledge never had to use the main hallways for his comings and goings. Rutledge, who liked to keep track of everyone else, did not allow anyone to do the same to him. He took most of his meals in private, and came and went as he pleased, sometimes with no indication of when he would return.

Jake knocked at the door and waited until he heard a muffled assent to enter.

He went into the suite, a series of four connected rooms that could be expanded into as large an apartment as one desired, up to fifteen rooms. "Good morning, Mr. Rutledge," he said, entering the study.

The hotelier sat at a massive mahogany desk fitted with a cupboard filled with drawers and cubbies. As usual, the desk was covered with folios, papers, books, correspondence, calling cards, a stamp box, and an array of writing implements. Rutledge was closing a letter, applying a seal precisely into a little pool of hot wax.

"Good morning, Valentine. How did the staff meeting go?"

Jake handed him the daily sheaf of manager reports. "Everything is going smoothly, for the most part. There have been few issues with the diplomatic contingent from Nagaraja."

"Oh?"

The tiny kingdom of Nagaraja, wedged between Burma and Siam, had just become a British ally. After offering to help the Nagarajans drive out the encroaching Siamese, Britain had now made the country one of its protectorates. Which was akin to being pinned beneath a lion's paw and being informed by the lion that you were perfectly safe. Since the British were currently fighting the Burmese and annexing provinces right and left, the Nagarajans hoped desperately to remain self-governing. Toward that end, the kingdom had sent a trio of high-level envoys on a diplomatic mission to England, bearing costly gifts in tribute to Queen Victoria.

"The reception manager," Jake said, "had to change their rooms three times when they first arrived yesterday afternoon."

Rutledge's brows rose. "There was a problem with the rooms?"

"Not the rooms themselves . . . the room *numbers,* which according to Nagarajan superstition were not auspicious. We finally settled them into suite 218. However, not long afterward, the second-floor manager detected the odor of smoke coming from the suite. It seems they were conducting an arrival-in-a-new-land ceremony, which involved starting a small fire on a bronze plate. Unfortunately the fire got out of hand, and the carpet was scorched."

A smile curved Rutledge's mouth. "As I recall, Nagarajans have ceremonies for nearly everything. See that an appropriate location is found for them to start as many sacred fires as they like without burning the hotel down."

"Yes, sir."

Rutledge riffled through the managers' reports. "What's our current occupancy rate?" he asked without looking up.

"Ninety-five percent."

"Excellent." Rutledge continued to peruse the reports.

In the silence that followed, Jake let his gaze wander over the desk. He saw a letter addressed to Miss Poppy Hathaway, from the Honourable Michael Bayning.

He wondered why it was in Rutledge's possession. Poppy Hathaway . . . one of the sisters of a family that stayed at the Rutledge during the London season. Like other families of the peerage who didn't own a residence in town, they were obligated either to let a furnished house or stay in a private hotel. The Hathaways had been loyal customers of the Rutledge for three years. Was it possible that Poppy was the girl Rutledge had been seen with that morning?

"Valentine," the hotelier said in an offhand manner, "One of the chairs in my curiosities room needs to be reupholstered. There was a slight mishap this morning."

Jake usually knew better than to ask questions, but he couldn't resist. "What kind of mishap, sir?"

"It was a ferret. I believe he was trying to make a nest in the cushions."

A *ferret?*

The Hathaways were definitely involved.

"Is the creature still at large?" Jake asked.

"No, it was retrieved."

"By one of the Hathaway sisters?" Jake guessed.

A warning glint appeared in the cool green eyes. "Yes, as a matter of fact." Setting the reports aside,

Rutledge leaned back in his chair. The position of ease was belied by the repeated tapping of his fingers as he rested his hand on the desk. "I have a few errands for you, Valentine. First, go to the residence of Lord Andover in Upper Brook Street. Arrange for a private meeting between myself and Andover within the next two days, preferably here. Make it clear that no one is to know about it, and impress upon Andover that the matter is one of great importance."

"Yes, sir." Jake didn't think there would be any difficulty in making the arrangements. Whenever Harry Rutledge wanted to meet with someone, they complied without delay. "Lord Andover is the father of Mr. Michael Bayning, isn't he?"

"He is."

What the devil was going on?

Before Jake could respond, Rutledge went on with the list. "Next, take this—" he handed Jake a narrow-bound folio tied with leather cord, "—to Sir Gerald at the War Office. Place it directly into his hands. After that, go to Watherston & Son, and buy a necklace or bracelet on my credit. Something nice, Valentine. And deliver it to Mrs. Rawlings at her residence."

"With your compliments?" Jake asked hopefully.

"No, with this note." Rutledge gave him a sealed letter. "I'm getting rid of her."

Jake's face fell. God. Another scene. "Sir, I'd rather go on an errand in east London and be pummeled by street thieves."

Rutledge smiled. "That will probably happen later in the week."

Jake gave his employer a speaking glance and left.

* * *

Poppy was well aware that in terms of marriageability, she had good points and bad points.

In her favor: Her family was wealthy, which meant she would have a handsome dowry.

Not in her favor: The Hathaways were neither a distinguished family nor blue-blooded, in spite of Leo's title.

In her favor: She was attractive.

Not in her favor: She was chatty and awkward, often at the same time, and when she was nervous, both problems worsened.

In her favor: The aristocracy could not afford to be as particular as they once had been. While the peerage's power slowly diminished, a class of industrialists and merchants was swiftly rising. Therefore, marriages between moneyed commoners and impoverished nobility occurred with increasing frequency. More and more often, the peerage had to figuratively hold its nose and mingle with those of low origins.

Not in her favor: Michael Bayning's father, the viscount, was a man of high standards, especially where his son was concerned.

"The viscount will certainly have to consider the match," Miss Marks had told her. "He may have impeccable lineage, but from all accounts, his fortune is waning. His son will have to marry a girl from a family of means. It may as well be a Hathaway."

"I hope you're right," Poppy had replied feelingly.

Poppy had no doubt that she would be happy as Michael Bayning's wife. He was intelligent, affectionate, quick to laugh . . . a born and bred gentleman. She loved him, not in a bonfire of passion, but in a warm, steady flame. She loved his tempera-

ment, the confidence that superseded any hint of arrogance. And she loved his looks, as unladylike as it
was to admit such a thing. But he had thick chestnut
hair and warm brown eyes, and his form was tall
and well exercised.

Once Poppy had met Michael, it had seemed almost too easy . . . in no time at all she had fallen in
love with him.

"I hope you're not trifling with me," Michael had
told her one evening as they browsed along the art
gallery of a London mansion during a soirée. "That
is, I hope I haven't mistaken what might be mere
politeness on your part for something more mean-
ingful." He had stopped with her in front of a large
landscape done in oils. "The truth is, Miss Hathaway . . . Poppy . . . every minute I spend in your
company gives me such pleasure that I can scarcely
bear to be apart from you."

And she had stared up at him in wonder. "Could
it be possible?" she whispered.

"That I love you?" Michael had whispered back,
a wry smile touching his lips. "Poppy Hathaway, it
is impossible *not* to love you."

She had taken an unsteady breath, her entire being filled with joy. "Miss Marks never told me what
a lady is supposed to do in this situation."

Michael had grinned and leaned a bit closer, as if
imparting a highly confidential secret. "You're supposed to give me discreet encouragement."

"I love you, too."

"That's not discreet." His brown eyes sparkled.
"But it's very nice to hear."

The courtship had been beyond circumspect. Michael's father, Viscount Andover, was protective of
his son. A good man, Michael had said, but stern.

And Michael had asked for sufficient time to approach the viscount and convince him of the rightness of the match. Poppy was entirely willing to give Michael however much time he needed.

The rest of the Hathaways, however, were not quite as amenable. To them, Poppy was a treasure, and she deserved to be courted openly and with pride.

"Shall I go and discuss the situation with Andover?" Cam Rohan had suggested as the family relaxed in the parlor of their hotel suite after supper. He lounged on the settee next to Amelia, who was holding their six-month-old baby. When the baby grew up, his *gadjo* name—*gadjo* being the word that Gypsies used for outsiders—would be Ronan Cole, but among the family he was called by his Romany name, Rye.

Poppy and Miss Marks occupied the other settee, while Beatrix lounged on the floor by the hearth, playing idly with a pet hedgehog named Medusa. Dodger sulked nearby in his basket, having learned through hard experience that it was unwise to tangle with Medusa and her quills.

Frowning contemplatively, Poppy looked up from her needlework. "I don't think that would help," she told her brother-in-law regretfully. "I know how persuasive you are . . . but Michael is very firm on how to handle his father."

Cam appeared to be thinking the matter over. With his black hair worn a trifle too long, his gleaming dark-honey complexion, and a diamond stud sparkling at one ear, Rohan looked far more like a pagan prince than a businessman who had garnered a fortune in manufacturing investments. Ever since he had married Amelia, Rohan had been the *de facto* head of the Hathaway family. No man alive would have been able to manage the unruly lot as adeptly as he did. His tribe, he called them.

"Little sister," he said to Poppy, sounding relaxed even though his gaze was intent, "as the Rom say, 'the tree without sunlight will bear no fruit.' I see no reason why Bayning should not ask for permission to court you, and then go about it openly in the usual way of the *gadjos*."

"Cam," Poppy said carefully, "I know the Rom has a more . . . well, straightforward . . . approach to courtship—"

At that, Amelia smothered a laugh. Cam pointedly ignored her. Miss Marks looked perplexed, clearly having no idea that the Romany tradition of courtship often involved stealing a woman right out of her bed.

"But you know as well as any of us," Poppy continued, "that it is a far more delicate process for the British peerage."

"Actually," Amelia said dryly, "from what I've seen, the British peerage negotiates marriages with all the romantic sensibilities of a bank transaction."

Poppy scowled at her older sister. "Amelia, whose side are you on?"

"For me, there is no side but yours." Amelia's blue eyes were filled with concern. "And that is why I don't care for this kind of covert courtship . . . arriving separately at events, never coming to take you and Miss Marks on a carriage drive . . . it bears the odor of shame. Embarrassment. As if you were some guilty secret."

"Are you saying you doubt Mr. Bayning's intentions?"

"Not at all. But I don't like his methods."

Poppy sighed shortly. "I am an unconventional choice for a peer's son. And therefore Mr. Bayning must proceed with caution."

"You're the most conventional person in the entire family," Amelia protested.

Poppy gave her a dark glance. "Being the most conventional Hathaway is hardly something to boast about."

Looking annoyed, Amelia glanced at her companion. "Miss Marks, my sister seems to believe that her family is so outlandish, so completely out of the ordinary, that Mr. Bayning must go through these exertions—sneaking about and so forth— instead of going to the viscount in an upstanding manner and saying 'Father, I intend to marry Poppy Hathaway and I would like your blessing.' Can you tell me *why* there is a need for such excessive caution on Mr. Bayning's part?"

For once, Miss Marks seemed at a loss for words.

"Don't put her on the spot," Poppy said. "Here are the facts, Amelia: You and Win are married to Gypsies, Leo is a notorious rake, Beatrix has more pets than the Royal Zoological Society, and I am socially awkward and can't carry on a proper conversation to save my life. Is it so difficult to understand why Mr. Bayning has to break the news to his father gently?"

Amelia looked as though she wanted to argue, but instead she muttered, "Proper conversations are very dull, in my opinion."

"Mine, too," Poppy said glumly. "That's the problem."

Beatrix looked up from the hedgehog, who had curled up in a ball in her hands. "Does Mr. Bayning make interesting conversation?"

"You wouldn't need to ask," Amelia said, "if he dared to come here for a visit."

"I suggest," Miss Marks said hastily, before Poppy could retort, "that as a family, we invite Mr. Bayning to accompany us to the Chelsea flower show, the day after next. That will allow us to spend the afternoon with Mr. Bayning—and perhaps we will gain some reassurance about his intentions."

"I think that's a lovely idea," Poppy exclaimed. Attending a flower show together was far more innocuous and discreet than Michael having to call on them at the Rutledge. "I'm sure that talking to Mr. Bayning will ease your worries, Amelia."

"I hope so," her sister replied, sounding unconvinced. A tiny frown pleated the space between her sister's slim brows. She turned her attention to Miss Marks. "As Poppy's chaperon, you have seen far more of this furtive suitor than I have. What is your opinion of him?"

"From what I have observed," the companion said carefully, "Mr. Bayning is well regarded and honorable. He has an excellent reputation, with no history of seducing women, spending beyond his means, or brawling in public venues. In short, he is the complete opposite of Lord Ramsay."

"That speaks well of him," Cam said gravely. His golden hazel eyes twinkled as he glanced down at his wife. A moment of silent communication passed between them before he murmured softly, "Why don't you send him an invitation, *monisha*?"

A sardonic smile flitted across Amelia's soft lips. "*You* would voluntarily attend a flower show?"

"I like flowers," Cam said innocently.

"Yes, scattered across meadows and marshes. But

you hate seeing them organized in raised beds and neat little boxes."

"I can tolerate it for an afternoon," Cam assured her. Idly he toyed with a loose lock of hair that had fallen on her neck. "I suppose it's worth the effort to gain an in-law like Bayning." He smiled as he added, "We need at least one respectable man in the family, don't we?"

Chapter Five

An invitation was sent to Michael Bayning the next day, and to Poppy's elation, it was accepted immediately. "It's only a matter of time now," she told Beatrix, barely restraining herself from hopping in excitement the way Dodger did. "I'm going to be Mrs. Michael Bayning, and I love him, I love everyone and everything . . . I even love your smelly old ferret, Bea!"

Late in the morning, Poppy and Beatrix dressed for a walk. It was a clear, warm day, and the hotel gardens, intercut with neatly graveled paths, were a symphony of blooms.

"I can hardly wait to go out," Poppy said, standing at the window and staring down at the extensive gardens. "It almost reminds me of Hampshire, the flowers are so beautiful."

"It doesn't remind me at all of Hampshire," Beatrix said, "It's too orderly. But I do like walking through the Rutledge rose garden. The air smells so sweet. Do you know, I spoke with the master gardener a few mornings ago, when Cam and Amelia and I went out, and he told me his secret recipe for making the roses so large and healthy."

"What is it?"

"Fish broth, vinegar and a dash of sugar. He sprinkles them with it right before they bloom. And they love it."

Poppy wrinkled her nose. "What a dreadful concoction."

"The master gardener said that old Mr. Rutledge is especially fond of roses, and people have brought him some of the exotic varieties you see in the garden. The lavender roses are from China, for example, and the Maiden's Blush variety comes from France, and—"

"*Old* Mr. Rutledge?"

"Well, he didn't actually say Mr. Rutledge was old. I just can't help thinking of him that way."

"Why?"

"Well, he's so awfully mysterious, and no one ever sees him. It reminds me of the stories of mad old King George, locked away in his apartments at Windsor Castle." Beatrix grinned. "Perhaps they keep Mr. Rutledge up in the attic."

"Bea," Poppy whispered urgently, filled with an overwhelming urge to confide in her, "There's something I'm bursting to tell you, but it must remain a secret."

Her sister's eyes lit with interest. "What is it?"

"First promise you won't tell anyone."

"I *promise* promise."

"Swear on something."

"I swear on St. Francis, the patron saint of all animals." Seeing Poppy's hesitation, Beatrix added enthusiastically, "If a band of pirates kidnapped me and took me to their ship and threatened to make me walk the plank over a shiver of starving sharks unless I told them your secret, I *still* wouldn't tell it. If I were tied by a villain and thrown before a herd of stampeding horses all shod in iron, and the *only way* to keep from being trampled was to tell the villain your secret, I—"

"All right, you've convinced me," Poppy said with a grin. Dragging her sister to the corner, she said softly, "I have met Mr. Rutledge."

Beatrix's blue eyes turned huge. "You have? When?"

"Yesterday morning." And Poppy told her the entire story, describing the passageway, the curiosities room, and Mr. Rutledge himself. The only thing she left out was the kiss, which, as far as she was concerned, had never happened.

"I'm so terribly sorry about Dodger," Beatrix said earnestly. "I apologize on his behalf."

"It's all right, Bea. Only . . . I do wish he hadn't lost the letter. So long as no one finds it, I suppose there's no problem."

"Then Mr. Rutledge is not a decrepit madman?" Beatrix asked, sounding disappointed.

"Heavens, no."

"What does he look like?"

"Quite handsome, actually. He's very tall, and—"

"As tall as Merripen?"

Kev Merripen had come to live with the Hathaways after his tribe had been attacked by Englishmen who had wished to drive the Gypsies out of the county. The boy had been left for dead, but the Hathaways had taken him in, and he had stayed for good. Recently he had married the second oldest sister, Winnifred. Merripen had undertaken the monumental task of running the Ramsay estate in

Leo's absence. The newlyweds were both quite happy to stay in Hampshire during the season, enjoying the beauty and relative privacy of Ramsay House.

"No one's as tall as Merripen," Poppy said. "But Mr. Rutledge is tall nonetheless, and he has dark hair and piercing green eyes . . ." Her stomach gave an unexpected little leap as she remembered.

"Did you like him?"

Poppy hesitated. "Mr. Rutledge is . . . unsettling. He's charming, but one has the feeling he's capable of nearly anything. He's like some wicked angel from a William Blake poem."

"I wish I could have seen him," Beatrix said wistfully. "And I wish even more that I could visit the curiosities room. I envy you, Poppy. It's been so long since anything interesting has happened to me."

Poppy laughed quietly. "What, when we've just gone through nearly the entire London season?"

Beatrix rolled her eyes. "The London season is about as interesting as a snail race. In January. With dead snails."

"Girls, I'm ready," came Miss Marks's cheerful summons, and she entered the room. "Make certain to fetch your parasols—you don't want to become sunbrowned." The trio left the suite and proceeded at a dignified pace along the hallway. Before they turned the corner to approach the grand staircase, they became aware of an unusual disturbance in the decorous hotel.

Men's voices tangled in the air, some agitated, at least one of them angry, and there was the sound of foreign accents, and heavy thumping, and a queer metallic rattling.

"What the devil . . ." Miss Marks said under her breath.

Rounding the corner, the three women stopped abruptly at the sight of a half dozen men clustered near the food lift. A shriek rent the air.

"Is it a woman?" Poppy asked, turning pale. "A child?"

"Stay here," Miss Marks said tensely. "I'll undertake to find out—"

The three of them flinched at a series of screams, the sounds blistered with panic.

"It is a child," Poppy said, striding forward despite Miss Marks's command to stay. "We must do something to help."

Beatrix had already run ahead of her. "It's not a child," she said over her shoulder. "It's a monkey!"

Chapter Six

There were few activities Harry enjoyed as much as fencing, even more so because it had become an obsolete art. Swords were no longer necessary as weapons or fashion accessories, and its practitioners were now mainly military officers and a handful of amateur enthusiasts. But Harry liked the elegance of it, the precision that required both physical and mental discipline. A fencer had to plan several moves in advance, something that came naturally to Harry.

A year earlier, he had joined a fencing club consisting of approximately a hundred members, including peers, bankers, actors, politicians, and soldiers from various ranks of the military. Thrice weekly, Harry and a few trusted friends met at the club, practicing with both foils and quarterstaffs beneath the watchful eye of a fencing master. Although the club had a changing room and shower baths, there was often a queue, so Harry usually left directly from practice.

This morning's practice had been especially vigorous, as the fencing master had taught them techniques for fighting off two opponents simultaneously. Although it had been invigorating, it was also challenging, and they had all been left bruised and tired. Harry had gotten a few hard strikes on his chest and bicep, and he was soaked in sweat.

When he returned to the hotel, he was still in his fencing whites, although he had removed the protective leather padding. He was looking forward to a shower bath, but it quickly became evident that the shower bath would have to wait.

One of his managers, a bespectacled young man named William Cullip, met him as he entered the back of the hotel. Cullip's face was drawn with anxiety. "Mr. Rutledge," he said apologetically, "I was told by Mr. Valentine to tell you immediately upon your return that we are having a . . . well, a difficulty . . ."

Harry stared at him and remained silent, waiting with forced patience. One could not rush Cullip, or the information would take forever to get out.

"It involves the Nagarajan diplomats," the manager continued.

"Another fire?"

"No, sir. It has to do with one of the articles of tribute the Nagarajans had planned to present to the Queen tomorrow. It has disappeared."

Harry frowned, reflecting on the collection of priceless gemstones, artwork and textiles the Nagarajans had brought. "Their possessions are stored in a locked basement room. How could something go missing?"

Cullip let out a ragged breath. "Well, sir, it has apparently left on its own."

Harry's brows lifted. "What the hell is going on, Cullip?"

"Among the items the Nagarajans brought for the Queen are a pair of rare animals . . . blue macaques . . . which are found only in the Nagarajan teak forest. They are to be housed at the zoological gardens at Regent's Park. Evidently each macaque was kept in its own crate, but somehow one of them learned to pick a lock, and—"

"The devil you say!" Incredulity was rapidly crushed by outrage. Yet somehow Harry managed to keep his voice quiet. "May I ask why no one bothered to inform me that we're harboring a pair of *monkeys* in my hotel?"

"There seems to be some confusion on that point, sir. You see, Mr. Lufton in reception is certain that he included it in his report, but Mr. Valentine says he never read anything about it, and he lost his temper and frightened a housemaid and two stewards, and now everyone is searching while at the same time making certain not to alert the guests—"

"Cullip." Harry gritted his teeth with the effort to stay calm. "How long has the macaque been missing?"

"We estimate at least forty-five minutes."

"Where is Valentine?"

"The last I heard, he had gone up to the third floor. One of the housemaids discovered what she thought might be droppings near the food lift."

"Monkey droppings near the food lift," Harry repeated, disbelieving his own ears. *Christ.* All the situation needed was for one of his elderly guests to be frightened into apoplexy from having a wild animal spring out from nowhere, or to have a woman or child bitten, or some other outrageous scenario.

It would be impossible to find the damned creature. The hotel was a virtual maze, riddled with hallways and concealed doors and passages. It could take days, during which the Rutledge would be in an uproar. He would lose business. And worst of all, he would be the butt of jokes for *years*. By the time the humorists got through with him . . .

"By God, heads are going to roll," Harry said with a lethal softness that caused Cullip to flinch. "Go to my apartments, Cullip, and get the Dreyse from the mahogany cabinet in my private office."

The young manager looked perplexed. "The Dreyse, sir?"

"A shotgun. It's the only percussion cap breechloader in the cabinet."

"A percussion . . ."

"The brown one," Harry said gently. "With a large bolt sticking out of the side."

"Yes, sir!"

"And for God's sake, don't point it at anyone. It's loaded."

Still gripping the foil, Harry raced up the back stairs. He took them two at a time, swiftly passing a pair of startled housemaids carrying baskets of linens.

Reaching the third floor, he headed to the food lift, where he found Valentine, all three of the Nagarajan diplomats, and Brimbley, the floor steward. A wood and metal crate had been positioned nearby. The men had gathered around the opening to the food lift, and were looking inside.

"Valentine," Harry said curtly, striding up to his right-hand man, "have you found it?"

Jake Valentine threw him a harassed glance. "He climbed up the rope pulley in the food lift. Now he's sitting on top of the movable frame. Every time we try to lower it, he hangs onto the rope and dangles above us."

"Is he close enough for me to reach him?"

Valentine's gaze flickered to the foil in his employer's grasp. His dark eyes widened as he understood that Harry intended to skewer the creature rather than let it roam freely through the hotel.

"It wouldn't be easy," Valentine said. "You'd probably only end up agitating him."

"Have you tried to lure it with food?"

"He won't take the bait. I reached up in the shaft with an apple, and he tried to bite my hand." Valentine cast a distracted glance at the food lift, where the other men were whistling and cooing to the obstinate monkey.

One of the Nagarajans, a slim middle-aged man dressed in a light suit with a richly patterned cloth draped over both shoulders, stepped forward. His expression was fraught with distress. "You are Mr. Rutledge? Good, yes, I thank you for coming to help retrieve this most important gift for Her Majesty. Very rare macaque. Very special. It must not be harmed."

"Your name?" Harry asked brusquely.

"Niran," the diplomat supplied.

"Mr. Niran, while I understand your concern for the animal, I have a responsibility to protect my guests."

The Nagarajan glowered. "If you damage our gift to the Queen, I fear it will not go well for you."

Leveling a hard stare at the diplomat, Harry said evenly, "If you don't find a way to get that animal out of my food lift and into that crate in five minutes, Niran, I'm going to make a kabob out of him."

This statement produced a stare of purest indignation, and the Nagarajan rushed to the opening of the food lift. The monkey gave an excited hoot, followed by a series of grunts.

"I have no idea what a kabob is," Valentine said to no one in particular, "but I don't think the monkey's going to like it."

Before Harry could reply, Valentine caught sight of something behind him, and he groaned. "Guests," the assistant muttered.

"Damn it," Harry said beneath his breath, and turned to face the approaching guests, wondering what he was going to say to them.

A trio of women rushed toward him, two of them in pursuit of a dark-haired girl. A small shock of recognition went through Harry as he recognized Catherine Marks and Poppy Hathaway. He guessed the third was Beatrix, who seemed determined to plow through him in her haste to reach the food lift.

Harry moved to block her way. "Good morning, miss. I'm afraid you can't go over there. Nor would you want to."

She stopped immediately, staring at him with eyes the same rich blue as her sister's. Catherine Marks regarded him with flinty composure, while Poppy took an extra breath, her cheeks infused with color.

"You don't know my sister, sir," Poppy said. "If there is a wild creature in the vicinity, she most definitely wants to see it."

"What makes you think there's a wild creature in my hotel?" Harry asked, as if the idea were inconceivable.

The macaque chose that moment to utter an enthusiastic screech.

Holding his gaze, Poppy grinned. Despite his annoyance at the situation and his lack of control over it, Harry couldn't help smiling back. She was even more exquisite than he had remembered, her eyes a dark, lucid blue. There were many beautiful women in London, but not one of them possessed her combination of intelligence and subtly off-kilter charm. He wanted to sweep her away somewhere, that very minute, and have her all to himself.

Schooling his expression, Harry recalled that although they had met the previous day, they weren't supposed to know each other. He bowed with impeccable politeness. "Harry Rutledge, at your service."

"I'm Beatrix Hathaway," the younger girl said, "and this is my sister Poppy and my companion Miss Marks. There's a monkey in the food lift, isn't there?" She seemed remarkably prosaic, as if discovering exotic animals in one's residence occurred all the time.

"Yes, but—"

"You'll never catch him that way," Beatrix interrupted.

Harry, who was never interrupted by anyone, found himself biting back another smile. "I assure you, we have the situation well in hand, Miss—"

"You need help," Beatrix told him. "I'll return directly. Don't do anything to upset the monkey. And don't try to poke him out with that sword—you may accidentally pierce him." With no further ado, she dashed back in the direction she had come from.

"It wouldn't be accidental," Harry muttered.

Miss Marks looked from Harry to her retreating charge, her mouth falling open. "Beatrix, do *not* run through the hotel like that. Stop at once!"

"I think she has a plan," Poppy remarked. "You'd better go after her, Miss Marks."

The companion threw her a beseeching glance. "Come with me."

But Poppy didn't move, only said innocently, "I'll wait here, Miss Marks."

"But it's not proper—" The companion looked from Beatrix's fast-disappearing form to Poppy's unmoving one. Deciding in a flash that Beatrix posed the greater problem, she turned with an unladylike curse and ran after her charge.

Harry found himself left with Poppy, who, like her sister, seemed remarkably unperturbed by the macaque's antics. They faced each other, he with his foil, she with her parasol.

Poppy's gaze traveled over his fencing whites, and rather than staying demurely silent or displaying the appropriate nervousness of a young lady with no companion to protect her . . . she launched into conversation. "My father called fencing 'physical chess,'" she said. "He very much admired the sport."

"I'm still a novice," Harry said.

"According to my father, the trick of it is to hold the foil as if it were a bird in your hand—close enough to prevent its escape, but not tight enough to crush it."

"He gave you lessons?"

"Oh, yes, my father encouraged all his daughters to try it. He said he knew of no other sport that would fall so directly in a woman's line."

"Of course. Women are agile and fast."

Poppy smiled ruefully. "Not enough to elude you, it seems."

The single comment managed, with wry humor, to gently mock herself and him.

Somehow they were standing closer together, although Harry wasn't certain who had stepped toward

whom. A delicious scent clung to her, sweet skin and
perfume and soap. Remembering how soft her mouth
had been, he wanted to kiss her so badly that it was
all he could do not to reach for her. He was stunned
to realize that he was a bit breathless.

"Sir!" Valentine's voice recalled him from his
thoughts. "The macaque is climbing up the rope."

"It has nowhere to go," Harry said curtly. "Try
moving the lift upward and trapping it against the
ceiling."

"You will injure the macaque!" the Nagarajan exclaimed.

"I can only hope so," Harry said, aggravated by
the distraction. He didn't want to be bothered with
the logistics of capturing an unruly macaque. He
wanted to be alone with Poppy Hathaway.

William Cullip arrived, carrying the Dreyse with
extreme care. "Mr. Valentine, here it is!"

"Thank you." Harry began to reach for it, but at
that second Poppy reared back in a startle reflex, her
shoulders colliding with his chest. Harry caught her
by the arms and felt the thrills of panic running
through her. Carefully, he turned her to face him.
Her face was bleached, her gaze not quite focused.
"What is it?" he asked softly, holding her against
him. "The shotgun? You're afraid of guns?"

She nodded, struggling to catch her breath.

Harry was shocked by the force of his own reaction to her, the tidal wave of protectiveness. She was
trembling and winded, one hand pressing on the
center of his chest. "It's all right," he murmured. He
couldn't recall the last time anyone had sought comfort from him. Perhaps no one ever had. He wanted
to draw her fully against him and soothe her. It

seemed he had always wanted this, waited for it, without even knowing.

In the same quiet tone Harry murmured, "Cullip, the shotgun won't be needed. Take it back to the cabinet."

"Yes, Mr. Rutledge."

Poppy stayed in the shelter of his arms, her head downbent. Her exposed ear looked so tender. The fragrance of her perfume teased him. He wanted to explore every part of her, hold her until she relaxed against him. "It's all right," he murmured again, stroking a circle on her back with his palm. "It's gone. I'm sorry you were frightened."

"No, *I'm* sorry, I . . ." Poppy drew back, her white face now infused with color. "I'm not usually skittish, it was only the surprise. A long time ago—" She stopped herself and fidgeted, and muttered, "I'm *not* going to babble."

Harry didn't want her to stop. He found everything about her endlessly interesting, although he couldn't explain why. She simply *was*.

"Tell me," he said in a low voice.

Poppy made a helpless gesture and gave him a wry glance as if to convey that she had warned him. "When I was a child, one of my favorite people in the world was my Uncle Howard, my father's brother. He had no wife or children of his own, so he lavished all his attention on us."

A reminiscent smile touched her lips. "Uncle Howard was very patient with me. My chattering drove everyone else to distraction, but he always listened as if he had all the time in the world. One morning he came to visit us while Father went shooting with some of the village men. When they returned with a

brace of birds, Uncle Howard and I went to the end of
the lane to meet them. But someone's rifle discharged
accidentally . . . I'm not certain if it was dropped, or
if the man was carrying it incorrectly . . . I remember
the sound if it, a boom like thunder, and there were a
few hard pinches on my arm, and another on my
shoulder. I turned to tell Uncle Howard, but he was
crumpling very slowly to the ground. He'd been fa-
tally wounded, and I had been hit by a few stray pel-
lets."

Poppy hesitated, her eyes glittering. "There was
blood all over him. I went to him and put my arms
beneath his head, and asked him what I should do.
And he whispered that I must always be a good girl,
so that we could meet again in heaven someday."
She cleared her throat and sighed shortly. "Forgive
me. I talk excessively. I shouldn't—"

"No," Harry said, overwhelmed by a baffling and
unfamiliar emotion, white-knuckled with it. "I could
listen to you all day."

She blinked in surprise, jostled out of her melancholy. A shy grin rose to her lips. "Aside from my
Uncle Howard, you're the first man ever to say that
to me."

They were interrupted by exclamations from the
men gathered around the rope lift, as the macaque
climbed higher.

"Bloody hell," Harry muttered.

"Please wait just a moment more," Poppy said to
him earnestly. "My sister is very good with animals.
She'll have him out with no injury."

"She has experience with primates?" Harry asked
sardonically.

Poppy considered that. "We've just been through
the London season. Does that count?"

Harry chuckled, with a genuine amusement that didn't often occur, and both Valentine and Brimbley glanced at him with astonishment.

Beatrix hurried back to them, clutching something in her arms. She paid no attention to Miss Marks, who was following and scolding. "Here we are," Beatrix said cheerfully.

"Our comfit jar?" Poppy asked.

"We've already offered him food, miss," Valentine said. "He won't take it."

"He'll take these." Beatrix strode confidently to the opening of the food lift. "Let's send the jar up to him."

"Have you adulterated the sweets?" Valentine asked hopefully.

All three of the Nagarajan envoys exclaimed anxiously to the effect that they did not want the macaque to be drugged or poisoned.

"No, no, no," Beatrix said, "He might fall down the shaft if I did that, and this precious animal must not be harmed."

The foreigners subsided at her reassurance.

"How may I help, Bea?" Poppy asked, approaching her.

Her younger sister handed her a length of heavy silk cord. "Tie this 'round the neck of the jar, please. Your knots are always much better than mine."

"A clove hitch?" Poppy suggested, taking the twine.

"Yes, perfect."

Jake Valentine regarded the two intent young women dubiously, and looked at Harry. "Mr. Rutledge—"

Harry gestured for him to be silent and allow the Hathaway sisters to proceed. Whether or not their attempt actually worked, he was enjoying this too much to stop them.

"Could you make some kind of loop for a handle at the other end?" Beatrix asked.

Poppy frowned. "An overhand knot, perhaps? I'm not sure I remember how."

"Allow me," Harry volunteered, stepping forward.

Poppy surrendered the end of the cord to him, her eyes twinkling.

Harry tied the end of the cord into an elaborate rope ball, first wrapping it several times around his fingers, then passing the free end back and forth. Not above a bit of showmanship, he tightened the whole thing with a deft flourish.

"Nicely done," Poppy said. "What knot is that?"

"Ironically," Harry replied, "it is known as the 'Monkey's Fist.'"

Poppy smiled. "Is it really? No, you're teasing."

"I never tease about knots. A good knot is a thing of beauty." Harry gave the rope end to Beatrix, and watched as she placed the jar atop the frame of the food lift cab. Then he realized what her plan was. "Clever," he murmured.

"It may not work," Beatrix said. "It depends on whether the monkey is more intelligent than we are."

"I'm rather afraid of the answer," Harry replied dryly. Reaching inside the food lift shaft, he pulled the rope slowly, sending the jar up to the macaque, while Beatrix kept hold of the silk cord.

All was quiet. The group held their breath *en masse* as they waited.

Thump.

The monkey had descended to the top of the cab. A few inquiring hoots and grunts echoed through the shaft. A rattle, a silence, and then a sharp tug at the line. Offended screams filled the air, and heavy thumps shook the food lift.

"We caught him," Beatrix exclaimed.

Harry took the line from her, while Valentine lowered the cab. "Please stand back, Miss Hathaway."

"Let me do it," Beatrix urged. "The macaque is much more likely to spring at you than me. Animals trust me."

"Nevertheless, I can't risk one of my guests being injured."

Poppy and Miss Marks both drew Beatrix away from the food lift opening. They all gasped as a large, blue black macaque appeared, his eyes huge and bright above a hairless muzzle, his head comically tufted with a shock of fur. The monkey was stocky and powerful in appearance, with hardly any tail to speak of. His expressive face contorted in fury, white teeth gleaming as it screeched.

One of the front paws appeared to be stuck in the comfit jar. The irate macaque tugged frantically to get it out, without success. His own clenched fist was the reason for his captivity—he refused to let go of the comfits even to remove his paw from the jar.

"Oh, isn't he beautiful!" Beatrix enthused.

"Perhaps to a female macaque," Poppy said dubiously.

Harry held the cord attached to the jar with one hand, his fencing foil with the other. The macaque was larger than he had expected, capable of inflicting considerable damage. And it was clearly considering whom to attack first.

"Come on, old fellow," Harry murmured, attempting to lead the monkey to the open crate.

Beatrix reached into her pocket, pulled out a few comfits, and went to toss them into the crate. "There you are, greedy boy," she said to the macaque. "Your treats are in there. Go on, and don't make such a fuss."

Miraculously, the monkey obeyed, dragging his jar with him. After casting a baleful glance at Harry, he entered his crate and scooped up the scattered comfits with his free paw.

"Give me the jar," Beatrix said patiently, tugging at the cord, and she pulled it out of the crate. She tossed a last handful of comfits to the monkey and closed the door. The Nagarajans hastened to lock it.

"I want it triple chained," Harry said to Valentine, "and the other monkey's crate chained as well. And then I want them delivered directly to Regent's Park."

"Yes, sir."

Poppy went to her sister, hugging her in an open display of affection. "Well done, Bea," she exclaimed. "How did you know the monkey wouldn't let go of the comfits in his hand?"

"Because it is a well-known fact that monkeys are nearly as greedy as people," Beatrix said, and Poppy laughed.

"Girls," Miss Marks said in a low voice, trying to hush them, draw them away. "This is unseemly. We must go."

"Yes, of course," Poppy said. "I'm sorry, Miss Marks. We'll go on with our walk."

However, the companion's attempt to urge the sisters to leave was foiled as the Nagarajans crowded around Beatrix.

"You have done us a *very* great service," the head

diplomat, Niran, told the girl. "Very great indeed. You have the gratitude of our country and our king, and you shall be recommended to Her Majesty Queen Victoria for your brave assistance—"

"No, thank you," Miss Marks interceded firmly. "Miss Hathaway does not wish to be recommended. You will harm her reputation by exposing her publicly. If you are indeed grateful for her kindness, we beg you to repay her with silence."

This produced more discussion and vigorous nodding.

Beatrix sighed and watched as the macaque was carried away in his crate. "I wish I had a monkey of my own," she said wistfully.

Miss Marks gave Poppy a long-suffering glance. "One might wish she were as eager to acquire a husband."

Smothering a grin, Poppy tried to look sympathetic.

"Have the food lift cleaned," Harry told Valentine and Brimbley. "Every inch of it."

The men hastened to comply, the older man using the pulleys to send the food lift down, while Valentine departed in swift, controlled strides.

Harry glanced at all three of the women, lingering an extra moment on Miss Marks's set face. "I thank you for your assistance, ladies."

"Not at all," Poppy said, her eyes dancing. "And if there are further problems with recalcitrant monkeys, do not hesitate to send for us."

Harry's blood quickened as lurid images filled his mind . . . her, against him, beneath him. That smiling mouth, his alone, her whispers curling into his ear. Her skin, soft and ivory pale in the darkness.

Skin heated by skin, sensation emerging as he touched her.

She was worth anything, he thought, even giving up the last remnants of his soul.

"Good day," he heard himself say, his voice husky but polite. And he forced himself to walk away.

For now.

Chapter Seven

"Now I understand what you meant earlier," Beatrix said to Poppy, when Miss Marks had gone on some undisclosed errand. Poppy had settled in her bed, while Beatrix had washed Dodger and was now drying him with a towel before the hearth. "What you were trying to say about Mr. Rutledge," she continued. "No wonder you found him unsettling." She paused to grin at the happy ferret, who was wriggling on a warm towel. "Dodger, you do like to be clean, don't you? You smell so lovely after a good washing."

"You always say that, and he always smells the same." Poppy raised herself on an elbow and watched them, her hair spilling around her shoulders. She felt too restless to nap. "Then you found Mr. Rutledge unsettling, too?"

"No, but I understand why *you* do. He watches you like one of those ambushing sort of predators. The kind that lie in wait before they spring."

"How dramatic," Poppy said with a dismissive laugh. "He's not a predator, Bea. He's only a man."

Beatrix made no reply, only made a project of smoothing Dodger's fur. As she leaned over him, he strained upward and kissed her nose affectionately. "Poppy," she murmured, "no matter how Miss Marks tries to civilize me—and I do try to listen to her—I still have my own way of looking at the world. To me, people are scarcely different from animals. We're all God's creatures, aren't we? When I meet someone, I know immediately what animal they would be. When we first met Cam, for example, I knew he was a fox."

"I suppose Cam is somewhat fox-like," Poppy said, amused. "What is Merripen? A bear?"

"No, unquestionably a horse. And Amelia is a hen."

"I would say an owl."

"Yes, but don't you remember when one of our hens in Hampshire chased after a cow that had strayed too close to the nest? That's Amelia."

Poppy grinned. "You're right."

"And Win is a swan."

"Am I also a bird? A lark? A robin?"

"No, you're a rabbit."

"A *rabbit*?" Poppy made a face. "I don't like that. Why am I a rabbit?"

"Oh, rabbits are beautiful soft animals who love to be cuddled. They're very sociable, but they're happiest in pairs."

"But they're timid," Poppy protested.

"Not always. They're brave enough to be companions to many other creatures. Even cats and dogs."

"Well," Poppy said in resignation, "it's better than being a hedgehog, I suppose."

"Miss Marks is a hedgehog," Beatrix said in a matter-of-fact tone that made Poppy grin.

"And you're a ferret, aren't you, Bea?"

"Yes. But I was leading to a point."

"Sorry, go on."

"I was going to say that Mr. Rutledge is a cat. A solitary hunter. With an apparent taste for rabbit."

Poppy blinked in bewilderment. "You think he is interested in . . . Oh, but Bea, I'm not at all . . . and I don't think I'll ever see him again . . ."

"I hope you're right."

Settling on her side, Poppy watched her sister in the flickering glow of the hearth, while a chill of uneasiness penetrated the very marrow of her bones.

Not because she feared Harry Rutledge.

Because she liked him.

Catherine Marks knew that Harry was up to something. He was *always* up to something. He certainly had no intention of inquiring after her welfare—he didn't give a damn about her. He considered most people, including Catherine, a waste of his time.

Whatever mysterious mechanism sent Harry Rutledge's blood pumping through his veins, it wasn't a heart.

In the years of their acquaintance, Catherine had never asked anything of him. Once Harry did someone a favor, it went into the invisible ledger he carried around in that infernally clever brain, and it was only a matter of time until he demanded repayment with interest. People feared him for good reason. Harry had powerful friends and powerful enemies, and it was doubtful that even they knew what category they fell in.

The valet, or assistant, whatever he was, showed her into Harry's palatial apartment. Catherine thanked him with a frosty murmur. She sat in a receiving room with her hands resting in her lap. The receiving room had been designed to intimidate visitors, all of it done in slick, pale fabrics and cold marble and priceless Renaissance art.

Harry entered the room, large and breathtakingly self-assured. As always, he was elegantly dressed and meticulously groomed.

Stopping before her, he surveyed her with insolent green eyes. "Cat. You look well."

"Go to the devil," she said quietly.

His gaze dropped to the white plait of her fingers, and a lazy smile crossed his face. "I suppose to you, I *am* the devil." He nodded toward the other side of the settee she occupied. "May I?"

Catherine gave a short nod and waited until he had seated himself. "Why did you send for me?" Her voice was brittle.

"It was an amusing scene this morning, wasn't it? Your Hathaways were a delight. They're certainly not your run-of-the-mill society misses."

Slowly Catherine raised her gaze to his, trying not to flinch as she stared into the vivid depths of green. Harry excelled at hiding his thoughts . . . but this morning he had stared at Poppy with a hunger that he was usually too well disciplined to reveal. And Poppy had no idea of how to defend herself against a man like Harry.

Catherine strove to keep her voice even. "I will not discuss the Hathaways with you. And I warn you to stay away from them."

"You *warn* me?" Harry repeated softly, his eyes bright with mocking amusement.

"I won't let you hurt anyone in my family."

"*Your* family?" One of his dark brows lifted. "You have no family."

"I meant the family I work for," Catherine said with icy dignity. "I meant my charges. Especially Poppy. I saw the way you looked at her this morning. If you try to harm her in any way—"

"I have no intention of harming anyone."

"Regardless of your intentions, it happens, doesn't it?" Catherine felt a stab of satisfaction as she saw his eyes narrow. "Poppy is far too good for you," she continued, "and she is out of your reach."

"Hardly anything is out of my reach, Cat." He said it without arrogance. It happened to be the truth. Which made Catherine all the more fearful.

"Poppy is practically betrothed," she replied sharply. "She is in love with someone."

"Michael Bayning."

Her heart began to hammer with alarm. "How do you know that?"

Harry ignored the question. "Do you really think that Viscount Andover, a man of notoriously exacting standards, would allow his son to marry a Hathaway?"

"I do. He loves his son, and therefore he will choose to overlook the fact that Poppy comes from an unconventional family. He could ask for no better mother for his future heirs."

"He's a peer. Bloodlines are everything to him. And while Poppy's bloodlines have led to an obviously charming result, they're far from pure."

"Her brother is a peer," Catherine snapped.

"Only by accident. The Hathaways are a twig on the farthest limb of the family tree. Ramsay may have inherited a title, but in terms of nobility, he's no more a peer than you or I. And Andover knows it."

"What a snob you are," Catherine observed in as calm a tone as she could manage.

"Not at all. I don't mind the Hathaways' common blood one bit. In fact, I like them all the better for it. All those anemic daughters of the peerage—none of them could hold a candle to the two girls I saw this morning." His smile became genuine for one dazzling moment. "What a pair. Catching a wild monkey with a comfit jar and string."

"Leave them alone," Catherine said. "You play with people as a cat does with mice. Entertain yourself with someone else, Harry. God knows you have no shortage of women who would do anything to please you."

"That's what makes them boring," he said gravely. "No, don't leave yet—there's something I want to ask. Has Poppy said anything to you about me?"

Mystified, Catherine shook her head. "Only that it was interesting to finally be able to put a face to the mysterious hotelier." She stared at him intently. "What else should she have told me?"

Harry adopted an innocent expression. "Nothing. I merely wondered if I had made an impression."

"I'm sure Poppy overlooked you entirely. Her affections are with Mr. Bayning, who, unlike you, is a good, honorable man."

"You wound me. Fortunately in matters of love, most women can be persuaded to choose a bad man over a good one."

"If you understood anything about love," Catherine said acidly, "you would know that Poppy would never choose *anyone* over the man she has already given her heart to."

"He can have her heart," came Harry's casual reply. "As long as I have the rest of her."

As Catherine spluttered in offended fury, Harry stood and went to the door. "Let me show you out. No doubt you'll want to go back and sound the alarms. For all the good it will do."

It had been a long time since Catherine had known such fathomless anxiety. Harry . . . Poppy . . . could he really have designs on her, or had he simply decided to torture Catherine with a cruel jest?

No, he had not been playacting. Of course Harry wanted Poppy, whose warmth and spontaneity and kindness was completely alien in his sophisticated world. He wanted a respite from his own inexhaustible needs, and once he was done with Poppy, he would have drained her of all the happiness and innocent charm that had attracted him in the first place.

Catherine didn't know what to do. She couldn't expose her own connection to Harry Rutledge, and he knew it.

The answer was to make certain that Poppy was betrothed to Michael Bayning, *publicly* betrothed, as soon as possible. Tomorrow Bayning would meet with the family and accompany them to the flower show. Afterward Catherine would find a way to hasten the courtship process. She would tell Cam and Amelia that they must press for the matter to be quickly resolved.

And if for some reason there was no betrothal—perish the thought—Catherine would suggest that she accompany Poppy on a trip abroad. Perhaps France or Italy. She would even tolerate the company of the galling Lord Ramsay, if he chose to go with them. Anything to keep Poppy safe from Harry Rutledge.

* * *

"Wake up, slugabed." Amelia strode into the bedroom wearing a dressing gown trimmed with cascades of soft lace, her dark hair gathered in a thick, neat braid over one shoulder. She had just come from feeding the baby. Having left him in the nursemaid's care, she was now set on the course of waking her husband.

Cam's natural preference was to stay up all hours of the night and rise late in the day. This habit was directly opposed to Amelia's early to bed, early to rise philosophy.

Going to one of the windows, she whisked open the curtains to admit the morning light, and was rewarded with a protesting groan from the bed. "Good morning," she said cheerfully. "The maid will be here soon to help me dress. You'd better put something on."

She busied herself at her dresser, sorting through a drawer of embroidered stockings. Out of the periphery of her vision she saw Cam stretch, his body lithe and powerful, his skin glowing like clover honey.

"Come here," Cam said in a sleep-darkened voice, drawing back the bed linens.

A laugh stirred in her throat. "Absolutely not. There is too much to be done. Everyone is busy except you."

"I intend to be busy. As soon as you come here. *Monisha,* don't make me chase you this early."

Amelia gave him a severe glance as she obeyed. "It's not early. In fact, if you don't wash and dress quickly, we'll be late to the flower show."

"How can you be late for flowers?" Cam shook his head and smiled, as he always did when she said something he considered to be *gadjo* nonsense. His gaze was hot and slumberous. "Come closer."

"Later." She gave a helpless gasp of laughter as he reached out with astonishing dexterity, snaring her wrist in his hand. "Cam, no."

"A good Romany wife never refuses her husband," he teased.

"The maid—" she said breathlessly as she was pulled across the mattress, and clasped against all that warm golden skin.

"She can wait." He unbuttoned her robe, his hand slipping past the lace, fingertips exploring the sensitive curves of her breasts.

Amelia's giggles died away. He knew so much about her—too much—and he never hesitated to take ruthless advantage. She closed her eyes as she reached up to the nape of his neck. The clean, silky locks of his hair slipped through her fingers like liquid.

Cam kissed her tender throat, while one of his knees nudged between hers. "It's either now," he murmured, "or behind the rhododendrons at the flower show. Your choice."

She writhed a little, not in protest but excitement as he trapped her arms in the confining sleeves of the dressing gown. "Cam," she managed to say as his head bent over her exposed breasts. "We're going to be so terribly late . . ."

He murmured his desire to her, speaking in Romany as he did whenever his mood turned uncivilized, and the exotic syllables fell hotly against her sensitive skin. And for the next several minutes he possessed her, consumed her, with a lack of inhibition that would have seemed barbaric had he not been so gentle.

"Cam," she said afterward, her arms clasped around his neck, "are you going to say something to Mr. Bayning today?"

"About pansies and primulas?"

"About his intentions toward my sister."

Cam smiled down at her as he fingered a loose lock of her hair. "Would you object if I did?"

"No, I want you to." A frown notched the space between her brows. "Poppy is adamant that no one should criticize Mr. Bayning for taking so long to speak to his father about courting her."

Gently Cam used the pad of his thumb to smooth away the little frown. "He's waited long enough. The Rom say of a man like Bayning, 'he would like to eat fish, but he would not like to get in the water.' "

Amelia responded with a humorless chuckle. "It's very frustrating, to know that he's tiptoeing around the issue like this. I wish Bayning would simply go to his father and have it out."

Cam, who knew something about the aristocracy from his days as the manager of an exclusive gaming club, said dryly, "A young man who stands to inherit as much as Bayning has to tread softly."

"I don't care. He has gotten my sister's hopes very high. If it all comes to naught, she'll be devastated. And he has kept her from being courted by other men, and wasted an entire season—"

"Shhh." Cam rolled to his side, taking her with him. "I agree with you, *monisha* . . . this shadow courtship must end. I'll make certain Bayning understands that it's time to take action. And I'll speak to the viscount, if that will help."

"Thank you." Amelia tucked her cheek into one of the hard curves of his chest, seeking comfort. "I'll be so glad when this is resolved. Lately I haven't been able to rid myself of the feeling that things won't turn out well for Poppy and Mr. Bayning. I hope I'm wrong. I want so badly for Poppy to be happy, and . . . what will we do, if he breaks her heart?"

"We'll take care of her," he murmured, cuddling her. "And love her. That's what a family is for."

Chapter Eight

Poppy was light-headed with nerves and excitement. Michael would soon arrive to accompany the family to the flower show. After all their subterfuge, this was the first step toward an openly acknowledged courtship.

She had dressed with extra care in a yellow walking dress trimmed with black velvet cord. The layered skirts were caught up at intervals with black velvet bows. Beatrix wore a similar ensemble, only hers was blue trimmed in chocolate.

"Lovely," Miss Marks had pronounced, smiling as they entered the receiving room of the family suite. "You will be the two most elegant young ladies at the flower show." She reached up to Poppy's upswept curls and anchored a pin more securely. "And I predict that Mr. Bayning will not be able to take his gaze off you," she added.

"He's a bit late," Poppy said tensely. "It's not like him. I hope he hasn't met with some difficulty."

"He will arrive soon, I'm sure."

Cam and Amelia entered the room, the latter

looking radiant in pink, her small waist cinched with a bronze leather belt that matched her walking boots.

"What a lovely day for an outing," Amelia said, her blue eyes twinkling. "Though I doubt you'll even notice the flowers, Poppy."

Putting a hand to her midriff, Poppy let out an unsteady sigh. "This is all so nerve-wracking."

"I know, dear." Amelia went to embrace her. "This makes me indescribably grateful that I never had to go through the London season. I would never have had your patience. Really, they should levy a tax on London bachelors until they marry. That would hasten the entire courtship process."

"I don't see why people have to marry at all," Beatrix said. "There was no one to marry Adam and Eve, was there? They lived together naturally. Why should any of us bother with a wedding if they didn't?"

Poppy gave a nervous laugh. "When Mr. Bayning is here," she said, "let's not bring up any outlandish debate topics, Bea. I'm afraid he's not used to our way of . . . well, our . . ."

"Colorful discussions," Miss Marks suggested.

Amelia grinned. "Don't worry, Poppy. We'll be so staid and proper, we'll be absolute bores."

"Thank you," Poppy said fervently.

"Do I have to be boring, too?" Beatrix asked Miss Marks, who nodded emphatically.

With a sigh, Beatrix went to a table in the corner and began to empty her pockets.

Poppy's stomach flipped as she heard a knock at the door. "He's here," she said breathlessly.

"I will answer," Miss Marks said. She gave Poppy a quick smile. "Breathe, dear."

Poppy nodded and tried to calm herself. She saw Amelia and Cam exchange a glance she could not interpret. The understanding between the pair was so absolute, it seemed they could read each other's thoughts.

She was tempted to smile as she remembered Beatrix's comment that rabbits were happiest in pairs. Beatrix had been right. Poppy wanted very much to be loved, to be part of a pair. And she had waited for so long, and she was still unwed when friends her age had already married and had two or three children. It seemed a common fate for Hathaways to find love later rather than sooner.

Poppy's thoughts were interrupted as Michael entered the room and bowed. A surge of gladness was tempered by the sight of his expression, more grim than she had ever imagined possible. His complexion was pale, his eyes reddened as if he'd had no sleep. He looked ill, as a matter of fact.

"Mr. Bayning," she said softly, her heart beating like a small animal fighting to free itself from a net. "Are you well? What is the matter?"

Michael's brown eyes, usually so warm, were bleak as he glanced at her family. "Forgive me," he said hoarsely. "I hardly know what to say." His breath seemed to shiver in his throat. "I am in some . . . some difficulty . . . it's impossible." His gaze settled on Poppy. "Miss Hathaway, I must speak with you. I don't know if it would be possible to have a moment alone . . ."

A difficult silence followed the request. Cam stared at the young man with an unfathomable expression, while Amelia gave a slight shake of her head as if to deny what was coming.

"I'm afraid that would not be proper, Mr. Bayning," Miss Marks murmured. "We have Miss Hathaway's reputation to consider."

"Of course." He passed a hand over his forehead, and Poppy realized that his fingers were trembling.

Something was very wrong indeed.

An icy calm settled over her. She spoke in a dazed voice that didn't sound quite like her own. "Amelia, perhaps you might stay in the room with us?"

"Yes, of course."

The rest of the family, including Miss Marks, left the room.

Poppy felt cold runnels of perspiration beneath her chemise, damp patches blossoming at the pits of her arms. She took a place on the settee and watched Michael with dilated eyes. "You may have a seat," she told him.

He hesitated and glanced at Amelia, who had gone to stand beside the window.

"Please do have a seat, Mr. Bayning," Amelia said, staring at the street outside. "I'm trying to pretend I'm not here. I'm so sorry you can't have more privacy than this, but I'm afraid Miss Marks is right. Poppy's reputation must be protected."

Although there was no trace of rebuke in her tone, Michael flinched visibly. Occupying the space next to Poppy, he took her hands and bent his head over them. His fingers were even colder than hers. "I had an unholy row with my father last night," he said, his voice muffled. "It seems one of the rumors reached him about my interest in you. About my intentions. He was . . . outraged."

"That must have been dreadful," Poppy said, knowing that Michael rarely, if ever, quarreled with his father. He held the viscount in awe, striving always to please him.

"Worse than dreadful." Michael took an unsteady breath. "I'll spare you the particulars. The result of a long, very ugly argument is that the viscount gave me an ultimatum. If I marry you, I will be cut off. He will no longer recognize me as his son, and I will be disinherited."

There was no sound in the room except for Amelia's swiftly indrawn breath.

Pain unfolded in Poppy's chest, crowding the breath from her lungs. "What reason did he give?" she managed to ask.

"Only that you do not fit the mold of a Bayning bride."

"If you allow time for his temper to cool . . . try to change his mind . . . I can wait, Michael. I'll wait forever."

Michael shook his head. "I cannot encourage you to wait. My father's refusal was absolute. It could take years to change his mind, if ever. And in the meantime, you deserve the chance to find happiness."

Poppy stared at him steadily. "I could only be happy with you."

Michael raised his head, his eyes dark and glittering. "I'm sorry, Poppy. Sorry for giving you any reason to hope, when it was never possible. My only excuse is that I thought I knew my father, when apparently I don't. I always believed I could convince him to accept the woman I loved, that my judgment would be enough. And I—" His voice cracked. He swallowed audibly. "I do love you. I . . . hell and damnation, I'll never forgive him for this." Releasing her hands, he reached into his coat pocket and extracted a packet of letters tied with cord. All the letters she had written to him. "I'm honor bound to return these."

"I won't give yours back," Poppy said, taking the letters in a shaking hand. "I want to keep them."

"That is your right, of course."

"Michael," Poppy said brokenly, "I love you."

"I . . . I can't give you any reason to hope."

They were both quiet and trembling, staring at each other in despair.

Amelia's voice pierced through the suffocating silence. She sounded blessedly rational. "The viscount's objections needn't stop you, Mr. Bayning. He can't prevent you from inheriting the title and entailed properties, can he?"

"No, but—"

"Take my sister to Gretna Green. We'll provide the carriage. My sister's dowry is large enough to secure a handsome annuity for you both. If you need more, my husband will increase it." Amelia leveled a steady, challenging gaze at him. "If you want my sister, Mr. Bayning, marry her. The Hathaways will help you weather what storms may come."

Poppy had never loved her sister more than she did at that moment. She stared at Amelia with a wobbly smile, her eyes brimming.

Her smile vanished, however, as Michael answered dully. "The title and real estate are entailed, but until my father dies, I would be abandoned to my own resources, which are nonexistent. And I can't live off the charity of my wife's family."

"It's not charity when it's family," Amelia countered.

"You don't understand how things are with the Baynings," Michael said. "This is a matter of honor. I'm the only son. I've been raised for one thing since I was born—to assume the responsibilities of my rank and title. It's all I've ever known. I can't live as an outcast, outside my father's sphere. I can't live with scandal and ostracism." He hung his head. "Sweet

God, I'm weary of arguing. My brain's gone in circles all night."

Poppy saw the impatience on her sister's face, and she knew that Amelia was prepared to fight him on every point, for her sake. But she held Amelia's gaze and shook her head, sending the silent message, *It's no use.* Michael had already decided on his course. He would never defy his father. Arguing would only make him more miserable than he already was.

Amelia closed her mouth and turned to stare out the window again.

"I'm sorry," Michael said after a long silence, still gripping Poppy's hands. "I never meant to deceive you. Everything I told you about my feelings—every word was true. My only regret is that I wasted your time. Valuable time for a girl in your position."

Although he hadn't meant that as a slight, Poppy winced.

A girl in her position.

Twenty-three. Unmarried. On the shelf after her third season.

Carefully she drew her hands from Michael's. "Not a moment was wasted," she managed to say. "I am the better for having known you, Mr. Bayning. Please don't have any regrets. I don't."

"Poppy," he said in an aching voice that nearly undid her.

She was terrified that she might burst into tears. "Please go."

"If I could make you understand—"

"I understand. I do. And I will be perfectly—" She broke off and swallowed hard. "Please go. *Please.*"

She was aware of Amelia coming forward, murmuring something to Michael, efficiently shepherding him out of the suite before Poppy lost her composure. Dear Amelia, who did not hesitate to take charge of a man much larger than herself.

A hen chasing a cow, Poppy thought, and she let out a watery giggle even as hot tears began to slide from her eyes.

After closing the door firmly, Amelia sat beside Poppy and reached out to grasp her shoulders. She stared into Poppy's blurred eyes. "You are," she said, her voice ragged with emotion, "such a lady, Poppy. And much kinder than he deserved. I am so proud of you. I wonder if he understands how much he has lost."

"The situation wasn't his fault."

Amelia tugged a handkerchief from her sleeve and gave it to her. "Debatable. But I won't criticize him, since it won't help matters. However, I must say . . . the phrase 'I can't' comes rather too easily to his lips."

"He is an obedient son," Poppy said, mopping at her tears, then giving up and simply wadding the handkerchief against her flooding eyes.

"Yes, well . . . from now on, I advise you to look for a man with his own means of support."

Poppy shook her head, her face still buried in the handkerchief. "There's no one for me."

She felt her sister's arms go around her. "There is. There is, I *promise* you. He's waiting. He'll find you. And someday Michael Bayning will be nothing but a distant memory."

Poppy began to cry in earnest, wracking sobs that caused her ribs to ache. "God," she managed to gasp. "This hurts, Amelia. And it feels as if it will never end."

Carefully Amelia guided Poppy's head to her

shoulder and kissed her wet cheek. "I know," she said. "I lived through it once. I remember what it was like. You'll cry, and then you'll be angry, and then despairing, and then angry again. But I know of a cure for heartbreak."

"What is it?" Poppy asked, letting out a shuddery sigh.

"Time . . . prayer . . . and most of all a family that loves you. You will always be loved, Poppy."

Poppy managed a wavering smile. "Thank God for sisters," she said, and wept against Amelia's shoulder.

Much later that night, there came a determined knock at the door of Harry Rutledge's private apartment. Jake Valentine paused in the act of laying out fresh clothes and polished black shoes for the morning. He went to answer the door and was confronted by a vaguely familiar–looking woman. She was small and slight, with light brown hair and blue gray eyes, and a pair of round spectacles perched on her nose. He considered her for a moment, trying to place her.

"May I help you?"

"I wish to see Mr. Rutledge."

"I'm afraid he's not at home."

Her mouth twisted at the well-worn phrase, used by servants when the master didn't wish to be disturbed. She spoke to him with scalding contempt. "Do you mean 'not at home' in the sense that he doesn't want to see me, or 'not at home' in the sense that he's actually gone?"

"Either way," Jake said implacably, "you won't see him tonight. But the truth is, he really isn't here. Is there a message I may convey to him?"

"Yes. Tell him that I hope he rots in hell for what he did to Poppy Hathaway. And then tell him that if he goes near her, I'll murder him."

Jake responded with a complete lack of alarm due to the fact that death threats against Harry were a more or less common occurrence. "And you are?"

"Just give him the message," she said curtly. "He'll know who it's from."

Two days after Michael Bayning had visited the hotel, the Hathaways' brother Leo, Lord Ramsay, came to call. Like other men-about-town, Leo leased a small Mayfair terrace during the season, and at the end of June retreated to his estate in the country. Although Leo could easily have chosen to live with the family at the Rutledge, he preferred privacy.

No one could deny that Leo was a handsome man, tall and broad shouldered, with dark brown hair and striking eyes. Unlike his sisters, his eyes were a light shade of blue, glacier colored with dark rims. Haunting. World-weary. He comported himself as a rake and did a thorough job of it, appearing never to care about anyone or anything. There were moments, however, when the mask was lifted just long enough to reveal a man of extraordinary feeling, and it was in those rare moments that Catherine was most apprehensive around him.

When they were in London, Leo was usually too busy to spend time with his family, for which Catherine was grateful. From the moment they had met, she had felt an intrinsic dislike for him, and he for her, flint and iron striking to create sparks of hatred. At times they competed to see who could say the most hurtful things to the other, each of them testing, prodding, trying to find places of vulnerability. They couldn't seem to help it, the constant urge to cut each other down to size.

Catherine answered the door of the family suite, and a jolt of reaction went through her as she was confronted by Leo's lanky, big-framed form. He was fashionably dressed in a dark coat with wide lapels, loose trousers with no creases, and a boldly patterned waistcoat with silver buttons.

He surveyed her with wintry eyes, an arrogant smile tilting the corners of his lips. "Good afternoon, Marks."

Catherine was stone-faced, her voice edged with scorn. "Lord Ramsay. I'm surprised you could tear yourself away from your amusements long enough to visit your sister."

Leo gave her a look of bemused mockery. "What have I done to earn a scolding? You know, Marks, if you ever learned to hold your tongue, your chances of attracting a man would rise exponentially."

Her eyes narrowed. "Why would I want to attract a man? I have yet to see anything they're good for."

"If for nothing else," Leo said, "you need us to help produce more women." He paused. "How is my sister?"

"Heartbroken."

Leo's mouth turned grim. "Let me in, Marks. I want to see her."

Catherine took a grudging step aside.

Leo went into the receiving room and found Poppy sitting alone with a book. He gave her an assessing glance. His normally bright-eyed sister was pale and drawn. She seemed unutterably weary, temporarily aged by grief.

Fury welled inside him. There were few people

that mattered to him in the world, but Poppy was one of them.

It was unfair that the people who longed for love the most, searched the hardest for it, found it so elusive. And there seemed no good reason why Poppy, the prettiest girl in London, shouldn't have been married by now. But Leo had gone through lists of acquaintances in his mind, pondering whether any of them would do for his sister, and none of them was remotely suitable. If one had the right temperament, he was an idiot or in his dotage. And then there were the lechers, the spendthrifts, and the reprobates. God help him, the peerage was a deplorable collection of male specimens. And he included himself in that estimation.

"Hello, sis," Leo said gently, approaching her. "Where are the others?"

Poppy managed a wan smile. "Cam is out on business matters, and Amelia and Beatrix are at the park, pushing Rye in the perambulator." She moved her feet to make room for him on the settee. "How are you, Leo?"

"Never mind that. What about you?"

"Never better," she said bravely.

"Yes, I can see that." Leo sat and reached for Poppy, gathering her close. He held her, patting her back, until he heard her sniffle. "That bastard," he said quietly. "Shall I kill him for you?"

"No," she said in a congested voice, "it wasn't his fault. He sincerely wanted to marry me. His intentions were good."

He kissed the top of her head. "Don't ever trust men with good intentions. They'll always disappoint you."

Refusing to smile at his quip, Poppy drew back to look at him. "I want to go home, Leo," she said plaintively.

"Of course you do, darling. But you can't yet."

She blinked. "Why not?"

"Yes, why not?" Catherine Marks asked tartly, sitting in a nearby chair.

Leo paused to send a brief scowl in the companion's direction before returning his attention to Poppy. "Rumors are flying," he said bluntly. "Last night I went to a drum, given by the wife of the Spanish ambassador—one of those things you go to only to be able to say you went—and I couldn't count the number of times I was asked about you and Bayning. Everyone seems to think that you were in love with Bayning, and that he rejected you because his father thinks you're not good enough."

"That's the truth."

"Poppy, this is London society, where the truth can get you into trouble. If you tell one truth, you'll have to tell another truth, and another, to keep covering up."

That elicited a genuine smile from her. "Are you trying to give me advice, Leo?"

"Yes, and although I always tell you to ignore my advice, this time you'd better take it. The last significant event of the season is a ball held by Lord and Lady Norbury next week—"

"We have just written our regrets," Catherine informed him. "Poppy does not wish to attend."

Leo glanced at her sharply. "Have the regrets been sent?"

"No, but—"

"Tear them up, then. That's an order." Leo saw

her narrow frame stiffen, and he got a perverse pleasure from the sight.

"But, Leo," Poppy protested, "I don't want to go to
a ball. People might be watching to see if I—"

"They will certainly be watching," Leo said.
"Like a flock of vultures. Which is why you have to
attend. Because if you don't, you'll be shredded by
the gossips, and mocked without mercy when next
season begins."

"I don't care," Poppy said. "I'll never go through
another season again."

"You may change your mind. And I want you to
have the choice. Which is why you're going to the
ball, Poppy. You'll wear your prettiest dress, and
blue ribbons in your hair, and show them all that you
don't give a damn about Michael Bayning. You're
going to dance and laugh, and hold your head high."

"Leo," Poppy groaned. "I don't know if I can."

"Of course you can. Your pride demands it."

"I don't have any reason to be proud."

"I don't either," Leo said. "But that doesn't stop
me, does it?" He glanced from Poppy's reluctant
expression to Catherine's unreadable one. "Tell her
I'm right, damn it," he told her. "She has to go, doesn't
she?"

Catherine hesitated uncomfortably. Much as it
galled her to admit it, Leo was indeed right. A confident, smiling appearance by Poppy at the ball
would do much to still the wagging tongues of London parlors. But her instincts urged that Poppy should
be taken to the safety of Hampshire as soon as possible. As long as she remained in town, she was in
Harry Rutledge's reach.

On the other hand . . . Harry never attended such

events, where desperate matchmaking mothers with unclaimed daughters scrabbled to snare every last available bachelor. Harry would never lower himself to go to the Norbury ball, especially since his appearance there would turn it into a veritable circus.

"Please control your language," Catherine said. "Yes, you are right. However, it will be difficult for Poppy. And if she loses her composure at the ball—if she gives way to tears—it will give the gossips even more ammunition."

"I won't lose my composure," Poppy said, sounding drained. "I feel as if I've cried enough for a lifetime."

"Good girl," Leo said softly. He glanced at Catherine's troubled expression and smiled. "It appears we've finally agreed on something, Marks. But don't worry—I'm sure it won't happen again."

Chapter Nine

The Norbury ball was held in Belgravia, a district of calm and quietness in the heart of London. One could be overwhelmed by the bustle and roar of traffic and activity on Knightsbridge or Sloane Street, cross over to Belgrave Square, and find oneself in an oasis of soothing decorum. It was a place of large marble embassies and grand white terraces, of solemn mansions with tall powdered footmen and stout butlers, and carriages conveying languid young ladies and their tiny overfed dogs.

The surrounding districts of London held little interest for those fortunate enough to live in Belgravia. Conversations were largely about local matters—who had taken a particular house, or what nearby street needed repairs, or what events had taken place at a neighboring residence.

To Poppy's dismay, Cam and Amelia had agreed with Leo's assessment of the situation. A show of pride and unconcern was called for if Poppy wished to stem the tide of gossip concerning Michael Bayning's rejection. "The *gadje* has a long memory of these matters," Cam had said sardonically. "God knows why they attach such importance to things of no consequence. But they do."

"It's only one evening," Amelia had told Poppy in concern. "Do you think you could manage an appearance, dear?"

"Yes," Poppy had agreed dully. "If you are there, I can manage it."

However, as she ascended the front steps to the mansion's portico, Poppy was swamped with regret and dread. The glass of wine she'd had to bolster her courage had pooled like acid in her stomach, and her corset had been laced too tightly.

She wore a white dress, layers of draped satin and pale blue illusion. Her waist was cinched with a belt of satin folds, the bodice deep and scooped and trimmed with another delicate froth of blue. After arranging her hair in a mass of pinned-up curls, Amelia had threaded a thin blue ribbon through it.

Leo had arrived, as promised, to accompany the family to the ball. He held out his arm for Poppy and escorted her up the stairs, while the family followed *en masse*. They entered the overheated house, which was filled with flowers, music, and the din of hundreds of simultaneous conversations. Doors had been removed from their hinges to allow for the circulation of guests from the ballroom to the supper and card rooms.

The Hathaways waited in a receiving line in the entrance hall.

"Look how dignified and polite they all are," Leo said, observing the crowd. "I can't stay long. Someone might influence me."

"You promised you would stay until after the first set," Poppy reminded him.

Her brother sighed. "For you, I will. But I despise these affairs."

"As do I," Miss Marks surprised them all by saying grimly, surveying the gathering as if it were enemy territory.

"My God. Something else we agree on." Leo gave the companion a half-mocking, half-uneasy glance. "We have to stop doing this, Marks. My stomach is starting to turn."

"*Please* do not say that word," she snapped.

"Stomach? Why not?"

"It is indelicate to refer to your anatomy." She gave his tall form a disdainful glance. "And I assure you, no one has any interest in it."

"You think not? I'll have you know, Marks, that scores of women have remarked on my—"

"Ramsay," Cam interrupted, giving him a warning glance.

When they had made it through the entrance hall, the family dispersed to make the rounds. Leo and Cam went to the card rooms, while the women headed to the supper tables. Amelia was instantly captured by a small group of chattering matrons.

"I can't eat," Poppy commented, glancing with revulsion at the long buffet of cold joints, beef, ham, and lobster salads.

"I'm starved," Beatrix. said apologetically. "Do you mind if I have something?"

"Not at all, we'll wait with you."

"Have a spoonful of salad," Miss Marks murmured to Poppy. "For appearance's sake. And smile."

"Like this?" Poppy attempted to turn the corners of her mouth upward.

Beatrix regarded her doubtfully. "No, that's not pretty at all. You look like a salmon."

"I feel like a salmon," Poppy said. "One that's been boiled, shredded and potted."

As the guests queued at the buffet, footmen filled their plates and carried them to nearby tables.

Poppy was still waiting in line when she was approached by Lady Belinda Wallscourt, a pretty young woman she had befriended during the Season. As soon as Belinda had come out into society, she was pursued by several eligible gentlemen, and had quickly become betrothed.

"Poppy," Lady Belinda said warmly, "how nice to see you here. There was uncertainty as to whether you would come."

"The last ball of the Season?" Poppy said with a forced smile. "I wouldn't miss it."

"I'm so glad." Lady Belinda gave her a compassionate glance. Her voice lowered. "It's terrible, what happened to you. I'm dreadfully sorry."

"Oh, there's nothing to be sorry about," Poppy said brightly. "I'm perfectly fine!"

"You're very brave," Belinda replied. "And Poppy, remember that someday you will meet a frog who will turn into a handsome prince."

"Good," Beatrix said. "Because all she's met so far are princes who turn into frogs."

Looking perplexed, Belinda managed a smile and left them.

"Mr. Bayning is not a frog," Poppy protested.

"You're right," Beatrix said. "That was very unfair to frogs, who are lovely creatures."

As Poppy parted her lips to object, she heard Miss Marks snicker. And she began to laugh as well, until they attracted curious glances from the queue at the buffet.

After Beatrix had finished eating, they wandered

to the ballroom. Music fluttered downward in continuous drifts from the orchestra playing in the upper gallery. The massive room glittered in the light of eight chandeliers, while the sweetness of abundant roses and greenery thickened the air.

Locked in the unforgiving bondage of her corset, Poppy filled her lungs with strained breaths. "It's too warm in here," she said.

Miss Marks glanced at her perspiring face, quickly produced a handkerchief, and guided her into one of the many cane openwork chairs at the side of the room. "It is quite warm," she said. "In a moment, I will locate your brother or Mr. Rohan to escort you outside for some air. But first let me see to Beatrix."

"Yes, of course," Poppy managed, seeing that two men had already approached Beatrix in hopes of entering their names on her dance card. Her younger sister was at ease with men in a way that Poppy could never manage. They seemed to adore Beatrix because she treated them as she did her wild creatures, gently humoring, showing patient interest.

While Miss Marks supervised Beatrix's dance card, Poppy settled back in her chair and concentrated on breathing around the iron prison of her corset. It was unfortunate that in this particular chair, she was able to hear a conversation from the other side of a garlanded column.

A trio of young women spoke in low tones that oozed with smug satisfaction.

"Of course Bayning wouldn't have her," one of them said. "She's pretty, I'll allow, but so maladroit, in the social sense. A gentleman I know said that he tried to talk to her at the private art viewing at the Royal Academy, and she was prattling about some ridiculous topic . . . something about a long-ago French balloon experiment when they sent a sheep up into the air in front of King Louis something-or-other . . . can you *imagine*?"

"Louis the sixteenth," Poppy whispered.

"But what would you expect?" came another voice. "Such an odd family. The only one good enough for society is Lord Ramsay, and he is quite wicked."

"A scapegrace," the other one agreed.

Poppy went from being overheated to chilled. She closed her eyes sickly, wishing she could disappear. It had been a mistake to come to the ball. She was trying to prove something to everyone . . . that she didn't care about Michael Bayning, when she did. That her heart wasn't broken, when it was. Everything in London was about appearances, pretenses . . . was it so unforgivable to be honest about one's feelings?

Apparently so.

She sat quietly, knitting her gloved fingers together until her thoughts were diverted by a stir near the main entrance of the ballroom. It seemed that some important person had arrived, perhaps royalty, or a military celebrity, or an influential politician.

"Who is he?" one of the young women asked.

"Someone new," the other said.

"And handsome."

"Divine," her companion agreed. "He must be a man of consequence—otherwise there wouldn't be such a to-do."

A light laugh. "And Lady Norbury wouldn't be fluttering so. See how she blushes!"

Curious despite herself, Poppy leaned forward to catch a glimpse of the newcomer. All she could make out was a dark head, taller than the others around him. He walked further into the ballroom, talking easily with his companions while the stout, bejeweled, and beaming Lady Norbury clung to his arm.

Recognizing him, Poppy sat back in her chair.

Harry Rutledge.

She couldn't fathom why he would be here, or why that made her smile.

Probably because she couldn't help recalling the last time she had seen him, dressed in fencing whites, trying to skewer a misbehaving monkey. Tonight Harry was forbiddingly handsome in full evening attire and a crisp white cravat. And he moved and conversed with the same charismatic ease that he appeared to do everything.

Miss Marks returned to Poppy, while Beatrix and a fair-haired man disappeared into the whirl of waltzing couples. "How do you—" she began, but stopped with a sharply indrawn breath. "Damn and blast," she whispered. "He's here."

It was the first time Poppy had ever heard her companion curse. Surprised by Miss Marks's reaction to Harry Rutledge's presence at the ball, Poppy frowned. "I noticed. But why do you—"

She broke off as she followed the direction of her companion's gaze.

Miss Marks wasn't looking at Harry Rutledge.

She was looking at Michael Bayning.

An explosion of pain filled Poppy's chest as she saw her former suitor across the room, slim and handsome, his gaze fixed on her. He had rejected her, exposed her to public mockery, and then he had come to a ball? Was he searching for a new girl to court now? Perhaps he had assumed that while he danced with eager young women in Belgravia, Poppy would be hiding in her hotel suite, weeping into her pillow.

Which was precisely what she wanted to be doing.

"Oh, God," Poppy whispered, staring into Miss Marks's concerned face. "Don't let him talk to me."

"He won't make a scene," her companion said softly. "Quite the opposite—a pleasantry or two will smooth the situation over for both of you."

"You don't understand," Poppy said hoarsely. "I can't *do* pleasantries right now. I can't face him. *Please*, Miss Marks—"

"I'll send him away," her companion said softly, squaring her narrow shoulders. "Don't worry. Collect yourself, dear." She moved in front of Poppy, blocking Michael's view, and went forward to speak to him.

"Thank you," Poppy whispered, even though Miss Marks couldn't hear. Horrified to feel the sting of desperate tears, she concentrated blindly on a section of floor in front of her. *Don't cry. Don't cry. Don't—*

"Miss Hathaway." Lady Norbury's jovial voice intruded on her frantic thoughts. "This gentleman has requested an introduction, you fortunate girl! It is my honor and delight to present Mr. Harry Rutledge, the hotelier."

A pair of highly polished black shoes came into her vision. Poppy glanced miserably up into his vivid green eyes.

Harry bowed, holding her gaze. "Miss Hathaway, how do you—"

"I'd love to waltz," Poppy said, practically leaping from her chair and seizing his arm. Her throat was so tight, she could hardly speak. "Let's go now."

Lady Norbury gave a disconcerted laugh. "What charming enthusiasm."

Poppy gripped Harry's arm as if it were a lifeline.

His gaze dropped to the clench of her fingers on the fine black wool of his sleeve. He covered her fingers with the reassuring pressure of his free hand, his thumb smoothing over the edge of her wrist. And even through two layers of white gloves, she felt the comfort in his touch.

At that moment Miss Marks returned, having just dispatched Michael Bayning. Her brows lowered in a scowl as she looked up at Harry. "No," she said shortly.

"No?" His lips twitched with amusement. "I haven't asked for anything yet."

Miss Marks gave him a cold stare. "Obviously you wish to dance with Miss Hathaway."

"You have objections?" he asked innocently.

"Several," Miss Marks said, her manner so curt that both Lady Norbury and Poppy looked askance.

"Miss Marks," Lady Norbury said, "I can vouch for this gentleman's character with all assurance."

The companion pressed her lips into a hyphen. She surveyed Poppy's glittering eyes and flushed face, seeming to understand how close she was to losing her composure. "When the dance is finished," she told Poppy grimly, "you will take his left arm, insist that he conduct you directly back to me, here, and then he will take his leave. Understood?"

"Yes," Poppy whispered, glancing over Harry's broad shoulder.

Michael was staring at her from across the room, his face ashen.

The situation was hideous. Poppy wanted to run from the ballroom. Instead, she would have to dance.

Harry led Poppy toward the crowd of waltzing couples and settled his gloved hand at her waist. She reached for him, one palm light and trembling at his shoulder, her other hand gripped securely in his. In one astute glance, Harry took in the entire scene: Poppy's unshed tears, Michael Bayning's set face, and the slew of curious gazes encompassing them.

"How can I help?" he asked gently.

"Take me away," she said. "As far as possible from here. Timbuktu."

Harry looked sympathetic and amused. "I don't think they're letting in Europeans these days." He drew Poppy into the current of dancers, swift counterclockwise turns in a clockwise pattern, and the only way to keep from stumbling was to follow him without hesitation.

Poppy was profoundly grateful to have something to focus on besides Michael. As she might have expected, Harry Rutledge was an excellent dancer. Poppy relaxed into his smooth, strong lead. "Thank you," she said. "You're probably wondering why I—"

"No, I don't wonder. It was written on your face, and Bayning's, for everyone to see. You're not very good at subterfuge, are you?"

"I've never needed to be." To Poppy's horror, her throat clenched and her eyes stung. She was about to burst into tears in front of everyone. As she tried to take a steadying breath, the corset squeezed her lungs, and she felt dizzy. "Mr. Rutledge," she wheezed, "Could you take me out to the terrace for some air?"

"Certainly." His voice was reassuringly calm. "One more circuit around the room, and we'll slip out."

In other circumstances, Poppy might have taken pleasure in the sureness of his lead, the music that gilded the air. She stared fixedly at the dark face of her unlikely rescuer. He was dazzling in the elegant clothes, his heavy dark hair brushed back in disciplined layers. But his eyes were underpinned by the ever-present hint of shadows. Windows to a restless soul. He didn't sleep enough, she thought, and wondered if anyone ever dared mention it to him.

Even through the haze of numb desolation, it occurred to Poppy that by asking her to dance, Harry Rutledge had singled her out in what could have been construed by many as a declaration of interest.

But that couldn't be true.

"Why?" she asked faintly, without thinking.

"Why what?"

"Why did you ask me to dance?"

Harry hesitated as if torn between the necessity of tact and the inclination toward honesty. He settled on the latter. "Because I wanted to hold you."

Thrown into confusion, Poppy focused on the simple knot of his white cravat. At another time, in another situation, she would have been extraordinarily flattered. At the moment, however, she was too absorbed in her despair over Michael.

With sneak-thief adroitness, Harry extricated her from the aggregate of dancers and led her to the row of French doors opening onto the terrace. She followed blindly, hardly caring if they were seen or not.

The air outside was a brace of coolness, dry and sharp in her lungs. Poppy breathed in rapid gasps, grateful to have escaped the smothering atmosphere of the ballroom. Hot tears slid from her eyes.

"Here," Harry said, guiding her to the far side of the balcony, which extended nearly the full width of the mansion. The lawn below was a quiet ocean. Harry brought Poppy to a shadowed corner. Reaching inside his coat pocket, he found a pressed square of fine linen and gave it to her.

Poppy blotted her eyes. "I can't begin to tell you," she said unsteadily, "how very sorry I am. You were so kind in asking me to dance, and now you're k-keeping company with a w-watering pot."

Looking amused and sympathetic, Harry leaned an elbow on the balcony railing as he faced her. His quietness relieved her. He waited patiently, as if he understood that no words could be an adequate plaster for her bruised spirit.

Poppy let out a slow breath, feeling soothed by the coolness of the night and the blessed lack of noise. "Mr. Bayning was going to offer for me," she told Harry. She blew her nose with a childlike gust. "But he changed his mind."

Harry studied her, his eyes catlike in the darkness. "What reason did he give?"

"His father didn't approve of the match."

"And that surprises you?"

"Yes," she said defensively. "Because he made promises to me."

"Men in Bayning's position are rarely, if ever, allowed to marry whomever they want. There's far more to consider than their personal preferences."

"More important than love?" Poppy asked with bitter vehemence.

"Of course."

"When all is said and done, marriage is a union of two people made by the same God. Nothing more, nothing less. Does that sound naïve?"

"Yes," he said flatly.

Poppy's lips quirked, although she felt nothing close to actual amusement. "I'm sure I've read too many fairy tales. The prince is supposed to slay the dragon, defeat the villain, and marry the servant girl, and carry her off to his castle."

"Fairy tales are best read as entertainment," Harry said. "Not as a guide to life." He removed his gloves methodically and tucked them into one of his coat pockets. Resting both his forearms on the railing, he sent her a sideways glance. "What does the servant girl do when the prince abandons her?"

"She goes home." Poppy's fingers tightened on the damp ball of the handkerchief. "I'm not suited for London and all its illusions. I want to return to Hampshire, where I can rusticate in peace."

"For how long?"

"Forever."

"And marry a farmer?" he asked skeptically.

"Perhaps." Poppy dried the residue of her tears. "I would make a wonderful farmwife. I'm good with cows. I know how to make hotchpotch. And I would appreciate the peace and quiet for my reading."

"Hotchpotch? What is that?" Harry seemed to have undue interest in the subject, his head inclined toward hers.

"A harvest vegetable broth."

"How did you learn to make it?"

"My mother." Poppy lowered her voice as if imparting highly confidential information. "The secret," she said wisely, "is a splash of ale."

They were standing too close. Poppy knew she should move away. But his nearness felt like shelter, and his scent was fresh and beguiling. The night air raised gooseflesh on her bare arms. How large and warm he was. She wanted to match herself against him and burrow inside the haven of his coat as if she were one of Beatrix's small pets.

"You're not meant to be a farmwife," Harry said.

Poppy gave him a rueful glance. "You think no farmer would have me?"

"I think," he said slowly, "that you should marry a man who would appreciate you."

She made a face. "Those are in short supply."

He smiled. "You don't need a supply. You just need one." He grasped Poppy's shoulder, his hand curving over the illusion-trimmed sleeve of her gown until she felt its warmth through the fragile gauze. His thumb toyed with the filmy edge of fabric, brushing her skin in a way that made her stomach tighten. "Poppy," he said gently, "what if I asked for permission to court you?"

She went blank as astonishment swept through her.

Finally, someone had asked to court her.

And it wasn't Michael, or any of the diffident, superior aristocrats she had met during three failed seasons. It was Harry Rutledge, an elusive and enigmatic man she had known only a matter of days.

"Why me?" was all she could manage.

"Because you're interesting and beautiful. Because saying your name makes me smile. Most of all because this may be my only hope of ever having hotchpotch."

"I'm sorry, but . . . no. It wouldn't be a good idea at all."

"I think it's the best idea I've ever had. Why can't we?"

Poppy's mind was spinning. She could hardly stammer out a reply. "I-I don't like courtship. It's very stressful. And disappointing."

His thumb found the soft ridge of her collarbone and traced it slowly. "It's arguable that you've ever had a real courtship. But if it pleases you, we'll dispense with it altogether. That would save time."

"I don't want to dispense with it," Poppy said,

increasingly flustered. She trembled as she felt his fingertips glide along the side of her neck. "What I mean is . . . Mr. Rutledge, I've just been through a very difficult experience. This is too soon."

"You were courted by a boy, who had to do as he was told." His hot breath feathered against her lips as he whispered, "You should try it with a man, who needs no one's permission."

A man. Well, he certainly was that.

"I don't have the luxury of waiting," Harry continued. "Not when you're so hell-bent on going back to Hampshire. You're the reason I'm here tonight, Poppy. Believe me, I wouldn't have come otherwise."

"You don't like balls?"

"I do. But the ones I attend are given by a far different crowd."

Poppy couldn't imagine what crowd he was referring to, or what kind of people he usually associated with. Harry Rutledge was too much of a mystery. Too experienced, too overwhelming in every way. He could never offer the quiet, ordinary, sane life she longed for.

"Mr. Rutledge, please don't take this as an affront, but you don't have the qualities I seek in a husband."

"How do you know? I have some excellent qualities you haven't even seen yet."

Poppy gave a shaky laugh. "I think you could talk a fish out of its skin," she told him. "But still, I don't—" She stopped with a gasp as he ducked his head and stole an off-center kiss from her lips, as if her laughter were something he could taste. She felt the imprint of his mouth even after he drew back, her excited nerves reluctant to release the sensation.

"Spend an afternoon with me," he urged. "Tomorrow."

"No, Mr. Rutledge. I'm—"

"Harry."

"Harry, I can't—"

"An hour?" he whispered. He bent to her again, and she turned her face away in confusion. He sought her neck instead, his lips brushing the vulnerable flesh with half-open kisses.

No one had ever done such a thing, even Michael. Who would have thought it would feel so delicious? Dazed, Poppy let her head fall back, her body accepting the steady support of his arms. He searched her throat with devastating care, touching his tongue to her pulse. His hand cradled her nape, the pad of his thumb tracing the satiny edge of her hairline. As her balance faltered, she reached around his neck.

He was so gentle, teasing color to the surface of her skin, chasing little shivers with his mouth. Blindly she followed, wanting the taste of him. As she angled her face toward his, her lips grazed the close-shaven surface of his jaw. His breath caught. "You should never cry over a man," he said against her cheek. His voice was soft, dark, like smoked honey. "No one is worth your tears." Before she could answer, he caught her mouth in a full, open kiss.

Poppy went weak, melting against him as he kissed her slowly. The tip of his tongue entered, played gently, and the feel of it was so strange and intimate and tantalizing that a wild tremor ran through her. His mouth lifted at once.

"I'm sorry. Did I frighten you?"

Poppy couldn't seem to think of an answer. It wasn't that he had frightened her, more that he had given her a glimpse of a vast erotic territory she had never encountered before. Even in her inexperience, she comprehended that this man had the power to turn her inside out with pleasure. And that was not something she had ever considered or bargained for.

She tried to swallow the heartbeat that had ascended in her throat. Her lips felt stung and swollen. Her body throbbed in unfamiliar places.

Harry framed her face in his hands, his thumbs stroking her crimson cheeks. "The waltz is over by now. Your companion is going to turn on me like a rat terrier for bringing you back late."

"She's very protective," Poppy managed to say.

"She should be." Harry lowered his hands, setting her free.

Poppy stumbled, her knees astonishingly weak. Harry grabbed her in a swift reflex, pulling her back against him. "Easy." She heard him laugh softly. "My fault. I shouldn't have kissed you like that."

"You're right," she said, her sense of humor tentatively reasserting itself. "I should give you a setdown . . . slap you or something . . . what is the usual response from ladies you've taken liberties with?"

"They encourage me to do it again?" Harry suggested in such a helpful manner that Poppy couldn't help smiling.

"No," she said. "I'm not going to encourage you."

They faced each other in darkness relieved only by the slivers of light shed by upper-floor windows. How capricious life was, Poppy thought. She should have been dancing with Michael tonight. But now she was Michael's castoff, and she was standing outside the ballroom, in the shadows with a stranger.

Interesting, that she could be so in love with one

man and yet find another so compelling. But Harry
Rutledge was one of the most fascinating people she
had ever met, with so many layers of charm and drive
and ruthlessness that she couldn't fathom what kind
of man he really was. She wondered what he was
like in his private moments.

She was almost sorry she would never find out.

"Give me a penance," Harry urged. "I'll do whatever you ask."

As their gazes caught and held in the shadows,
Poppy realized that he actually meant it. "How large
a penance?" she asked.

Harry tilted his head a little, studying her intently. "Ask for anything."

"What if I wanted a castle?"

"Done," he said promptly.

"Actually, I don't want a castle. Too drafty. What
about a diamond tiara?"

"Certainly. A modest one suitable for daytime
wear, or something more elaborate?"

Poppy began to smile, when a few minutes earlier
she had thought she would never smile again. She felt
a surge of liking and gratitude. She couldn't think of
anyone else who would have been able to console her
in these circumstances. But the smile turned bitter-
sweet as she looked up at him once more.

"Thank you," she said. "But I'm afraid no one
can give me the one thing I truly want."

Rising on her toes, she pressed her lips sweetly to
his cheek. It was a friendly kiss.

A good-bye kiss.

Harry looked down at her intently. His gaze
flicked to something beyond her, before his mouth
came down over hers with smoldering demand. Con-

founded by his sudden aggression, thrown off balance, she reached out for him reflexively. It was the wrong reaction, the wrong time and place . . . wrong to feel a surge of pleasure as he tasted and sweetly delved inside her mouth . . . but, as she was discovering, there were some temptations impossible to resist. And his kisses seemed to wring a helpless response from every part of her, a bonfire of feeling. She couldn't catch up with her own pulse, her own breath. Her nerves lit with sparks of sensation, while stars cascaded all around her, little bursts of light striking the tiles of the terrace floor with the sound of breaking crystal . . .

Trying to ignore the harsh noise, Poppy leaned harder against him. But Harry eased her away with a quiet murmur, and guided her head to his chest as if he were trying to protect her.

Her lashes lifted, and she went cold and still as she saw that someone . . . *several* someones . . . had come out to the balcony.

Lady Norbury, who had dropped a glass of champagne in her surprise. And Lord Norbury, and another elderly couple.

And Michael, with a blonde woman on his arm.

They all stared at Poppy and Harry in shock.

Had the angel of death appeared at that moment, complete with black wings and a gleaming scythe, Poppy would have run to him with open arms. Because being caught on the balcony kissing Harry Rutledge was not just a scandal . . . it would be the stuff of legend. She was ruined. Her life was ruined. Her family was ruined. Everyone in London would know by sunrise.

Dumbstruck by the sheer awfulness of the situation, Poppy looked helplessly up at Harry. And for one confusing moment, she thought she saw a flicker of predatory satisfaction in his eyes. But then his expression changed.

"This might be difficult for us to explain," he said.

Chapter Ten

As Leo made his way through the Norbury mansion, he was privately amused as he saw some of his friends—young lords whose debauchery had put even *his* past exploits to shame—now starched and buttoned up and impeccably mannered. Not for the first time, Leo reflected how unfair it was that men were allowed to get away with so much more than women.

This business of manners, for example . . . he had seen his sisters struggling to remember hundreds of inane points of etiquette that were expected of upper-class society. Whereas Leo's main interest in the rules of etiquette was how to break them. And he, as a man with a title, was unfailingly excused for nearly anything. Ladies at a supper party were criticized behind their backs if they used the wrong fork for the fish course, while a man could drink to excess or make some off-color remark, and everyone pretended not to notice.

Nonchalantly, Leo entered the ballroom and stood to the side of the triple-width doorway, surveying the scene. Dull, dull, dull. There was the ever-present row of virgins and their chaperones, and clusters of gossiping women that reminded him of nothing so much as a hen yard.

His attention was snared by the sight of Catherine Marks, standing in the corner and watching as Beatrix and her partner danced.

Marks looked tense as usual, her slender dark-clad figure as straight as a ramrod. She never missed an opportunity to disdain Leo and treat him as if he had all the intellectual prowess of an oyster. And she was resistant to any attempts at charm or humor. Like any sensible man, Leo did his best to avoid her.

But to his chagrin, Leo couldn't stop himself from wondering what Catherine Marks would look like after a good, thorough tupping. Her spectacles cast aside, her silky hair loose and tumbled, her pale body released from the contraption of stays and laces . . .

Suddenly nothing at the ball seemed quite so interesting as his sisters' companion.

Leo decided to go bother her.

He sauntered to her. "Hello, Marks. How is the—"

"*Where have you been?*" she whispered violently, her eyes flashing furiously behind her spectacles.

"In the card room. And then I had a plate of supper. Where else should I have been?"

"You were supposed to have been helping with Poppy."

"Helping with what? I promised I would dance with her, and here I am." Leo paused and glanced around them. "Where is she?"

"I don't know."

He frowned. "How can you not know? You mean to say you've lost her?"

"The last time I saw Poppy was approximately ten minutes ago, when she went to dance with Mr. Rutledge."

"The hotel owner? He never appears at these things."

"He did this evening," Miss Marks said grimly, keeping her tone low. "And now they've disappeared. *Together.* You must find her, my lord. *Now.* She is in danger of being ruined."

"Why haven't you gone after her?"

"Someone has to keep an eye on Beatrix, or she'll disappear as well. Besides, I didn't want to draw attention to Poppy's absence. Go find her, and be quick about it."

Leo scowled. "Marks, in case you hadn't noticed, other servants don't snap out orders to their masters. So if you don't mind—"

"You're not my master," she had the nerve to say, glaring insolently at him.

Oh, I'd like to be, Leo thought in a quick, angry flush of arousal, every hair on his body standing erect. Along with a certain feature of his anatomy. He decided to leave before her effect on him became obvious. "All right, settle your feathers. I'll find Poppy."

"Start looking in all the places where you would take a woman to compromise her. There can't be that many."

"Yes, there can. You'd be amazed at the variety of places I've—"

"Please," she muttered. "I'm feeling nauseous enough at the moment."

Casting an assessing glance around the ballroom, Leo spied the row of French doors at the far end. He headed for the balcony, trying to go as fast as possible without appearing to be in a hurry. It was his cursed luck to be snared in two separate conversations on the way, one with a friend who wanted his opinion of a certain lady, the other with a dowager who thought the punch was "off" and wanted to know if he'd tried it.

Finally Leo made it to one of the doors and slipped outside.

His eyes widened as he beheld an astonishing tableau. Poppy, clasped in the arms of a tall black-haired man . . . being watched by a small group of people who had come onto the balcony through another set of doors. And one of them was Michael Bayning, who looked sick with jealousy and outrage.

The black-haired man lifted his head, murmured something to Poppy, and leveled a cool glance at Michael Bayning.

A glance of triumph.

It only lasted a moment, but Leo saw it, and recognized it for what it was.

"Holy hell," Leo whispered.

His sister was in considerable trouble.

When a Hathaway caused a scandal, they never did it by half measures.

By the time Leo steered Poppy back into the ballroom and collected Miss Marks and Beatrix, the scandal had started to spread. In no time at all, Cam and Amelia had found them, and the family drew together in a protective cluster around Poppy.

"What happened?" Cam asked, looking deceptively relaxed, his hazel eyes alert.

"Harry Rutledge happened," Leo muttered. "I'll

explain everything shortly. For now, let's leave here as quickly as possible and meet Rutledge at the hotel."

Amelia leaned close to murmur into Poppy's scarlet ear. "It's all right, dear. Whatever it is, we'll fix it."

"You can't," Poppy whispered. "No one can."

Leo looked past his sisters and saw the subdued uproar of the crowd. Everyone was staring at them. "It's like watching an ocean wave," he remarked. "One can literally see the scandal sweep through the room."

Cam looked sardonic and resigned. *"Gadjos,"* he muttered. "Leo, why don't you take your sister and Miss Marks in your carriage? Amelia and I will make our farewells to the Norburys."

In a daze of wretchedness, Poppy allowed Leo to usher her outside to his carriage. All of them were silent until the vehicle had pulled away from the mansion with a sharp lurch.

Beatrix was the first to speak. "Have you been compromised, Poppy?" she asked with concern. "As Win was last year?"

"Yes, she has," Leo replied, while Poppy let out a little moan. "It's a bad habit our family's gotten into. Marks, you'd better write a poem about it."

"This disaster could have been avoided," the companion told him tersely, "had you found her sooner."

"It could also have been avoided if you hadn't lost her in the first place," Leo shot back.

"I'm responsible," Poppy broke in, her voice muffled against Leo's shoulder. "I went off with Mr. Rutledge. I had just seen Mr. Bayning in the ballroom, and I was distraught, and Mr. Rutledge asked me to dance but I needed air and we went out to the balcony—"

"No, *I'm* responsible," Miss Marks said, looking equally as upset. "I let you dance with him."

"It does no good to assign blame," Leo said. "What's done is done. But if anyone is responsible, it's Rutledge, who apparently came to the ball on a hunting expedition."

"What?" Poppy lifted her head and looked at him in bewilderment. "You think he . . . no, it was an accident, Leo. Mr. Rutledge didn't intend to compromise me."

"It was deliberate," Miss Marks said. "Harry Rutledge never gets 'caught' doing anything. If he was seen in a compromising situation, it was because he wanted to be seen."

Leo looked at her alertly. "How do you know so much about Rutledge?"

The companion flushed. It seemed to require an effort for her to hold his gaze. "His reputation, of course."

Leo's attention was diverted as Poppy buried her face against his shoulder. "I'm going to die of humiliation," she said.

"No, you won't," Leo replied. "I'm an expert on humiliation, and if it were fatal, I'd have died a dozen times by now."

"You can't die a dozen times."

"You can if you're a Buddhist," Beatrix said helpfully.

Leo smoothed Poppy's shining hair. "I hope Harry Rutledge is," he said.

"Why?" Beatrix asked.

"Because there's nothing I'd rather do than kill him repeatedly."

* * *

Harry received Leo and Cam Rohan in his private library. Any other family in the situation would have been predictable . . . they would have demanded that he do the right thing, and terms of compensation would have been discussed, and arrangements would have been made. Because of Harry's vast fortune, most families would have accepted the results with good grace. He wasn't a peer, but he was a man of influence and means.

However, Harry knew better than to expect a predictable response to the situation from either Leo or Cam. They were not conventional, and they would have to be dealt with carefully. That being said, Harry wasn't worried in the least. He had negotiated over matters of far greater consequence than a woman's honor.

Pondering the events of the night, Harry was filled with immoral triumph. No, not triumph . . . elation. It was all turning out to be so much easier than he had expected, especially with Michael Bayning's unanticipated appearance at the Norbury ball. The idiot had practically handed Poppy to Harry on a silver platter. And when an opportunity presented itself, Harry took it.

Besides, Harry felt he *deserved* Poppy. Any man who allowed scruples to get in the way of having a woman like her was a fool. He recalled the way she had looked in the ballroom, pale and fragile and distraught. When Harry had approached her, there had been no mistaking the relief in her expression. She had turned to him, she had let him take her away.

And as Harry had brought her outside to the terrace, his satisfaction had been quickly supplanted by an entirely new sensation . . . the desire to ease someone else's pain. The fact that he had helped to bring about her heartbreak in the first place was regrettable. But the end justified the means. And once she was his, he would do more for her, take better care of her, than Michael Bayning ever could.

Now he had to deal with Poppy's family, who were understandably outraged that he had compromised her. That didn't worry him in the slightest. He had no doubt of his ability to persuade Poppy to marry him. And no matter how much the Hathaways objected, they would ultimately have to come to terms.

Marrying him was the only way to redeem Poppy's honor. Everyone knew it.

Keeping his expression neutral, Harry offered wine as Leo and Cam entered the library, but they refused.

Leo went to the fireplace mantel and leaned beside it with his arms folded across his chest. Cam went to a leather-upholstered chair and settled into it, stretching out his long legs and crossing them at the ankles.

Harry wasn't deceived by their comfortable postures. Anger, masculine discord, permeated the room. Remaining relaxed, Harry waited for one of them to speak.

"You should know, Rutledge," Leo said in a pleasant tone, "that I had planned to kill you right away, but Rohan says we should talk for a few minutes first. Personally, I think he's trying to delay me so he can have the pleasure of killing you himself. And even if Rohan and I don't kill you, we probably won't be able to stop my brother-in-law Merripen from killing you."

Harry half sat on the edge of the heavy mahogany library table. "I suggest you wait until Poppy and I marry, so she can at least be made a respectable widow."

"Why do you assume," Cam asked, "that we would allow you to have Poppy?"

"If she doesn't marry me after this, no one will receive her. For that matter, I doubt any of the rest of your family would be welcome in London parlors."

"I don't think we're welcome as it is," Cam replied, his hazel eyes narrowed.

"Rutledge," Leo said with deceptive casualness, "before I came into the title, the Hathaways lived outside London society for so many years that we couldn't give a monkey's arse as to whether we're received or not. Poppy doesn't have to marry anyone, for any reason, other than her own desire to do so. And Poppy is of the opinion that you and she would never suit."

"The opinions of women are frequently changed," Harry said. "Let me talk to your sister tomorrow. I'll convince her to make the best of the situation."

"Before you convince her," Cam said, "you're going to have to convince us. Because what little I know about you makes me damned uneasy."

Of course Cam Rohan would have some knowledge of him. Cam's former position at the gentlemen's gaming club would have made him privy to all kinds of private information. Harry was curious as to how much he had found out.

"Why don't you tell me what you know," Harry invited idly, "and I'll confirm if it's true."

The amber-shaded eyes regarded him without blinking. "You're originally from New York City, where your father was a hotelier of middling success."

"Buffalo, actually," Harry said.

"You didn't get on with him. But you found mentors. You apprenticed at an engineering works, where you became known for your abilities as a mechanic and draftsman. You patented several innovations in valves and boilers. At the age of twenty, you left America and came to England for undisclosed reasons."

Cam paused to observe the effects of his recitation.

Harry's ease had evaporated, the muscles of his shoulders drawing upward. He forced them back down and resisted the temptation to reach up and ease a cramp of tension at the back of his neck. "Go on," he invited softly.

Cam obliged. "You put together a group of private investors and bought a row of houses with very little capital of your own. You leased the houses for a short time, razed them and bought the rest of the street, and built the hotel as it now stands. You have no family, save your father in New York, with whom you have no communication. You have a handful of loyal friends and a host of enemies, many of whom seem to like you in spite of themselves."

Harry reflected that Cam Rohan must have had impressive connections to have unearthed such information. "There are only three people in England who know that much about me," he muttered, wondering which one of them had talked.

"Now there are five," Leo said. "And Rohan forgot to mention the fascinating discovery that you've become a favorite with the War Office after designing some modifications to the standard issue army rifle. But lest we assume that you are only allied with the British government, you also seem to have dealings with foreigners, royalty and criminals alike. It rather gives one the impression that the only side you're ever on is your own."

Harry smiled coolly. "I've never lied about myself or my past. But I keep things private whenever possible. And I owe allegiance to no one." He went to the sideboard and poured a brandy. Holding the bowl in the palms of his hands to warm it, he glanced at both men. He'd bet his fortune that Cam knew more that he wasn't revealing. But this discussion, brief as it was, made it clear that there would be no helpful family coercion to make Poppy an honest woman. The Hathaways didn't give a damn about respectability, nor did they need his money, nor his influence.

Which meant that he would have to focus solely on Poppy.

"Whether you approve or not," he told Cam and Leo, "I'm going to propose to your sister. The choice is hers. And if she accepts, no power on earth will stop me from marrying her. I understand your concerns, so let me assure you that she will want for nothing. She'll be protected, cherished, even spoiled."

"You have no bloody idea how to make her happy," Cam said quietly.

"Rohan," Harry said with a faint smile, "I excel at making people happy—or at least making them think they are." He paused to survey their set faces. "Are you going to forbid me to speak to her?" he asked in a tone of polite interest.

"No," Leo said. "Poppy's not a child, nor a pet. If she wants to speak to you, she shall. But be aware that, whatever you say or do in the effort to convince her to marry you, it will be counterweighed by the opinions of her family."

"And there's one more thing to be aware of," Cam said, with a wintry softness that disguised all hint of feeling. "If you succeed in marrying her, we're not losing a sister. You're gaining an entire family—who will protect her at any cost."

That was almost enough to give Harry pause.

Almost.

Chapter Eleven

"My brother and Mr. Rohan don't like you," Poppy told Harry the next morning, as they walked slowly through the rose garden behind the hotel. As the news of the scandal traveled through London like wildfire, it was necessary to do something about it with all expediency. Poppy knew that as a gentleman, Harry Rutledge was bound to offer for her, to save her from social disgrace. However, she wasn't certain if a lifetime of being married to the wrong man was any better than being a pariah. She didn't know Harry well enough to make any judgments about his character. And her family was emphatically *not* in favor of him.

"My companion doesn't like you," she continued, "and my sister Amelia says she doesn't know you well enough to decide, but she's inclined not to like you."

"What about Beatrix?" Harry asked, the sun striking glimmers in his dark hair as he looked down at her.

"She likes you. But then, she likes lizards and snakes."

"What about you?"

"I can't abide lizards or snakes."

A smile touched his lips. "Let's not fence today, Poppy. You know what I'm asking."

She responded with an unsteady nod.

It had been a hellish night. She had talked and cried and argued with her family until the early hours of the morning, and then she'd found it nearly impossible to sleep. And then more arguing and conversation this morning, until her chest was a cauldron of roiling emotions.

Her safe, familiar world had been turned upside down, and the peace of the garden was an unspeakable relief. Strangely, it made her feel better to be in Harry Rutledge's presence, even though he was partially responsible for the mess she was in. He was calm and self-assured, and there was something in his manner, sympathy woven with pragmatism, that soothed her.

They paused in a long arbor draped in sheets of roses. It was a tunnel of pink and white blossoms. Beatrix wandered along a nearby hedgerow. Poppy had insisted on taking her in lieu of Miss Marks or Amelia, both of whom would have made it impossible for her to have even marginal privacy with Harry.

"I like you," Poppy admitted bashfully. "But that's not enough to build a marriage on, is it?"

"It's more than many people start with." Harry studied her. "I'm sure your family has talked to you."

"At length," Poppy said. Her family had framed the prospect of marriage with Harry Rutledge in such dire terms that she had already decided to refuse him. She twisted her mouth in an apologetic grimace. "And after hearing what they had to say, I'm sorry to tell you that I—"

"Wait. Before you make a decision, I'd like to hear what *you* have to say. What your feelings are."

Well. That was a change. Poppy blinked in disconcertion as she reflected that her family and Miss Marks, well intentioned as they had been, had told her what they thought she should do. Her own thoughts and feelings hadn't received much attention.

"Well . . . you're a stranger," she said. "And I don't think I should make a decision about my future when I'm in love with Mr. Bayning."

"You still have hopes of marrying him?"

"Oh, no. All possibility of that is gone. But the feelings are still there, and until enough time passes for me to forget him, I don't trust my own judgment."

"That's very sensible of you. Except that some decisions can't be put off. And I'm afraid this is one of them." Harry paused before asking gently, "If you go back to Hampshire under the cloud of scandal, you know what to expect, don't you?"

"Yes. There will be . . . unpleasantness, to say the least." It was a mild word for the disdain, pity and scorn she would receive as a fallen woman. And worse, it might ruin Beatrix's chances of marrying well. "And my family won't be able to shield me from it," she added dully.

"But I could," Harry said, reaching for the braided coil at the top of her head, using a fingertip to nudge an anchoring pin further into place. "I could if you marry me. Otherwise, I'm powerless to do anything for you. And no matter how anyone else advises you, Poppy, you're the one who will bear the brunt of the scandal."

Poppy tried, but couldn't quite manage, a weary smile. "So much for my dreams of a quiet, ordinary life. My choice is either to live as a social outcast or as the wife of a hotelier."

"Is the latter choice so unappealing?"

"It's not what I've always hoped for," she said frankly.

Harry absorbed that, considered it, while reaching out to skim his fingers over clusters of pink roses. "It wouldn't be a peaceful existence in a country cottage," he acknowledged. "We would live at the hotel most of the year. But there are times we could go to the country. If you want a house in Hampshire as a wedding present, it's yours. And a carriage of your own, and a team of four at your disposal."

Exactly what they said he'd do, Poppy thought, and sent him a wry glance. "Are you trying to bribe me, Harry?"

"Yes. Is it working?"

His hopeful tone made her smile. "No, although it was a very good effort." Hearing the rustling of foliage, Poppy called out, "Beatrix, are you there?"

"Two rows away," came her sister's cheerful reply. "Medusa found some worms!"

"Lovely."

Harry gave Poppy a bemused glance. "Who . . . or should I say *what* . . . is Medusa?"

"Hedgehog," she replied. "Medusa's getting a bit plump, and Beatrix is exercising her."

To Harry's credit, he remained composed as he remarked, "You know, I pay my staff a fortune to keep those *out* of the garden."

"Oh, have no fear. Medusa is merely a guest hedgehog. She would never run away from Beatrix."

"Guest hedgehog," Harry repeated, a smile working across his mouth. He paced a few impatient steps before turning to face her. A new urgency filtered through his voice. "Poppy. Tell me what your worries are, and I'll try to answer them. There must be some terms we can come to."

"You are persistent," she said. "They told me you would be."

"I'm everything they told you and worse," Harry said without hesitation. "But what they didn't tell you is that you are the most desirable and fascinating woman I've ever met, and I would do anything to have you."

It was insanely flattering to have a man like Harry Rutledge pursuing her, especially after the hurt inflicted by Michael Bayning. Poppy flushed with cheek-stinging pleasure, as if she'd been lying too long in the sun. She found herself thinking, *Perhaps I'll consider it, just for a moment, in a purely hypothetical sense. Harry Rutledge and me . . .*

"I have questions," she said.

"Ask away."

Poppy decided to be blunt. "Are you dangerous? Everyone says you are."

"To you? No."

"To others?"

Harry shrugged innocently. "I'm a hotelier. How dangerous could I be?"

Poppy gave him a dubious glance, not at all deceived. "I may be gullible, Harry, but I'm not brainless. You know the rumors . . . you're well aware of your reputation. Are you as unscrupulous as you're made out to be?"

Harry was quiet for a long moment, his gaze fixed on a distant cluster of blossoms. The sun threw its light into the filter of branches, scattering leaf shadows over the pair in the arbor.

Eventually he lifted his head and looked at her directly, his eyes greener than the sunstruck rose leaves. "I'm not a gentleman," he said. "Not by birth, and not by character. Very few men can afford to be honorable while trying to make a success of themselves. I don't lie, but I rarely tell everything I know. I'm not a religious man, nor a spiritual one. I act in my own interests, and I make no secret of it. However, I always keep my side of a bargain, I don't cheat, and I pay my debts."

Pausing, Harry fished in his coat pocket, pulled out a penknife, and reached up to cut a rose in full bloom. After neatly severing the stem, he occupied himself with stripping the thorns with the sharp little blade. "I would never use physical force against a woman, or anyone weaker than myself. I don't smoke, take snuff, or chew tobacco. I always hold my liquor. I don't sleep well. And I can make a clock from scratch." Removing the last thorn, he handed the rose to her, and slipped the knife back into his pocket.

Poppy concentrated on the satiny pink rose, running her fingers along the top edges of the petals.

"My full name is Jay Harry Rutledge," she heard him say. "My mother is the only one who ever called me Jay, which is why I don't like it. She left my father and me when I was very young. I never saw her again."

Poppy looked at him with wide eyes, understanding that this was a sensitive subject he rarely, if ever, discussed. "I'm sorry," she said softly, although she kept her tone carefully devoid of pity.

He shrugged as if it was of no importance. "It was a long time ago. I barely remember her."

"Why did you come to England?"

Another pause. "I wanted to have a go at the hotel business. And whether I was a success or failure, I wanted to be far away from my father."

Poppy could only guess at the wealth of information buried beneath the spare words. "That's not the entire story," she said rather than asked.

The ghost of a smile touched his lips. "No."

She looked down at the rose again, feeling her cheeks color. "Do you . . . would you . . . want children?"

"Yes. Hopefully more than one. I didn't like being an only child."

"Would you want to raise them at the hotel?"

"Of course."

"Do you think it a suitable environment?"

"They would have the best of everything. Education. Travel. Lessons in anything that interested them."

Poppy tried to imagine bringing up children in a hotel. Could such a place ever feel like home? Cam had once told her that the Rom believed the entire world was their home. As long as you were with your family, you were home. She looked at Harry, wondering what it would be like to live intimately with him. He seemed so self-contained and invulnerable. It was hard to think of him doing ordinary things such as shaving, or having his hair trimmed, or staying in bed with a head cold.

"Would you keep your wedding vows?" she asked.

Harry held her gaze. "I wouldn't make them otherwise."

Poppy decided that her family's worries about letting her talk to Harry had been entirely justified. Because he was so persuasive, and appealing, that she was beginning to consider the idea of marrying him, and seriously weigh the decision.

Fairy-tale dreams had to be set aside if she was to embark on marriage with a man she didn't love and hardly knew. But adults had to take responsibility for their actions. And then it occurred to Poppy that she was not the only one taking a risk. There was no guarantee for Harry that he would end up with the kind of wife he needed.

"It's not fair for me to ask all the questions," she told him. "You must have some as well."

"No, I've already decided that I want you."

Poppy couldn't prevent a bemused laugh. "Do you make all your decisions so impulsively?"

"Not usually. But I know when to trust my instincts."

It seemed Harry was about to add something else when he saw a movement on the ground from the periphery of his vision. Following his gaze, Poppy saw Medusa pushing her way through the rose arbor, waddling innocently across the path. The little brown and white hedgehog looked like a walking scrub brush. To Poppy's surprise, Harry lowered to his haunches to retrieve the creature.

"Don't touch her," Poppy warned. "She'll roll into a ball and sink her quills into you."

But Harry settled his hands on the ground, palms up, on either side of the inquisitive hedgehog. "Hello, Medusa." Gently he worked his hands beneath her. "Sorry to interrupt your exercise. But believe me, you don't want to run into any of my gardeners."

Poppy watched incredulously as Medusa relaxed and settled willingly into the warm masculine hands. Her spines flattened, and she let him lift and turn her so she was tummy upward. Harry stroked the soft white fur of her underbelly while Medusa's delicate snout lifted and she regarded him with her perpetual smile.

"I've never seen anyone except Beatrix handle her like that," Poppy said, standing beside him. "You have experience with hedgehogs?"

"No." He slanted a smile at her. "But I have some experience with prickly females."

"Excuse me," Beatrix's voice interrupted them, and she came into the tunnel of roses. She was disheveled, bits of leaves clinging to her dress, her hair straggling over her face. "I seem to have lost track of . . . oh, there you are, Medusa!" She broke into a grin as she saw Harry cradling the hedgehog in his hands. "Always trust a man who can handle a hedgehog, that's what I always say."

"Do you?" Poppy asked dryly. "I've never heard you say that."

"I only say it to Medusa."

Harry carefully transferred the pet to Beatrix's hands. " 'The fox has many tricks,' " he quoted, " 'the hedgehog only one.' " He smiled at Beatrix as he added, "But it's a good one."

"Archilochus," Beatrix said promptly. "You read Greek poetry, Mr. Rutledge?"

"Not usually. But I make an exception for Archilochus. He knew how to make a point."

"Father used to call him a 'raging iambic,' " Poppy said, and Harry laughed.

And in that moment, Poppy made her decision.

Because even though Harry Rutledge had his flaws, he admitted them freely. And a man who could charm a hedgehog and understand jokes about ancient Greek poets was a man worth taking a risk on.

She wouldn't be able to marry for love, but she could at least marry for hope.

"Bea," she murmured, "might you allow us a few moments alone?"

"Certainly. Medusa would love to grub about in the next row."

"Thank you, dear." Poppy turned back to Harry, who was dusting his hands. "May I ask one more question?"

He looked at her alertly and spread his hands as if to show he had nothing to hide.

"Would you say that you're a good man, Harry?"

He had to think about that. "No," he finally said. "In the fairy tale you mentioned last night, I would probably be the villain. But it's possible the villain would treat you far better than the prince would have."

Poppy wondered what was wrong with her, that she should be amused rather than frightened by his confession. "Harry. You're not supposed to court a girl by telling her you're the villain."

He gave her an innocent glance that didn't deceive her in the least. "I'm trying to be honest."

"Perhaps. But you're also making certain that whatever anyone says about you, you've already admitted it. Now you've made all criticism of you ineffectual."

Harry blinked as if she'd surprised him. "You think I'm *that* manipulative?"

She nodded.

Harry seemed stunned that she could see through him so easily. Instead of being annoyed, however, he stared at her with stark longing. "Poppy, I have to have you."

Reaching her in two steps, he took her into his arms. Her heart thumped with sudden force, and she let her head fall back naturally as she waited for the warm pressure of his mouth. When nothing happened, however, she opened her eyes and glanced at him quizzically.

"Aren't you going to kiss me?"

"No. I don't want your judgment clouded." But he brushed his lips against her forehead before he continued. "Here are your choices, as I see them. First, you could go to Hampshire in a cloud of social scorn, and content yourself with the knowledge that at least you didn't get trapped into a loveless marriage. Or you could marry a man who wants you beyond anything, and live like a queen." He paused. "And don't forget the country house and carriage."

Poppy could not contain a smile. "Bribery again."

"I'll throw in the castle and tiara," Harry said ruthlessly. "Gowns, furs, a yacht—"

"Hush," Poppy whispered, and touched his lips gently with her fingers, not knowing how else to make him stop. She took a deep breath, hardly able to believe what she was about to say. "I'll settle for a betrothal ring. A small, simple one."

Harry stared at her as if he were afraid to trust his own ears. "Will you?"

"Yes," Poppy said, her voice a bit suffocated. "Yes, I will marry you."

Chapter Twelve

This was the phrase of Poppy's wedding day: "It's not too late to change your mind."

She had heard it from every member of her family, or some variation thereof, since the early hours of the morning. That was, she'd heard it from everyone except Beatrix, who thankfully didn't share the Hathaways' general animosity toward Harry.

In fact, Poppy had asked Beatrix why she hadn't objected to the betrothal.

"I think it might turn out to be a good pairing," Beatrix said.

"You do? Why?"

"A rabbit and a cat can live together peaceably. But first the rabbit has to assert itself—charge the cat a time or two—and then they become friends."

"Thank you," Poppy said dryly. "I'll have to remember that. Although I daresay Harry will be surprised when I knock him over like a ninepin."

The wedding and the reception afterward would be as large and heavily attended as humanly possible, as if Harry intended for half of London to witness the ceremony. As a result, Poppy would spend most of her wedding day amidst a sea of strangers.

She had hoped that she and Harry might become better acquainted in the three weeks of their betrothal, but she had scarcely seen him except for the two occasions when he had come to take her on a drive. And Miss Marks, who had accompanied them, had glowered so fiercely that it had embarrassed and infuriated Poppy.

The day before the wedding, her sister Win and brother-in-law Merripen had arrived. To Poppy's relief, Win had elected to remain neutral on the controversy of the marriage. She and Poppy sat together in a richly appointed hotel suite, talking over the matter at length. And just as in the days of their childhood, Win assumed the role of peacemaker.

The light from a fringed lamp slid over Win's blond hair in a brilliant varnish. "If you like him, Poppy," she said gently, "if you've found things to esteem in him, then I'm sure I will, too."

"I wish Amelia felt that way. And Miss Marks, too, for that matter. They're both so . . . well, opinionated . . . that I can hardly discuss anything with either of them."

Win smiled. "Remember, Amelia has taken care of all of us for a very long time. And it's not easy for her to relinquish her role as our protector. But she will. Remember when Leo and I left for France, how difficult it was for her to see us off? How afraid she was for us?"

"I think she was more afraid for France."

"Well, France survived the Hathaways," Win said, smiling. "And you will survive becoming Harry Rutledge's wife on the morrow. Only . . . if I may say my piece . . . ?"

"Certainly. Everyone else has."

"The London season is like one of those Drury Lane melodramas in which marriage is always the ending. And no one ever seems to give any thought as to what happens after. But marriage isn't the end of the story, it's the beginning. And it demands the efforts of both partners to make a success of it. I hope Mr. Rutledge has given assurances that he will be the kind of husband that your happiness requires?"

"Well . . ." Poppy paused uncomfortably. "He told me I would live like a queen. Although that's not quite the same thing, is it?"

"No," Win said, her voice soft. "Be careful, dear, that you don't end up as the queen of a lonely kingdom."

Poppy nodded, stricken and uneasy, trying to hide it. In her gentle way, Win had offered more devastating advice than all the sharp warnings of the other Hathaways combined. "I'll consider that," she said, staring at the floor, at the tiny printed flowers of her dress, anywhere other than into her sister's perceptive gaze. She twisted her betrothal ring around her finger. Although the current fashion was for diamond clusters, or colored stones, Harry had bought her a single rose-cut diamond, shaped at the top with facets that mimicked the inner spiral of a rose.

"I asked for something small and simple," she had told Harry when he had given it to her.

"It's simple," he had countered.

"But not small."

"Poppy," he had told her with a smile, "I never do anything in a small way."

Spying the clock ticking busily on the mantel, Poppy brought her thoughts back to the present. "I won't change my mind, Win. I promised Harry that

I would marry him, and so I shall. He has been kind to me. I would never repay him by jilting him at the altar."

"I understand." Win slid her hand over Poppy's, and pressed warmly. "Poppy . . . has Amelia had a 'certain talk' with you yet?"

"You mean the 'what to expect on my wedding night' talk?"

"Yes."

"She was planning to tell me later tonight, but I'd just as soon hear it from you." Poppy paused. "However, having spent so much time with Beatrix, I should tell you that I know the mating habits of at least twenty-three different species."

"Heavens," Win said with a grin. "Perhaps you should be leading the discussion, dear."

The fashionable, the powerful, and the wealthy usually married at St. George's in Hanover Square, located in the middle of Mayfair. In fact, so many peers and virgins had been united in holy wedlock at St. George's that it was unofficially and quite vulgarly known as the "London Temple of Hymen."

A pediment with six massive columns fronted the impressive but relatively simple structure. St. George's had been designed with a deliberate lack of ornamentation so as not to detract from the beauty of the architecture. The interior was similarly austere, with a canopied pulpit built several feet higher than the box pews. But there was a magnificent work of stained glass above the front altar, depicting the Tree of Jesse and an assortment of biblical figures.

Surveying the crowd packed inside the church, Leo wore a carefully blank expression. So far he had given away two sisters in marriage. Neither of those

weddings had begun to approach this kind of gran-
deur and visibility. But they had far eclipsed it in
genuine happiness. Amelia and Win had both been
in love with the men they had chosen to marry.

It was unfashionable to marry for love, a mark of
the *bourgeoisie*. However, it was an ideal the Hathaways had always aspired to.

This wedding had nothing to do with love.

Dressed in a black morning coat with silver trousers and a white cravat, Leo stood beside the side
door of the vestry room, where ceremonial and sacred objects were kept. Altar and choir robes hung
in a row along one wall. This morning the vestry
doubled as a waiting room for the bride.

Catherine Marks came to stand on the other side
of the doorway as if she were a fellow sentinel guard-
ing the castle gate. Leo glanced at her covertly. She
was dressed in lavender, unlike her usual drab colors. Her mousy brown hair was pulled back into
such a tight chignon as to make it difficult for her to
blink. The spectacles sat oddly on her nose, one of
the wire earpieces crimped. It gave her the appearance of a befuddled owl.

"What are you looking at?" she asked testily.

"Your spectacles are crooked," Leo said, trying
not to smile.

She scowled. "I tried to fix them, but it only made
them worse."

"Give them to me." Before she could object, he
took them from her face and began to fiddle with the
bent wire.

She spluttered in protest. "My lord, I didn't ask
you to—if you damage them—"

"How did you bend the earpiece?" Leo asked,
patiently straightening the wire.

"I dropped them on the floor, and as I was searching, I stepped on them."

"Nearsighted, are you?"

"Quite."

Having reshaped the earpiece, Leo scrutinized the spectacles carefully. "There." He began to give them to her and paused as he stared into her eyes, all blue, green, and gray, contained in distinct dark rims. Brilliant, warm, changeable. Like opals. Why had he never noticed them before?

Awareness chased over him, making his skin prickle as if exposed to a sudden change in temperature. She wasn't plain at all. She was beautiful, in a fine, subtle way, like winter moonlight, or the sharp linen smell of daisies. So cool and pale . . . delicious. For a moment, Leo couldn't move.

Marks was similarly still, locked with him in a moment of peculiar intimacy.

She snatched the spectacles from him and replaced them firmly on her nose. "This is a mistake," she said. "You shouldn't have let it happen."

Struggling through layers of bemusement and stimulation, Leo gathered that she was referring to his sister's wedding. He sent her an irritable glance. "What do you suggest I do, Marks? Send Poppy to a nunnery? She has the right to marry whomever she pleases."

"Even if it ends in disaster?"

"It won't end in disaster, it will end in estrangement. And I've told Poppy as much. But she's bound and determined to marry him. I always thought Poppy was too sensible to make this kind of mistake."

"She is sensible," Marks said. "But she's also lonely. And Rutledge took advantage of that."

"How could she be lonely? She's constantly surrounded by people."

"That can be the worst loneliness of all."

There was a disturbing note in her voice, a fragile sadness. Leo wanted to touch her . . . gather her close . . . pull her face into his neck . . . and that caused a twinge of something like panic. He had to do something, anything, to change the mood between them.

"Cheer up, Marks," he said briskly. "I'm sure that someday you, too, will find that one special person you can torment for the rest of your life."

He was relieved to see her familiar scowl reassert itself.

"I've yet to meet a man who could compete with a good strong cup of tea."

Leo was about to reply when he heard a noise from inside the vestry where Poppy was waiting.

A man's voice, taut with urgency.

Leo and Marks looked at each other.

"Isn't she supposed to be alone?" Leo asked.

The companion nodded uncertainly.

"Is it Rutledge?" Leo wondered aloud.

Marks shook her head. "I just saw him outside the church."

Without another word, Leo grasped the door handle and opened the portal, and Marks followed him inside the vestry.

Leo stopped so abruptly that the companion bumped into him from behind. His sister, clad in a high-necked white lace gown, was silhouetted against a row of black and purple robes. Poppy looked angelic, bathed in light from a narrow rectangular window, a veil cascading down her back from a neat coronet of white rosebuds.

And she was confronting Michael Bayning—who looked like a madman, his eyes wild, his clothes disheveled.

"Bayning," Leo said, closing the door with an efficient swipe of his foot. "I wasn't aware you'd been invited. The guests are being seated in the pews. I suggest you join them." He paused, his voice iced with quiet warning. "Or better yet, leave altogether."

Bayning shook his head, desperate fury gleaming in his eyes. "I can't. I must talk with Poppy before it's too late."

"It's already too late," Poppy said, her complexion nearly as white as her dress. "Everything's decided, Michael."

"You must know what I've found out." Michael threw a pleading glance at Leo. "Let me have just a moment alone with her."

Leo shook his head. He was not without sympathy for Bayning, but he couldn't see that any good would come of this. "Sorry, old fellow, but someone has to think of appearances. This has the earmarks of a last tryst before the wedding. And while that would be scandalous enough between the bride and groom, it's even more objectionable between the bride and someone else." He was aware of Marks coming to stand beside him.

"Let him speak," the companion said.

Leo threw her an exasperated glance. "Blast it, Marks, do you ever tire of telling me what to do?"

"When you stop needing my advice," she said, "I'll stop giving it."

Poppy hadn't taken her gaze off Michael. It was like something from a dream, a nightmare, having him come to her when she was dressed in her wedding gown, minutes away from marrying another man. Dread filled her. She didn't want to hear what Michael had to say, but neither could she turn him away.

"Why are you here?" she managed to ask.

Michael looked anguished and imploring. He held out something . . . a letter. "Do you recognize this?"

Taking the letter in lace-gloved fingers, Poppy stared at it closely. "The love letter," she said, bewildered. "I lost it. Where . . . where did you find it?"

"My father. Harry Rutledge gave it to him." Michael raked a hand through his hair with distracted roughness. "That bastard went to my father and exposed our relationship. He put the worst possible light on it. Rutledge turned my father against us before I ever had a chance to explain our side of it."

Poppy turned even colder, and her mouth went dry, and her heart labored with slow, painful thumps. At the same time, her brain was working too fast, racing through a chain of conclusions, each more unpleasant than the last.

The door opened, and all of them turned to watch as someone else entered the vestry.

"Of course," Poppy heard Leo say dourly. "The drama only needed you to be complete."

Harry came into the small, overcrowded room, looking suave and astonishingly calm. He approached Poppy, his green eyes cool. He wore his self-control like impenetrable armor. "Hello, darling." He reached out to run a hand lightly over the transparent lace of her veil.

Even though he hadn't touched her directly, Poppy stiffened. "It's bad luck," she whispered through dry lips, "for you to see me before the ceremony."

"Fortunately," Harry said, "I'm not superstitious."

Poppy was filled with confusion, anger, and a dull ache of horror. Staring up into Harry's face, she saw no trace of remorse in his expression.

"In the fairy tale . . ." he had told her, *"I would probably be the villain."*

It was true.

And she was about to marry him.

"I told her what you did," Michael said to Harry. "How you made it impossible for us to marry."

"I didn't make it impossible," Harry said. "I merely made it difficult."

How young and noble and vulnerable Michael appeared, a wronged hero.

And how large and cruel and contemptuous Harry was. Poppy couldn't believe she had ever found him charming, that she had *liked* him, that she had thought some form of happiness would be possible with him.

"She was yours, if you'd truly wanted her," Harry continued, a pitiless smile touching his lips. "But I wanted her more."

Michael launched at him with a choked cry, his fist raised.

"No," Poppy gasped, and Leo started forward. Harry was faster, however, seizing Michael's arm and twisting it behind his back. Expertly he shoved him up against the door.

"Stop it!" Poppy said, rushing to them, hitting Harry's shoulder and back with her fist. "Let him go! Don't do this!"

Harry didn't seem to feel her blows. "Out with it, Bayning," he said coldly. "Did you come here merely to complain, or is there some point to all this?"

"I'm taking her away from here. Away from you!"

Harry gave a chilling smile. "I'll send you to hell first."

"Let . . . him . . . go," Poppy said in a voice she had never used before.

It was enough to make Harry listen. His gaze connected with hers in a flash of unholy green. Slowly he released Michael, who swung around, his chest heaving with the anguished force of his breaths.

"Come with me, Poppy," Michael pleaded. "We'll go to Gretna. I no longer give a damn about my father or my inheritance. I can't let you marry this monster."

"Because you love me?" she asked in a half whisper. "Or because you want to save me?"

"Both."

Harry watched her intently, taking in every nuance of her expression. "Go with him," he invited gently. "If that's what you want."

Poppy wasn't at all deceived. Harry would go to any lengths to get what he wanted, no matter what destruction or pain he caused. He would never let her go. He was merely testing her, curious to see what choice she would make.

One thing was clear: she and Michael would never be happy together. Because Michael's righteous fury would eventually wear off, and then all the reasons that had seemed so important before would regain their validity. He would come to regret having married her. He would lament the scandal and the disinheritance, and the lifelong disapproval of his father. And eventually Poppy would come to be the focus of his resentment.

She had to send Michael away—it was the best thing she could do for him.

As for her interests . . . all choices seemed equally bad.

"I suggest you get rid of both these idiots," Leo told her, "and let me take you home to Hampshire."

Poppy stared at her brother, her lips touched with a hopeless smile. "What kind of life would I have in Hampshire after this, Leo?"

His only reply was grim silence. Poppy turned her attention to Miss Marks, who looked anguished. In their shared gaze, Poppy saw that her companion understood her precarious situation more accurately than the men did. Women were judged and condemned far more harshly than men in these matters. Poppy's elusive dream of a simple, peaceful life had already vanished. If she didn't go through with the wedding, she would never marry, never have children, never have a place in society. The only thing left was to make the best of her situation.

She faced Michael with unyielding resolve. "You must go," she said.

His face contorted. "Poppy, I haven't lost you. You're not saying—"

"Go," she insisted. Her gaze switched to her brother. "Leo, please escort Miss Marks to her seat in the congregation. The wedding will start soon. And I need to speak to Mr. Rutledge alone."

Michael stared at her in disbelief. "Poppy, you can't marry him. Listen to me—"

"It's over, Bayning," Leo said quietly. "There's no undoing the part you've played in this bloody mess. Let my sister deal with it as she chooses."

"*Christ.*" Michael lurched toward the door like a drunken man.

Poppy longed to comfort him, to follow him, to reassure him of her love. Instead, she stayed in the vestry with Harry Rutledge.

After what seemed an eternity, the other three left, and Poppy and Harry faced each other.

It was clear he was indifferent to the fact that she now knew him for what he was. Harry wanted neither forgiveness nor redemption . . . he regretted nothing.

A lifetime, Poppy thought. *With a man I can never trust.*

To marry a villain, or never to marry at all. To be Harry Rutledge's wife, or live as an object of disgrace, to have mothers scold their children for speaking to her as if their innocence would be contaminated by her presence. To be propositioned by men who thought she was immoral or desperate. That was her future if she didn't become his wife.

"Well?" Harry asked quietly. "Will you go through with it or not?"

Poppy felt foolish standing there in her bridal finery, bedecked in flowers and a veil, all of it symbolizing hope and innocence when there was none left. She longed to tear off her betrothal ring and throw it at him. She wanted to crumple to the floor like a hat someone had stepped on. A brief thought came to her, that she wanted to send for Amelia, who would take charge of the situation and manage everything.

Except that Poppy was no longer a child whose life could be managed.

She stared into Harry's implacable face and hard eyes. He looked mocking, supremely confident that he'd won. No doubt he assumed he'd be able to run circles around her for the rest of their lives.

To be sure, she had underestimated him.

But he had underestimated her, too.

All of Poppy's sorrow and misery and helpless

anger swirled together into some new bitter amal-gam. She was surprised by the calmness of her own voice as she spoke to him. "I will never forget that you took away the man I loved and put yourself in his place. I'm not certain I can ever forgive you for that. The only thing I am absolutely certain of is that I will never love you. Do you still want to marry me?"

"Yes," Harry said without hesitation. "I've never wanted to be loved. And God knows no one's done it yet."

Chapter Thirteen

Poppy had forbidden Leo to tell the rest of the family about what had happened with Michael Bayning before the wedding. "You may tell them anything you wish after the breakfast," she had said. "But for my sake, please keep quiet until then. I won't be able to endure all those rituals—the breakfast, the wedding cake, the toasts—if I have to look into their eyes and know that *they* know."

Leo had looked angry. "You expect me to take you to the front of this church and give you to Rutledge for reasons I don't understand."

"You don't have to understand. Just help me through this."

"I don't want to help if it results in you becoming Mrs. Harry Rutledge."

But because she had asked it of him, Leo had played his part in the elaborate ceremony with grim-faced dignity. With a shake of his head, he had offered his arm, and they had followed Beatrix to the front of the church where Harry Rutledge was waiting.

The service was mercifully short and unemotional. There was only one moment when Poppy felt a sharp pang of unease, as the minister said, ". . . if any man can show any just cause why they may not lawfully be joined together, let him now speak; or else hereafter forever hold his peace." It seemed the whole world stilled for the two or three seconds that followed his pronouncement. Poppy's pulse quickened. She realized she expected, hoped, to hear Michael's vehement protest ring out through the church.

But there was only silence. Michael had gone.

The ceremony went on.

Harry's hand was warm as it closed around her cold one. They repeated their vows, and the minister gave the ring to Harry, who slid it firmly onto Poppy's finger.

Harry's voice was quiet and steady. "With this ring I thee wed, with my body I thee worship, and with all my worldly goods I thee endow."

Poppy didn't meet his gaze, but instead stared at the gleaming circlet on her finger. To her relief, there was no kiss to follow. The custom of kissing the bride was in bad taste, a plebeian practice that was never done at St. George's.

Finally bringing herself to look up at Harry, Poppy flinched at the satisfaction in his eyes. She took his arm, and they walked back down the aisle together, toward the future and a fate that seemed anything but benevolent.

Harry knew that Poppy thought of him as a monster. He acknowledged that his methods had been unfair, selfish, but there had been no other way to have Poppy as his wife. And he couldn't work up even a second's worth of regret for having taken her away from Bayning. Perhaps he was amoral, but it was the only way he knew to make his way in the world.

Poppy was his now, and he would make certain that she would not be sorry for marrying him. He would be as kind as she would allow. And in his experience, women would forgive anything if one offered the right incentives.

Harry was relaxed and in good spirits the rest of the day. A procession of "glass coaches," elaborate carriages with gold empire decorations and abundant windows, conveyed the wedding party to the Rutledge Hotel, where a huge formal breakfast was held in the hotel banquet room. The windows were crowded with onlookers, eager to catch a glimpse of the glittering scene. Greek pillars and arches had been placed all around the room, swathed in tulle and masses of flowers.

A regiment of servants brought out silver platters and trays of champagne, and the guests settled in their chairs to enjoy the repast. They were given individual servings of goose dressed with cream and herbs and covered with a steaming golden crust . . . bowls of melons and grapes, boiled quail eggs scattered lavishly on crisp green salad, baskets of hot muffins, toast and scones, flitches of fried smoked bacon . . . plates of thinly sliced beefsteak, the pink strips littered with fragrant shavings of truffle. Three wedding cakes were brought out, thickly iced and stuffed with fruit.

As was the custom, Poppy was served first, and Harry could only guess at the effort it took for her to eat and smile. If anyone noticed that the bride was subdued, it was assumed that the event was overwhelming for her, or perhaps that, like all brides, she was nervously anticipating the wedding night.

Poppy's family regarded her with protective concern, especially Amelia, who seemed to sense that something was wrong. Harry was fascinated by the Hathaways, the mysterious connections between them, as if they shared some collective secret. One could almost see the wordless understanding that passed between them.

Although Harry knew a great deal about people, he knew nothing about being part of a family.

After Harry's mother had run off with one of her lovers, his father had tried to get rid of every remaining trace of her existence. And he had done his best to forget that he even had a son, leaving Harry to the hotel staff and a succession of tutors.

Harry had few memories of his mother, only that she had been beautiful and had had golden hair. It seemed she had always been going out, away from him, forever elusive. He remembered crying for her once, clutching his hands in her velvet skirts, and she had tried to make him let go, laughing softly at his persistence.

In the wake of his parents' abandonment, Harry had taken his meals in the kitchen with the hotel employees. When he was sick, one or another of the maids had taken care of him. He saw families come and go, and he had learned to view them with the same detachment that the hotel staff did. Deep down Harry harbored a suspicion that the reason his mother had left, the reason his father never had anything to do with him, was because he was unlovable. And therefore he had no desire to be part of a family. Even if or when Poppy bore him children, Harry would never allow anyone close enough to form an attachment. He would never let himself be shackled that way. And yet he sometimes knew a fleeting envy for those who were capable of it, like the Hathaways.

The breakfast wore on, with endless rounds of toasting. When Harry saw the betraying droop of Poppy's shoulders, he deduced she'd had enough. He rose and made a short, gracious speech, offering his thanks for the honor of the guests' presence on such a significant day.

It was the signal for the bride to retire along with her bridesmaids. They would soon be followed by the general company, who would disperse to attend a variety of amusements for the rest of the day. Poppy paused at the doorway. As if she could feel Harry's gaze on her, she turned to glance over her shoulder.

A warning flashed in her eyes, and it aroused him instantly. Poppy would not be a complacent bride, nor had he expected her to be. She would try to exact compensation for what he had done, and he would indulge her . . . up to a point. He wondered how she would react when he came to her that evening.

Harry tore his gaze away from his bride as he was approached by Kev Merripen, Poppy's brother-in-law, a man who managed to stay relatively inconspicuous despite his size and striking appearance. He was a Romany Gypsy, tall and black haired, his austere exterior concealing a nature of dark intensity.

"Merripen," Harry said pleasantly. "Did you enjoy the breakfast?"

The Rom was in no mood for small talk. He

stared at Harry with a gaze promising death. "Something is wrong," he said. "If you've done something to harm Poppy, I will find you and rip your head from your—"

"Merripen!" came a cheerful exclamation as Leo suddenly appeared beside them. Harry didn't miss the way Leo jabbed a warning elbow against the Gypsy's ribs. "All charm and lightness, as usual. You're supposed to congratulate the bridegroom, *phral*. Not threaten to dismember him."

"It's not a threat," the Rom muttered. "It's a promise."

Harry met Merripen's gaze directly. "I appreciate your concern for her. I assure you, I'll do everything in my power to make her happy. Poppy will have anything she wants."

"I believe a divorce would top the list," Leo mused aloud.

Harry leveled a cool stare at Merripen. "I'd like to point out that your sister married me voluntarily. Michael Bayning should have had the bollocks to come to the church and carry her out bodily if necessary. But he didn't. And if he wasn't willing to fight for her, he didn't deserve her." He saw from Merripen's quick blink that he had scored a point. "Moreover, after going through these exertions to marry Poppy, the last thing I would do is mistreat her."

"What exertions?" the Rom asked suspiciously, and Harry realized that he hadn't yet been told the entire story.

"Never mind that," Leo told Merripen. "If I told you now, you'd only make an embarrassing scene at Poppy's wedding. And that's supposed to be my job."

They exchanged a glance, and Merripen muttered something in Romany.

Leo smiled faintly. "I have no idea what you just said. But I suspect it's something about battering Poppy's new husband into forest mulch." He paused. "Later, old fellow," he said. A look of grim understanding passed between them.

Merripen gave him a curt nod and left without another word to Harry.

"And that was one of his good moods," Leo remarked, staring after his brother-in-law with rueful affection. He returned his attention to Harry. Suddenly, his eyes were filled with a world-weariness that should have taken lifetimes to acquire. "I'm afraid no amount of discussion would ease Merripen's concern. He's lived with the family since he was a boy, and my sisters' welfare is everything to him."

"I will take care of her," Harry said.

"I'm sure you'll try. And whether you believe it or not, I hope you succeed."

"Thank you."

Leo focused on him with an astute gaze that would have troubled a man with a conscience. "Incidentally, I'm not going with the family when they depart for Hampshire on the morrow."

"Business in London?" Harry asked politely.

"Yes, a few last parliamentary obligations. And a bit of architectural dabbling—a hobby of mine. But mainly I'm staying for Poppy's sake. You see, I expect she'll want to leave you quite soon, and I intend to escort her home."

Harry smiled contemptuously, amused by his new brother-in-law's effrontery. Did Leo have any idea how many ways Harry could ruin him, and how easily it could be done? "Tread carefully," Harry said softly.

It was a sign of either naïveté or courage that Leo didn't flinch. He actually smiled, though there was no humor in it. "There's something you don't seem to understand, Rutledge. You've managed to acquire Poppy, but you don't have what it takes to keep her. Therefore, I won't be far away. I'll be there when she needs me. And if you harm her, your life won't be worth a bloody farthing. No man is untouchable—not even you."

After a maid had helped Poppy change from her wedding garments into a simple dressing gown, she brought a glass of iced champagne and tactfully left.

Grateful for the silence of the private apartments, Poppy sat at her dressing table and unpinned her hair slowly. Her mouth ached from smiling, and the tiny muscles of her forehead felt strained. She drank the champagne and made a project of brushing her hair in long strokes, letting it fall in mahogany waves. The boar bristles felt good against her scalp.

Harry had not yet come to the apartment. Poppy considered what she would say to him once he appeared, but nothing came to mind. With dreamlike slowness, she wandered through the rooms. Unlike the icy formality of the receiving area, the rest of the rooms had been decorated in plush fabrics and warm colors, with abundant places for sitting, reading, relaxing. Everything was immaculate, the windowpanes polished to stunning clarity, the Turkish carpeting clean swept and scented of tea leaves. There were fireplaces with marble or carved wood mantels and tiled hearths, and many lamps and sconces to keep the rooms well lit in the evening.

An extra bedroom had been added for Poppy. Harry had told her that she could have as many rooms for her own use as she wished—the apartments had been designed so that connecting spaces could be opened up with ease. The counterpane on the bed was a soft shade of robin's egg blue, the fine linen sheets embroidered with tiny blue flowers. Pale blue satin and velvet curtains swathed the windows. It was a beautiful, feminine room, and Poppy would have taken great pleasure in it, had the circumstances been different.

She tried to decide if she was most angry with Harry, Michael, or herself. Perhaps equally with all three of them. And she was increasingly nervous, knowing it wouldn't be long until Harry arrived. Her gaze fell to the bed. She reassured herself with the thought that Harry would not force her to submit to him. His villainy would not lend itself to crude violence.

Her stomach dropped as she heard someone entering the apartments. She took a deep breath, and another, and waited until Harry's broad-shouldered form appeared in the doorway.

He paused, watching her, his features impassive. His cravat had been removed, the shirt opened to reveal the strong line of his throat. Poppy steeled herself not to move as Harry approached her. He reached out to touch her shining hair, letting it slide through his fingers like liquid fire. "I've never seen it down before," he said. He was close enough that she could smell a hint of shaving soap, and the tang of champagne on his breath. His fingers smoothed over her cheek, detecting the trembling within her stillness.

"Afraid?" he asked softly.

Poppy forced herself to meet his gaze. "No."

"Maybe you should be. I'm much nicer to people who are afraid of me."

"I doubt that," she said. "I think the opposite is true."

A smile touched his lips.

Poppy was disoriented by the complex mixture of emotions he stirred in her, the antagonism and attraction and curiosity and resentment. Pulling away from him, she went to her dressing table and examined a small porcelain box with a gilded top.

"Why did you go through with it?" she heard him ask quietly.

"I thought it best for Michael." She felt a twinge of satisfaction as she saw how that had annoyed him.

Harry half sat on the bed, his posture informal. His gaze didn't stray from her. "Had there been a choice, I would have done all this the ordinary way. I would have courted you openly, won you fairly. But you'd already decided on Bayning. This was the only alternative."

"No, it wasn't. You could have let me be with Michael."

"It's doubtful he ever would have offered for you. He deceived you, and himself, by assuming he could persuade his father to accept the match. You should have seen the old man when I showed him the letter—he was mortally offended by the notion of his son taking a wife so far beneath him."

That hurt, as perhaps Harry had intended, and Poppy stiffened.

"Then why didn't you let it all play out? Why not wait until Michael had abandoned me, and then come forward to pick up the pieces?"

"Because there was a chance Bayning might have

dared to run off with you. I couldn't risk it. And I knew that sooner or later you'd realize that what you had with Bayning was nothing but infatuation."

Poppy gave him a glance of purest contempt. "What do you know of love?"

"I've seen how people in love behave. And what I witnessed in the vestry this morning was nothing close to it. Had you truly wanted each other, no force in the world could have stopped you from walking out of that church together."

"You wouldn't have allowed it!" she shot back in outrage.

"True. But I would have respected the effort."

"Neither of us gives a damn about your respect."

The fact that she was speaking for Michael as well as herself . . . "us" . . . caused Harry's face to harden. "Whatever your feelings for Bayning are, you're my wife now. And he'll go on to marry some blue-blooded heiress as he should have done in the first place. Now all that's left to decide is how you and I will go on."

"I would prefer a marriage in name only."

"I don't blame you," Harry said calmly. "However, the marriage isn't legal until I bed you. And, unfortunately, I never leave loopholes."

He was going to insist on his rights, then. Nothing would dissuade him from getting what he wanted. Poppy's eyes and nose stung. But she would have rather died than cry in front of him. She shot him a look of revulsion, while her heart pounded until she felt its reverberations in her temples and wrists and ankles.

"I'm overwhelmed by such a poetic declaration. By all means, let's complete the contract." She began on the gilded buttons at the front of her dressing gown, her fingers stiff and shaking. Her breath trembled in her throat. "All I ask is that you make it quick."

Harry pushed away from the bed with graceful ease and came to her. One of his warm hands covered both of hers, and her fingers stilled. "Poppy." He waited until she could bring herself to look up at him. Amusement glinted in his eyes. "You make me feel like a vile ravisher," he said. "It's only fair to tell you that I've never forced myself on a woman. A simple refusal would probably be enough to deter me."

He was lying, her instincts told her. But . . . perhaps he wasn't. Damn him for toying with her like a cat with a mouse.

"Is that true?" she asked with offended dignity.

Harry gave her a guileless glance. "Refuse me, and we'll find out."

The fact that such a despicable human being could be so handsome was proof that the universe was vastly unfair, or at least very badly organized. "I'm not going to refuse you," she said, pushing his hand away. "I'm not going to entertain you with virginal theatrics." She continued to unfasten the buttons of her dressing gown. "And I'd like to have done with this so I won't have anything to dread."

Obligingly Harry removed his coat and went to drape it over a chair. Poppy dropped her dressing robe to the floor and kicked off her slippers. The cool air wafted beneath the hem of her thin cambric nightgown and lingered in icy curls around her ankles. She could scarcely think, her head filled with fears and worries. The future she had once hoped for was gone, and another was being created,

one with infinite complications. Harry would know
her in a way no one else ever had, or ever would. But
it wouldn't be anything like her sisters' marriages . . . it would be a relationship built on something far different from love and trust.

Her sister Win's information on marital intimacy
had been garnished with flowers and moonbeams,
with the barest description of the physical act. Win's
advice had been to trust one's husband, and to relax,
and to understand that sexual closeness was a wonderful part of love. None of that had any relevance to
the situation Poppy now found herself in.

The room was utterly silent. *This means nothing
to me,* she thought, trying to make herself believe it.
She felt as if she were in a stranger's body as she
undid her nightgown and pulled it over her head and
let it fall to the carpeting in a limp heap. Gooseflesh
rose everywhere, the tips of her breasts contracting
in the chill.

She went to the bed and turned back the covers
and slipped in. Drawing the bed linens up to her
breasts, she settled back against the pillows. Only
then did she glance at Harry.

Her husband had paused in the act of unfastening
a shoe, his foot propped on a chair. He had already
removed his shirt and waistcoat, and the muscles of
his long back were bunched and tense. He stared at
her over his shoulder, his thick lashes half lowered.
His color was high, as if sun flushed, and his lips
were parted as if he'd forgotten something he'd been
about to say. Letting out a breath that wasn't entirely
steady, he turned back to his shoe.

His body was beautifully made, but Poppy took
no pleasure in it. In fact, she resented it. She would
have preferred a few signs of vulnerability, a touch of

softness around the middle, a set of narrow shoulders, anything that would put him at a disadvantage. But he was lean and strong and powerfully proportioned. Still clad in his trousers, Harry came to stand beside the bed. Despite her efforts to appear indifferent, Poppy couldn't stop her fingers from curling into the embroidered sheets.

His hand went to her bare shoulder, his fingertips drifting to her throat and back again. He paused as he found a tiny, nearly invisible scar on her shoulder— the place a stray shotgun pellet had once lodged. "From the accident?" he asked huskily.

Poppy nodded, unable to speak. She realized he would become familiar with every small and unique detail of her body . . . she had given him that right. He found three more scars on her arm, stroking each one as if he could soothe those long-ago injuries. Slowly his hand went to a lock of hair that lay in a fine mahogany river over her chest, following it beneath the sheets and blankets.

She gasped as she felt his thumb brush over the bud of her nipple, circling, sending runners of heat to the pit of her stomach. His hand left her for a moment, and when he reached for her breast again, his thumb was damp from his own mouth. Another teasing, acute circle, moisture enhancing the caress. Her knees drew up slightly, her hips tilting as if her entire body had become a vessel to contain sensation. His other hand slid softly beneath her chin, tilting her face up to his.

He bent to kiss her, but Poppy turned her face away.

"I'm the same man who kissed you on the terrace," she heard him say. "You liked it well enough then."

Poppy could hardly speak with his hand cupping

her breast. "Not anymore." A kiss meant more to her
than a simple physical gesture. It was a gift of love,
of affection, or at the very least liking, and she felt
none of those things for him. He might have the
right to her body, but not to her heart.

His hands left her, and she felt him nudge her
gently to the side.

Poppy obeyed, her pulse racing as he joined her on
the bed. He reclined on his side, his feet extending
much farther than hers along the mattress. She forced
her fingers to loosen from the covers as he drew them
away from her.

Harry's gaze slid over her slim, exposed body, the
curves of her breasts, the clamped seam of her
thighs. Heat surfaced everywhere, a flush that deepened as he drew her against him. His chest was warm
and hard, with a covering of dark hair that tickled
her breasts.

Poppy shivered as his hand moved along her spine,
pressing her close. The intimacy of being clasped
against a half-naked man, breathing the scent of his
skin, was almost more than her dazed mind could
comprehend. He pressed her bare legs apart, the fabric of his trousers smooth and cool. And he held her
like that, his hand roaming slowly over her back until
the teeth-chattering shivers eased.

His mouth traced the taut side of her neck. He
spent a long time kissing her there, investigating
the hollow behind her ear, the edge of her hairline,
the front of her throat. His tongue found the hectic
throb of her pulse, lingering until she gasped and
tried to push him away. His arms tightened, one
hand coming to the bare curve of her bottom, keeping her against him.

"Don't you like that?" he asked against her throat.

"No," Poppy said, trying to work her arms between them.

Harry pressed her back to the mattress, his eyes bright with diabolical amusement. "You're not going to admit to liking any of this, are you?"

She shook her head.

His hand cradled the side of her face, his thumb brushing her closed lips. "Poppy, if there's nothing else about me that pleases you, at least give this a chance."

"I can't. Not when I remember that I should be doing this with . . . him." As angry and resentful as she was, Poppy couldn't quite bring herself to say Michael's name.

As it was, it provoked even more of a reaction from Harry than she'd expected. He gripped her jaw, his hand closing in a strong, not-quite-painful vise, his eyes flaring with fury. She stared back at him defiantly, almost willing him to do something awful, to prove that he was as contemptible as she thought him.

But Harry's voice, when he finally spoke, was scrupulously controlled. "Then I'll see if I can put him out of your thoughts." The bedclothes were pushed away with ruthless insistence, robbing her of any means of concealment. She started upward, but he pushed her back down. His hand curved beneath her breast, plumping it upward, and he bent until his breath fell against the peak in light, repeated shocks.

He traced the aureole with his tongue, caught it tenderly with his teeth, playing with the sensitive flesh. Delight fed into her veins with every swirl and lick and soft tug. Poppy's hands clenched into fists as she tried to keep them by her sides. It seemed important not to touch him voluntarily. But he was

skilled and persistent, arousing deep and writhing
impulses, and her body was apparently inclined to
choose pleasure over principle.

She reached up to his head, the dark hair thick
and soft between her fingers. Gasping, she guided
him to her other breast. He complied with a hoarse
murmur, his lips opening over the heat-stung bud.
His hands glided over her body, charting the curves
of her waist and hips. The tip of his middle finger
circled the rim of her navel and wove in a teasing
path across the flat of her stomach, along the valley
where her legs pressed together . . . from her knees
to the top of her thighs . . . back again.

Stroking gently, Harry whispered, "Open for me."

Poppy was quiet, resisting, panting as if each
breath were being torn from her throat. The pressure
of tears rose behind her closed eyes. Experiencing
any pleasure at all with Harry seemed like a be-
trayal.

And he knew it. His voice was soft against her ear
as he said, "What happens in this bed is only between us. There's no sin in submitting to your husband, and nothing to gain by denying what enjoyment
I might be able to give you. Let it happen, Poppy.
You don't have to be virtuous with me."

"I'm not trying to be," she said unsteadily.

"Then let me touch you."

At her silence, Harry pushed her resistless legs
apart. His palm coursed along her inner thigh until
his thumb brushed soft, private curls. The ragged
rhythms of their breathing rustled through the quiet
room. His thumb nestled into the curls, grazing
against a place so sensitive that she jerked with a
muffled protest.

He gathered her closer into hard muscle and smoothness and crisp hair. Reaching down again, he teased the yielding flesh apart. An irresistible urge came to press upward into his hand. But she forced herself to lay passive, even though the effort to hold still was exhausting.

Finding the entrance to her body, Harry stroked the softness until he had elicited a slick of hot serum. He fondled her, one of his fingers nudging inside. Startled, she stiffened and whimpered.

Harry kissed her throat. "Shhh . . . I'm not hurting you. Easy." He stroked within her, his finger gently crooking as if to urge her forward. Over and over, so patiently. The pleasure acquired a new tension, her limbs weighted with thickening layers of sensation. His finger withdrew, and he began to play with her idly.

Sounds climbed in her throat, but she swallowed them back. She wanted to move, to twist in the restless heat. Her hands itched to grip the flexing muscles of his shoulders. Instead, she lay with martyred stillness.

But he knew how to make her body respond, how to coax delight from her unwilling flesh. She couldn't stop her hips from riding upward, her heels delving into the cool pliancy of the mattress. He slid along her front, kissing lower and lower, his mouth measuring tender distances across her body. When he nuzzled into the soft, private curls, however, she stiffened and tried to move away. Her mind was reeling. No one had told her about this. It couldn't be right.

As she wriggled, his hands slid beneath her bottom, gripping her in place, and his tongue found her in wet, fluent strokes. Carefully he guided her into a deliberate rhythm, urging her upward, and again, while he stroked in voluptuous countermeasure. Wicked mouth, merciless tongue. Hot breath, flowing over her. The feeling built and built, until it came to a startling summit and flared in all directions. A cry escaped her, and another, as dense spasms rolled through her. There was no escaping, no holding back. And he stayed with her, prolonging the descent with soft licks, extorting a few last twitches of pleasure as she lay trembling beneath him.

Then came the worst part, when Harry took her into his arms to comfort her . . . and she let him.

She could hardly help but feel how aroused he was, his body taut and solid, his heartbeat swift beneath her ear. He ran his hand over the supple curve of her spine. With a pang of reluctant excitement, she wondered if he would take her now.

But Harry surprised her by saying, "I won't force the rest of it on you tonight."

Her voice sounded strange and thick to her own ears. "You . . . you needn't stop. As I told you—"

"Yes, you want to have done with it," Harry said sardonically. "So you'll have nothing left to dread." Releasing her, he rolled away and stood, adjusting the front of his trousers with casual unconcern. Poppy's face flamed. "But I've decided to let you dread it a bit longer. Just remember that if you have any idea about requesting an annulment, I'll have you on your back and divested of your virginity before you can blink." He drew the covers over her and paused. "Tell me, Poppy . . . Did you think of him at all just now? Was his face, his name in your mind while I was touching you?"

Poppy shook her head, refusing to look at him.

"That's a start," he said softly. He extinguished the lamp and left.

She lay alone in the darkness, shamed and sated and confused.

Chapter Fourteen

Sleep was always difficult for Harry. Tonight it was impossible. His mind, accustomed to working on multiple problems simultaneously, now had a new and endlessly interesting subject to ponder.

His wife.

He had learned a great deal about Poppy in one day. She had shown that she was exceptionally strong under duress, not a woman to go to pieces in a difficult situation. And although she loved her family, she had not run to them for shelter.

Harry admired the way Poppy had dealt with her wedding day. Even more, he admired the way she had dealt with *him*. No virginal theatrics, as she had put it.

He thought of those blistering minutes before he had left her, when she had been sweet and yielding, her beautiful body blazing in response. Aroused and restless, Harry lay in his bedroom, on the other side of the apartment from hers. The thought of Poppy sleeping in the place where he lived was more than sufficient to keep him awake. No woman had ever stayed in his apartments before. He had always conducted his liaisons away from his residence, never spending a full night with anyone. It made him uncomfortable, the notion of actually sleeping in a bed with another person. Just why that seemed more intimate than the sexual act was not something Harry cared to ponder.

Harry was relieved when daybreak approached, the sky's low roof enameled with dull silver. He arose, washed, and dressed. He let in a housemaid, who stirred the grate and brought freshly ironed copies of the *Morning Chronicle,* the *Globe,* and the *Times.* As per their usual routine, the floor waiter would arrive with breakfast, and then Jake Valentine would deliver the managers' reports and take his morning list.

"Will Mrs. Rutledge want breakfast as well, sir?" the maid asked.

Harry wondered how long Poppy would sleep. "Tap on her door and ask."

"Yes, sir."

He saw the way the maid's gaze darted from the direction of his bedroom to Poppy's. Although it was common for upper-class couples to maintain separate bedrooms, the maid evinced a touch of surprise before she schooled her expression. Vaguely annoyed, Harry watched her leave the dining area.

He heard the housemaid's murmur, and Poppy's reply. The muffled sound of his wife's voice caused a pleasant ripple of awareness across his nerves.

The housemaid returned to the dining area. "I'll be bringing a tray for Mrs. Rutledge as well. Will there be anything else, sir?"

Harry shook his head, returning his attention to the papers as she left. He tried to read an article at least three times before finally giving up and staring in the direction of Poppy's room.

Finally she appeared, wearing a dressing gown made of blue taffeta, heavily embroidered with flowers. Her hair was loose, the brown locks shot with gleaming fire. Her expression was neutral, her eyes guarded. He wanted to peel the intricately stitched garment away from her, kiss her exposed body until she was flushed and panting.

"Good morning," Poppy murmured, not quite meeting his gaze.

Harry stood and waited until she came to the small table. It didn't escape him that she tried to avoid being touched by him as he seated her. *Patience,* he reminded himself. "Did you sleep well?" he asked.

"Yes, thank you." It was clear that politeness rather than concern motivated her to ask, "And you?"

"Well enough."

Poppy glanced at the variety of papers on the table. Picking one up, she held it so that any view of her face was obstructed as she read. Since it appeared that she was not inclined to converse, Harry occupied himself with another paper.

The silence was broken only by the rustling of flimsy news pages.

Breakfast was brought in, and two housemaids set out porcelain plates and flatware and crystal glasses.

Harry saw that Poppy had asked for crumpets, their flat, porous tops gently steaming. He began on his own breakfast of poached eggs on toast, cutting into the condensed yellow yolks and spreading the soft insides across the crisp bread.

"There's no need for you to awaken early if you

don't wish," he said, sprinkling a pinch of salt over his eggs. "Many ladies of London sleep until noon."

"I like to rise when the day begins."

"Like a good farmwife," Harry said, casting her a brief smile.

But Poppy showed no reaction to the reminder, only applied herself to drizzling honey over the crumpets.

Harry paused with his fork held in midair, mesmerized by the sight of her slim fingers twirling the honey stick, meticulously filling each hole with thick amber liquid. Realizing that he was staring, Harry took a bite of his breakfast. Poppy replaced the honey stick in a small silver pot. Discovering a stray drop of sweetness on the tip of her thumb, she lifted it to her lips and sucked it clean.

Harry choked a little, reached for his tea, and took a swallow. The beverage scalded his tongue, causing him to flinch and curse.

Poppy gave him an odd look. "Is there anything the matter?"

Nothing. Except that watching his wife eating breakfast was the most erotic act he had ever seen. "Nothing at all," Harry said scratchily. "Tea's hot."

When he dared to look at Poppy again, she was consuming a fresh strawberry, holding it by the green stem. Her lips rounded in a luscious pucker as she bit neatly into the ripe flesh of the fruit. *Christ.* He moved uncomfortably in his chair, while all the unsatisfied desire of the previous night reawakened with a vengeance. Poppy ate two more strawberries, nibbling slowly, while Harry tried to ignore her. Heat collected beneath his clothing, and he used a napkin to blot his forehead.

Poppy lifted a bite of honey-soaked crumpet to her mouth, and gave him a perplexed glance. "Are you feeling well?"

"It's too warm in here," Harry said irritably, while lurid thoughts went through his mind. Thoughts involving honey, and soft feminine skin, and moist pink—

A knock came at the door.

"Come in," Harry said curtly, eager for any kind of distraction.

Jake Valentine entered the apartments more cautiously than usual, looking a bit surprised as he saw Poppy sitting at the breakfast table. Harry supposed the novelty of the situation would take a little getting used to on all sides.

"Good morning," Valentine said, uncertain whether to address only Harry or include Poppy.

She solved the dilemma by giving him an artless smile. "Good morning, Mr. Valentine. I hope there are no fugitive monkeys in the hotel today?"

Valentine grinned. "Not that I'm aware of, Mrs. Rutledge. But the day's still young."

Harry experienced a new sensation, a poisonous resentment that crept all through his body. Was it . . . jealousy? It had to be. He tried to suppress the feeling, but it lingered in the pit of his stomach. He wanted Poppy to smile at him like that. He wanted her playfulness, her charm, her attention.

Stirring a lump of sugar into his tea, Harry said coolly, "Tell me about the staff meeting."

"Nothing to report, really." Valentine handed him the sheaf of paper. "The sommelier asked that you approve a list of wines. And Mrs. Pennywhistle raised the problem of cutlery and flatware disappearing from trays when guests request food in their room."

Harry's eyes narrowed. "It's not an issue in the dining room?"

"No, sir. It seems that few guests are inclined to take the flatware straight from the dining room. But in the privacy of their own rooms . . . well, the other morning, an entire breakfast service went missing. As a result, Mrs. Pennywhistle proposed that we purchase a set of tinware to be used strictly for private dining."

"My guests, using tin knives and forks?" Harry shook his head emphatically. "No, we'll have to find some other way of discouraging petty thievery. We're not a damned coaching inn."

"That's what I thought you'd say." Valentine watched Harry leaf through the top few pages. "Mrs. Pennywhistle said that whenever Mrs. Rutledge prefers, she would be honored to escort her around the hotel offices and kitchens, and introduce her to the staff."

"I don't think—" Harry began.

"That would be lovely," Poppy interrupted. "Please tell her that I will be ready after breakfast."

"There's no need," Harry said. "It's not as if you'll have a hand in running the place."

Poppy turned to him with a polite smile. "I would never dream of interfering. But since this is my new home, I would like to become more familiar with it."

"It's not a home," Harry said.

Their gazes met.

"Of course it is," Poppy said. "People live here. Don't you consider it your home?"

Jake Valentine shifted his weight uncomfortably. "If you'll give me my morning list, Mr. Rutledge . . ."

Harry barely heard him. He continued to stare at

his wife, wondering why the question seemed important to her. He tried to explain his reasoning. "The mere fact of people living here doesn't make it a home."

"You have no feelings of domestic affection for this place?" Poppy asked.

"Well," Valentine said awkwardly, "I'll go now."

Neither of them took notice of his hasty departure.

"It's a place I happen to own," Harry said. "I value it for practical reasons. But I attach no sentiment to it."

Her blue eyes searched his, curious and perceptive, oddly compassionate. No one had ever looked at him that way before. It made his nerves prickle defensively. "You've spent all your life in hotels, haven't you?" she murmured. "Never a house with a yard and a tree."

Harry was unable to fathom why any of that should signify. He brushed away the subject and tried to reassert his control. "Let me be clear, Poppy . . . this is a business. And my employees are not to be treated as relations, or even as friends, or you'll create a management problem. Do you understand?"

"Yes," she said, still staring at him. "I'm beginning to."

This time it was Harry's turn to lift the newspaper, avoiding her gaze. Uneasiness stirred within him. He did not want any form of understanding from her. He merely wanted to enjoy her, browse over her as he did his room of treasures. Poppy would have to comply with the limits he set. And in return he would be a lenient husband—as long as she understood that he would always have the upper hand.

* * *

"Everyone—" Mrs. Pennywhistle, the head house-keeper said emphatically, "From myself down to the laundry maids, is so *very* delighted that Mr. Rutledge has finally found a bride. And on behalf of the entire staff, we hope you will feel welcome here. You have three hundred people available to serve your every need."

Poppy was touched by the woman's obvious sincerity. The housekeeper was a tall, broad-shouldered woman with a ruddy complexion and an air of barely suppressed liveliness.

"I promise you," Poppy said with a smile, "I won't require the assistance of three hundred people. Although I will need your help in finding a lady's maid. I've never needed one before, but now without my sisters and my companion . . ."

"Certainly. We have a few girls among the staff who could be easily trained for such a purpose. You may interview them, and if none seems suitable, we will advertise."

"Thank you."

"I expect that from time to time you may wish to view the housekeeping accounts and ledgers, and the supply lists and inventory. I am at your disposal, of course."

"You are very kind," Poppy said. "I'm glad of the chance to meet some of the hotel staff. And to see some of the places I was never able to visit as a guest. The kitchens, especially."

"Our chef, Monsieur Broussard, will be in raptures to show you his kitchen and boast of his achievements." She paused and added *sotto voce*, "Fortunately for us, his vanity is matched by his talent."

They began to descend the grand staircase. "How

long have you been employed here, Mrs. Pennywhistle?" Poppy asked.

"Well nigh ten years . . . since the beginning."
The housekeeper smiled at a distant memory. "Mr.
Rutledge was so very young, lanky as a beanpole,
with a sharp American accent and a habit of talking
so fast, one could scarcely follow him. I worked in
my father's tea shop in the Strand—I managed it for
him—and Mr. Rutledge was a frequent customer.
One day he came in and offered me the position I
currently hold, although the hotel was still only a
row of private houses. Nothing compared to what it
is now. Of course I said yes."

"Why 'of course'? Didn't your father want you to
stay at his shop?"

"Yes, but he had my sisters to help him. And there
was something about Mr. Rutledge that I've never
seen in any man before or since . . . an extraordinary
force of character. He is very persuasive."

"I've noticed," Poppy said dryly.

"People want to follow him, or to be part of whatever it is he's involved in. It's why he was able to
accomplish all this—" Mrs. Pennywhistle gestured
at their surroundings, "—at such an early age."

It occurred to Poppy that she could learn much
about her husband from those who worked for him.
She hoped at least a few of them would be as willing
to talk as Mrs. Pennywhistle. "Is he a demanding
master?"

The housekeeper chuckled. "Oh, yes. But fair,
and always reasonable."

They went to the front office, where two men, one
elderly, one in his middle years, were conferring
over an enormous ledger, which lay open across an
oak desk. "Gentlemen," the housekeeper said, "I

am touring Mrs. Rutledge around the hotel. Mrs. Rutledge, may I present Mr. Myles, our general manager, and Mr. Lufton, the concierge."

They bowed respectfully, regarding Poppy as if she were a visiting monarch. The younger of the two, Mr. Myles, beamed and blushed until the top of his balding head was pink. "Mrs. Rutledge, it is a very great honor indeed! May we offer our sincere congratulations on your marriage—"

"*Most* sincere," Mr. Lufton chimed in. "You are the answer to our prayers. We wish you and Mr. Rutledge every happiness."

Slightly taken aback by their enthusiasm, Poppy smiled and nodded to each of them in turn. "Thank you, gentlemen."

They proceeded to show her the office, which housed a long row of arrival ledgers, managers' logs, books containing histories and customs of foreign countries, dictionaries for various languages, maps of all kinds, and floor plans of the hotel. The plans, tacked on a wall, were marked in pencil to indicate which rooms were vacant or under repair.

Two leather-bound books had been set apart from the rest, one red, one black.

"What are these volumes?" Poppy asked.

The men glanced at each other, and Mr. Lufton replied cautiously. "There are very rare occasions on which a guest has proved so . . . well, difficult—"

"Impossible," Mr. Myles chimed in.

"That regrettably we must enter them in the black book, which means they are no longer precisely welcome—"

"Undesirable," Mr. Myles added.

"And we are unable to allow them back."

"*Ever,*" Mr. Myles said emphatically.

Amused, Poppy nodded. "I see. And the purpose of the red book?"

Mr. Lufton proceeded to explain. "That is for certain guests who are a bit more demanding than usual."

"Problem guests," Mr. Myles clarified.

"Those who have special requests," Mr. Lufton continued, "or don't like their rooms cleaned at certain times; those who insist on bringing pets, things of that sort. We don't discourage them from staying, but we do make a note of their peculiarities."

"Hmmm." Poppy picked up the red book and cast a mischievous glance at the housekeeper. "I wouldn't be surprised if the Hathaways were mentioned a few times in this book."

Silence greeted her comment.

Seeing the frozen looks on their faces, Poppy began to laugh. "I knew it. Where is my family mentioned?" She opened the book and glanced over a few pages at random.

The two men were instantly distressed, hovering as if searching for an opportunity to seize the book. "Mrs. Rutledge, please, you mustn't—"

"I'm sure you're not in there," Mr. Myles said anxiously.

"I'm sure we are," Poppy countered with a grin. "In fact, we probably have our own chapter."

"Yes—I mean, *no*—Mrs. Rutledge, I beg of you—"

"Very well," Poppy said, surrendering the red book. The men sighed with relief. "However," she said, "I may borrow this book someday. I'm sure it would make excellent reading material."

"If you are done teasing these poor gentlemen, Mrs. Rutledge," the housekeeper said, her eyes twinkling, "I see that many of our employees have gathered outside the door to meet you."

"Lovely!" Poppy went to the reception area, where she was introduced to housemaids, floor managers, maintenance staff, and hotel valets. She repeated everyone's name, trying to memorize as many of them as possible, and she asked questions about their duties. They responded eagerly to her interest, volunteering information about the various parts of England they had come from and how long they had worked at the Rutledge.

Poppy reflected that despite the many occasions she had stayed at the hotel as a guest, she had never given much thought to the employees. They had always been nameless and faceless, moving in the background with quiet efficiency. Now she felt immediate kinship with them. She was part of the hotel just as they were . . . all of them existing in Harry Rutledge's sphere.

After the first week of living with Harry, it was clear to Poppy that her husband kept a schedule that would have killed a normal man. The only time she was sure to see him was in the mornings at breakfast; he was busy the rest of the day, often missing supper, and seldom retiring before midnight.

Harry liked to occupy himself with two or more things at once, making lists and plans, arranging meetings, reconciling arguments, doing favors. He was constantly approached by people who wanted him to apply his brilliant mind to some problem or other. People visited him at all hours, and it seemed a quarter hour couldn't pass without someone, usually Jake Valentine, tapping on the apartment door.

When Harry wasn't busy with his various intrigues, he meddled with the hotel and its staff. His demands for perfection and the highest quality of service were relentless. The employees were paid generously and treated well, but in return they were expected to work hard and, above all, to be loyal. If one of them were injured or ill, Harry sent for a doctor and paid for their treatments. If someone suggested a way to improve the hotel or its service, the idea was sent directly to Harry, and if he approved, he gave a handsome bonus. As a result, Harry's desk was always laden with piles of reports, letters and notes.

It didn't seem to have occurred to Harry to suggest a honeymoon for himself and his new bride, and Poppy suspected he had no desire to leave the hotel. Certainly she had no desire for a honeymoon with a man who had betrayed her.

Since their wedding night, Poppy had been nervous around Harry, especially when they were alone. He made no secret of his desire for her, his interest in her, but so far there had been no more advances. In fact, he had gone out of his way to be polite and considerate. It seemed as if he were trying to get her accustomed to him, to the altered circumstances of her life. And she appreciated his patience, because it was all so very new. Ironically, however, his self-imposed restraint gave their occasional moments of contact—the touch of his hand on her arm, the press of his body when they stood close in a crowd—a charge of vibrant attraction.

Attraction without trust . . . not a comfortable thing to feel for one's own husband.

Poppy had no idea how long he would continue this conjugal reprieve. She was only grateful that

Harry was so consumed with his hotel. Although . . .
she couldn't help thinking that this sunrise-to-
midnight agenda was not at all good for him. If someone Poppy cared for had been working so relentlessly,
she would have urged him to ease his pace, to take
some time to rest.

Simple compassion got the better of her one afternoon when Harry came into their apartment unexpectedly, carrying his coat in one hand. He had
spent most of the day with the Chief Officer of the
LFEE, the London Fire Engine Establishment. Together they had meticulously gone through the hotel
to examine its safety procedures and equipment.

If, heaven forbid, a fire should ever break out at
the Rutledge, the employees had been trained to
help as many guests as possible leave the building
expediently. Escape ladders were routinely counted
and inspected, and floor plans and exit routes were
examined. Firemarks had been mortared onto the
outside of the building to designate it as one the
LFEE had been paid to protect.

As Harry entered the apartment, Poppy saw that
the day had been especially demanding. His face
was etched with weariness.

He paused at the sight of Poppy curled in the corner of the settee, reading a book balanced on her
drawn-up knees.

"How was the luncheon?" Harry asked.

Poppy had been invited to join a group of well-
to-do young matrons, who held an annual charity
bazaar. "It went nicely, thank you. They are a pleasant group. Although they do seem a bit too fond of
forming committees. I've always thought a commit-
tee takes a month to accomplish something a single
person could have done in ten minutes."

Harry smiled. "The goal of such groups isn't to be efficient. It's to have something to occupy their time."

Poppy took a closer look at him, and her eyes widened. "What happened to your clothes?"

Harry's white linen shirt and dark blue silk waistcoat had been streaked with soot. There were more black smudges on his hands, and one on the edge of his jaw.

"I was testing one of the safety ladders."

"You climbed down a ladder outside the building?" Poppy was amazed that he would have taken such an unnecessary risk. "Couldn't you have asked someone else to do it? Mr. Valentine, perhaps?"

"I'm sure he would have. But I wouldn't provide equipment for my employees without trying it myself. I still have concerns about the housemaids—their skirts would make their descent more difficult. However, I draw the line at trying *that* out." He cast a rueful glance at his palms. "I have to wash and change before going back to work."

Poppy returned her attention to her book. But she was intensely aware of the quiet sounds coming from the other room, the opening of drawers, the splash of water and soap, the thud of a discarded shoe. She thought of him being unclothed, at that very moment, and a dart of warmth went through her stomach.

Harry came back into the room, clean and impeccable as before. Except . . .

"A smudge," Poppy said, conscious of a flutter of amusement. "You missed a spot."

Harry glanced down over his front. "Where?"

"Your jaw. No, not that side." She picked up a napkin and gestured for him to come to her.

Harry leaned over the back of the settee, his face descending toward hers. He held very still as she wiped the soot from his jaw. The scent of his skin drifted to her, fresh and clean, with a slight smoky tinge like cedarwood.

Wishing to prolong the moment, Poppy stared into his fathomless green eyes. They were shadowed from lack of sleep. Good heavens, did the man ever pause for even a moment?

"Why don't you sit with me?" Poppy asked impulsively.

Harry blinked, clearly thrown off guard by the invitation. "Now?"

"Yes, now."

"I can't. There's too much to—"

"Have you eaten today? Aside from a few bites of breakfast?"

Harry shook his head. "I haven't had time."

Poppy pointed to the place on the settee beside her in wordless demand.

To her surprise, Harry actually obeyed. He came around the end of the settee and sat in the corner, staring at her. One of his dark brows arched questioningly.

Reaching for the tray beside her, Poppy lifted a plate laden with sandwiches, tarts, and biscuits. "The kitchen sent up far too much for one person. Have the rest."

"I'm really not—"

"Here," she insisted, pushing the plate into his hands.

Harry took a sandwich and began to consume it slowly. Taking her own teacup from the tray, Poppy poured fresh tea and added a spoonful of sugar. She gave it to Harry.

"What are you reading?" he asked, glancing at the book in her lap.

"A novel by a naturalist author. As of yet, I can't find anything resembling a plot, but the descriptions of the countryside are quite lyrical." She paused, watching him drain the teacup. "Do you like novels?"

He shook his head. "I usually read for information, not entertainment."

"You disapprove of reading for pleasure?"

"No, it's just that I don't often manage to find the time for it."

"Perhaps that's why you don't sleep well. You need an interlude between work and bedtime."

There was a dry, perfectly timed pause before Harry asked, "What would you suggest?"

Aware of his meaning, Poppy felt a bloom of color emerge from head to toe. Harry seemed to enjoy her discomfiture, not in a mocking way, but as if he found her charming.

"Everyone in my family loves novels," Poppy finally said, pushing the conversation back into line. "We gather in the parlor nearly every evening, and one of us reads aloud. Win is the best at it—she invents a different voice for each character."

"I'd like to hear you read," Harry said.

Poppy shook her head. "I'm not half as entertaining as Win. I put everyone to sleep."

"Yes," Harry said. "You have the voice of a scholar's daughter." Before she could take offense, he added, "Soothing. Never grates. Soft . . ."

He was extraordinarily tired, she realized. So much that even the effort to string words together was defeating him.

"I should go," he muttered, rubbing his eyes.

"Finish your sandwiches first," Poppy said authoritatively.

He picked up a sandwich obediently. While he ate, Poppy paged through the book until she found what she wanted . . . a description of walking through the countryside, under skies filled with fleecy clouds, past almond trees in blossom and white campion nestled beside quiet brooks. She read in a measured tone, occasionally stealing a glance at Harry while he polished off the entire plate of sandwiches. And then he settled deeper into the corner, more relaxed than she had ever seen him.

She read a few pages more, about walking past hedges and meadows, through a wood dressed with a counterpane of fallen leaves, while soft pale sunshine gave way to a quiet rain . . .

And when she finally reached the end of the chapter, she looked at Harry once more.

He was asleep.

His chest rose and fell in an even rhythm, his long lashes fanned against his skin. One hand was palm down against his chest, while the other lay half open at his side, the strong fingers partially curled.

"Never fails," Poppy murmured with a private grin. Her talent at putting people to sleep was too much even for Harry's relentless drive. Carefully she set the book aside.

This was the first time she'd ever been able to view Harry at her leisure. It was strange to see him so utterly disarmed. In sleep, the lines of his face were relaxed and almost innocent, at odds with his usual expression of command. His mouth, always so purposeful, looked as soft as velvet. He looked like a boy lost in a solitary dream. Poppy felt an urge to safeguard the sleep Harry so badly needed, to cover him with a blanket, and stroke the dark hair from his brow.

Several tranquil minutes passed, the silence disturbed only by distant sounds of activity in the hotel and from the street. This was something Poppy had not known she needed . . . time to contemplate the stranger who had taken utter possession of her life.

Trying to understand Harry Rutledge was like taking apart one of the intricate clockwork mechanisms he had constructed. One could examine every gear and ratchet wheel and lever, but that didn't mean one would ever comprehend what made it all work.

It seemed that Harry had spent his life wrestling with the world and trying to bend it to his will. And toward that end he had made a great deal of progress. But he was clearly dissatisfied, unable to enjoy what he had achieved, which made him very different from the other men in Poppy's life, especially Cam and Merripen.

Because of their Romany heritage, her brothers-in-law didn't view the world as something to be conquered, but rather something to roam through freely. And then there was Leo, who preferred to view life as an objective observer instead of as an active participant.

Harry was nothing short of a brigand, scheming to conquer everyone and everything in sight. How could such a man ever be restrained? How would he ever find peace?

Poppy was so lost in the peaceful stillness of the room that she started when she heard a tap at the door. Her nerves jangled unpleasantly. She made no response, wishing the blasted noise would go away. But there it was again.

Tap. Tap. Tap.

Harry awakened with an inarticulate murmur, blinking with the confusion of someone who had been too quickly roused from sleep. "Yes?" he said gruffly, struggling to sit up.

The door opened, and Jack Valentine entered. He looked apologetic as he saw Harry and Poppy together on the settee. Poppy could barely refrain from scowling, even though he was only doing his job. Valentine came to hand Harry a folded note, murmured a few cryptic words, and left the apartment.

Harry scanned the note with a bleary glance. Tucking it into his coat pocket, he smiled ruefully at Poppy. "I seem to have nodded off while you were reading." He stared at her, his eyes warmer than she had ever seen them. "An interlude," he murmured for no apparent reason, and a corner of his mouth hitched upward. "I'd like another one soon."

And he left while she was still struggling to form a reply.

Chapter Fifteen

Only the wealthiest of London ladies possessed
their own carriages and horses, as it cost a fortune to
maintain such a convenience. Women without their
own stables, or those who lived alone, were compelled to "job" the horses, brougham, and coachman,
hiring it all from a livery service or jobmaster whenever they needed to knock about London.

Harry had insisted that Poppy must have her own
carriage and pair, and had sent for a designer from a
carriage works to come to the hotel. After consulting
with Poppy, the carriage maker was commissioned
to build a vehicle specifically to her taste. Poppy was
left rather bemused by the process, and even a bit
nettled because her insistence on asking the prices
of materials had caused a tiff. "You're not here to
question how much any of this costs," Harry had
told her. "Your only task is to choose what you like."

But in Poppy's experience, that had always been
part of choosing something . . . viewing what was
available and then comparing costs until one arrived
at something that was neither the most expensive

nor the least. Harry, however, seemed to view this approach as an affront, as if she were questioning his ability to provide for her.

Finally it was decided that the outside would be done in elegant black lacquer, the inside upholstered in green velvet and beige leather with brass bead trim, and the interior paneling would feature decorative paintwork. There would be green silk curtains and venetian blinds in lieu of mahogany shutters . . . morocco leather sleeping cushions . . . decorative welding on the outside steps, plated carriage lamps and matching door handles . . . it had never occurred to Poppy that there would be so much to decide.

She spent what was left of the afternoon in the kitchen with the chef, Monsieur Broussard, the pastry chef, Mr. Rupert, and Mrs. Pennywhistle. Broussard was involved in the creation of a new dessert . . . or more aptly, trying to re-create a dessert he had remembered from childhood.

"My great-aunt Albertine always made this with no recipe," Broussard explained ruefully as he pulled a bain-marie, or water bath, from the oven. Nestled inside were a half dozen perfect little steaming apple puddings. "I watched her every time. But it has all slipped from my mind. Fifteen times I have tried it, and still it's not perfect . . . but *quand on veut, on peut.*"

"When one wants, one can," Poppy translated.

"Exactement." Broussard carefully removed the dishes from the hot water.

Chef Rupert drizzled cream sauce over each pudding, and topped them with delicate pastry leaves. "Shall we?" he asked, handing out spoons.

Solemnly, Poppy, Mrs. Pennywhistle, and the two chefs each took a pudding and sampled it. Poppy's mouth was filled with cream, soft tart apple, and crisply imploding pastry. She closed her eyes to better enjoy the textures and flavors, and she heard satisfied sighs from Mrs. Pennywhistle and Chef Rupert.

"Still not right," Monsieur Broussard fretted, scowling at the dish of pudding as if it were deliberately being obstinate.

"I don't care if it's not right," the housekeeper said. "That is the best thing I've ever tasted in my life." She turned to Poppy. "Don't you agree, Mrs. Rutledge?"

"I think it's what angels must eat in heaven," Poppy said, digging into the pudding. Chef Rupert had already shoved another spoonful into his mouth.

"Maybe a touch more lemon and cinnamon . . ." Monsieur Broussard mused.

"Mrs. Rutledge."

Poppy twisted to see who had spoken her name. Her smile dimmed as she saw Jake Valentine entering the kitchen. It wasn't that she didn't like him. In fact, Valentine had been very personable and kind. However, he seemed to have been appointed as a watchdog, enforcing Harry's mandate that Poppy should refrain from keeping company with the employees.

Mr. Valentine looked no happier than Poppy as he spoke. "Mrs. Rutledge, I've been sent to remind you that you have an appointment at the dressmaker's."

"I do? Now?" Poppy looked at him blankly. "I don't remember making an appointment."

"It was made for you. At Mr. Rutledge's request."

"Oh." Reluctantly Poppy set down her spoon. "When must I leave?"

"In a quarter hour."

That would give her just enough time to tidy her

hair and fetch a walking cloak. "I have enough clothes," Poppy said. "I don't need more."

"A lady in your position," Mrs. Pennywhistle said wisely, "needs many dresses. I've heard it said that fashionable ladies never wear the same frock twice."

Poppy rolled her eyes. "I've heard that as well. And I think it's ridiculous. Why should it matter if a lady is seen in the same frock twice? Except to provide evidence that her husband is wealthy enough to buy her more clothes than a person needs."

The housekeeper smiled sympathetically. "Shall I walk with you to your apartments, Mrs. Rutledge?"

"No, thank you. I'll go along the servants' hallway. None of the guests will see me."

Valentine said, "You shouldn't go unescorted."

Poppy heaved an impatient sigh. "Mr. Valentine?"

"Yes?"

"I want to walk to my apartment by myself. If I can't even do that, this entire hotel will start to feel like a prison."

He nodded with reluctant understanding.

"Thank you." Murmuring good-bye to the chefs and the housekeeper, Poppy left the kitchen.

Jake Valentine shifted his weight uncomfortably as the other three glared at him. "I'm sorry," he muttered. "But Mr. Rutledge has decided that his wife shouldn't fraternize with the employees. He says it makes all of us less productive, and there are more suitable ways for her to occupy herself."

Although Mrs. Pennywhistle was usually disinclined to criticize the master, her face grew taut with annoyance. "Doing what?" she asked curtly. "Shopping for things she neither needs nor wants? Reading fashion periodicals by herself? Riding in the park with a footman in attendance? No doubt there are many fashion-plate wives who would be more than pleased by such a shallow existence. But that lonely young woman is from a close family, and she is accustomed to a great deal of affection. She needs someone to do things with . . . a companion . . . and she needs a husband."

"She has a husband," Jake protested.

The housekeeper's eyes narrowed. "Have you noticed *nothing* odd about their relationship, Valentine?"

"No, and it's not appropriate for us to discuss it."

Monsieur Broussard regarded Mrs. Pennywhistle with keen interest. "I'm French," he said. "I have no problem discussing it."

Mrs. Pennywhistle lowered her voice, mindful of the scullery maids who were washing pots in the adjoining room. "There is some doubt as to whether they've had conjugal relations yet."

"Now see here—" Jake began, outraged at this violation of his employer's privacy.

"Have some of this, *mon ami*," Broussard said, shoving a pastry plate at him. As Jake sat and picked up a spoon, the chef gave Mrs. Pennywhistle an encouraging glance. "What gives you the impression that he has not yet, er . . . sampled the watercress?"

"Watercress?" Jake repeated incredulously.

"*Cresson.*" Broussard gave him a superior look. "A metaphor. And much nicer than the metaphors you English use for the same thing."

"I never use metaphors," Jake muttered.

"*Bien sur,* you have no imagination." The chef turned back to the housekeeper. "Why is there doubt about the relations between Monsieur and Madame Rutledge?"

"The sheets," she said succinctly.

Jake nearly choked on his pastry. "You have the housemaids *spying on them*?" he asked around a mouthful of custard and cream.

"Not at all," the housekeeper said defensively. "It's only that we have vigilant maids who tell me everything. And even if they didn't, one hardly needs great powers of observation to see that they do not behave like a married couple."

The chef looked deeply concerned. "You think there's a problem with his carrot?"

"Watercress, carrot—is *everything* food to you?" Jake demanded.

The chef shrugged. *"Oui."*

"Well," Jake said testily, "there is a string of Rutledge's past mistresses who would undoubtedly testify there is nothing wrong with his carrot."

"Alors, he is a virile man . . . she is a beautiful woman . . . why are they not making salad together?"

Jake paused with the spoon raised halfway to his lips as he recalled the business with the letter from Bayning and the secret meeting between Harry Rutledge and Viscount Andover. "I think," he said uncomfortably, "that to win her hand in marriage, Mr. Rutledge may have . . . well, manipulated events to make things turn out the way he wanted. Without taking her feelings into consideration."

The other three looked at him blankly.

Chef Rupert was the first to speak. "But he does that to everyone."

"Apparently Mrs. Rutledge doesn't like it," Jake muttered.

Mrs. Pennywhistle leaned her chin on her hand and tapped her jaw thoughtfully. "I believe she would be a good influence on him, were she ever inclined to try."

"Nothing," Jake said decisively, "will ever change Harry Rutledge."

"Still," the housekeeper mused, "I think the two of them may need a bit of help."

"From whom?" Chef Rupert asked.

"From all of us," the housekeeper replied. "It's all to our benefit if the master is happy, isn't it?"

"*No,*" Jake said firmly. "I've never known anyone more ill equipped for happiness. He wouldn't know what to do with it."

"All the more reason he should try it," Mrs. Pennywhistle declared.

Jake gave her a warning glance. "We are *not* going to meddle in Mr. Rutledge's personal life. I forbid it."

Chapter Sixteen

Sitting at her dressing table, Poppy brushed powder on her nose and applied rose-petal salve to her lips. That night she and Harry were to attend a supper given in one of the private dining rooms, a highly formal affair attended by foreign diplomats and government officials to honor the visiting monarch of Prussia, King Frederick William IV. Mrs. Pennywhistle had shown Poppy the menu, and Poppy had remarked wryly that with ten courses, she expected the supper would last half the night.

Poppy was dressed in her best gown, a violet silk that shimmered with tones of blue and pink as the light moved over it. The unique color had been achieved with a new synthetic dye, and it was so striking that little ornamentation was needed. The bodice was intricately wrapped, leaving the tops of her shoulders bare, and the full, layered skirts rustled softly as she moved.

Just as she set down the powder brush, Harry came to the doorway and surveyed her leisurely.

"No woman will compare to you tonight," he murmured.

Poppy smiled and murmured her thanks. "You look very fine," she said, although "fine" seemed an entirely inadequate word to describe her husband.

Harry was severely handsome in the formal scheme of black and white, his cravat crisp and snowy, his shoes highly polished. He wore the elegant clothes with unselfconscious ease, so debonair and beguiling that it was easy to forget how calculating he was.

"Is it time to go downstairs yet?" Poppy asked.

Pulling a watch from his pocket, Harry consulted it. "Fourteen . . . no, thirteen minutes."

Her brows lifted as she saw how battered and scratched the watch was. "My goodness. You must have carried that for a long time."

He hesitated before showing it to her. Poppy took the object carefully. The watch was small but heavy in her palm, the gold casing warm from his body. Flipping it open, she saw that the scarred and scratched metal had not been inscribed or adorned in any way.

"Where did it come from?" she asked.

Harry tucked the watch into his pocket. His expression was inscrutable. "From my father, when I told him I was leaving for London. He said his father had given it to him years before, with the advice that when he became a success, he should celebrate by purchasing a much finer watch. And so my father passed it on to me with the same counsel."

"But you've never bought one for yourself?"

Harry shook his head.

A perplexed smile touched her lips. "I would say that you've had more than enough success to merit a new watch."

"Not yet."

She thought he must be joking, but there was no humor in his expression. Perturbed and fascinated, Poppy wondered how much more wealth he intended to gain, how much power he wanted to accrue, before he considered it enough.

Perhaps there was no such thing as "enough" for Harry Rutledge.

She was distracted from her thoughts as he pulled something from one of his coat pockets, a flat rectangular leather case.

"A present," Harry said, giving it to her.

Her eyes rounded with surprise. "You didn't need to give me anything. Thank you. I didn't expect . . . *oh*." This last as she opened the case and beheld a diamond necklace arranged on the velvet lining like a pool of glittering fire. It was a heavy garland of sparkling flowers and quatrefoil links.

"Do you like it?" Harry asked casually.

"Yes, of course, it's . . . breathtaking." Poppy had never imagined owning such jewelry. The only necklace she possessed was a single pearl on a chain. "Shall I . . . shall I wear it tonight?"

"I think it would be appropriate with that gown." Harry took the necklace from the case, stood behind Poppy, and fastened it gently around her neck. The cold weight of the diamonds and the warm brush of his fingers at her nape elicited a shiver. He remained behind her, his hands settling lightly on the curves of her neck, moving in a warm stroke to the tops of her shoulders. "Lovely," he murmured. "Although nothing is as beautiful as your bare skin."

Poppy stared into the looking glass, not at her flushed face, but at his hands on her skin. They were both still, watching their shared reflection as if they were two forms encased in ice.

His hands moved sensitively, as if he were touching a priceless work of art. With the tip of his middle finger, he traced the line of her collarbone to the hollow at the base of her throat.

Feeling agitated, Poppy pulled away from his hands and stood to face him, coming around the little chair. "Thank you," she managed to say. Cautiously she moved to embrace him, her arms sliding over his shoulders.

It was more than Poppy had intended to do, but there was something in Harry's expression that touched her. She had sometimes seen the same expression on Leo's face in childhood, when he had been caught in mischief and had gone to their mother with a bouquet of flowers or some little treasure.

Harry's arms went around her, pulling her farther up against him. He smelled delicious, and he was warm and hard beneath the layers of linen, silk and wool. The soft gust of his breath against her neck was ragged at the finish.

Closing her eyes, Poppy let herself lean against him. He kissed the side of her throat, working up to the juncture of her neck and jaw. She felt warm from the bottom of her feet to the top of her head. She found something surprising in the embrace, a sense of security. They fit nicely together, softness and hardness, pliancy and tension. It seemed that every curve of her was perfectly reconciled with his masculine contours. She wouldn't have minded standing against him, with him, for a while longer.

But Harry chose to take more than had been offered. His hand went to the side of her head, easing her back at just the right angle to kiss her. His mouth descended swiftly. Poppy arched and twisted away from him, nearly causing an awkward collision of their heads.

She turned to face him, refusal stamped on her expression.

The evasion seemed to have stunned Harry. Sparks of wrath kindled in his eyes, as if she had been vastly unfair. "It seems the ban on virginal theatrics has been lifted."

Poppy replied with stilted dignity. "I don't think it's theatrical to pull away when I don't want to be kissed."

"A diamond necklace for one kiss. Is that such a bad bargain?"

Her cheeks went scarlet. "I appreciate your generosity. But you're wrong to think that you can buy or bargain for my favors. I'm not a mistress, Harry."

"Obviously. Because in return for such a necklace, a mistress would go to that bed, lie there willingly and offer to do whatever I wanted."

"I've never denied you your marital rights," she said. "If you wish, I'll go to that bed willingly and do whatever you want, this very moment. But not because you gave me a necklace, as if it were part of some transaction."

Far from being appeased, Harry regarded her with gathering outrage. "The thought of you laid out like a martyr on the sacrificial altar is not what I had in mind."

"Why isn't it enough that I'm willing to submit to you?" Poppy asked, her own temper flaring. "Why must I be *eager* to lie with you, when you're not the husband I wanted?"

The very second the words left her lips, Poppy

regretted them. But it was too late. Harry's eyes turned to ice. His lips parted, and she braced herself, knowing he was about to say something decimating.

Instead, he turned and walked from the room.

Submit.

The word hovered, wasplike, in Harry's mind. Stinging repeatedly.

Submit to him . . . as if he were some loathsome toad, when some of the most beautiful women in London had begged for his attentions. Sensuous, accomplished women with clever mouths and hands, willing to satisfy his most exotic desires . . . in fact, he could have one of them tonight.

When his temper had eased enough that he could function normally, Harry went back into Poppy's bedroom and informed her that it was time to go down to supper. She sent him a wary glance, seeming to want to say something, but she had the sense to keep her mouth shut.

"You're not the husband I wanted."

And he never would be. No amount of scheming or manipulation could change it.

But Harry would continue to play out his hand. Poppy was legally his, and God knew he had money on his side. Time would have to take care of the rest.

The formal dinner was a great success. Every time Harry glanced at the other end of the long table, he saw that Poppy was acquitting herself splendidly. She was relaxed and smiling, taking part in conversation, appearing to charm her companions. It was exactly as Harry had expected: the same qualities that were considered faults in an unmarried girl were admired in a married woman. Poppy's acute observations and her enjoyment of lively debate made her far more interesting than a demure society miss with a modest downcast gaze.

She was breathtaking in the violet gown, her slender neck encircled with diamonds, her hair rich with dark fire. Nature had blessed her with abundant beauty. But it was her smile that made her irresistible, a smile so sweet and brilliant that it warmed him from the inside out.

Harry wished she would smile at him like that. She had, in the beginning. There had to be something that would induce her to warm to him, to like him again. Everyone had a weakness.

In the meantime, Harry stole glances of her whenever he could, his lovely and distant wife . . . and he drank in the smiles she gave to other people.

The next morning Harry awoke at his usual hour. He washed and dressed, sat at the breakfast table with a newspaper, and glanced at Poppy's door. There was no sign of her. He assumed she would sleep late, since they had retired long after midnight.

"Don't wake Mrs. Rutledge," he told the maid. "She needs to rest this morning."

"Yes, sir."

Harry ate his breakfast alone, trying to focus on the newspaper, but his gaze kept dragging to Poppy's closed door.

He had gotten used to seeing her every morning. He liked to start his day with her. But Harry was aware that he had been nothing less than boorish the previous night, giving her jewelry and demanding a demonstration of gratitude. He should have known better.

It was just that he wanted her so damned badly. And he had become accustomed to having his way, especially where women were concerned. He reflected that it probably wouldn't hurt him to learn to consider someone else's feelings.

Especially if that would hasten the process of getting what he wanted.

After receiving the morning managers' reports from Jake Valentine, Harry went with him to the basement of the hotel to assess the damage from some minor flooding due to faulty drainage. "We'll need an engineering assessment," Harry said, "And I want an inventory of the damaged storage items."

"Yes, sir," Valentine replied. "Unfortunately there were some rolled-up Turkish carpets in the flooded area, but I don't know if the staining—"

"Mr. Rutledge!" An agitated housemaid descended to the bottom of the stairs and rushed over to them. She could barely speak between labored breaths. "Mrs. Pennywhistle said . . . to come fetch you because . . . Mrs. Rutledge . . ."

Harry looked at the housemaid sharply. "What is it?"

"She's injured, sir . . . took a fall . . ."

Alarm shot through him. "Where is she?"

"Your apartments, sir."

"Send for a doctor," Harry told Valentine, and he ran for the stairs, taking them two and three at a time. By the time he reached his apartments, full-scale panic roared through him. He tried to push it back enough to think clearly. There was a congregation of maids around the door, and he shouldered his way through them into the main room. "Poppy?"

Mrs. Pennywhistle's voice echoed from the tiled bathing room. "We're in here, Mr. Rutledge."

Harry reached the bathing room in three strides,

his stomach lurching in fear as he saw Poppy on the floor, reclining against the housekeeper's supportive arms. Toweling had been draped over her for modesty's sake, but her limbs were naked and vulnerable looking in contrast to the hard gray tiling.

Harry dropped to his haunches beside her. "What happened, Poppy?"

"I'm sorry." She looked pained and mortified and apologetic. "It was so silly. I stepped out of the bath and slipped on the tiles, and my leg went out from beneath me."

"Thank heavens one of the maids had come to clear the breakfast dishes," Mrs. Pennywhistle told him, "and she heard Mrs. Rutledge cry out."

"I'm all right," Poppy said. "I just twisted my ankle a bit." She gave the housekeeper a gently chiding glance. "I'm perfectly capable of getting up, but Mrs. Pennywhistle won't let me."

"I was afraid to move her," the housekeeper told Harry.

"You were right to keep her still," Harry replied, examining Poppy's leg. The ankle was discolored and already beginning to swell. Even the light brush of his fingers was enough to make her flinch and inhale quickly.

"I don't think I'll need a doctor," Poppy said. "If you could just wrap it with a light binding, and perhaps I could have some willow bark tea—"

"Oh, you're seeing a doctor," Harry said, suffused with grim concern. Glancing at Poppy's face, he saw the residue of tears, and he reached out to her with extreme gentleness, his fingers caressing the side of her face. Her skin was as smooth as fine-milled soap. There was a red mark in the center of her lower lip, where she must have bitten it.

Whatever she saw in his expression caused her eyes to widen and her cheeks to flush.

Mrs. Pennywhistle eased up from the floor. "Well," she said briskly, "Now that she's in your care, Mr. Rutledge, shall I fetch some bandages and salve? We may as well treat the ankle until the doctor arrives."

"Yes," Harry said curtly. "And send for another doctor—I want a second opinion."

"Yes, sir." The housekeeper fled.

"We haven't even gotten a first opinion yet," Poppy protested. "And you're making far too much of this. It's just a minor sprain, and . . . what are you doing?"

Harry had laid two fingers on the top of her foot, two inches below the ankle, feeling for her pulse. "Making certain your circulation hasn't been compromised."

Poppy rolled her eyes. "My goodness. All I need is to sit somewhere with my foot up."

"I'm going to carry you to bed," he said, sliding one arm behind her back, the other beneath her knees. "Can you put your arms around my neck?"

She blushed from head to toe, and complied with an inarticulate murmur. He lifted her in a slow, easy movement. Poppy fumbled a little as the toweling began to slip from her body, and she gasped in pain.

"Did I jostle your leg?" Harry asked in concern.

"No. I think . . ." She sounded sheepish. "I think I may have hurt my back a little as well."

Harry let out a few quiet curses that caused her brows to raise, and he carried her into the bedroom. "From now on," he told her sternly, "you're not to step out of the bathing tub unless there's someone to help you."

"I can't do that," she protested.

"Why not?"

"I don't need help with my bath every night. I'm not a child!"

"Believe me," Harry said, "I'm aware of that." He set her down gently and arranged the covers over her. After easing the damp towel away from her, he adjusted her pillows. "Where are your nightgowns?"

"The bottom dresser drawer."

Harry went to the dresser, jerked the drawer open, and pulled out a white gown. Returning to the bed, he helped Poppy into the nightgown, his face tautening with concern as she winced with every movement. She needed something for the pain. She needed a doctor.

Why the hell was it so *quiet* in the apartment? He wanted people running, fetching things. He wanted action.

After tucking the covers around Poppy, he left the room in rapid strides.

Three maids were still in the hallway, talking amongst themselves. Harry scowled, and the maids blanched simultaneously.

"S-sir?" one of them asked nervously.

"Why are you all standing here?" he demanded. "And where is Mrs. Pennywhistle? I want one of you to find her immediately, and tell her to hurry! And I want the other two of you to start fetching things."

"What kind of things, sir?" one of them quavered.

"Things for Mrs. Rutledge. A hot water bottle. Ice. Laudanum. A pot of tea. A book. I don't give a damn, just start bringing things!"

The two maids scampered away like terrified squirrels.

A half minute passed, and still no one appeared.

Where the devil was the doctor? Why was everyone so bloody *slow?*

He heard Poppy calling for him, and he turned on his heels and raced back into the apartments. He was at her bedside in an instant.

Poppy was huddled in a small, motionless heap.

"Harry," her voice came from beneath the bedclothes, "are you yelling at people?"

"No," he said instantly.

"Good. Because this is not a serious situation, and it certainly doesn't merit—"

"It's serious to me."

Poppy pushed the covers away from her strained face and looked at him as if he were someone she had met before but couldn't quite place. A faint smile touched her lips. Tentatively her hand crept to Harry's, her small fingers curving around his palm.

That simple clasp did something strange to Harry's heartbeat. His pulse drove in erratic surges, and his chest turned hot with some unknown emotion. He took her entire hand in his, their palms gently pressing. He wanted to hold her in his arms, not in passion, but to give comfort. Even though his embrace was the last thing she wanted.

"I'll be back in a moment," he said, striding from the room. He rushed to a sideboard in his private library, poured a small glass of French brandy, and brought it back to Poppy. "Try this."

"What is it?"

"Brandy."

She tried to sit up, wincing with every movement. "I don't think I'll like it."

"You don't have to like it. Just drink it." Harry

tried to help her, feeling unaccountably awkward . . .
he, who had always navigated his way around the
female form with absolute confidence. Carefully he
wedged another pillow behind her back.

She sipped the brandy and made a face. *"Ugh."*

Had Harry not been so worried, he might have
found some amusement in her reaction to the brandy,
a heritage vintage that had been aged at least a hundred years. As she continued to sip the brandy, Harry
pulled a chair beside the bed.

By the time Poppy had finished the brandy, some
of the fine-grooved tension had gone from her face.
"That actually helped a bit," she said. "My ankle still
hurts, but I don't think I care as much."

Harry took the glass from her and set it aside.
"That's good," he said gently. "Would you mind if I
left you again momentarily?"

"No, you're only going to yell at the staff again,
and they're already doing their best. Stay with me."
She reached for his hand.

That mystifying feeling again . . . the sense of
puzzle pieces fitting together. Such an innocent connection, one hand in another, and yet it was enor-
mously satisfying.

"Harry?" The soft way she said his name caused
the hair to rise pleasurably on his arms and the back
of his neck.

"Yes, love?" he asked hoarsely.

"Would you . . . would you mind rubbing my
back?"

Harry fought to conceal his reaction. "Of course,"
he said, striving to keep his tone casual. "Can you
turn to your side?" Reaching for her lower back, he
found the little reefs of muscle on either side of her
spine. Poppy pushed the pillows aside and lay flat on

her stomach. He worked up to her upper shoulders, finding the knotted muscles.

A soft groan escaped her, and Harry paused.

"Yes, there," she said, and the full-throated pleasure in her voice went straight to Harry's groin. He continued to knead her back, his fingers coaxing and sure. Poppy sighed deeply. "I'm keeping you from your work."

"I have nothing planned."

"You always have at least ten things planned."

"Nothing's more important than you."

"You almost sound sincere."

"I am sincere. Why wouldn't I be?"

"Because your work is more important to you than anything, even people."

Annoyed, Harry held his tongue and continued to massage her.

"I'm sorry," Poppy said after a minute. "I didn't mean that. I don't know why I said it."

The words were an instant balm to Harry's anger. "You're hurting. And you're tipsy. It's all right."

Mrs. Pennywhistle's voice came from the threshold. "Here we are. Hopefully this will suffice until the doctor arrives." She brought a tray laden with supplies, including rolled linen bandages, a pot of salve, and two or three large green leaves.

"What are these for?" Harry asked, picking up one of the leaves. He gave the housekeeper a questioning glance. "Cabbage?"

"It's a very effective remedy," the housekeeper explained. "It reduces swelling and makes bruises disappear. Only make certain to break the spine of the leaf and crush it a bit, then wrap it around the ankle before you tie the bandage."

"I don't want to smell like cabbage," Poppy protested.

Harry gave her a severe glance. "I don't give a damn what it smells like, if it will make you better."

"That's because you're not the one who has to wear a vegetable leaf on your leg!"

But he had his way, of course, and Poppy reluctantly endured the poultice.

"There," Harry said, tying off a neat bandage around it. He drew the hem of Poppy's nightgown back over her knee. "Mrs. Pennywhistle, if you wouldn't mind—"

"Yes, I'll see if the doctor's arrived," the housekeeper said. "And I'll have a brief talk with the housemaids. For some reason they're piling the strangest assortment of objects near the doorway . . ."

The doctor had indeed arrived. Stoic soul that he was, he ignored Harry's muttered comment that he hoped the doctor didn't *always* take so long when there was a medical emergency, or half his patients would probably expire before he ever crossed the threshold.

After examining Poppy's ankle, the doctor diagnosed a light sprain, and he prescribed cold compresses for the swelling. He left a bottle of tonic for the pain, a pot of liniment for the pulled muscle in her shoulder, and advised that above all Mrs. Rutledge must rest.

Were it not for her discomfort, Poppy would have actually enjoyed the rest of the day. Apparently Harry had decided that she should be waited on hand and foot. Chef Broussard sent up a tray of pastry, fresh fruit, and creamed eggs. Mrs. Pennywhistle brought a selection of cushions to make her more comfortable. Harry had dispatched a footman to the bookshop, and the servant had returned with an armload of new publications.

Soon thereafter, a maid brought Poppy a tray of neat boxes tied with ribbons. Opening them, Poppy discovered that one was filled with toffee, another with boiled sweets, and another with Turkish delight. Best of all, one box was filled with a new confection called "eating-chocolates" that had been all the rage at the London Exhibition.

"Where did these come from?" Poppy asked Harry when he returned to her room after a brief visit to the front offices.

"From the sweet shop."

"No, *these.*" Poppy showed him the eating-chocolates. "No one can get them. The makers, Fellows and Son, have closed their shop while they move to a new location. The ladies at the philanthropic luncheon were talking about it."

"I sent Valentine to the Fellows residence to ask them to make a special batch for you." Harry smiled as he saw the paper twists scattered across the counterpane. "I see you've sampled them."

"Have one," Poppy said generously.

Harry shook his head. "I don't like sweets." But he bent down obligingly as she gestured for him to come closer. She reached out to him, her fingers catching the knot of his necktie.

Harry's smile faded as Poppy exerted gentle tension, drawing him down. He was suspended over her, an impending weight of muscle and masculine drive. As her sugared breath blew against his lips, she sensed the deep tremor within him. And she was aware of a new equilibrium between them, a balance of will and curiosity. Harry held still, letting her do as she wished.

She tugged him closer until her mouth brushed his. The contact was brief but vital, striking a glow of heat.

Poppy released him carefully, and Harry drew back.

"You won't kiss me for diamonds," he said, his voice slightly raspy, "but you will for chocolates?"

Poppy nodded.

As Harry turned his face away, she saw his cheek tauten with a smile. "I'll put in a daily order, then."

Chapter Seventeen

Accustomed as Harry was to arranging everyone's schedule, he seemed to take it for granted that Poppy would allow him to do the same for her. When she told him that she preferred to make her own decisions about planning her days, Harry had countered that if she insisted on socializing with the hotel employees, he would find better uses for her time.

"I like to spend time with them," Poppy protested. "I can't treat everyone who lives and works here as nothing more than cogs in a machine."

"The hotel has been run this way for years," Harry said. "It's not going to change. As I've told you before, you'll create a management problem. From now on, no more visiting the kitchens. No more chats with the master gardener while he prunes the roses. No cups of tea with the housekeeper."

Poppy frowned. "Does it ever occur to you that your employees are people with thoughts and feelings? Have you thought to ask Mrs. Pennywhistle if her hand injury has healed?"

Harry frowned. "Hand injury?"

"Yes, she accidentally closed her fingers in the door. And when was the last time Mr. Valentine went on holiday?"

Harry's expression went blank.

"Three years," Poppy said. "Even the housemaids go on holiday to see their families, or go to the country. But Mr. Valentine is so devoted to his job that he forgoes all his personal time. And you've probably never offered a word of praise or thanks for it."

"I pay him a salary," Harry said indignantly. "Why the devil are you so interested in the personal lives of the hotel staff?"

"Because I can't live with people and see them day to day and not care about them."

"Then you can bloody well start with me!"

"You want me to care about you?" Her incredulous tone seemed to exasperate him.

"I want you to behave like a wife."

"Then stop trying to control me as you do everyone else. You've allowed me no choice in anything—not even the choice of whether or not to marry you in the first place!"

"And there's the heart of the matter," Harry said. "You'll never stop trying to punish me for taking you away from Michael Bayning. Has it occurred to you that it wasn't nearly as great a loss to him as it was to you?"

Poppy's eyes narrowed suspiciously. "What do you mean?"

"He's found consolation from any number of women since the wedding. He's fast becoming known as the biggest whoremonger in town."

"I don't believe you," Poppy said, turning ashen. It wasn't possible. She couldn't conceive of Michael—*her* Michael—behaving in such a way.

"It's all over London," Harry said ruthlessly. "He drinks, gambles, and squanders money. And the devil knows how many bawdy-house diseases he's caught by now. It might console you that the viscount is probably regretting his decision to forbid the match between you and his son. At this rate, Bayning won't live long enough to inherit the title."

"You're lying."

"Ask your brother. You should thank me. Because as much as you despise me, I'm a better bargain than Michael Bayning."

"I should *thank* you?" Poppy asked thickly. "After what you've done to Michael?" A dazed smile crossed her lips, and she shook her head. She put her hands to her temples, as if to stave off an encroaching headache. "I need to see him. I must speak to him—" She broke off as he seized her arms in a harsh grip that was just short of painful.

"Try," Harry said softly, "and you'll both regret it."

Shoving his hands away, Poppy stared at his hard features and thought, *this is the man I'm married to.*

Unable to endure one more minute of proximity to his wife, Harry left for the fencing club. He was going find someone, anyone, who wanted to practice, and he was going to fight until his muscles were sore and his frustration was spent. He was sick with need, half mad with it. But he didn't want Poppy to accept him out of duty. He wanted her willing. He wanted her warm and welcoming, the way she would have been with Michael Bayning. Harry would be damned if he'd take anything less.

There had never been a woman he'd wanted and hadn't gotten, until now. Why did his skills fail him when it came to seducing his own wife? It was becoming clear that as his craving for Poppy increased, his ability to charm her was decreasing at a proportionate rate.

The one brief kiss she'd given him had been more pleasurable than entire nights Harry had spent with other women. He could try to ease his needs with someone else, but that wouldn't begin to satisfy him. He wanted something that only Poppy seemed able to provide.

Harry spent two hours at the club, dueling at lightning speed, until the fencing master had flatly refused to allow anymore. "That's enough, Rutledge."

"I'm not finished," Harry said, tearing off his mask, his chest heaving with the force of his breaths.

"I say you are." Approaching him, the fencing master said quietly, "You're relying on brute force instead of using your head. Fencing requires precision and control, and this evening you're lacking both."

Offended, Harry schooled his features and said calmly, "Give me another chance. I'll prove you wrong."

The fencing master shook his head. "If I let you go on, there is every chance of an accident occurring. Go home, friend. Rest. You look tired."

The hour was late by the time Harry returned to the hotel. Still clad in fencing whites, he went into the hotel through the back entrance. Before he could ascend the stairs to his apartments, he was met by Jake Valentine.

"Good evening, Mr. Rutledge. How was your fencing?"

"Not worth discussing," Harry said shortly. His

eyes narrowed as he saw the tension in his assistant's manner. "Is there anything the matter, Valentine?"

"A maintenance issue, I'm afraid."

"What is it?"

"The carpenter was repairing a section of flooring that happens to be located directly above Mrs. Rutledge's room. You see, the last guest who stayed there complained of a creaking board, and so I—"

"Is my wife all right?" Harry interrupted.

"Oh, *yes,* sir. Beg pardon, I didn't mean to worry you. Mrs. Rutledge is quite well. But unfortunately the carpenter struck a nail into a plumbing pipe, and there was a significant leak in the ceiling of Mrs. Rutledge's room. We had to take out a section of the ceiling to reach the pipe and stop the flooding. The bed and carpet are ruined, I'm afraid. And the room is uninhabitable at present."

"Bloody hell," Harry muttered, running a hand through his sweat-dampened hair. "How long until the repairs are done?"

"We estimate two to three days. The noise will undoubtedly be a problem for some of the guests."

"Apologize on behalf of the hotel and cut their room rates."

"Yes, sir."

With annoyance, Harry realized that Poppy would have to stay in his bedroom. Which meant that he would have to find another place to sleep. "I'll stay in a guest suite for the time being," he said. "Which ones are empty?"

Valentine's face was expressionless. "I'm afraid we're at full occupancy tonight, sir."

"There isn't one room available? In this *entire* hotel?"

"No, sir."

Harry scowled. "Set up a spare bed in my apartments, then."

Now the valet looked apologetic. "I've already thought of that, sir. But we have no spare beds. Three have been requested and set up in guest suites, and the other two were loaned to Brown's Hotel earlier in the week."

"Why did we do that?" Harry demanded incredulously.

"You told me that if Mr. Brown ever asked a favor, I should oblige him."

"I do too many damned favors for people!" Harry snapped.

"Yes, sir."

Rapidly Harry considered his alternatives . . . he could check into another hotel, he could prevail on a friend to allow him to stay overnight . . . but as he glanced at Valentine's implacable face, he knew how that would appear. And he'd go hang before he gave anyone reason to speculate he wasn't sleeping with his own wife. With a mumbled curse, he brushed by the valet and headed up the private staircase, his overworked leg muscles aching in vicious protest.

The apartment was ominously silent. Was Poppy asleep? No . . . a lamp had been lit in his room. His heart began to thud heavily as he followed the soft spill of light through the hallway. Reaching the doorway of his room, he looked inside.

Poppy was in his bed, an open book in her lap.

Harry filled his gaze with her, taking in the demure white nightgown, the frills of lace on her sleeves, the rope of shiny braided hair trailing over one shoulder. Her cheeks were stained with a high flush. She looked soft and sweet and clean, her knees drawn up beneath the covers.

Violent desire surged through him. Harry was afraid to move, afraid he might actually leap on her with no thought given to her virginal sensibilities. Appalled by the extent of his own need, Harry fought to restrain it. He tore his gaze away and stared hard at the floor, willing himself back into control.

"My bedroom was damaged." he heard Poppy say awkwardly. "The ceiling—"

"I heard." His voice was low and rough.

"I'm so sorry to inconvenience you—"

"It's not your fault." Harry brought himself to look at her again. A mistake. She was so pretty, so vulnerable, her slender throat rippling with a visible swallow. He wanted to ravish her. His body felt thick and hot with arousal, a merciless pulse pounding all through him.

"Is there somewhere else you can sleep?" she asked with difficulty.

Harry shook his head. "The hotel is fully occupied," he said gruffly.

She looked down at the book in her lap, remaining silent.

And Harry, who had never been less than perfectly articulate, grappled with words as if they were a wall of bricks tumbling over him. "Poppy . . . sooner or later . . . you're going to have to let me . . ."

"I understand," she murmured, her head bent.

Harry's sanity began to dissolve in a rush of heat. He was going to take her, now, here. But as he started for her, he saw how tightly Poppy was gripping the book, the tips of her fingers white. She wouldn't look at him.

She did not want him.

Why that mattered, he had no bloody idea.

But it did.

Bloody hell.

Somehow, with all his force of will, Harry mustered a cool tone. "Some other time, perhaps. I don't have the patience to tutor you tonight."

Leaving the bedroom, he went to the bathing room, to wash and douse himself with cold water. Repeatedly.

"Well?" Chef Broussard asked as Jake Valentine entered the kitchen the next morning.

Mrs. Pennywhistle and Chef Rupert, who were standing by the long table, looked at him expectantly.

"I told you it was a bad idea," Jake said, glaring at the three of them. Sitting on a tall stool, he grabbed a warm croissant from a platter of pastries, and shoved half of it into his mouth.

"It didn't work?" the housekeeper asked gingerly.

Jake shook his head, swallowing the croissant and gesturing for a cup of tea. Mrs. Pennywhistle poured a cup, dropped in a lump of sugar, and gave it to him.

"From what I could tell," Jake growled, "Rutledge spent the night on the settee. I've never seen him in such a foul mood. He nearly took my head off when I brought him the managers' reports."

"Oh, dear," Mrs. Pennywhistle murmured.

Broussard shook his head in disbelief. "What is the matter with you British?"

"He's not British, he was born in America," Jake snapped.

"Oh, yes," Broussard said, recalling the indelicate fact. "Americans and romance. It's like watching a bird try to fly with one wing."

"What will we do now?" Chef Rupert asked in concern.

"Nothing," Jake said. "Not only has our meddling *not* helped, it's made the situation worse. They're scarcely speaking to each other."

Poppy went through the day in a state of gloom, unable to stop worrying about Michael, knowing there was nothing she could do for him. Although his unhappiness was not her fault—and given the same choices, she wouldn't change anything she'd done—Poppy felt responsible all the same, as if by marrying Harry, she had assumed a portion of his guilt.

Except that Harry was incapable of feeling guilty about anything.

Poppy thought it would make things far less complicated if she could simply bring herself to hate Harry. But in spite of his innumerable flaws, something about him touched her, even now. His determined solitude . . . his refusal to make emotional connections to the people around him, or even to think of the hotel as his home . . . these things were alien to Poppy.

How in heaven's name, when all she had ever wanted was someone to share affection and intimacy with, had she ended up with a man who was capable of neither? All Harry wanted was the use of her body, and the illusion of a marriage.

Well, she had much more to give than that. And he would have to take all of her or nothing.

In the evening, Harry came to the apartments to have dinner with Poppy. He informed her that, after the meal was concluded, he was going to meet with visitors in their apartment library room.

"A meeting with whom?" Poppy asked.

"Someone from the War Office. Sir Gerald Hubert."

"May I ask what it is about?"

"I'd rather you didn't."

Staring into his inscrutable features, Poppy felt a chill of unease. "Am I to play hostess?" she asked.

"That won't be necessary."

The evening was cold and wet, rain striking in heavy sheets against the roof and windows, and washing the filth from the streets in muddy streams. The stilted dinner concluded, and a pair of maids cleared away the dishes and brought tea.

Stirring a spoonful of sugar into the dark liquid, Poppy stared at Harry thoughtfully. "What rank is Sir Gerald?"

"Assistant adjutant general."

"What is he in charge of?"

"Financial administration, personnel management, provost services. He's pushing for reforms to increase the army's strength. Badly needed reforms, in light of the tensions between the Russians and the Turks."

"If a war starts, will Britain be drawn into it?"

"Almost certainly. But it's possible that diplomacy will resolve the issue before it comes to war."

"Possible but not likely?"

Harry smiled cynically. "War is always more profitable than diplomacy."

Poppy sipped her tea. "My brother-in-law Cam told me that you improved the design of the standard army rifle. And now the War Office is indebted to you."

Harry shook his head to indicate that it had been nothing. "I scratched out a few ideas when the subject came up at a supper party."

"Obviously the ideas turned out to be very effective," Poppy said. "As most of your ideas are."

Harry turned a glass of port idly in his hands. His gaze lifted to hers. "Are you trying to ask something, Poppy?"

"I don't know. Yes. It seems likely that Sir Gerald will want to discuss weaponry with you, won't he?"

"Undoubtedly. He is bringing Mr. Edward Kinloch, who owns an arms manufactory." Seeing her expression, Harry gave her a quizzical glance. "You don't approve?"

"I think a brain as clever as yours should be put to better use than coming up with more efficient ways to kill people."

Before Harry could reply, there came a knock at the door, and the visitors were announced.

Harry stood and helped Poppy rise from her chair, and she went with him to welcome his guests.

Sir Gerald was a large and stocky man, his florid face supported by a scaffolding of thick white whiskers. He wore a silver gray military coat trimmed with regimental buttons. The scent of tobacco smoke and heavy cologne wafted from him with each movement.

"An honor, Mrs. Rutledge," he said with a bow. "I see the reports of your beauty are not at all exaggerated."

Poppy forced a smile. "Thank you, Sir Gerald."

Harry, standing beside her, introduced the other man. "Mr. Edward Kinloch."

Kinloch bowed impatiently. Clearly, meeting Harry Rutledge's wife was an unwelcome distraction. He wanted to get about the business at hand. Everything about him, the narrow, dark suit of clothes, the ungenerous tightness of his smile, the guarded eyes, even the flat hair subjugated by a gleaming layer of pomade, spoke of rigid containment. "Madam."

"Welcome, gentlemen," Poppy murmured. "I will leave you to your discussion. May I send for refreshments?"

"Why, thank you—" Sir Gerald began, but Kinloch interrupted.

"That is very gracious of you, Mrs. Rutledge, but it won't be necessary."

Sir Gerald's jowls drooped in disappointment.

"Very well," Poppy said pleasantly. "I will take my leave. I bid you good evening."

Harry showed the visitors to his library, while Poppy stared after them. She didn't like her husband's visitors, and she especially didn't like the subject they intended to discuss. Most of all, she loathed the idea of her husband's diabolical cleverness being applied to improve the art of war.

Retreating to Harry's bedroom, Poppy tried to read, but her mind kept returning to the conversation that was taking place in the library. Finally, she gave up the attempt and set the book aside.

She argued silently with herself. Eavesdropping was wrong. But really, in the spectrum of sin, how bad was it? What if one eavesdropped for a good reason? What if there was a beneficial result of the eavesdropping, such as preventing another person from making a mistake? Furthermore, wasn't it her duty as Harry's wife to be his helpmate whenever possible?

Yes, he might need her advice. And certainly the best way to be helpful was to find out what he was discussing with his guests.

Poppy tiptoed across the apartment to the library door, which had been left slightly ajar. Keeping herself tucked out of sight, she listened.

". . . you can feel the recoil power in the kick of the gun against your shoulder," Harry was saying in a matter-of-fact tone. "There might be a way to turn that to practical effect, using the recoil to draw in another bullet. Or better yet, I could devise a metallic casing that contains powder, bullet, and primer all in one. The recoil force would automatically eject the casing and draw in another, so the weapon could fire repeatedly. And it would have far more power and precision than any firearm yet developed."

His statements were met with silence. Poppy guessed that Kinloch and Sir Gerald, like herself, were struggling to take in what Harry had just described.

"My God," Kinloch finally said, sounding breathless. "That is so far beyond anything we . . . that is *leaps* ahead of what I'm currently manufacturing . . ."

"Can it be done?" Sir Gerald asked tersely. "Because if so, it would give us an advantage over every army in the world."

"Until they copy it," Harry said dryly.

"However," Sir Gerald continued, "in the time it would take them to reproduce our technology, we will have expanded the Empire . . . consolidated it so firmly . . . that our supremacy would be unchallenged."

"It wouldn't go unchallenged for long. As Benjamin Franklin once said, empire is like a great cake—most easily diminished around the edges."

"What do Americans know about empire building?" Sir Gerald asked with a scornful snort.

"I should remind you," Harry murmured, "that I'm American by birth."

Another silence.

"With whom do your loyalties lie?" Sir Gerald asked.

"With no country in particular," Harry replied. "Does that pose a problem?"

"Not if you'll give us the rights to the weapon design. And license it exclusively to Kinloch."

"Rutledge," came Kinloch's hard, eager voice, "how long would it take for you to develop these ideas and create a prototype?"

"I have no idea." Harry sounded amused by the other men's fervor. "When I have spare time, I'll work on it. But I can't promise you—"

"Spare time?" Now Kinloch was indignant. "A fortune rests on this, not to mention the future of the Empire. By God, if I had your abilities, I wouldn't rest until I had brought this idea to fruition!"

Poppy felt ill as she heard the naked greed in his voice. Kinloch wanted profits. Sir Gerald wanted power.

And if Harry obliged them . . .

She couldn't bear to listen any longer. As the men continued to talk, she slipped away silently.

Chapter Eighteen

After bidding farewell to Sir Gerald and Edward Kinloch, Harry turned and set his back against the inside door of his apartments. The prospect of designing the new gun and integrated bullet casings would ordinarily have been an interesting challenge.

At present, however, it was nothing but an annoying distraction. There was only one problem he was interested in solving, and it had nothing to do with mechanical wizardry.

Rubbing the back of his neck, Harry went to his bedroom in search of a nightshirt. Although he usually slept naked, it would hardly be comfortable to do so on the settee. The prospect of spending another night there caused him to question his own sanity. He was faced with the choice of sleeping in a comfortable bed with his enticing wife, or alone on a narrow piece of furniture . . . and he was going to opt for the latter?

His wife regarded him from the bed, her gaze accusatory. "I can't believe you're even considering it," she said without preamble.

It took his distracted brain a moment to comprehend that she was not referring to their sleeping arrangements, but the meeting he'd just concluded. Had he not been so weary, Harry might have thought to advise his wife that now was not the night to pick an argument.

"How much did you hear?" he asked calmly, turning to rummage in one of the dresser drawers.

"Enough to understand that you may design a new kind of weapon for them. And if so, you would be responsible for so much carnage and suffering—"

"No, I wouldn't." Harry tugged off his necktie and coat, tossing them to the floor instead of laying them neatly on a chair. "The soldiers carrying the guns would be responsible for it. And the politicians and military men who sent them out there."

"Don't be disingenuous, Harry. If you didn't invent the weapons, no one would have them in the first place."

Giving up the search for the nightshirt, Harry untied his shoes and cast them on the heap of his discarded clothing. "Do you think people will ever stop developing new ways to kill each other? If I don't do this, someone else will."

"Then let someone else. Don't let it be your legacy."

Their gazes met, clashing. *For God's sake,* he wanted to beg her, *don't push me tonight.* The effort to carry on a coherent conversation was draining away what little self-restraint he had left.

"You know that I'm right," Poppy persisted, flinging back the covers and hopping out of bed to confront him. "You know how I feel about guns. Doesn't that matter to you at all?"

Harry could see the outline of her body in the

thin white nightgown. He could even see the tips of her breasts, rosy and firm in the chill of the room. Right and wrong . . . no, he didn't give a damn about useless moralizing. But if it would soften her toward him, if it would cause her to yield even a little of herself, he would tell Sir Gerald and the entire British government to go swive themselves. And somewhere in the depths of his soul, a fracture began as he experienced something entirely new . . . the desire to please another person.

Yielding to the feeling before he even knew what it was, he opened his mouth to tell Poppy that she could have her way. He would send word to the War Office tomorrow that the deal was off.

Before he could get out a word, however, Poppy said quietly. "If you keep your promise to Sir Gerald, I'm going to leave you."

Harry wasn't aware of reaching out for her, only that she was in his grip, and that she was gasping. "That's not a choice for you," he managed to say.

"You can't make me stay if I don't want to," she said. "And I won't compromise on this, Harry. You will do as I ask, or I will leave."

All hell broke loose inside him. Leave him, would she?

Not in this life, or the next.

She thought him a monster . . . well, he would prove her right. He would be everything she thought him and worse. He jerked her against him, hot blood teeming in his groin as he felt the cambric slide over her firm, smooth body. Grasping her braid in his hand, he pulled the ribbon loose. His mouth went to the curve of her neck and shoulder, and the scents of soap and perfume and female skin inundated his senses.

"Before I make a decision," he said in a guttural tone, "I think I'll have a sample of what I might be forgoing."

Her hands came up to his shoulders as if to push him away.

But she wasn't struggling. She was holding onto him.

Harry had never been so aroused, desperate beyond pride. He held her, absorbing the feel of her with his whole body. Her hair was loose, fiery silk sliding over his arms. He took handfuls of it, lifted the soft locks to his face. She smelled like roses, the intoxicating residue of perfumed soap or bath oil. He hunted for more of the scent, drawing it in with deep breaths.

Tugging the front of her nightgown open, Harry sent tiny cloth-covered buttons pattering to the carpet. Poppy quivered but offered no resistance as he tugged the garment to her waist, letting the sleeves trap her arms. His hand went to one of her breasts, their shapes lush and beautiful in the muted light. He touched her with the backs of his fingers, drifting down until one of the pink buds was caught lightly between his knuckles. He pulled, just a little. At the feel of the gentle tug, Poppy gasped and bit her lip.

Guiding Poppy backward, Harry stopped when her hips bumped against the edge of the mattress. "Lie down," he said, his voice rougher than he had intended. He helped her to lie back, supporting her with his arms, easing her to the bed. Bending over her flushed body, he savored all that rose-scented skin, wooing her with kisses . . . slow traveling kisses, wet and artful and fiendishly patient kisses. He licked his way to the tip of one breast and captured the taut point, flicking with his tongue. Poppy moaned, her body drawing into a helpless arch as he suckled her for long minutes.

Easing the muslin gown away from her, Harry dropped it to the floor. He stared at her with equal parts hunger and reverence. She was unspeakably beautiful, reclining in sweet abandon before him . . . lost, aroused, uncertain. Her gaze was distant, as if she were trying to encompass too many sensations at once.

Harry tore off the rest of his clothing and lowered himself over her. "Touch me," he was mortified to hear himself rasp . . . something he had never asked of anyone before.

Slowly her arms lifted, one hand sliding around his neck. Her fingers laced through the shorter locks that curled slightly against his nape. The tentative caress drew a groan of pleasure from him. He lay beside her, easing a hand between her thighs.

Accustomed as he was to fine, intricate things, to delicate mechanisms, Harry was sensitive to every subtle response of her body. He discovered where and how she most liked to be stroked, what aroused her. What made her wet. Following the moisture, he slipped a finger inside, and she accepted it easily. When he tried to add another, however, she flinched and instinctively reached down to push his hand away. Withdrawing, he caressed her with a gentle palm, coaxing her to relax.

Pressing her back on the bed, Harry loomed over her. He heard her breathing quicken as he settled between her thighs. But he didn't try to enter her, only let her feel the pressure of him, the length fitting against the soft feminine rise. He knew how to tease, how to make her want him. He moved in the gentlest intimation of a thrust, sliding along dampness and sweetly vulnerable flesh, and then he rotated his hips slowly, every movement a syllable that added to a greater meaning.

Her lashes half lowered, and there was a faint, intent pull between her fine brows . . . she wanted what he was giving her, she wanted the tension and torment and relief. Desire had brought a mist of perspiration over her skin, until the scent of roses deepened and acquired a hint of musk, so wildly arousing and heady that he could have let himself go right then. But he rolled to his side, away from the enticing cradle of her hips.

He slid his hand over her mound and slipped his fingers inside her again, his touch coaxing and careful. This time her body relaxed and welcomed him. Kissing her throat, he caught the vibration of every moan against his lips. A faint, rhythmic clenching began around his knuckles as he thrust his fingers in her oh so gently. Every time she took them to the hilt, he let the heel of his hand brush her intimately. She panted and began to lift upward repeatedly.

"Yes," Harry whispered, letting his hot breath fill the shell of her ear. "Yes. When I'm inside you, this is how you move. Show me what you want, and I'll give it to you, as much as you need, as long as you want . . ."

She clamped on his fingers, tightening, convulsing, coming in erotic shivers. He teased out every last luscious ripple, relishing her climax, lost in the feel of her.

Levering his body over hers, he pushed her thighs wide and lowered himself between them. Before her sated flesh had begun to close, he centered himself where she was wet and ready for him. He stopped thinking altogether. He pushed into the resisting ring, finding it even more difficult than he'd expected despite the abundant moisture.

Poppy whimpered in pained surprise, her body stiffening.

"Hold onto me," Harry said hoarsely. She obeyed, her arms coming around his neck. He reached down and pulled her hips upward, trying to make it easier for her as he pressed deeper, harder, her flesh unbelievably tight and hot and sweet, and he gave her more, unable to help himself, until he was fully buried in the soft heat of her.

"Oh, God," he whispered, shaking with the effort to hold still, to let her adjust around him.

Every nerve clamored for movement, for the sliding, teasing friction that would bring him release. He nudged gently. But Poppy grimaced, her legs straining on either side of his. He waited longer, caressing her with his hands.

"Don't stop," she choked. "It's all right."

But it wasn't. He pushed again, and a pained sound escaped her. Again, and she braced and clenched her teeth. Every time he moved, it caused her agony.

Resisting her tight grip on his neck, Harry drew back far enough to look at her face. Poppy was white with distress, her lips bloodless. Holy hell, was it this painful for all virgins?

"I'll wait," he said raggedly. "It will be easier in a moment."

She nodded, her mouth stiff, her eyes tightly shut.

And they both held still and fast, while he tried to soothe her. But nothing changed. Despite Poppy's compliance, this was sheer misery for her.

Harry buried his face in her hair and cursed. And

he withdrew, despite the vicious protest of his loins, when every impulse screamed for him to hammer into her.

She couldn't stifle a gasp of relief as the painful intrusion was removed. Hearing the sound, Harry nearly exploded with murderous frustration.

He heard her murmur his name, her voice questioning.

Ignoring her, Harry left the bed and staggered toward the bathing room. He braced his hands on the tiled wall and closed his eyes, struggling for self-control. After a few minutes, he drew water and washed himself. He found smears of blood . . . Poppy's blood. That was only to be expected. But the sight of it made him want to howl.

Because the last thing he wanted on earth was to cause his wife even a moment's pain. He would die before hurting her, no matter what the consequences to himself.

Dear God, what had happened to him? He had never wanted to feel this way about anyone, never even imagined it possible.

He had to make it stop.

Sore and bewildered, Poppy lay on her side and listened to the sounds of Harry washing. It burned where he had taken her. The residue of blood was sticky between her thighs. She wanted to leave the bed and wash as well, but the thought of performing such an intimate task in front of Harry . . . no, she wasn't ready for that yet. And she was unsure, because even in her innocence, she knew that he had not finished making love to her.

But why?

Had there been something she should have done?

Had she made some kind of mistake? Perhaps she should have been more stoic. She had tried her best, but it had hurt dreadfully, even though Harry had been gentle. Surely he knew that it was painful for a virgin the first time. Why, then, had he seemed angry with her?

Feeling inadequate and defensive, Poppy crept from the bed and found her nightgown. She put it on and hastily retreated beneath the covers as Harry came back into the room. Without a word, he picked up his discarded clothes and began to dress.

"You're going out?" she heard herself ask.

Harry didn't look at her. "Yes."

"Stay with me," she blurted out.

Harry shook his head. "I can't. We'll talk later. But right now I—" He broke off as if words failed him.

Poppy curled on her side, gripping the edges of the bedclothes. Something was terribly wrong—she couldn't fathom what it was, and she was too afraid to ask.

Pulling on his coat, Harry started for the doorway.

"Where are you going?" Poppy asked unsteadily.

He sounded distant. "I don't know."

"When will you—"

"I don't know that, either."

She waited until he had left before she let a few tears slip out, and she blotted them with the sheet. Was Harry going to another woman?

Miserably, she reflected that her sister Win's advice about marital relations had been insufficient. There should have been a bit less about roses and moonlight and a bit more practical information.

She wanted to see her sisters, especially Amelia. She wanted her family, who would pet and praise and make much of her, and offer the reassurance she badly needed. It was more than a little disheartening to have failed at marriage after a mere three weeks.

Most of all, she needed advice about husbands.

Yes, it was time to retreat and consider what to do. She would go to Hampshire.

A hot bath soothed her smarting flesh and eased the strained muscles on the insides of her thighs. After drying and powdering herself, she dressed in a wine-colored traveling gown. She packed a few belongings in a small valise, including undergarments and stockings, a silver-backed brush, a novel, and an automaton that Harry had made—a little woodpecker on a tree trunk—which she usually kept on her dressing table. However, she left the diamond necklace that Harry had given her, setting the velvet-lined case in a drawer.

When she was ready to depart, she rang the bell-pull and sent a maid to fetch Jake Valentine.

The tall, brown-eyed young man appeared in an instant, making no effort to mask his concern. His gaze skimmed quickly over her traveling clothes. "May I be of service, Mrs. Rutledge?"

"Mr. Valentine, has my husband left the hotel?"

He nodded, a frown puckering his forehead.

"Did he tell you when he would return?"

"No, ma'am."

Poppy wondered if she could trust him. His loyalty to Harry was well-known. However, she had no choice but to ask for his help. "I must ask a favor of you, Mr. Valentine. However, I fear it may put you in a difficult position."

His brown eyes warmed with rueful amusement. "Mrs. Rutledge, I'm nearly always in a difficult position. Please don't hesitate to ask me for anything."

She squared her shoulders. "I need a carriage. I'm going to visit my brother at his terrace in Mayfair."

The smile vanished from his eyes. He glanced at the valise by her feet. "I see."

"I am very sorry to ask you to ignore your obligations to my husband but . . . I would prefer you didn't let him know where I've gone until morning. I will be perfectly safe in my brother's company. He is going to convey me to my family in Hampshire."

"I understand. Of course I will help you." Valentine paused, appearing to choose his words carefully. "I hope you will be returning soon."

"So do I."

"Mrs. Rutledge . . ." he started, and cleared his throat uncomfortably. "I shouldn't overstep my bounds. But I feel it necessary to say—" He hesitated.

"Go on," Poppy said gently.

"I've worked for Mr. Rutledge for more than five years. I daresay I know him as well as anyone. He's a complicated man . . . too smart for his own good, and he doesn't have much in the way of scruples, and he forces everyone around him to live by his terms. But he has changed many lives for the better. Including mine. And I believe there's good in him, if one looks deep enough."

"I think so, too," Poppy said. "But that's not enough to found a marriage on."

"You mean something to him," Valentine insisted. "He's formed an attachment to you, and I've never seen that before. Which is why I don't think anyone in the world can manage him except for you."

"Even if that's true," Poppy managed to say, "I don't know if I *want* to manage him."

"Ma'am . . ." Valentine said feelingly, "*Someone* has to."

Amusement broke through Poppy's distress, and she ducked her head to hide a smile. "I'll consider it," she said. "But at the moment I need some time away. What do they call it in the rope ring . . . ?"

"A breather," he said, bending to pick up her valise.

"Yes, a breather. Will you help me, Mr. Valentine?"

"Of course." Valentine bid her to wait but a few minutes, and went to summon the carriage. Comprehending the need for discretion, he had the vehicle brought to the back of the hotel, where Poppy could depart unobserved.

She felt a pang of regret, leaving the Rutledge and its employees. In no time at all it had become home . . . but things could not stay the way they were. Something would have to yield. And that something—or someone, rather—was Harry Rutledge.

Valentine returned to escort her to the back entrance. Opening an umbrella to shelter her from the rain, Valentine guided her outside to the waiting vehicle.

Poppy climbed onto the block step that had been placed beside the carriage, and turned to face the valet. With the added height of the step, they stood nearly eye to eye. Raindrops glittered in the light from the hotel as they fell in jewel-like strands from the points of the umbrella.

"Mr. Valentine . . ."

"Yes, ma'am?"

"You do think he'll follow me, don't you?"

"Only to the ends of the earth," he said gravely.

That drew a smile from her, and she turned to climb into the carriage.

Chapter Nineteen

It had taken Mrs. Meredith Clifton three months of dedicated pursuit before she had finally seduced Leo, Lord Ramsay. Or more accurately, was about to seduce him. As the young and nubile wife of a distinguished British naval officer, she was frequently left to her own devices while her husband was off at sea. Meredith had bedded every man in London worth bedding—excluding the handful of tiresomely faithful married ones, of course—but then she had heard about Ramsay, a man reputedly as sexually audacious as herself.

Leo was a man of tantalizing contradictions. He was a handsome man, dark haired and blue eyed, with a clean and wholesome appeal . . . and yet he was rumored to be capable of shocking debauchery. He was cruel but gentle, callous but perceptive, selfish but charming. And from what she had heard, he was a vastly accomplished lover.

Now, in Leo's bedroom, Meredith stood quietly while he undressed her. He took his time about unfastening the row of buttons at her back. Sidling back, she let the backs of her fingers brush his trousers. The feel of him caused her to purr.

She heard Leo laugh, and he pushed her exploring hand away. "Patience, Meredith."

"You can't know how much I've anticipated this night."

"That's a shame. I'm terrible in bed." Gently he spread her dress open.

She shivered as she felt the exploratory stroke of his fingertips on her upper back. "You're teasing, my lord."

"You'll find out soon, won't you?" He brushed aside the wisps of hair at her nape and kissed her there, letting his tongue brush her skin.

That light, erotic touch caused Meredith to gasp. "Are you ever serious about anything?" she managed to ask.

"No. I've found that life is far kinder to shallow people." Turning her, Leo drew her up against his tall, well-muscled frame.

And in one long, slow blaze of a kiss, Meredith realized that she had finally met a predator more seductive, less inhibited, than anyone she had ever met. His sensual power was no less potent for being completely devoid of emotion or tenderness. This was pure, unashamed physicality.

Consumed in the kiss, Meredith gave an agitated little cry when he stopped.

"The door," Leo said.

Another tentative knock.

"Ignore it," Meredith said, trying to slide her arms around his lean waist.

"I can't. My servants won't let me ignore them. Believe me, I've tried." Releasing her, Leo went to the door, opened it a crack, and said curtly, "There had better be a fire or a felony in progress, or I swear you'll be sacked."

Another murmur from the servant, and Leo's tone changed, the arrogant drawl vanishing. "Good God. Tell her I'll be down at once. Get her some tea or something." Raking his hand through the short dark brown layers of his hair, he went to a wardrobe and began to hunt through a row of jackets. "I'm afraid you'll have to ring for a maid to help you dress, Meredith. When you're ready, my servants will make certain you're escorted out to your carriage at the back."

Her mouth fell open. "What? *Why?*"

"My sister has arrived unexpectedly." Pausing in his search, Leo threw an apologetic glance over his shoulder. "Another time, perhaps?"

"Most certainly not," Meredith said indignantly. *"Now."*

"Impossible." He pulled out a coat and shrugged into it. "My sister needs me."

"*I* need you! Tell her to return tomorrow. And if you don't send her away, you'll never have another chance with me."

Leo smiled. "My loss, I'm sure."

His indifference aroused Meredith even further. "Oh Ramsay, *please*," she said heatedly. "It's ungentlemanly to leave a lady wanting!"

"It's more than ungentlemanly, darling. It's a crime." Leo's face softened as he approached her. Taking her hand, he lifted it to kiss the backs of her fingers one by one. His eyes glinted with rueful amusement. "This is certainly not what I had planned for this evening. My apologies. Let's try again someday. Because, Meredith . . . I'm actually *not* terrible in bed." He kissed her lightly, and smiled with such skillfully manufactured warmth that she almost believed it was real.

Poppy waited in the small front parlor of the terrace. At the sight of her brother's tall form entering the room, she stood and flew to him. "Leo!"

He gathered her close. After a brief, hard hug, he held her at arms' length. His gaze swept over her. "You've left Rutledge?"

"Yes."

"You lasted a week longer than I expected," he said, not unkindly. "What's happened?"

"Well, to start with—" Poppy tried to sound pragmatic even though her eyes watered. "I'm not a virgin anymore."

Leo gave her a mock-shamed glance. "Neither am I," he confessed.

A reluctant giggle escaped her.

Leo rummaged in his coat for a handkerchief, without success. "Don't cry, darling. I have no handkerchief, and in any case, virginity is nearly impossible to find once you've lost it."

"That's not why I'm weepy," she said, blotting her wet cheek on his shoulder. "Leo . . . I'm in a muddle. I need to think about some things. Will you take me to Hampshire?"

"I've been waiting for you to ask."

"I'm afraid we'll have to depart immediately. Because if we wait too long, Harry may prevent us from going at all."

"Sweetheart, the devil himself couldn't stop me from taking you home. That being said . . . yes, we'll go right away. I prefer to avoid confrontation whenever possible. And I doubt Rutledge will take it well when he discovers you've left him."

"No," she said emphatically. "He'll take it quite badly. But I'm not leaving him because I want to end my marriage. I'm leaving him because I want to save it."

Leo shook his head, smiling. "There's Hathaway logic for you. What worries me is that I almost understand."

"You see—"

"No, you can explain once we're on our way. For the moment, wait here. I'll send for the driver and tell the servants to ready the carriage."

"I'm sorry to cause trouble—"

"Oh, they're used to it. I'm the master of hasty departures."

There must have been some truth to Leo's claim, because a trunk was packed and the carriage was readied with astonishing speed. Poppy waited by the parlor fire until Leo came to the doorway. "We'll be off now," he said. "Come."

He took her to his carriage, a comfortable and well-sprung vehicle with deep-upholstered seats. After arranging some cushions in the corner, Poppy settled back in preparation for a long journey. It would take the full night to reach Hampshire, and although the macadamized roadways were in decent repair, there were many rough stretches.

"I'm sorry to have come to you at such a late hour," she told her brother. "No doubt you would be sleeping soundly right now had I not arrived."

That produced a swift grin. "I'm not sure about that," Leo said. "But no matter—it's time to go to Hampshire. I want to see Win and that merciless brute she married, and I need to check on the estate and tenants."

Poppy smiled slightly, knowing how fond Leo

was of the so-called "merciless brute." Merripen had earned Leo's everlasting gratitude for rebuilding and managing the estate. They communicated frequently by letter, maintained two or three running arguments at any given time, and thoroughly enjoyed baiting each other.

Reaching to the dark brown shade that covered the window nearest her, Poppy lifted it to glance at the broken buildings, brick facings plastered with bills, and battered shop fronts, all of them bathed in the twilight gloom of street lamps. London at night was unsavory, unsafe, uncontrolled. Harry was out there somewhere. She had no doubt he could take care of himself, but the thought of what he might be doing—or whom he might be doing it with—filled her with melancholy. She sighed heavily.

"I loathe London in the summer," Leo said. "The Thames is working up to an unholy stench this year." He paused, his gaze resting on her. "I suppose that look on your face isn't caused by worry over public sanitation. Tell me what you're thinking, sis."

"Harry left the hotel tonight after—" Poppy broke off, unable to find a word to describe just what it was they had done. "I don't know how long he'll stay out, but at best, we're only about ten or twelve hours ahead of him. Of course, he may decide not to follow me, which would be rather anticlimactic but also a relief. Still—"

"He'll follow," Leo said flatly. "But you won't have to see him if you don't wish it."

Poppy shook her head morosely. "I've never had such mixed-up feelings about anyone. I don't understand him. Tonight in bed, he—"

"Wait," Leo said. "Some things are better discussed between sisters. I'm sure this is one of them.

We'll reach Ramsay House by morning, and you can ask Amelia anything you like."

"I don't think she would know anything about this."

"Why not? She's a married woman."

"Yes, but it's . . . well . . . a masculine problem."

Leo blanched. "I wouldn't know anything about that, either. I don't have masculine problems. In fact, I don't even like saying the phrase 'masculine problems.'"

"Oh." Crestfallen, Poppy pulled a lap blanket over herself.

"Damn it. What exactly are we calling a 'masculine problem'? Did he have trouble running the flag up? Or did it fall to half-staff?"

"Do we have to speak about this metaphorically, or—"

"Yes," Leo said firmly.

"All right. He . . ." Poppy frowned in concentration as she searched for the right words, ". . . left me while the flag was still flying."

"Was he drunk?"

"No."

"Did you do or say something to make him leave?"

"Just the opposite. I asked him to stay, and he wouldn't."

Shaking his head, Leo rummaged in a side compartment beside his seat and swore. "Where the blazes is my liquor? I told the servants to stock the carriage with drink for the journey. I'm going to fire the bloody lot of them."

"There's water, isn't there?"

"Water is for washing, not drinking." He muttered something about an evil conspiracy to keep him sober, and sighed. "One can only guess as to Rutledge's motivations. It's not easy for a man to stop in the middle of lovemaking. It puts us in a devil of a temper." Folding his arms across his chest, he watched her speculatively. "I propose the radical notion of actually asking Rutledge why he left you tonight, and discussing it like two rational beings. But before your husband reaches Hampshire, you'd better decide on something, and that's whether you're going to forgive him for what he did to you and Bayning."

She blinked in surprise. "Do you think I should?"

"The devil knows I wouldn't want to, were I in your place." He paused. "On the other hand, I've been forgiven for many things I should never have been forgiven for. The point is, if you can't forgive him, there's no use in trying to talk about anything else."

"I don't think Harry cares about being forgiven," Poppy said glumly.

"Of course he does. Men love to be forgiven. It makes us feel better about our inability to learn from our mistakes."

"I don't know if I'm ready," Poppy protested. "Why must I do it so soon? There's no time limit for forgiveness, is there?"

"Sometimes there is."

"Oh, Leo . . ." She felt crushed under a weight of uncertainty and hurt and yearning.

"Try to sleep," her brother murmured. "We'll have two hours, more or less, before it's time to change horses."

"I can't sleep for worrying," Poppy said, although a yawn had already overtaken her.

"There's no point in worrying. You already know

what you want to do—you just aren't ready to admit it yet."

Poppy settled deeper into the corner, closing her eyes. "You know a lot about women, don't you, Leo?"

There was a smile in his voice. "I should hope so, with four sisters." And he watched over her while she slept.

After returning to the hotel drunk as a boiled owl, Harry staggered to his apartments. He had gone to a tavern, flamboyantly decorated with mirrors, tiled walls, and expensive prostitutes. It had taken approximately three hours to drink himself into a suitable state of numbness that he could go back home. Despite the artful advances of more than a few lightskirts, Harry took no notice of any of them.

He wanted his wife.

And he knew that Poppy would never soften toward him unless he began with a sincere apology for taking her away from Michael Bayning. The problem was, he couldn't. Because he wasn't at all sorry about what he'd done, he was only sorry that she was unhappy about it. He would never regret having done what was necessary to marry her, because she was what he had wanted most in his life.

Poppy was every fine, good, unselfish impulse that he would never have. She was every caring thought, loving gesture, happy moment, that he would never know. She was every minute of peaceful sleep that would forever elude him. According to the law of universal balance, Poppy had been put into the world to compensate for Harry and his wickedness. Which was probably why, as the opposite of two magnetic forces, Harry was so damnably drawn to her.

Therefore, the apology was not going to be sincere. But it would be made. And then he would ask to begin again with her.

Lowering himself to the narrow settee, which he loathed with a passion, Harry fell into a drunken stupor that almost passed for sleep.

The morning light, weak though it was, entered his brain like a stiletto. Groaning, Harry cracked his eyes open and took inventory of his abused body. He was dry mouthed, exhausted, and aching, and if there had ever been a time in his life he had needed a shower bath more, he couldn't remember it. He slitted a glance at the closed door of his bedroom, where Poppy still slept.

Remembering her gasp of pain the previous night, when he had thrust into her, Harry felt a cold, sick heaviness in the pit of his stomach. She would be sore this morning. She might need something.

She probably hated him.

Swamped with dread, Harry lurched upward from the settee and went to the bedroom. He opened the door and let his eyes adjust to the semidarkness.

The bed was empty.

Harry stood there blinking while apprehension swept over him. He heard himself whisper her name.

In seconds he had reached the bellpull, but there was no need to call for anyone. As if by magic, Valentine was at the apartment door, his brown eyes alert in his lean face.

"Valentine," Harry began hoarsely, "where is—"

"Mrs. Rutledge is with Lord Ramsay. I believe they are traveling to Hampshire as we speak."

Harry grew very, very calm, as he always did when a situation was dire. "When did she leave?"

"Last night, while you were out."

Resisting the urge to kill his valet where he stood, Harry asked softly, "And you didn't tell me?"

"No, sir. She asked me not to." Valentine paused, looking momentarily bemused, as if he, too, couldn't believe that Harry hadn't already killed him. "I have a carriage and team ready, if you intend to—"

"Yes, I intend to." Harry's tone was as crisp as the strike of a chisel through granite. "Pack my clothes. I'm leaving within the half hour."

Rage hovered nearby, so powerful that Harry could scarcely own it as his. But he shoved the feeling aside. Giving in to it would accomplish nothing. The undertaking for now was to wash and shave, change his clothes, and deal with the situation.

Any hint of concern or contrition burned to ashes. Any hope of being kind or gentlemanly had gone. He would keep Poppy no matter how he had to do it. He would lay out the law, and when he was through, she would never dare leave him again.

Poppy awakened from a jolting sleep and sat up, rubbing her eyes. Leo was dozing in the seat opposite hers, his broad shoulders hunched and one arm curled behind his head as he leaned against a paneled wall.

Nudging aside the little curtain over one of the windows, Poppy saw her beloved Hampshire ... sun crossed, green, peaceful. She had been in London too long—she had forgotten how beautiful the world could be. The carriage passed flushes of poppies and oxeye daisies and vibrant stands of lavender. The landscape was rich with wet meadows and chalk streams. Brilliant blue kingfishers and swifts darted through the sky, while green woodpeckers rattled the trees.

"Almost there," she whispered.

Leo awakened, yawning and stretching. His eyes narrowed in a protesting squint as he lifted a cloth panel for a glimpse of the passing countryside.

"Isn't it wonderful?" Poppy asked, smiling. "Have you ever seen such views?"

Her brother dropped the panel. "Sheep. Grass. Thrilling."

Before long the carriage reached the Ramsay lands and passed the gatekeeper's house, which had been constructed of blue gray brick and cream stone. Owing to recent and extensive renovations, the landscape and manor were new looking, although the house had retained its haphazard charm. The estate was not a large one, certainly nothing compared to the massive neighboring estate owned by Lord Westcliff. But it was a jewel, the land fertile and varied, with fields irrigated by channels that had been dug from a nearby stream to the upper fields.

Before Leo had inherited the title, the estate had fallen into decay and disrepair, abandoned by many of the tenants. Now, however, it had been turned into a thriving and progressive enterprise, mostly due to the efforts of Kev Merripen. And Leo, though he was almost embarrassed to admit it, had come to care about the estate and was doing his best to acquire the vast amounts of knowledge necessary to make it run efficiently.

Ramsay House was a cheerful combination of architectural styles. Originally an Elizabethan manor house, it had been altered as successive generations had grafted on additions and wings. The result was an asymmetrical building with bristling chimney stacks, rows of leaded-glass windows, and a gray slate roof with hips and bays. Inside, there were interesting niches and nooks, odd-shaped rooms, hidden doors and staircases, all adding to an eccentric charm that perfectly suited the Hathaway family.

Roses in bloom hugged the exterior of the house. Behind the manor, white-graveled walking paths led to gardens and fruit orchards. Stables and a live-stock yard were set to one side of the manor, while at a farther distance there was a timber yard in full production.

The carriage stopped on the front drive before a set of timbered doors with glass insets. By the time the footmen had gone to alert the household of their arrival and Leo had assisted Poppy from the vehicle, Win had come running from the house. She flung herself at Leo. He grinned and caught her easily, swinging her around.

"Dear Poppy," Win exclaimed. "I missed you dreadfully!"

"What about me?" Leo asked, still holding her. "Haven't you missed me?"

"Perhaps a little," Win said with a grin, and kissed his cheek. She went to Poppy and embraced her. "How long will you stay?"

"I'm not sure," Poppy said.

"Where is everyone?" Leo asked.

Win kept her slender arm around Poppy's back as she turned to reply. "Cam is visiting Lord Westcliff at Stony Cross Park, Amelia is inside with the baby, Beatrix is roaming the woods, and Merripen is with some of the tenants, lecturing them on new tech-niques of hoeing."

The word caught Leo's attention. "I know all

about that. If you don't want to go to a brothel, there are certain districts of London—"

"*Hoeing,* Leo," Win said. "Breaking ground with farm implements."

"Oh. Well, I know nothing about that."

"You'll find out a great deal about it once Merripen learns you're here." Win tried to look severe, although her eyes were twinkling. "I do hope you'll behave, Leo."

"Of course I will. We're in the country. There's nothing else to do." Heaving a sigh, Leo shoved his hands in his pockets and observed their picturesque surroundings as if he'd just been assigned a cell at Newgate. Then, with perfectly calibrated offhandedness he asked, "Where's Marks? You didn't mention her."

"She is well, but . . ." Win paused, obviously searching for words. "She had a small mishap today, and she's rather upset. Of course, any woman would be, considering the nature of the problem. Therefore, Leo, I insist that you *not* tease her. And if you do, Merripen has already said that he will give you such a drubbing—"

"Oh, please. As if I'd care enough to notice some problem of Marks's." He paused. "What is it?"

Win frowned. "I wouldn't tell you, except that the problem is obvious and you'll notice immediately. You see, Miss Marks dyes her hair, which I never knew before, but apparently—"

"Dyes her hair?" Poppy repeated in surprise. "But why? She's not old."

"I have no idea. She won't explain why. But there are some unfortunate women who start to gray in their twenties, and perhaps she's one of them."

"Poor thing," Poppy said. "It must embarrass her. She's certainly taken great pains to keep it secret."

"Yes, poor thing," Leo said, sounding not at all sympathetic. In fact, his eyes fairly danced with glee. "Tell us what happened, Win."

"We think the London apothecary who mixed her usual solution must have gotten the proportions wrong. Because when she applied the dye this morning, the result was . . . well, distressing."

"Did it fall out?" Leo asked. "Is she bald?"

"No, not at all. It's just that her hair is . . . green."

To look at Leo's face, one would think it was Christmas morning. "What shade of green?"

"Leo, *hush*," Win said urgently. "You are not to torment her. It's been a very trying experience. We mixed a peroxide paste to take the green out, and I don't know if it worked or not. Amelia was helping her to wash it a little while ago. And no matter what the result is, you are to say *nothing*."

"You're telling me that tonight, Marks will be sitting at the supper table with hair that matches the asparagus, and I'm not supposed to remark on it?" He snorted. "I'm not that strong."

"Please, Leo," Poppy murmured, touching his arm. "If it were one of your sisters, you wouldn't mock."

"Do you think that little shrew would have any mercy on me, were the situations reversed?" He rolled his eyes as he saw their expressions. "Very well, I'll try not to jeer. But I make no promises."

Leo sauntered toward the house in no apparent hurry. He didn't deceive either of his sisters.

"How long do you think it will take him to find her?" Poppy asked Win.

"Two, perhaps three minutes," Win replied, and they both sighed.

In precisely two minutes and forty-seven seconds, Leo had located his archenemy in the fruit orchard behind the house. Marks sat on a low stone wall, her narrow frame slightly hunched, her elbows close together. She had some kind of cloth wrapped around her head, a knotted turban that concealed her hair entirely.

Seeing the dispirited droop of her slender frame, anyone else might have been moved to pity. But Leo had no compunction about taking a few jabs at Catherine Marks. From the beginning of their acquaintance, she had never missed an opportunity to nag, insult or deflate him. On the few occasions he had said something charming or nice—purely as an experiment, of course—she willfully misinterpreted him.

Leo had never understood why they had started off on such bad footing, or why she was so determined to hate him. And even more perplexing, why it mattered. Prickly, narrow-minded, sharp-tongued, secretive woman, with her stern mouth and haughty little nose . . . she *deserved* green hair, and she deserved to be mocked for it.

The time for revenge was at hand.

As Leo approached nonchalantly, Marks lifted her head, the sunlight flashing on the lenses of her spectacles. "Oh," she said sourly. "You're back."

She said it as if she had just discovered a vermin infestation.

"Hello, Marks," Leo said cheerfully. "Hmmm. You look different. What can it be?"

She glowered at him.

"Is it some new fashion, that wrapping on your head?" he asked with polite interest.

Marks maintained a stony silence.

The moment was delicious. He knew, and she knew that he knew, and mortified color was creeping over her face.

"I brought Poppy with me from London," Leo volunteered.

Her eyes turned alert behind the spectacles. "Did Mr. Rutledge come, too?"

"No. Although I imagine he's not far behind us."

The companion stood from the stone wall and brushed at her skirts. "I must see Poppy—"

"There'll be time for that." Leo moved to block her way. "But before we return to the house, I think you and I should reacquaint ourselves. How are things with you, Marks? Anything interesting happen lately?"

"You're no better than a ten-year-old," she said vehemently. "All ready to sneer at someone else's misfortune. You immature, mean-spirited—"

"I'm sure it's not that bad," Leo said kindly. "Let me have a look, and I'll tell you if—"

"Stay away from me!" she snapped, and tried to dart around him.

Leo blocked her easily, a muffled laugh escaping him as she tried to shove him. "Are you trying to push me out of the way? You don't have the strength of a butterfly. Here—your headgear is askew—let me help you with it—"

"Don't touch me!"

They struggled, one of them playful, the other frantic and flailing.

"One glance," Leo begged, a laugh ending in a grunt as she twisted and jabbed a sharp elbow against his midriff. He snatched at the kerchief, managing to loosen it. "Please. It's all I want from life, to see you with—" another swipe, and he snagged the edge of the cloth, "—your hair all—"

But Leo broke off as the kerchief pulled free, and the hair that spilled out was not any conceivable shade of green. It was blond . . . pale amber and champagne and honey . . . and there was so much of it, cascading in shimmering waves to the middle of her back.

Leo went still, holding her in place as his astonished gaze raked over her. They both gulped for breath, worked up and winded like racehorses. Marks couldn't have looked more appalled if he had just stripped her naked. And the truth was, Leo couldn't have been any more confounded—or aroused—if he were actually viewing her naked. Though he certainly would have been willing to try it.

Such a commotion had risen in him, Leo hardly knew how to react. Just hair, just locks of hair . . . but it was like setting a previously undistinguished painting in the perfect frame, revealing its beauty in full luminous detail. Catherine Marks in the sunlight was a mythical creature, a nymph, with delicate features and opalescent eyes.

The most confounding realization was that it wasn't really hair color that had concealed all this from him . . . he had never noticed how stunning she was because she had deliberately kept him from seeing it.

"Why," Leo asked, his voice husky, "would you conceal something so beautiful?" Staring at her, nearly devouring her, he asked more softly still, "What are you hiding from?"

Her lips trembled, and she gave a brief shake of her head, as if to answer would prove fatal to them both. And, wrenching free of him, she picked up her skirts and ran headlong to the house.

Chapter Twenty

"Amelia," Poppy said as she lay her head on her sister's shoulder, "you've done me a terrible disservice, making marriage look so easy."

Amelia laughed softly, hugging her. "Oh, dear. If I've given that impression, I do apologize. It's not. Especially when both individuals are strong willed."

"The ladies' periodicals advise to let one's husband have his way most of the time."

"Oh, lies, lies. Only let your husband *think* he's having his way. That's the secret to a happy marriage."

They both snickered, and Poppy sat up.

Having put Rye down for his morning nap, Amelia had gone with Poppy to the family parlor, where they sat together on the settee. Although Win had been invited to join them, she had tactfully declined, sensitive to the fact that Amelia had a more maternal relationship with Poppy than she did.

During the two years that Win had spent away at a health clinic in France, recovering from the damages of scarlet fever, Poppy had grown even closer to their oldest sister. When Poppy wished to divulge her most private thoughts and problems, Amelia was the one she always felt most comfortable with.

A tea tray had been brought in, and there was a plate of treacle tarts made according to their mother's old recipe, strips of buttery shortbread topped with lemon syrup and sweet crumbs.

"You must be exhausted," Amelia remarked, putting a gentle hand to Poppy's cheek. "I think you need a nap more than little Rye."

Poppy shook her head. "Later. I must try to settle some things first, because I think Harry may arrive by nightfall. Of course, he may not, but—"

"He will," came a voice from the doorway, and Poppy looked up to behold her former companion. "Miss Marks," she exclaimed, jumping to her feet.

A brilliant smile broke out on Miss Marks's face, and she came to Poppy swiftly, catching her in a warm embrace. Poppy could tell that she had been outside. Instead of her usual pristine soap-and-starch smell, she carried the scents of earth and flowers and summer heat. "Nothing's the same without you here," Miss Marks said. "It's so much quieter."

Poppy laughed.

Drawing back, Miss Marks added hastily, "I didn't mean to imply—"

"Yes, I know." Still smiling, Poppy viewed her quizzically. "How pretty you look. Your hair . . ." Instead of being scraped back and tightly pinned, the thick, fine locks flowed around her back and shoulders. And the nondescript shade of brown had been lightened to brilliant pale gold. "Is that your natural color?"

A blush swept over Miss Marks's face. "I'm going to darken it again as soon as possible."

"Must you?" Poppy asked, perplexed. "It's so lovely this way."

Amelia spoke from the settee. "I wouldn't advise applying any chemicals for a while, Catherine. Your hair may be too fragile."

"You may be right," Miss Marks said with a frown, self-consciously reaching up to finger the light, glinting strands.

Poppy looked askance at them both, having never heard Amelia call the companion by her first name before.

"May I sit with you both?" Miss Marks asked Poppy gently. "I want very much to hear what has transpired since the wedding. And—" There was a quick, oddly nervous pause. "I have some things to tell you, that I believe are relevant to your situation."

"Please do," Poppy said. Throwing a quick glance at Amelia, she saw that her older sister was already aware of what Miss Marks intended to tell her.

They sat together, the sisters on the settee and Catherine Marks on a nearby chair.

A long, supple shape streaked through the doorway and paused. It was Dodger, who caught sight of Poppy, did a few hops of joy, and raced to her.

"Dodger," Poppy exclaimed, almost happy to see the ferret. He loped to her, regarded her with bright eyes and chirped happily as she petted him. After a moment, he left her lap and stole toward Miss Marks.

The companion glanced at him sternly. "Don't come near me, you loathsome weasel."

Undeterred, he stopped by her feet and executed a slow roll, showing her his belly. It was a source of amusement to the Hathaways that Dodger adored Miss Marks, no matter that she despised him. "Go

away," she told him, but the lovestruck ferret continued his efforts to entice her.

Sighing, she reached down and removed one of
her shoes, a sturdy black leather affair that laced up
to the ankle. "It's the only way to keep him quiet,"
she said dourly.

Immediately, the ferret's chatter ceased, and he
buried his head inside the shoe.

Suppressing a grin, Amelia turned her attention
to Poppy. "Did you have a row with Harry?" she
asked gently.

"Not really. Well, it began as one, but—" Poppy
felt a wash of heat over her face. "Ever since the
wedding we've done nothing more than circle
around each other. And then last evening it seemed
that we would finally—" The words seemed to
bottle up in her throat, and she had to force them out
in a jumble. "I'm so afraid it will always be this way,
this push and pull . . . I think he cares for me, but he
doesn't want me to care for him. It's as if he both
wants and fears affection. And that leaves me in an
impossible position." She let out a shaky, mirthless
laugh and looked at her sister with a helpless grimace, as if to ask *what can be done with such a
man?*

Instead of replying, Amelia turned her gaze to
Miss Marks.

The companion appeared vulnerable, uneasy, turmoil churning beneath the veneer of composure.
"Poppy. I may be able to shed some light on the situation. On what makes Harry so unreachable."

Startled by the familiar way she had referred to
Harry, Poppy stared at her without blinking. "You
have some knowledge of my husband, Miss Marks?"

"Please call me Catherine. I would like very much

for you to consider me as a friend." The fair-haired woman drew in a tense breath. "I was acquainted with him in the past."

"What?" Poppy asked faintly.

"I should have told you before. I'm sorry. It's not something I can speak of easily."

Poppy was silent with amazement. It wasn't often that someone she had known for a long time was suddenly revealed in a new and surprising way. A connection between Miss Marks and Harry? That was profoundly unnerving, especially since both of them had kept it secret. She suffered a chill of confusion as an awful thought occurred to her. "Oh, God. Were you and Harry—"

"*No*. Nothing like that. But it's a complicated story, and I'm not certain how to . . . well, let me start by telling you what I know about Harry."

Poppy responded with a dazed nod.

"Harry's father, Arthur Rutledge, was an exceptionally ambitious man," Catherine said. "He built a hotel in Buffalo, New York, around the time they had started to expand the port and the harbor. And he made a moderate success of it, although he was by all accounts a poor manager—proud and obstinate and domineering. Arthur didn't marry until he was in his forties. He chose a local beauty, Nicolette, known for her high spirits and charm. She was less than half his age, and they had little in common. I don't know if Nicolette married him solely for his money, or if there was affection between them at the beginning. Unfortunately, Harry was born a bit too early on in the marriage—there was a great deal of speculation as to whether or not Arthur was the father. I think the rumors helped to bring about an estrangement. Whatever the cause, the marriage turned bitter. After Harry's birth, Nicolette was indiscreet in her affairs, until finally she ran away to England with one of her lovers. Harry was four years old at the time."

Her expression turned pensive. She was so deep in thought, in fact, that she didn't appear to notice that the ferret had crawled into her lap. "Harry's parents had taken little enough notice of him before. After Nicolette left, however, he was utterly neglected. Worse than neglected—he was deliberately isolated. Arthur put him in a kind of invisible prison. The hotel staff was instructed to have as little to do with the boy as possible. He was often locked alone in his room. Even when he took his meals in the kitchen, the employees were afraid to talk to him, for fear of reprisal. Arthur had made certain that Harry was given food, clothing, and education. No one could say Harry was being maltreated, you see, because he wasn't beaten or starved. But there are ways to break someone's spirit other than physical punishment."

"But why?" Poppy asked with difficulty, trying to absorb the idea of it, a child being brought up in such a cruel manner. "Was the father so vindictive that he could blame a child for his mother's actions?"

"Harry was a reminder of past humiliation and disappointment. And in all likelihood, Harry isn't even Arthur's son."

"That's no excuse," Poppy burst out. "I wish . . . oh, someone should have helped him."

"Many of the hotel staff felt terrible guilt over what was being done to Harry. The housekeeper, in particular. At one point she noticed that she hadn't seen the child in two days, and she went looking for him. He had been locked in his room with no food . . . Arthur had been so busy, he had forgotten to let him out. And Harry was only five."

"No one had heard him crying? Hadn't he made any noise?" Poppy asked unsteadily.

Catherine looked down at the ferret, stroking him compulsively. "The cardinal rule of the hotel was never to bother the guests. It had been drilled into him since birth. So he waited quietly, hoping someone would remember him, and come for him."

"Oh, no," Poppy whispered.

"The housekeeper was so horrified," Catherine continued, "that she managed to find out where Nicolette had gone, and she wrote letters describing the situation in the hopes that they might send for him. Anything, even living with a mother like Nicolette, would be better than the terrible isolation that was imposed on Harry."

"But Nicolette never sent for him?"

"Not until much later, when it was too late for Harry. Too late for everyone, as it turned out. Nicolette took ill with a wasting disease. It was a long, slow decline, but when the end approached, it progressed quickly. She wanted to see what had become of her son before she died, and so she wrote asking him to come. He left for London on the next available ship. He was an adult by then, twenty years of age or so. I don't know what his motives for seeing his mother were. No doubt he had many questions. I suspect there was always an uncertainty in his mind, as to whether she had left because of him." She paused, momentarily preoccupied with her own thoughts. "Most often, children blame themselves for how they are treated."

"But it wasn't his fault," Poppy exclaimed, her

heart wrenched with compassion. "He was only a little boy. No child deserves to be abandoned."

"I doubt anyone has ever said as much to Harry," Catherine said. "He won't discuss it."

"What did his mother say when he found her?"

Catherine looked away for a moment, seeming unable to speak. She stared at the curled-up ferret in her lap, stroking his sleek fur. Eventually she managed to reply in a strained voice, her gaze still averted. "She died the day before he reached London." Her fingers twined into a tight basket. "Forever eluding him. I suppose to Harry, any hope of finding answers, any hope of affection, died along with her."

The three women were silent.

Poppy was overwhelmed.

What would it do to a child, to be raised in such a barren and loveless environment? It must have seemed as if the world itself had betrayed him. What a cruel burden to carry.

I will never love you, she had told him on their wedding day. And his reply . . .

I've never wanted to be loved. And God knows no one's done it yet.

Poppy closed her eyes sickly. This was not a problem to be solved in a conversation, or in a day, or even a year. This was a wound to the soul.

"I wanted to tell you before," she heard Catherine say. "But I was afraid it might have inclined you more strongly in Harry's favor. You've always been so easily moved to compassion. And the truth is, Harry won't ever want your sympathy, and probably not your love. I don't think it likely that he can become the kind of husband you deserve."

Poppy looked at her through tear-hazed eyes. "Then why are you telling me this?"

"Because even though I've always believed that Harry is incapable of love, I'm not entirely sure. I've never been sure about anything regarding Harry."

"Miss Marks—" Poppy began, and checked herself. "Catherine. What is the association between you and he? How is it that you know all this about him?"

A curious series of expressions crossed Catherine's face . . . anxiety, sorrow, pleading. She began to tremble visibly, until the ferret in her lap awoke and hiccupped.

As the silence drew out, Poppy threw a questioning glance at Amelia, who gave her a subtle nod as if to say, *Be patient.*

Catherine removed her spectacles and polished the perspiration-misted edges of the lenses. Her entire face had gone damp with nervousness, the fine skin gleaming with the luster of a pearl. "A few years after Nicolette came to England with her paramour," she said, "she had another child. A daughter."

Poppy was left to make the connection on her own. She found herself pressing her knuckles gently against her mouth. "You?" she eventually managed to get out.

Catherine lifted her face, the spectacles still in her hand. A poetic, fine-boned face, but there was something direct and decisive in the lovely symmetry of her features. Yes, there was something of Harry in that face. And a quality in her reserve that spoke of deep-trammeled emotions.

"Why have you never mentioned it?" Poppy asked, bewildered. "Why hasn't my husband? Why is your existence a secret?"

"It's for my protection. I took a new name. No one can ever know why."

There was much more Poppy wanted to ask, but it

seemed Catherine Marks had reached the limits of her tolerance. Murmuring another apology beneath her breath, and another, she stood and set the sleepy ferret onto the rug. Snatching up her discarded shoe, she left the room. Dodger shook himself awake and followed her instantly.

Left alone with her sister, Poppy contemplated the little pile of tarts on the nearby table. A long silence passed.

"Tea?" she heard Amelia ask.

Poppy responded with a distracted nod.

After the tea was poured, they both reached for tarts, using their fingers to cradle the heavy strips of pastry, biting carefully. Tart lemon, sugar syrup, the pie crust velvety and crumbly. It was one of the tastes of their childhood. Poppy washed it down with a sip of hot milky tea.

"Things that remind me of our parents," Poppy said absently, "and that lovely cottage in Primrose Place . . . they always make me feel better. Like eating these tarts. And flower-print curtains. And reading Aesop's fables."

"The smell of Apothecary's Roses," Amelia reminisced. "Watching the rain fall from the thatched eaves. And remember when Leo caught fireflies in jars, and we tried to use them as candlelight for supper?"

Poppy smiled. "I remember never being able to find the cake pan, because Beatrix was forever making it into a bed for her pets."

Amelia gave an unladylike snort of laughter. "What about the time one of the chickens was so frightened by the neighbor's dog, it lost all its feathers? And Bea got Mother to knit a little sweater for it."

Poppy spluttered in her tea. "I was mortified. Everyone in the village came to see our bald chicken strutting around in a sweater."

"As far as I know," Amelia said with a grin, "Leo's never eaten poultry since. He says he can't have something for dinner if there's a chance it once wore clothes."

Poppy sighed. "I never realized how wonderful our childhood was. I wanted us to be ordinary, so people wouldn't refer to us as 'those peculiar Hathaways.'" She licked a tacky spot of syrup from a fingertip, and glanced ruefully at Amelia. "We're never going to be ordinary, are we?"

"No, dear. Although, I must confess, I've never fully understood your desire for an ordinary life. To me, the word implies dullness."

"To me, it means safety. Knowing what to expect. There have been so many terrible surprises for us, Amelia . . . Mother and Father dying, and the scarlet fever, and the house burning . . ."

"And you believe you would have been safe with Mr. Bayning?" Amelia asked gently.

"I thought so." Poppy shook her head in bemusement. "I was so certain that I would be content with him. But in retrospect, I can't help thinking . . . Michael didn't fight for me, did he? Harry said something to him on the morning of our wedding, right in front of me . . . 'She was yours, if you'd wanted her, but I wanted her more.' And even though I hated what Harry had done . . . part of me liked it that Harry didn't think of me as being beneath him."

Drawing her feet up onto the settee, Amelia regarded her with fond concern. "I suppose you know already that the family can't let you go back with

Harry until we're satisfied that he will be kind to you."

"But he has been," Poppy said. And she told Amelia about the day when she had sprained her ankle, and Harry had taken care of her. "He was thoughtful and gentle and . . . well, loving. And if that was a glimpse of who Harry really is, I . . ." She stopped and traced the edge of her teacup, staring intently into the empty bowl of it. "Leo said something to me on the way here, that I had to decide whether or not to forgive Harry for the way our marriage started. I think I must, Amelia. For my own sake as well as Harry's."

"To err is human," Amelia said, "to forgive, absolutely galling. But yes, I think it's a good idea."

"The problem is, *that* Harry—the one who took care of me that day—doesn't surface nearly often enough. He keeps himself ridiculously busy, and he meddles with everyone and everything in that blasted hotel to avoid having to think about anything personal. If I could get him away from the Rutledge, to some quiet, peaceful place, and just . . ."

"Keep him in bed for a week?" Amelia suggested, her eyes twinkling.

Glancing at her sister in surprise, Poppy flushed and tried to stifle a laugh.

"It might do wonders for your marriage," Amelia continued. "It's lovely to talk to your husband after you've been to bed together. They just lie there feeling grateful and say yes to everything."

"I wonder if I could convince Harry to stay here with me for a few days," Poppy mused. "Is the gamekeeper's cottage in the woods still empty?"

"Yes, but the caretaker's house is much nicer, and at a more convenient distance from the house."

"I wish . . ." Poppy hesitated. "But it would be impossible. Harry would never agree to stay away from the hotel so long."

"Make it a condition of your returning to London with him," Amelia suggested. "Seduce him. For heaven's sake, Poppy, it's not that difficult."

"I don't know anything about it," Poppy protested.

"Yes, you do. Seduction is merely encouraging a man to do something he already wants to do."

Poppy gave her a bemused glance. "I don't understand why you're giving me this advice now, when you were so against the marriage in the first place."

"Well, now that you're married, there's not much anyone can do except try to make the best of it." A thoughtful pause. "Sometimes when you're making the best of a situation, it turns out far better than you could have hoped for."

"Only you," Poppy said, "could make seducing a man sound like the most pragmatic option."

Amelia grinned and reached for another tart. "What I mean to suggest is, why don't you try making a headlong dash at him? Try to make a real go of it. Show him what kind of marriage you want."

"Charge at him," Poppy murmured, "like a rabbit at a cat."

Amelia gave her a perplexed glance. "Hmmm?"

Poppy smiled. "Something Beatrix advised me to do early on. Perhaps she's wiser than the rest of us."

"I wouldn't doubt it." Lifting her free hand, Amelia pushed aside the edge of a white lace curtain, sunlight falling over her shining sable hair, gilding her fine features. A laugh escaped her. "I see her now, coming back from her ramble in the wood. She'll be thrilled to discover that you and Leo are here. And it appears she's carrying something in her apron. Lord, it could be anything. Lovely, wild girl . . . Catherine has done wonders with her, but you know she'll never be more than half tame."

Amelia said this without worry or censure, merely accepting Beatrix for what she was, trusting that fate would be kind. Undoubtedly that was Cam's influence. He'd always had the good sense to give the Hathaways as much freedom as possible, making room for their eccentricities where someone else might have crushed them. The Ramsay estate was their safe harbor, their haven, where the rest of the world dared not intrude.

And Harry would be there soon.

Chapter Twenty-one

Harry's journey to Hampshire had been long, dull, and uncomfortable, with no companionship except his own smoldering thoughts. He had tried to rest, but as a man who found sleep difficult in even the best of circumstances, trying to doze in a jolting carriage in the daytime was impossible. He had occupied himself with making up extravagant threats to bully his wife into obedience. Then he had fantasized about what he would do to Poppy in her chastised state, until those thoughts had made him aroused and aggravated.

Damn her, he would not be *left*.

Harry had never been given to introspection, finding the territory of his own heart too treacherous and tricky to examine. But it was impossible to forget the earlier time in his life, when every bit of softness and pleasure and hope had disappeared, and he'd had to fend for himself. Survival had meant never allowing himself to need another person again.

Harry tried to divert his thoughts by staring at the

passing scenery, the summer sky still light as the hour approached nine. Of all the places in England he had visited, he had not yet gone to Hampshire. They were traveling south of the Downs, toward the thick wood and fertile grasslands near the New Forest and Southampton. The prosperous market town of Stony Cross was located in one of the most picturesque regions of England. But the town and its environs possessed something more than mere scenic appeal—a mystical quality, something difficult to put his finger on. It seemed they were traveling to a place out of time, the ancient woods harboring creatures that could only exist in myth. As evening deepened, mist collected in the valley and crept across the roads in an otherworldly haze.

The carriage turned onto the private road of the Ramsay estate, past two sets of open gates and a caretaker's house made of blue gray stone. The main house was a composite of architectural styles that shouldn't have looked right together but somehow did.

Poppy was there. The knowledge spurred him, made him desperate to reach her. It was more than desperation. Losing Poppy was the one thing he couldn't recover from, and knowing that made him feel fearful and furious and caged. The feelings catalyzed into one impetus: He would not be kept apart from her.

With all the patience of a baited badger, Harry strode to the front door, not waiting for a footman. He shoved his way into the entrance hall, two stories high with immaculate cream paneling and a curving stone staircase at the back.

Cam Rohan was there to greet him, casually

dressed in a collarless shirt, trousers, and an open leather jerkin. "Rutledge," he said pleasantly. "We were just finishing supper. Will you have some?"

Harry gave an impatient shake of his head. "How is Poppy?"

"Come, let's have some wine, and we'll discuss a few things—"

"Is she having supper as well?"

"No."

"I want to see her. Now."

Cam's pleasant expression didn't change. "I'm afraid you'll have to wait."

"Let me rephrase—I'm *going* to see her, if I have to turn this place into matchsticks."

Cam received this imperturbably, his shoulders hitching in a shrug. "Outside, then."

This ready acceptance of a brawl both surprised and gratified Harry. His blood was teeming with violence, his temper on the brink of explosion.

Some part of his mind recognized that he wasn't quite himself, that the precise workings of his mind were off-kilter, his self-control dismantled. His usual cool logic had deserted him. All he knew was that he wanted Poppy, and if he had to fight for her, so be it. He would fight until he bloody well dropped.

He followed Cam through the entrance, down a side hallway, and out to a small open conservatory and garden where a pair of torches burned.

"I'll say this for you," the Rom remarked conversationally, "it's in your favor that your first question was not 'Where is Poppy' but '*How* is Poppy.'"

"Devil take you and your opinions," Harry growled, stripping off his coat and tossing it aside. "I'm not asking for permission to take my wife back.

She's mine, and I'll have her, and be damned to all of you."

Cam turned to face him, the torchlight gleaming in his eyes and over the black layers of his hair. "She's part of my tribe," he said, beginning to circle him. "You'll go back without her, unless you can find a way to make her want you."

Harry circled as well, the chaos of his thoughts settling as he focused on his opponent. "No rules?" he asked gruffly.

"No rules."

Harry threw the first punch, and Cam dodged easily. Adjusting, calculating, Harry retreated as Cam threw a right. A pivot, and then Harry connected with a left cross. Cam had reacted a fraction too late, deflecting some of the blow's force, but not all.

A quiet curse, a rueful grin, and Cam renewed his guard. "Hard and fast," he said approvingly. "Where did you learn to fight?"

"New York."

Cam lunged forward and flipped him to the ground. "West London," he returned.

Tucking into a roll, Harry gained his footing instantly. As he came up, he used his elbow in a backward jab into Cam's midriff.

Cam grunted. Grabbing Harry's arm, he hooked a foot around his ankle and took him down again. They rolled once, twice, until Harry sprang away and retreated a few steps.

Breathing hard, he watched as Cam leapt to his feet.

"You could have put a forearm to my throat," Cam pointed out, shaking a swath of hair from his forehead.

"I didn't want to crush your windpipe," Harry said acidly, "before I made you tell me where my wife is."

Cam grinned. Before he could reply, however, there was a commotion as all the Hathaways poured from the conservatory. Leo, Amelia, Win, Beatrix, Merripen, and Catherine Marks. Everyone except Poppy, Harry noted bleakly. Where the hell was she?

"Is this the after-dinner entertainment?" Leo asked sardonically, emerging from the group. "Someone might have asked me—I would have preferred cards."

"You're next, Ramsay," Harry said with a scowl. "After I finish with Rohan, I'm going to flatten you for taking my wife away from London."

"No," Merripen said with deadly calm, stepping forward, "I'm next. And I'm going to flatten *you* for taking advantage of my kinswoman."

Leo glanced from Merripen's grim face to Harry's, and rolled his eyes. "Forget it, then," he said, going back into the conservatory. "After Merripen's done, there won't be anything left of him." Pausing beside his sisters, he spoke quietly to Win out of the side of his mouth. "You'd better do something."

"Why?"

"Because Cam only wants to knock a bit of sense into him. But Merripen actually intends to kill him, which I don't think Poppy would appreciate."

"Why don't *you* do something to stop him, Leo?" Amelia suggested acidly.

"Because I'm a peer. We aristocrats always try to get someone else to do something before we have to do it ourselves." He gave her a superior look. "It's called *noblesse oblige.*"

Miss Marks's brows lowered. "That's not the definition of *noblesse oblige*."

"It's my definition," Leo said, seeming to enjoy her annoyance.

"Kev," Win said calmly, stepping forward, "I would like to talk to you about something."

Merripen, attentive as always to his wife, gave her a frowning glance. "Now?"

"Yes, now."

"Can't it wait?"

"No," Win said equably. At his continued hesitation, she said, "I'm expecting."

Merripen blinked. "Expecting what?"

"A baby."

They all watched as Merripen's face turned ashen. "But how . . ." he asked dazedly, nearly staggering as he headed to Win.

"*How*?" Leo repeated. "Merripen, don't you remember that special talk we had before your wedding night?" He grinned as Merripen gave him a warning glance. Bending to Win's ear, Leo murmured, "Well done. But what are you going to tell him when he discovers it was only a ploy?"

"It's not a ploy," Win said cheerfully.

Leo's smile vanished, and he clapped a hand to his forehead. "Christ," he muttered. "Where's my brandy?" And he disappeared into the house.

"I'm sure he meant to say 'congratulations,'" Beatrix remarked brightly, following the group as they all went inside.

Cam and Harry were left alone.

"I should probably explain," Cam said to Harry, looking somewhat apologetic. "Win used to be an invalid, and although she's recovered, Merripen is still afraid that childbirth may be difficult for her." He paused. "We all are," he admitted. "But Win is determined to have children—and God help anyone who tries to say no to a Hathaway."

Harry shook his head in bemusement. "Your family—"

"I know," Cam said. "You'll get used to us eventually." A pause, and then he asked in a matter-of-fact tone, "Do you want to take up the fight again, or shall we dispense with the rest of it and go have a brandy with Ramsay?"

One thing was clear to Harry: His in-laws were not normal people.

One of the loveliest aspects of Hampshire summers was that even when the days were sun drenched and warm, most evenings were cool enough for a fire. Alone in the caretaker's house, Poppy snuggled by the small, crackling hearth and read a book by lamplight. She read the same page repeatedly, unable to concentrate as she waited for Harry. She had seen his carriage pass the cottage on the way to Ramsay House, and she knew it was only a matter of time before they sent him to her. "You won't see him," Cam had told her, "until I've decided that his temper has cooled sufficiently."

"He would never hurt me, Cam."

"All the same, little sister, I intend to have a few words with him."

She wore a dressing gown borrowed from Win, a ruffled pale pink garment with a white lace inset at the top. The bodice was very low, exposing her cleavage, and since Win was more slender, the garment was a bit too snug, nearly causing her breasts to spill over the lace. Knowing that Harry liked her hair down, she had brushed it and left it loose, a feathery, fiery curtain.

There was a sound from outside, a hard strike against the door. Poppy looked up sharply, her heartbeat quickening, her stomach turning over in a lazy somersault. She set the book aside and went to the door, turning the key in the lock, pulling at the knob.

She found herself standing face-to-face with her husband, who was one step below the stoop.

This was a new version of Harry, exhausted and rumpled and brutish, a day beyond a shave. Somehow the masculine dishevelment suited him, giving his handsomeness a raw, unvarnished appeal. He looked as if he were contemplating at least a dozen ways to punish her for having escaped him. His gaze raised gooseflesh all over her.

With a deep, arid breath, she stood back to let Harry in. Carefully, she closed the door.

The silence was pressing, the air charged with emotions she couldn't even name. A pulse drummed in the backs of her knees, the insides of her elbows, and the pit of her belly as Harry's gaze raked over her. "If you ever try to leave me again," he said with quiet menace, "the consequences will be worse than you could imagine." And he went on to say something to the effect that there were rules she would have to obey, and there were things he would not tolerate, and if she needed to be taught a lesson, he would be damned happy to oblige.

Despite his blistering tone, Poppy felt a wave of tenderness. He looked so hard faced and alone. So in need of comfort.

Before she gave herself a chance to reconsider, she went forward in two strides, removing all distance between them. Taking his stiff jaw in her hands, she stood on her toes and brought herself against him, and silenced him with her mouth.

She felt the shock of that tender contact jolt all through Harry. His breath slammed in his throat, and he seized her upper arms, pushing her back just far enough to stare at her incredulously. She felt how strong he was, able to break her in two if he chose. He was motionless, riveted by whatever he saw in her expression.

Eager and intent, Poppy strained upward to put her mouth to his again. He allowed it for just a moment, then pushed her back. A swallow rippled visibly down his throat. If the first kiss had startled him into silence, the second had utterly disarmed him.

"Poppy," he said hoarsely, "I didn't want to hurt you. I tried to be gentle."

Poppy laid her hand softly along his cheek. "Is that why you think I left, Harry?"

He seemed stunned by the caress. His lips parted in a wordless question, his features stamped with exquisite frustration. She saw the moment when he stopped trying to make sense of anything.

Bending over her with a groan, he kissed her.

The shared heat of their mouths, the sinuous brush of tongue against tongue, filled her with pleasure. She answered him ardently, withholding nothing, letting him search and stroke inside her as he wished. His arms went around her, one hand clasping beneath her bottom to pull her closer.

Caught up on her toes, Poppy felt her body list forward, chests, stomachs, hips pressing together. He was aggressively aroused, his flesh jutting boldly against her, every hint of friction wringing out deep and resonant delight.

His lips dragged along the side of her throat, and

he bent her backward until her breasts strained the front of the dressing gown. He nuzzled into the valley of compressed flesh, stroking between her breasts with his tongue. His hot breath mingled in the white lace, his mouth dampening her skin. Roughly he sought the tip of her breast, but it was tucked too tightly beneath the soft pink fabric. She arched desperately, wanting his mouth there, everywhere, wanting everything.

She tried to say something, perhaps suggest they go to the bedroom, but it came out as a moan. Her knees were close to buckling. Harry tugged at the front of the bodice, discovering the row of concealed hook-and-eye closures. He opened the bodice with stunning swiftness and stripped the dressing gown away, leaving her naked.

Reaching for her, he turned her away from him and pushed the gleaming fall of her hair aside. His mouth descended to the nape of her neck, kissing, almost biting, his tongue playing, while his hands slid over her smooth front. He cupped a breast, gently pinching the hardening peak while his other hand slid between her thighs.

Poppy jumped a little, gasping in anticipation as he parted her. Instinctively she tried to widen her stance for him, offering herself, and his approving purr vibrated against her neck. He held her in a deep fondling embrace, feeling her, filling her with his fingers until she arched back against him, her bare bottom cradling the shape of his erection. He coaxed sensation from her, pleasuring her vulnerable flesh.

"Harry," she panted, "I'm going to f-fall—"

They sank to the carpeted floor in a sort of slow, grappling collapse, with Harry still behind her. He muttered against her back, imprinting words of need and praise against her skin. The texture of his mouth, wet velvet surrounded by the bristle of his jaw, caused her to shiver in pleasure. He kissed his way along the curve of her spine, following it to the small of her back.

Poppy turned around to reach for the placket of his shirt. Her fingers were unusually clumsy as she undid the four buttons. Harry held still, his chest rising and falling rapidly as he watched her with volatile green eyes. He stripped off his open waistcoat, pulled his leather braces to the sides, and tugged the shirt over his head. His chest was magnificent, broad reaches of curved muscle and tough-knit hardness covered by a light fleece of hair. She stroked him with a trembling hand and reached down to his trousers, trying to find the concealed placket at the front.

"Let me," Harry said brusquely.

"I will," she insisted, determined to learn this bit of wifely knowledge. She felt his stomach against her knuckles, hard as a board. Finding the elusive button, she worked on it with both hands while Harry forced himself to wait. They both jumped as her delving fingers inadvertently brushed against his erection.

He made a choked sound, something between a groan and a laugh. "Poppy." He was breathless. "Damn it, *please* let me do it."

"It wouldn't be so difficult—" she protested, finally managing to free the button, "—if your trousers weren't so tight."

"They're not usually."

Comprehending what he meant, she paused and met his gaze, and a shy, rueful grin curved her mouth. He took her head in his hands, staring at her with a longing that raised the hairs on the back of her neck.

"Poppy," he said raggedly, "I thought about you every minute of that twelve-hour carriage drive. About how to make you come back with me. I'll do anything. I'll buy you half of bloody London, if that will suffice."

"I don't want half of London," she said faintly. Her fingers tightened on the waist of his trousers. This was Harry as she had never seen him before, all defenses down, speaking to her with raw honesty.

"I know I should apologize for coming between you and Bayning."

"Yes, you should," she said.

"I can't. I'll never be sorry about it. Because if I hadn't done it, you'd be his now. And he only wanted you if it was easy for him. But I want you any way I can get you. Not because you're beautiful or clever or kind or adorable, although the devil knows you're all those things. I want you because there's no one else like you, and I don't ever want to start a day without seeing you."

As Poppy opened her mouth to reply, he smoothed his thumb across her lower lip, coaxing her to wait until he had finished. "Do you know what a balance wheel is?"

She shook her head slightly.

"There's one in every clock or watch. It rotates back and forth without stopping. It's what makes the ticking sound . . . what makes the hands move forward to mark the minutes. Without it, the watch wouldn't work. You're my balance wheel, Poppy." He paused, his fingers compulsively following the fine curve of her jaw up to the lobe of her ear. "I spent today trying to think of what I could apologize for and maybe sound at least half sincere. And I finally came up with something."

"What is it?" she whispered.

"I'm sorry I'm not the husband you wanted." His voice turned gravelly. "But I swear on my life, if you'll tell me what you need, I'll listen. I'll do anything you ask. Just don't leave me again."

Poppy stared at him in wonder. Perhaps most women wouldn't find this talk of watch mechanisms to be terribly romantic, but she did. She understood what Harry was trying to say, perhaps even more than he himself did.

"Harry," she said softly, daring to reach out and caress his jaw, "what am I to do with you?"

"Anything," he said with a heartfelt vehemence that almost made her laugh. Leaning forward, Harry pressed his face into the silky mass of her hair.

She continued to work on his trousers, popping the last two buttons from their holes. Her fingers trembled as she gripped him tentatively. He let out a growl of pleasure, his arms sliding around her back. Unsure of how to touch him, she clasped him, squeezed gently, drew her fingertips up the hot length. She was fascinated by him, the silk and hardness and contained force of him, the way his entire body shivered as she stroked him.

His mouth sought hers in a full-open kiss, obliterating all thought. He rose above her, powerful and predatory, famished for the pleasures that were still so new to her. As he lowered her to the carpet, she realized that he was going to take her, now, here, instead of seeking the more civilized comforts of the bedroom. But he hardly seemed aware of where they were, his eyes focused only on her, his color high, his lungs pumping like hearth bellows.

Murmuring his name, she lifted her arms to him. He struggled out of the rest of his clothes and bent to feast on her breasts . . . hot, wet mouth . . . restless tongue. She kept trying to pull him farther over her, seeking the weight of his body, needing to be anchored. She groped for the hard, aching length of him, and urged him against her.

"No," he said thickly. "Wait . . . I have to make sure you're ready."

But she was determined, her grip insistent, and somewhere amid his groans and pants, a husky laugh emerged. He mounted her, adjusted her hips, and paused as he struggled for a measure of self-restraint.

Poppy wriggled helplessly as she felt the gradual pressure of his entry . . . torturously slow . . . maddening, heavy, sweet.

"Does it hurt?" Harry panted, hanging over her, bracing his weight on his arms to keep from crushing her. "Shall I stop?"

The concern on his face was her undoing, filling her with warmth. Her arms slid around his neck, and she pressed kisses on his cheek, neck, ear, everywhere she could reach. Her body held him tightly down below. "I want more of you, Harry," she whispered. "All of you."

He groaned her name and surged into her, alert to every subtle response . . . lingering when it pleased her, pressing deeper when she lifted, every slow plunge tamping more sensation inside her. She let her hands glide over his sleek, flexing back, the burning silk of his skin, loving the feel of him.

Following the long lines of muscle, she went lower until her palms smoothed circles over the tight curves of his backside. His response was electric, his thrusts turning more forceful, a quiet grunt escaping his throat. He liked that, she thought with a smile, or would have smiled if her mouth hadn't been so thoroughly occupied with his. She wanted to discover more about him, all the ways to please him, but the accumulating pleasure reached a tipping point and began to spill powerfully, inundating her, drowning all thought.

Her body clenched him in strong spasms, extorting release, pulling it from him. He let out a harsh cry and sank into her with a last thrust, shuddering violently. It was indescribably satisfying to feel him climax inside her, his body powerful and yet vulnerable in that ultimate moment. And better still to have him lower into her arms, his head dropping on her soft shoulder. Here was the closeness she had always craved.

She cradled his head, his hair a silky tickle against her inner wrist, his breath flowing over her in hot rushes. His unshaven bristle was scratchy against the tender skin of her breast, but she wouldn't have moved him for all the world.

Their breathing slowed, and Harry's weight became crushingly heavy. Poppy realized he was falling asleep. She pushed at him. "Harry."

He lurched upward, blinking, his gaze disoriented.

"Come to bed," Poppy murmured, rising. "The bedroom is just over there." She murmured a few encouragements, urging him to follow. "Did you bring a traveling bag?" she asked. "Or a gentleman's case?"

Harry glanced at her as if she'd spoken in a foreign language. "Case?"

"Yes, with your clothes, toiletries, that sort of . . ." Perceiving how utterly exhausted he was, she smiled and shook her head. "Never mind. We'll sort it out in the morning." She towed him to the bedroom.

"Come . . . we'll sleep . . . we'll talk later. A few more steps . . ."

The wooden bed was utilitarian, but easily large enough for two, and it was made up with quilts and fresh white linens. Harry went to it without hesitation, climbing beneath the covers—collapsing, really—and he fell asleep with startling immediacy.

Poppy paused to look down at the large, unshaven man in her bed. Even in his unkempt state, his dark-angel handsomeness was breathtaking. His lids trembled infinitesimally as he succumbed to encroaching dreams. Complex, remarkable, driven man. Not incapable of love . . . not at all. He merely needed to be shown how.

And just as she had a few days earlier, Poppy thought, *this is the man I'm married to.*

Except that now, she felt a stirring of gladness.

Chapter Twenty-two

Harry had never known such sleep, so deep and restorative that it seemed he had never experienced real sleep before, only an imitation. He felt drugged when he awoke, drunk on sleep, steeped in it.

Squinting his eyes open, he discovered that it was morning, the curtained windows limned with sunlight. He felt no overwhelming need to leap out of bed as he usually did. Rolling to his side, he stretched lazily. His hand encountered empty space.

Had Poppy shared the bed with him? A frown gathered on his forehead. Had he slept all night with someone for the first time and missed it? Turning to his stomach, he levered himself to the other side of the bed, hunting for her scent. Yes . . . there was a flowery hint of her on the pillow, and the sheets carried a whiff of her skin, a lavender-tinged sweetness that aroused him with every breath.

He wanted to hold Poppy, to reassure himself that the previous night hadn't been a dream.

In fact, it had been so preposterously good that he

felt a twinge of worry. *Had* it been a dream? Frowning, he sat up and scrubbed his fingers through his hair.

"Poppy," he said, not really calling out for her, just saying her name aloud. Quiet as the sound was, she appeared in the doorway as if she'd been waiting for him.

"Good morning." She was already dressed for the day in a simple blue gown, her hair in a loose braid tied with a white ribbon. How apt it was that she'd been named for the showiest of wildflowers, rich and vivid, a gleaming finish to the bloom. Her blue eyes surveyed him with such attentive warmth that he felt a catch in his chest, a dart of pleasure-pain.

"The shadows are gone," Poppy said softly. Seeing that he didn't follow, she added, "Beneath your eyes."

Self-consciously, Harry looked away and rubbed the back of his neck. "What time is it?" he asked gruffly.

Poppy went to a chair, where his clothes had been set in a folded pile, and rummaged for his pocket watch. Flipping open the gold case, she went to the windows and parted the curtains. Vigorous sunlight pushed into the room. "Half past eleven," she said, closing the watch with a decisive snap.

Harry stared at her blankly. Holy hell. Half the day was over. "I've never slept so late in my life."

His disgruntled surprise seemed to amuse Poppy. "No stack of managers' reports. No one rapping at the door. No questions or emergencies. Your hotel is a demanding mistress, Harry. But today, you belong to me."

Harry absorbed that, a tug of inner resistance

quickly vanishing into the pull of his enormous attraction to her.

"Will you dispute it?" she asked, looking vastly pleased with herself. "That you're mine today?"

Harry found himself smiling back at her, unable to help himself. "Yours to command," he said. His smile turned rueful as he became uncomfortably aware of his unwashed state, his unshaven face. "Is there a bathing room?"

"Yes, through that door. The house is plumbed. There's cold water pumped directly from a well to the bathtub, and I have cans of hot water ready on the cookstove." She tucked the watch back into his waistcoat. Straightening, she glanced over his naked torso with covert interest. "They sent your things from the main house this morning, along with some breakfast. Are you hungry?"

Harry had never been so ravenous. But he wanted to wash and shave, and put on fresh clothes. He felt out of his element, needing to recapture a measure of his usual equanimity. "I'll wash first."

"Very well." She turned to go to the kitchen.

"Poppy—" He waited until she glanced back at him. "Last night . . ." he forced himself to ask, ". . . after what we . . . was it all right?"

Comprehending his concern, Poppy's expression cleared. "Not all right." She paused only a second before adding, "It was wonderful." And she smiled at him.

Harry entered the cottage kitchen area, which was essentially a portion of the main room, with a small cast-iron cookstove, a cupboard, a hearth, and a pine table that served both as workstation and dining surface. Poppy had set out a feast of hot tea, boiled eggs, Oxford sausages, and massive pasties—thick flaky crusts wrapped around fillings.

"These are a Stony Cross specialty," Poppy said, gesturing to a plate bearing two hefty baked loaves. "One side is filled with meat and sage, and the other side is filled with fruit. It's an entire meal. You start with the savory end, and . . ." Her voice faded as she glanced up at Harry, who was clean and dressed and freshly shaven.

He looked the same as always, and yet intrinsically different. His eyes were clear and unshadowed, the green irises brighter than hawthorn leaves. Every hint of tension had vanished from his face. It seemed as if he had been replaced by a Harry from a much earlier time in his life, before he'd mastered the art of hiding every thought and emotion. He was so devastating that Poppy felt hot flutters of attraction in her stomach, and her knees lost all their starch.

Harry glanced down at the oversized pastry with a crooked grin. "Which end do I start with?"

"I have no idea," she replied. "The only way to find out is to take a bite."

His hands went to her waist, and he turned her gently to face him. "I think I'll start with you."

As his mouth lowered to hers, she yielded easily, her lips parting. He drew in the taste of her, delighting in her response. The casual kiss deepened, altered into something patient and deeply hungering . . . heat opening into more heat, a kiss with the layered merosity of exotic flowers. Eventually Harry lifted his mouth, his hands coming to her face as if he were cupping water to drink. He had a unique way of touching, she thought dazedly, his fingers gentle and artful, sensitive to nuance.

"Your lips are swollen," he whispered, the tip of his thumb brushing the corner of her mouth.

Poppy pressed her cheek against one of his palms. "We've had many kisses to make up for."

"More than kisses," he said, and the look in those vivid eyes brought a heartbeat into her throat. "As a matter of fact—"

"Eat, or you'll starve," she said, trying to push him into a chair. He was so much larger, so solid, that the idea of compelling him to do anything was laughable. But he yielded to the urging of her hands, and sat, and began to peel an egg.

After Harry had consumed an entire pastie, two eggs, an orange, and a mug of tea, they went for a walk. At Poppy's urging, he left off his coat and waistcoat, a state of undress that could have gotten him arrested in certain parts of London. He even left the top buttons of his shirt undone and rolled up his sleeves. Charmed by Poppy's eagerness, he took her hand and let her tug him outside.

They went across a field to a nearby wood, where a broad, leaf-carpeted path cut through the forest. The massive yews and furrowed oaks tangled their boughs in a dense roof, but the depth of shade was pierced by blades of sunlight. It was a place of abundant life, plants growing on plants. Pale green lichen frosted the oak branches, while tresses of woodbine dangled to the ground.

After Harry's ears had adjusted to the absence of city clamor, he became aware of new sounds . . . a rippling chorus of birdcalls, leaf rustlings, the burble of a nearby brook, and a rasp like a nail being drawn along the teeth of a comb.

"Cicadas," Poppy said. "This is the only place

you'll see them in England. They're usually found only in the tropics. Only a male cicada makes that noise—it's said to be a mating song."

"How do you know he's not commenting on the weather?"

Sending him a provocative sideways glance, Poppy murmured, "Well, mating is rather a male preoccupation, isn't it?"

Harry smiled. "If there's a more interesting subject," he said, "I have yet to discover it."

The air was sweet, spiced heavily with woodbine and sun-heated leaves and flowers he didn't recognize. As they went deeper into the wood, it seemed they had left the world far behind them.

"I talked with Catherine," Poppy said.

Harry glanced at her alertly.

"She told me why you came to England," Poppy continued. "And she told me that she's your half sister."

Harry focused on the path before them. "Does the rest of the family know?"

"Only Amelia and Cam and I."

"I'm surprised," he admitted. "I would have thought she'd prefer death over telling anyone."

"She impressed upon us the need for secrecy, but she wouldn't explain why."

"And you want me to?"

"I was hoping you might," she said. "You know I would never say or do anything to harm her."

Harry was quiet, turning over thoughts in his mind, reluctant to refuse Poppy anything. And yet he had made a promise to Catherine. "They're not my secrets to reveal, love. May I talk to Cat first, and tell her what I'd like to explain to you?"

Her hand tightened on his. "Yes, of course." A

quizzical smile curved her lips. "Cat? That's what you call her?"

"Sometimes."

"Do you . . . is there fondness between you?"

The hesitant question provoked a laugh as dry as the rustle of corn husks. "I don't know, actually. Neither of us is exactly comfortable with affection."

"She's a bit more comfortable with it than you, I think."

Glancing at her warily, Harry saw that there was no censure on her face. "I'm trying to improve," he said. "It's one of the things Cam and I discussed last evening—he said it's characteristic of Hathaway women, this need for demonstrations of affection."

Amused and fascinated, Poppy made a face. "What else did he say?"

Harry's mood altered with quicksilver speed. He threw her a dazzling grin. "He compared it to working with Arabian horses . . . they're responsive, quick, but they need their freedom. You never master an Arabian . . . you become its companion." He paused. "At least, I think that's what he said. I was half dead from exhaustion, and we were drinking brandy."

"That sounds like Cam." Poppy raised her gaze heavenward. "And after dispensing this advice, he sent you to me, the horse."

Harry stopped and pulled her against him, nudging her braid aside to kiss her neck. "Yes," he whispered. "And what a nice ride it was."

She flushed and squirmed with a protesting laugh, but he persisted in kissing her, working his way up to her mouth. His lips were warm, beguiling, determined. But as soon as he gained access to her mouth, he gentled, his mouth soft against hers. He liked to tease, to seduce. Warmth swept through her, arousal flowing through her veins, prickling sweetly in hidden places.

"I love kissing you," he murmured. "It was the worst punishment you could have devised, not letting me do this."

"It wasn't a punishment," Poppy protested. "It's just that a kiss means something special to me. And after what you'd done, I was afraid to be close to you."

All hint of amusement left Harry's expression. He smoothed her hair and drew the backs of his fingers softly along the side of her face. "I won't betray you again. I know you have no reason to trust me, but in time I hope—"

"I do trust you," she said earnestly. "I'm not afraid now."

Harry was baffled by her words, and even more by the intensity of his response to them. An unfamiliar feeling welled up in him, a deep, overwhelming ardor. His voice sounded a bit strange to his own ears as he asked, "How can you trust me when you have no way of knowing if I'm worthy of it?"

The corners of her lips tilted upward. "That's what trust is, isn't it?"

Harry couldn't help kissing her again, adoration and arousal pumping through him. He could barely feel the shape of her body through her skirts, and his hands shook with the urge to pull up the bunches of fabric, remove every obstruction between them. A quick glance along both directions of the path revealed that they were alone and unobserved. It would be so easy to lay her into the soft carpet of leaves and moss, push up her dress, and take her right there in the forest. He pulled her to the side of the path, his fingers clenching in a swath of her skirts.

But he forced himself to stop, breathing hard with the effort to check his desire. He had to be careful with Poppy, considerate of her. She deserved better than to have her husband throwing himself on her in the woods.

"Harry?" she murmured in confusion as he turned her to face away from him.

He held her from behind, his arms crossed around her front. "Say something to distract me," he said, only half joking. He took a deep breath. "I'm a hairsbreadth away from ravishing you right here."

Poppy was silent for a moment. Either she was struck mute with horror, or she was considering the possibility. Evidently it was the latter, because she asked, "It can be done outside?"

Despite his fierce arousal, Harry couldn't help smiling against her neck. "Love, there's hardly any place it can't be done. Against trees or walls, in chairs or bathtubs, on staircases or tables . . . balconies, carriages—" He let out a quiet groan. "Damn it, I've got to stop this, or I won't be able to walk back."

"None of those ways sound very comfortable," Poppy said.

"You'd like chairs. Chairs I can vouch for."

A chuckle rippled through her, causing her back to press against his chest.

They both waited until Harry had calmed himself sufficiently to let go of her. "Well," he said, "this has been a delightful walk. Why don't we go back, and—"

"But we're not even halfway done yet," she protested.

Harry glanced from her expectant face to the long path that extended before them, and he sighed. They linked hands and resumed traversing the ground woven with sun and shadows.

After a minute, Poppy asked, "Do you and Catherine visit each other, or correspond?"

"Hardly ever. We don't get on well."

"Why not?"

It wasn't a subject that Harry liked to think about, much less discuss. And this business of having to talk freely with someone, withholding nothing . . . it was like being perpetually naked, except that Harry would have preferred being literally naked in lieu of revealing his private thoughts and feelings. However, if that was the price of having Poppy, he'd bloody well pay it.

"At the time I first met Cat," he said, "she was in a difficult situation. I did as much as possible to help her, but I wasn't kind about it. I've never had much kindness to spare. I could have been better to her. I could have—" He gave an impatient shake of his head. "What's done is done. I did make certain that she would be financially independent for the rest of her life. She doesn't have to work, you know."

"Then why did she apply for a position with the Hathaways? I can't imagine why she would have wanted to subject herself to the hopeless task of making ladies of Beatrix and me."

"I imagine she wanted to be with a family. To know what it was like. And to keep from being lonely or bored." He stopped and gave her a questioning glance. "Why do you say it was a hopeless task? You're very much a lady."

"Three failed London seasons," she pointed out.

Harry made a scoffing sound. "That had nothing to do with being ladylike."

"Then why?"

"The biggest obstacle was your intelligence. You don't bother to hide it. One of the things Cat never taught you was how to flatter a man's vanity—because she doesn't have any damned idea of how to do it. And none of those idiots could tolerate the idea of having a wife who was smarter than himself. Second, you're beautiful, which meant they would always have to worry about you being the target of other men's attentions. On top of that, your family is . . . your family. Basically you were too much to manage, and they all knew they were better off finding dull, docile girls to marry. All except Bayning, who was so taken with you that the attraction eclipsed any other considerations. God knows I can't hold that against him."

Poppy gave him a wry glance. "If I'm so forbiddingly intelligent and beautiful, then why did *you* want to marry me?"

"I'm not intimidated by your brains, your family, or your beauty. And most men are too afraid of me to look twice at my wife."

"Do you have many enemies?" she asked quietly.

"Yes, thank God. They're not nearly as inconvenient as friends."

Although Harry was perfectly serious, Poppy seemed to find that highly amusing. After her laughter slowed, she stopped and turned to face him with her arms folded. "You need me, Harry."

He stopped before her, his head inclined over hers. "I've become aware of that."

The sounds of stonechats perched overhead filled

the pause, their chirps sounding like pebbles being struck together.

"I've something to ask you," Poppy said.

Harry waited patiently, his gaze resting on her face.

"May we stay in Hampshire for a few days?"

His eyes turned wary. "For what purpose?"

She smiled slightly. "It's called a holiday. Haven't you ever gone on holiday before?"

Harry shook his head. "I'm not sure what I would do."

"You read, walk, ride, spend a morning fishing or shooting, perhaps go calling on the neighbors . . . tour the local ruins, visit the shops in town . . ." Poppy paused as she saw the lack of enthusiasm on his face. ". . . Make love to your wife?"

"Done," he said promptly.

"May we stay a fortnight?"

"Ten days."

"Eleven?" she asked hopefully.

Harry sighed. Eleven days away from the Rutledge. In close company with his in-laws. He was tempted to argue, but he wasn't fool enough to risk the ground he'd gained with Poppy. He'd come here with the expectation of a royal battle to get her back to London. But if Poppy would take him willingly into her bed, and then accompany him back with no fuss, it was worth a concession on his part.

Still . . . eleven days . . .

"Why not?" he muttered. "I'll probably go mad after three days."

"That's all right," Poppy said cheerfully. "No one around here would notice."

To Mr. Jacob Valentine
The Rutledge Hotel
Embankment and Strand
London

Valentine,
*   I hope this letter finds you well. I am writing to apprise you that Mrs. Rutledge and I have decided to remain in Hampshire until month's end.*
*   In my absence, carry on as usual.*

Yours truly,
J.H. Rutledge

Jake looked up from the letter with jaw-slackening disbelief. *Carry on as usual?*

Nothing was usual about this.

"Well, what does it say?" Mrs. Pennywhistle prompted, while nearly everyone in the front office strained to hear.

"They're not coming back until month's end," Jake said, dazed.

A strange, lopsided smile touched the house-keeper's lips. "Bless my soul. She's done it."

"Done what?"

Before she could reply, the elderly concierge sidled up to them and asked in a discreet tone, "Mrs. Pennywhistle, I couldn't help but overhear your conversation . . . am I to understand that Mr. Rutledge is taking a *holiday*?"

"No, Mr. Lufton," she said with an irrepressible grin. "He's taking a honeymoon."

Chapter
Twenty-three

In the following days, Harry learned a great deal about his wife and her family. The Hathaways were an extraordinary group of individuals, lively and quick-witted, with an instant collective willingness to try any ideas that came to them. They teased and laughed and squabbled and debated, but there was an innate kindness in the way they treated each other.

There was something almost magical about Ramsay House. It was a comfortable, well-run home, filled with sturdy furniture and thick carpets, and piles of books everywhere ... but that didn't account for the extra something. One felt it immediately after crossing the front threshold, something as intangible but life-giving as sunlight. A something that had always escaped Harry.

Gradually he came to realize that it was love.

The second day after Harry's arrival in Hampshire, Leo toured him around the estate. They rode to visit some of the tenant farms, and Leo stopped to talk to various tenants and laborers. He exchanged informed comments with them about the weather, the soil, and the harvest, displaying a depth of knowledge that Harry would not have expected.

In London, Leo played the part of disaffected rake to perfection. In the country, however, the mask of indifference dropped. It was clear that he cared about the families who lived and worked on the Ramsay estate, and he intended to make a success of it. He had designed a clever system of irrigation that brought water along stone channels they had dug from the nearby river, relieving many of the tenants of the chore of hauling water. And he was doing his utmost to bring modern methods to local farming, including convincing his tenants to plant a new variety of hybrid wheat developed in Brighton that produced higher yields and stronger straw.

"They're slow to accept change in these parts," Leo told Harry ruefully. "Many of them still insist on using the sickle and scythe instead of the threshing machine." He grinned. "I've told them the nineteenth century is going to be over before they ever decide to take part in it."

It occurred to Harry that the Hathaways were making a solid success of the estate not in spite of their lack of aristocratic heritage, but *because* of it. No traditions or habits had been passed on to them. There had been no one to protest "but this is how we've always done it." As a result, they approached estate management as both a business and a scientific undertaking, because they knew no other way to proceed.

Leo showed Harry the estate timber yard, where the backbreaking work of cutting, hauling, and adsizing logs was all done by hand. Massive logs were carried on shoulders or with lug hooks, creating countless opportunities for injury.

After supper that evening, Harry sketched some plans for moving timber with a system of rollers, run planks, and dollies. The system could be constructed at a relatively low expense, and it would allow for faster production and greater safety for the estate laborers. Merripen and Leo were both immediately receptive to the idea.

"It was very kind of you to draw up those schemes," Poppy told Harry later, when they had gone to the caretaker's house for the night. "Merripen was very appreciative."

Harry shrugged casually, unfastening the back of her gown and helping to draw her arms from the sleeves. "I merely pointed out a few obvious improvements they could make."

"Things that are obvious to you," she said, "aren't necessarily obvious to the rest of us. It was very clever of you, Harry." Stepping out of the gown, Poppy turned to face him with a satisfied smile. "I'm very glad my family is getting the chance to know you. They're beginning to like you. You're being very charming, and not at all condescending, and you don't make a fuss about things like finding a hedgehog in your chair."

"I'm not fool enough to compete with Medusa for chair space," he said, and she laughed. "I like your family," he said, unhooking the front of her corset, gradually freeing her from the web of cloth and stays. "Seeing you with them helps me to understand you better."

The corset made a soft *thwack* as he tossed it to the floor. Poppy stood before him in her chemise and drawers, flushing as he studied her intently.

An uncertain smile crossed her face. "What do you understand about me?"

Harry hooked a gentle finger beneath the strap of her chemise, easing it downward. "That it's your nature to form close attachments to the people around you." He moved his palm over the curve of her bared shoulder in a circling caress. "That you are sensitive, and devoted to those you love, and most of all . . . that you need to feel safe." He eased the other strap of her chemise down, and felt the shivers that chased through her body. He drew her against him, his arms closing around her, and she molded to him with a sigh.

After a while, he murmured softly into the pale, fragrant curve of her neck. "I'm going to make love to you all night, Poppy. And the first time, you're going to feel very safe. But the second time, I'm going to be a little bit wicked . . . and you'll like that even more. And the third time—" he paused with a smile as he heard her breath catch. "The third time, I'm going to do things that will mortify you when you remember them tomorrow." He kissed her gently. "And you'll love that most of all."

Poppy couldn't quite fathom Harry's mood, devilish yet tender as he finished undressing her. He laid her back on the mattress with her legs dangling, and stood between them as he leisurely removed his shirt. As his gaze traveled over her, she blushed and tried to cover herself with her arms.

Flashing a grin, Harry bent over her, pulling her hands away. "Love, if you only knew what pleasure it gives me to look at you . . ." He kissed her lips, teasing them open, his tongue slipping inside the warm interior of her mouth. The hair on his chest brushed over the tips of her breasts, a sweet and ceaseless stimulation that drew a moan from low in her throat.

His lips wandered along the arch of her throat to her breasts. Capturing a nipple, he stroked with his tongue, making it taut and stingingly sensitive. At the same time, his hand went to her other breast, his thumb circling and prodding the peak.

She strained upward, her body trembling and flushed. His hands drifted over her in light paths, across her stomach, lower, down to the place where a sweet erotic ache had centered. Finding the humid, delicately layered flesh, he teased her with his thumbs, opened her, making her ready for him.

Her knees drew up, and she reached for him with an incoherent sound, trying to draw him over her. Instead, he sank to his knees and gripped her hips, and she felt his mouth on her.

She quivered beneath the gentle articulation of his tongue, every intricate movement provoking, tormenting, until her eyes fluttered closed and she began to breathe in wrenching sighs. His tongue entered her and lingered for an excruciating moment. "Please," she whispered. "Please, Harry."

She felt him stand, heard the rustle of trousers and linens being dropped. There was hot, gentle pressure at the entrance of her body, and she made a shuddering sound of relief. He pushed inside as deeply as she could accept him, a deliciously substantial invasion. She was stretched, utterly filled, and she worked her hips against him, trying to take even more. A slow rhythm began, his body pressing hers at just the right angle, driving the pitch of feeling higher with each luscious ingress.

Her eyes flew open as the accumulated sensation rolled up to her, relentless in its strength and velocity, and she saw his sweat-misted face above hers. He was watching her, savoring her pleasure, bending to take her helpless cries into his mouth.

When the last spasms had faded, and she was as limp as a discarded stocking, Poppy found herself cradled in Harry's arms. They reclined together on the bed, her soft limbs tangled with his harder, longer ones.

She stirred in drowsy surprise as she felt that he was still aroused. He kissed her and sat up, his hand playing in the loose fire of her hair.

Gently he guided her head to his lap. "Make it wet," he whispered. Her mouth closed carefully over the pulsing head, slid as far down as she could, and lifted. Intrigued, she nuzzled the silken hardness, her tongue flicking out like a cat's.

Harry turned her so that she was positioned face-down on the mattress. Hoisting her hips upward, he covered her from behind, his fingers sliding between her thighs. She felt a leap of excitement, her body responding instantly to his touch.

"Now," he whispered into her hot ear, "I'm going to be wicked. And you'll let me do anything, won't you?"

"Yes, yes, yes . . ."

Harry held her with firm pressure, cupping her as he pulled her against his solid weight. She felt him move her in an insinuating rocking motion, with his aroused flesh poised at the wet cove of her body. He entered her, but just barely, and each time she rocked backward, he let her have a little more. Murmuring his name, she pushed back more strongly, trying to impale herself fully. But he only laughed softly and kept her where he wanted her, maintaining the voluptuous, metrical pitch.

He was utterly in control, appropriating her flesh with dizzying skill, letting her writhe and gasp for long minutes. Dragging the length of her hair to one side, he kissed the back of her neck, his mouth strong and gnawing. Everything he did drove her pleasure higher, and he knew it, gloried in it. Poppy felt the oncoming rush of fulfillment, her senses preparing for the hot tumble of release, and only then did he take her fully, driving hard and deep into her center.

Harry held her until she stopped trembling, her body limp with satisfaction. And then he pressed her to her back and whispered one word into her ear.

"Again."

It was a long and searing night, filled with unthinkable intimacy. After the third time, they snuggled in the darkness with Poppy's head on Harry's shoulder. It was lovely to lie with someone this way, talking about anything and everything, their bodies relaxed in the aftermath of passion.

"You fascinate me in every way," Harry whispered, his hand playing gently in her hair. "There are mysteries in your soul that will take a lifetime to uncover . . . and I want to know every one of them."

No one had ever called her mysterious before. While Poppy didn't think of herself that way, she rather liked it. "I'm not all *that* mysterious, am I?"

"Of course you are." Smiling, he lifted her hand and pressed a kiss into the tender cup of her palm. "You're a woman."

Poppy went for a walk with Beatrix the next afternoon, while the rest of the family dispersed on various errands: Win and Amelia went to visit an ailing friend in the village, Leo and Merripen met with a prospective new tenant, and Cam had gone to a horse auction in Southampton.

Harry sat at a desk in the library with a detailed report from Jake Valentine. Relishing the peace and quiet—rare in the Hathaway household—he began to read. However, the sound of a floorboard creaking snagged his attention, and he looked toward the threshold.

Catherine Marks was standing there, book in hand, her cheeks pink. "Forgive me," she said. "I didn't mean to disturb you. I meant to return a book, but—"

"Come in," Harry said at once, rising from his chair. "You're not interrupting anything."

"I'll just be a moment." She hurried to a bookshelf, replaced the volume, and paused to glance at him. Light from the window gleamed on her spectacles, obscuring her eyes.

"Stay in here if you like," Harry said, feeling unaccountably awkward.

"No, thank you. It's a lovely day, and I thought I might walk through the gardens, or—" She stopped and shrugged uncomfortably.

God, how ill at ease they were with each other. Harry contemplated her for a moment, wondering what was troubling her. He had never known what to do with her, this unwanted half sister, what place in his life he could find for her. He had never wanted to care for Catherine, and yet she had always tugged at him, worried him, perplexed him.

"May I walk with you?" he asked huskily.

She blinked in surprise. Her answer was long in coming. "If you wish."

He went out with her to a small hedged garden, with heavy drifts of white and yellow daffodils all around. Squinting against the abundant sunshine, they walked along a graveled path.

Catherine gave him an unfathomable glance, her eyes like opals in the daylight. "I don't know you at all, Harry."

"You probably know me as well as anyone," Harry said. "Except for Poppy, of course."

"No, I don't," she said earnestly. "The way you've been this week . . . I would never have expected it of you. This affection you seem to have developed for Poppy—I find it quite astonishing."

"It's not an act," he said.

"I know. I can see that you're sincere. It's just that before the wedding, you said it didn't matter if Poppy's heart belonged to Mr. Bayning, as long as—"

"As long as I had the rest of her," Harry said, smiling in self-contempt. "I was an arrogant swine. I'm sorry, Cat." He paused. "I understand now why you feel so protective of Poppy and Beatrix. Of all of them. They're the closest thing to a family you've ever known."

"Or you."

An uncomfortable silence passed before Harry brought himself to admit, "Or I."

They stopped at a bench set alongside the path, and Catherine seated herself. "Will you?" she asked, gesturing to the space beside her.

He obliged, lowering to the bench and leaning forward with his elbows braced on his knees.

They were quiet but oddly companionable, both of them wishing for some kind of affinity, not knowing quite how to achieve it.

Harry decided to start with honesty. Taking a deep breath, he said gruffly, "I've never been kind to you, Cat. Especially when you needed it most."

"I would dispute that," she said, surprising him. "You rescued me from a very unpleasant situation, and you've given me the means to live handsomely without having to find employment. And you never demanded anything in return."

"I owed that much to you." He stared at her, taking in the rich golden glitter of her hair, the small oval of her face, the porcelain fineness of her skin. A frown pulled at his brow. Averting his gaze, he reached up to rub the back of his neck. "You look too damned much like our mother."

"I'm sorry," Catherine whispered.

"No, don't be sorry. You're beautiful, just as she was. More so. But sometimes it's difficult to see the resemblance, and not remember . . ." He let out a taut sigh. "When I found out about you, I resented you for having had so many more years with her than I'd had. It was only later that I realized I was the fortunate one."

A bitter smile touched her lips. "I don't think either of us could be accused of having had an excess of good fortune, Harry."

He responded with a humorless chuckle.

They continued to sit side by side, still and silent, close but not touching. The two of them had been raised not knowing how to give or receive love. The world had taught them lessons that would have to be unlearned. But sometimes life was unexpectedly generous, Harry mused. Poppy was proof of that.

"The Hathaways were a stroke of luck for me," Catherine said, as if she had read his thoughts. She removed her spectacles and cleaned them with the edge of her sleeve. "Being with them these past three years . . . it's given me hope. It has been a time of healing."

"I'm glad of it," Harry said gently. "You deserve that, and more." He paused, searching for words. "Cat, I have something to ask you . . ."

"Yes?"

"Poppy wants to know more about my past. What may I tell her, if anything, about the part when I found you?"

Catherine replaced her spectacles and stared into a nearby blaze of daffodils. "Tell her everything," she said eventually. "She can be trusted with my secrets. And yours."

Harry nodded, silently amazed by a statement he once could never have imagined her making. "There's one more thing I want to ask of you. A favor. I understand the reasons we can't acknowledge each other in public. But in private, from now on, I hope you'll do me the honor of . . . well, letting me act as your brother."

She glanced at him with wide eyes, seeming too stunned to reply.

"We won't have to tell the rest of the family until you're ready," Harry said. "But I would rather not hide our relationship when we're in private. You're my only family."

Catherine reached beneath her spectacles to wipe at an escaping tear.

A feeling of compassion and tenderness came over Harry, something he had never felt for her before. Reaching out, he drew her close and kissed her forehead gently. "Let me be your big brother," he whispered.

She watched in wonder as he went back to the house.

For a few minutes afterward Catherine sat alone on the bench, listening to the drone of a bee, the high, sweet chirps of common swifts, and the softer, more melodious twitters of skylarks. She wondered at the change that had come over Harry. She was half afraid he was playing some kind of game with her, with all of them, except . . . it had to be real. The emotion on his face, the sincerity in his eyes, all of it was undeniable. But how could someone's character alter so greatly?

Perhaps, she mused, it wasn't so much that Harry was being altered as he was being revealed . . . layer by layer, the defenses coming off. Perhaps Harry was becoming—or would become in time—the man he had always been meant to be. Because he had finally found someone who mattered.

Chapter Twenty-four

The mail coach had arrived at Stony Cross, and a footman was dispatched to fetch a stack of letters and parcels addressed to Ramsay House. The footman brought the deliveries to the back of the house, where Win and Poppy lounged on furniture that had been brought out to the brick-paved terrace. The largest parcel was addressed to Harry.

"More reports from Mr. Valentine?" Poppy asked, sipping sweet red wine as she curled next to Win on a chaise.

"It would appear so," Harry said with a self-mocking grin. "It appears the hotel is managing brilliantly in my absence. Perhaps I should have taken a holiday sooner."

Merripen went to Win and slipped his fingers beneath her chin. "How are you feeling?" he asked softly.

She smiled up at him. "Splendid."

He bent to kiss the top of Win's blond head, and sat in a nearby chair. One could see that he was trying to be at ease with the idea of his wife carrying a child, but his concern for her practically radiated from every pore.

Harry took the other chair and opened his parcel. After reading the first few lines of the top page, he made a sound of discomfort and winced visibly. "Good God."

"What is it?" Poppy asked.

"One of our regular guests—Lord Pencarrow—injured himself late last evening."

"Oh, dear." Poppy's brow furrowed. "And he's such a nice old gentleman. What happened? Did he take a fall?"

"Not exactly. He slid down the banister of the grand staircase, from the mezzanine level to the ground floor." Harry paused uncomfortably. "He made it all the way to the end of the balustrade—where he crashed into the pineapple ornament on top of the newel post."

"Why would a man in his eighties do such a thing?" Poppy asked in bewilderment.

Harry sent her a sardonic smile. "I imagine he was in his cups."

Merripen was cringing. "One can only be glad his child-siring years are behind him."

Harry paused to read a few more lines. "Apparently a doctor was summoned, and in his opinion the damage is not permanent."

"Is there any other news?" Win asked hopefully. "Something a bit more cheerful?"

Obligingly Harry continued to read, this time out loud. "I'm sorry to report another unfortunate incident that occurred Friday evening at eleven o'clock, involving—" He broke off, his gaze skimming swiftly down the page.

Before Harry managed to school his expression

into impassiveness, Poppy saw that something was very wrong. He shook his head, not quite meeting her gaze. "It's nothing of interest."

"May I see?" Poppy asked gently, reaching for the page.

His fingers tightened on it. "It's not important."

"Let me," she insisted, tugging at the sheet of paper.

Win and Merripen were both quiet, exchanging a glance.

Settling back on the chaise, Poppy glanced over the letter. ". . . involving Mr. Michael Bayning," she read aloud, "who appeared in the lobby without notice or warning, thoroughly inebriated and in a hostile temperament. He demanded to see you, Mr. Rutledge, and refused to accept that you were not in the hotel. To our alarm, he brandished a—" She stopped and took an extra breath, "a revolver, and made threats against you. We tried to bring him to the front office to calm him in private. A scuffle ensued, and regrettably Mr. Bayning was able to fire a shot before I was able to disarm him. Thankfully no one was injured, although there were many anxious queries from hotel patrons afterward, and the office ceiling must be repaired. Mr. Lufton took a bad fright from the incident and experienced pains in his chest, but the doctor prescribed a day of bed rest and said he should be right as rain tomorrow. As for Mr. Bayning, he was returned home safely, and I took the initiative to reassure his father that no charges would be pressed, as the viscount seemed quite concerned about the possibility of scandal . . ."

Poppy fell silent, feeling ill, shivering even though the sun was warm.

"Michael," she whispered.

Harry glanced sharply at her.

The carefree young man she had known would never have resorted to such sordid, irresponsible melodrama. Part of her ached for him, and part of her was appalled, and part was simply furious. Coming to her home—for that was how she thought of the hotel—making a scene, and worst of all, endangering people. He might have seriously injured someone, perhaps even killed someone. Dear God, there were children in the hotel—hadn't Michael spared a thought for their safety? And he had frightened poor Mr. Lufton into apoplexy.

Poppy's throat went tight, anger and misery stinging like pepper. She wished she could go to Michael right then and shout at him. And she wanted to shout at Harry as well, because no one could deny that the incident was a consequence of his perfidy.

Occupied with her roiling thoughts, she wasn't aware of how much time had passed before Harry broke the silence.

He spoke in the way she most hated: the amused, silky, callous tone of a man who didn't give a damn about anything.

"He ought to be more clever in his murder attempt. Done properly, he could make a wealthy widow of you, and then you'd both have your happy ending."

Harry knew instantly that he shouldn't have said it—the comment was the kind of cold-blooded sarcasm he had always resorted to when he felt the need to defend himself. He regretted it even before he saw Merripen out of the periphery of his vision. The Rom was giving him a warning shake of his head and drawing a finger across his throat.

Poppy was red faced, her brows drawn in a scowl. "What a dreadful thing to say!"

Harry cleared his throat. "I'm sorry," he said brusquely. "I was joking. It was in poor—" He ducked as something came flying at him. "What the devil—"

She had thrown something at him, a cushion.

"I don't want to be a widow, I don't want Michael Bayning, and I don't want you to joke about such things, you tactless *clodpole!*"

As all three of them stared at her openmouthed, Poppy leapt up and stalked away, her hands drawn into fists.

Bewildered by the immediate force of her fury—it was like being stung by a butterfly—Harry stared after her dumbly. After a moment, he asked the first coherent thought that came to him. "Did she just say she doesn't want Bayning?"

"Yes," Win said, a smile hovering on her lips. "That's what she said. Go after her, Harry."

Every cell in Harry's body longed to comply. Except that he had the feeling of standing on the edge of a cliff, with one ill-chosen word likely to send him over. He gave Poppy's sister a desperate glance. "What should I say?"

"Be honest with her about your feelings," Win suggested.

A frown settled on Harry's face as he considered that. "What's my second option?"

"I'll handle this," Merripen told Win before she could reply. Standing, he slung a great arm across Harry's shoulders and walked him to the side of the terrace. Poppy's furious form could be seen in the distance. She was walking down the drive to the caretaker's house, her skirts and shoes kicking up tiny dust storms.

Merripen spoke in a low, not unsympathetic tone, as if compelled to guide a hapless fellow male away from danger. "Take my advice, *gadjo* . . . never argue with a woman when she's in this state. Tell her you were wrong and you're sorry as hell. And promise never to do it again."

"I'm still not exactly certain what I did," Harry said.

"That doesn't matter. Apologize anyway." Merripen paused and added in whisper, "And whenever your wife is angry . . . for God's sake, don't try logic."

"I heard that," Win said from the chaise.

Harry caught up with Poppy by the time she was halfway to the caretaker's house. She didn't glance at him, only glared ahead with her jaw set.

"You think I drove him to it," Harry said quietly, keeping pace with her. "You think I ruined his life as well as yours."

That fueled Poppy's outrage until she wasn't certain whether she might cry or slap him. Blast him, he was going to drive her mad.

She had been in love with a prince, and she had ended up in the arms of a villain, and it would be so much easier if she could continue to view everything in those simplistic terms. Except that her prince was not nearly as perfect as he had seemed . . . and her villain was a caring, passionate man.

It was finally becoming clear to her that love wasn't about finding someone perfect to marry. Love was about seeing through to the truth of a person, and accepting all their shades of light and dark. Love was an ability. And Harry had it in abundance, even if he wasn't ready to come to terms with it yet.

"Don't presume to tell me what I think," she said. "You're wrong on both counts. Michael is responsible for his own behavior, which in this case was—" she paused to deliver a vicious kick to a stray pebble, "—revoltingly self-indulgent. Immature. I'm sorely disappointed in him."

"I can't blame him," Harry said. "I would have done far worse, were I in his position."

"Of that I have no doubt," Poppy said acidly.

He scowled but remained silent.

Approaching another pebble, Poppy kicked it with a vicious swipe of her foot. "I hate it when you say cynical things," she burst out. "That stupid remark about making me a wealthy widow—"

"I shouldn't have," Harry said quickly. "That was unfair, and wrong. I should have considered that you were distressed because you still care for him, and—"

Poppy stopped dead in her tracks, staring at him with scornful astonishment. "*Oh!* How a man whom everyone considers so intelligent can be such an *imbecile*—" Shaking her head, she continued to storm along the drive.

Bewildered, Harry followed at her heels.

"Does it not occur to you," her words came winging over her shoulder like angry bats, "that I might not like the idea of someone making threats against your life? That I might be just the *least* little bit bothered by someone coming to our home waving a gun about with the intention of shooting you?"

It took Harry a long time to answer. In fact, they had nearly reached the house by the time he replied, his voice thick and odd. "You're concerned for my safety? For . . . me?"

"Someone has to be," she muttered, stomping to the front door. "I'm sure I don't know why it's me."

Poppy reached for the handle, but Harry stunned her by flinging it open, whisking her inside, and slamming it shut. Before she could even draw breath, he had pushed her back up against the door, a bit rough in his eagerness.

She had never seen him look quite this way, incredulous, anxious, yearning.

His body crowded hers, his breath falling in swift strikes against her cheek. She saw a visible pulse in the strong plane of his throat. "Poppy ... Are you ..." He was forced to pause, as if he were fumbling to speak in a foreign language.

Which he was, in a way.

Poppy knew what Harry wanted to ask, and yet she didn't want him to. He was forcing the issue—it was too soon—she wanted to beg him to be patient, for both their sakes.

He managed to get the words out. "Are you starting to care for me, Poppy?"

"No," she said firmly, but that didn't seem to put him off at all.

Harry leaned his face against hers, his lips parting against her cheek in a nuzzling half kiss. "Not even a little?" he whispered.

"Not the slightest bit."

He pressed the side of his cheek to hers, his lips playing with the wisps of hair at her ear. "Why won't you say it?"

He was so large and warm, and everything in her wanted to surrender to him. A fine trembling started inside her, radiating outward from her bones to her skin. "Because if I did, you wouldn't be able to run from me fast enough."

"I would never run from you."

"Yes, you would. You'd turn distant and push me

away, because you're not nearly ready to take such a risk yet."

Harry pressed the front of his body all along hers, his forearms braced on either side of her head. "Say it," he urged, tender and predatory. "I want to hear what it sounds like."

Poppy had never thought it was possible to be amused and aroused at the same time. "No, you don't." Slowly, her arms went around his lean waist.

If only Harry knew the extent of what she felt for him. The very second she judged that he was ready, the moment she was certain it wouldn't cause their marriage to lose ground, she would tell him how dearly she loved him. She could hardly wait.

"I'll make you say it," Harry said, his sensuous mouth covering hers, his hands going to the fastenings of her bodice.

Poppy couldn't control a shiver of anticipation. No, he wouldn't . . . but for the next few hours, she would certainly enjoy letting him try.

Chapter Twenty-five

To the Hathaways' general surprise, Leo elected to return to London the same day as the Rutledges. His original intention had been to stay in Hampshire the remainder of the summer, but he had decided instead to take on a small commission to design a conservatory addition to a Mayfair mansion. Poppy wondered privately if his change of plan had anything to do with Miss Marks. She suspected they had quarreled, because it seemed they were going to great extremes to avoid each other now. Even more than usual.

"You can't go," Merripen had said in outrage when Leo told him he was heading back to London. "We're preparing to sow the turnip crop. There is much to be decided, including the composition of the manure, and how best to approach the harrowing and plowing, and—"

"Merripen," Leo had interrupted sarcastically, "I know you consider my help to be invaluable in these matters, but I believe that somehow you'll all manage to drill turnip seed competently without my involvement. As for the manure composition, I can't help you there. I have a very democratic view of excrement—it's all shit to me."

Merripen had responded with a volley of Romany that no one except Cam could understand. And Cam refused to translate a word of it, claiming there were no English equivalents and that was a good thing.

After making his farewells, Leo left for London in his carriage. Harry and Poppy were slower to depart, having a last cup of tea, a last lingering glimpse of the green summer-dressed estate.

"I'm almost surprised you're letting me take her," Harry said to Cam after handing his wife into the carriage.

"Oh, we voted this morning, and it was a unanimous decision," his brother-in-law replied in a matter-of-fact tone.

"You voted on my marriage?"

"Yes, we decided you fit in with the family quite well."

"Oh, God," Harry said, just as Cam closed the carriage door.

After a pleasant and uneventful journey, the Rutledges arrived in London. To discerning outsiders, particularly the hotel employees, it was clear that Poppy and Harry had acquired the mysterious and intangible bond of two people who had made a promise to each other. They were a couple.

Although Poppy was happy to return to the Rutledge, she had a few private concerns about how her relationship with Harry would proceed—if perhaps he might slip back into his former habits. To her reassurance, Harry had firmly set a new course, and he seemed to have no intention of deviating from it.

The differences in him were observed with gratified wonder by the hotel staff the first full day of his return. Poppy had brought back gifts, including jars of honey for the managers and everyone in the front office, a length of bobbin lace for Mrs. Pennywhistle, cured Hampshire hams and sides of smoked bacon for Chef Broussard and Chef Rupert and the kitchen staff, and for Jake Valentine, a sheep hide that had been tanned and polished with smooth stones until the material had been worked into butter-soft glove leather.

After delivering the presents, Poppy sat in the kitchen and chattered animatedly about her visit to Hampshire. ". . . and we found a dozen truffles," she told Chef Broussard, "each one nearly as large as my fist. All at the roots of a beech tree, and barely a half inch beneath the soil. And guess how we discovered them? My sister's pet ferret! He ran over to them and started nibbling."

Broussard sighed dreamily. "When I was a boy, I lived in Périgord for a time. The truffles there would make one weep. So delicious and dear, they were usually only eaten by nobles and their kept women." He looked at Poppy expectantly. "How did you prepare them?"

"We chopped some leeks and sautéed them in butter and cream, and—" She paused as she noticed the staff in a sudden flurry of activity, scrubbing, chopping, stirring. Glancing over her shoulder, she saw that Harry had entered the kitchen.

"Sir," Mrs. Pennywhistle said, while she and Jake stood to face him.

Harry motioned for them to stay seated. "Good

morning," he said with a slight smile. "Forgive me for interrupting." He came to stand beside Poppy, who was perched on a stool. "Mrs. Rutledge," he murmured, "I wonder if I might steal you away for just a few minutes? There's a . . ." His voice faded as he stared into his wife's face. She had looked up at him with a flirting little grin that had apparently disrupted his train of thought.

And who could blame him? Jake Valentine thought, both amused and similarly mesmerized. Although Poppy Rutledge had always been a beautiful woman, there was an extra glow about her now, a new brilliance in her blue eyes.

"The carriage maker," Harry said, recollecting himself. "They've just delivered your carriage. I hoped you might come look at it, and make certain everything is to your satisfaction."

"Yes, I'd love to." Poppy took another bite of her brioche, a warm puff of glazed bread touched with butter and jam. She held the last bit up to Harry's lips. "Help me finish?"

They all watched in astonishment as Harry took the tidbit obligingly into his mouth. And, holding her wrist in his hand, he nipped at her fingertip to remove a little spot of jam. "Delicious," he said, helping her from the stool. He glanced at the three of them. "I'll return her shortly. And Valentine . . ."

"Yes, sir?"

"It's come to my attention that you haven't gone on holiday in far too long. I want you to arrange something for yourself immediately."

"I wouldn't know what to do on holiday," Jake protested, and Harry smiled.

"That, Valentine, is why you need one."

After Harry had escorted his wife from the

kitchen, Jake looked at the others with a dumb-
founded expression. "He's an entirely different man,"
he said dazedly.

Mrs. Pennywhistle smiled. "No, he'll always be
Harry Rutledge. It's just that now . . . he's Harry
Rutledge with a heart."

As the hotel was a virtual clearinghouse of gossip,
Poppy was privy to scandals and private disclosures
concerning people from every part of London. To
her dismay, there were persistent rumors about the
continuing decline of Michael Bayning . . . his frequent public drunkenness, gambling, brawling, and
all manner of behavior unbecoming to a man of his
position. Some of the rumors were linked to Poppy,
of course, and her precipitate wedding to Harry. It
saddened Poppy profoundly to hear what a mess
Michael was making of his life, and she wished
there were something she could do about it.

"It's the one subject I can't discuss with Harry,"
she told Leo, visiting his terrace one afternoon. "It
puts him in a dreadful temper—he gets very quiet
and stern faced, and last night we actually quarreled
about it."

Taking a cup of tea from her, Leo arched a sardonic brow at the information. "Sis, as much as I
would prefer to take your side in all things . . . why
should you *want* to discuss Michael Bayning with
your husband? And what the devil is there to argue
about? That chapter in your life is closed. Were I
married—and thank God I never will be—I
wouldn't welcome the subject of Bayning with any
more enthusiasm than Harry apparently does."

Poppy frowned into her own cup of tea, slowly
stirring a sugar lump into the steaming amber liq-

uid. She waited until it had thoroughly dissolved
before replying. "I'm afraid Harry took exception to
a request I made. I said I wanted to visit Michael,
and that perhaps I might be able to talk some sense
into him." As she saw Leo's expression, she added
defensively, "Only for a few minutes! A *supervised*
visit. I even told Harry he was welcome to accompany me. But he forbade me in a very overbearing
manner, without even letting me explain why I—"

"He should have put you over his knee," Leo informed her. As her mouth fell open, he set his tea
down, made her do the same, and took both her
hands in his. His expression was a comical mixture
of reproof and sympathy. "Darling Poppy, you
have a kind heart. And I've no doubt that for you,
visiting Bayning is a mission of mercy comparable
to Beatrix rescuing a rabbit from a snare. But this
is where it becomes clear that you are still woe-
fully ignorant of men. Since it falls to me to explain to you . . . we're not nearly as civilized as
you seem to think. In fact, we were much happier
in the days when we could simply chase off a rival
at spearpoint. Therefore, asking Harry to allow
you—by all accounts, the only person on earth he
actually gives a damn about—to visit Bayning and
soothe his wounded feelings . . ." Leo shook his
head.

"But Leo," Poppy protested, "you remember the
days when you were doing the same things that Michael is doing. I would have thought you'd have
sympathy for him."

Letting go of her hands, Leo smiled, but it didn't
reach his eyes. "The circumstances were a bit different. I had to watch a girl I loved die in my arms. And
yes, afterward I behaved very badly. Even worse

than Bayning. But a man on that path can't be rescued, sweetheart. He has to follow it off a cliff. Perhaps Bayning will survive the fall, perhaps not. In either case . . . no, I have no sympathy for him."

Poppy picked up her tea and took a hot, bracing swallow. Presented with Leo's viewpoint, she felt uncertain and even a bit sheepish. "I'll let the matter drop, then," she said. "I may have been wrong to ask it of Harry. Perhaps I should apologize to him."

"Now that," Leo said softly, "is one of the things I've always adored about you, sis. The willingness to reconsider, and even change your mind."

After her visit to her brother had concluded, Poppy went to the jeweler's shop on Bond Street. She retrieved a gift that she'd had made for Harry, and returned to the hotel.

Thankfully, she and Harry had planned to have supper sent up to their apartment that night. It would allow her the time and privacy she needed to discuss their argument of the previous evening. And she would apologize. In her desire to help Michael Bayning, she hadn't stopped to consider Harry's feelings, and she wanted very much to atone.

The situation reminded her of something her mother had often said about marriage: "Never remember his mistakes, but always remember your own."

After taking a perfumed bath, Poppy donned a light blue dressing gown and brushed out her hair, leaving it loose in the way he liked.

Harry entered the apartment as the clock struck seven. He looked more like the Harry she remembered from the beginning of their marriage, his face grim and tired, his gaze wintry.

"Hello," she murmured, going to kiss him. Harry

held still, not rebuffing her, but he was hardly warm or encouraging. "I'll send for dinner," she said. "And then we can—"

"None for me, thank you. I'm not hungry."

Taken aback by his flat tone, Poppy regarded him with concern. "Did something happen today? You look all in."

Harry shrugged out of his coat and laid it on a chair. "I've just returned from a meeting at the War Office, where I told Sir Gerald and Mr. Kinloch that I've decided not to work on the new gun design. They receive my decision as nothing short of treason. Kinloch even threatened to lock me in a room somewhere until I'd come up with a set of drawings."

"I'm sorry." Poppy grimaced in sympathy. "That must have been dreadful. Are you . . . are you disappointed that you won't be doing the work for them?"

Harry shook his head. "As I told them, there are better things I could do for my fellow countrymen. Working on agricultural technology, for one thing. Putting food in a man's belly is a vast improvement over inventing a more efficient way to put a bullet in him."

Poppy smiled. "That was well done of you, Harry."

But he didn't return the smile, only leveled a cool, speculative stare at her. His head tilted a bit. "Where were you today?"

Poppy's pleasure dissolved as she understood.

He was suspicious of her.

He thought she had gone to visit Michael.

The injustice of that, and the hurt of being mistrusted, caused her face to stiffen. She answered in a brittle voice. "I went out for an errand or two."

"What kind of errand?"

"I'd rather not say."

Harry's face was hard and implacable. "I'm afraid I'm not giving you a choice. You will tell me where you went and whom you saw."

Reddening in outrage, Poppy whirled away from him and clenched her fists. "I don't have to account for every minute of my day, not even to you."

"Today you do." His eyes narrowed. "Tell me, Poppy."

She laughed incredulously. "So you can verify my statements, and decide whether I'm lying to you?"

His silence was answer enough.

Hurt and furious, Poppy went to her reticule, which had been set on a small table, and rummaged in it. "I went to visit Leo," she snapped without looking at him. "He'll vouch for me, and so will the driver. And afterward I went to Bond Street to pick up something I had bought for you. I had wanted to wait for an appropriate moment to give it to you, but apparently that's not possible now."

Extracting an object encased in a small velvet pouch, she resisted the temptation to throw it at him. "Here's your proof," she muttered, pushing it into his hands. "I knew you would never get one of these on your own."

Harry opened the pouch slowly, and let the object slide into his hand.

It was a pocket watch with a solid gold casing, exquisitely simple except for the engraved initials *JHR* on the lid.

There was a perplexing lack of reaction from Harry. His dark head was bent so that Poppy couldn't even see his face. His fingers closed around the watch, and he let out a long, deep breath.

Wondering if she had done the wrong thing, Poppy turned blindly to the bellpull. "I hope you like it," she said evenly. "I'll ring for dinner now. I'm hungry, even if you're—"

All at once Harry seized her from behind, wrapping his arms around her, one hand still gripped around the watch. His entire body was trembling, powerful muscles threatening to crush her. His voice was low and remorseful.

"I'm sorry."

Poppy relaxed against him as he continued to hold her. She closed her eyes.

"Damn it," he said into the loose sheaf of her hair, "I'm so sorry. It's just that the thought of you having any feelings for Bayning . . . it . . . doesn't bring out the best in me."

"There's an understatement," Poppy said darkly. But she turned in his arms and pressed against him, her hand sliding up to the back of his head.

"It tortures me," he admitted gruffly. "I don't want you to care for any man but me. Even if I don't deserve it."

Poppy's hurt faded as she reflected that the experience of being loved was still very new to Harry. The problem wasn't a lack of trust in her, it was a result of his own self-doubt. Harry would probably always be possessive where she was concerned.

"Jealous," she accused softly, pulling his head down to her shoulder.

"Yes."

"Well, there's no need for it. The only feelings I have for Michael Bayning are pity and kindness." She brushed her lips against his ear. "Did you see the engraving on the watch? No? . . . It's inside the lid. Look."

But Harry didn't move, didn't do anything except hold her as if she were a lifeline. She suspected he was too overcome to do anything at the moment. "It's a quote by Erasmus," she said helpfully. "My father's favorite monk, after Roger Bacon. The watch is inscribed,'It is the chiefest point of happiness that a man is willing to be what he is.'" At Harry's continued silence, she couldn't help throwing more words into the void. "I want you to be happy, you exasperating man. I want you to understand that I love you for exactly what you are."

Harry's breathing turned hard and rough. He held her in a grip that would have taken a hundred men to break. "I love you, Poppy," he said raggedly. "I love you so much that it's absolute hell."

She tried to suppress a smile. "Why is it hell?" she asked sympathetically, stroking his nape.

"Because I have so much to lose now. But I'm going to love you anyway, because there doesn't seem to be any way to stop doing it." He kissed her forehead, eyelids, cheeks. "I have so much love for you, I could fill rooms with it. Buildings. You're surrounded by it wherever you go, you walk through it, breathe it . . . it's in your lungs, and under your tongue, and between your fingers and toes . . ." His mouth moved passionately over hers, urging her lips apart.

It was a kiss to level mountains and shake stars from the sky. It was a kiss to make angels faint and demons weep . . . a passionate, demanding, soul-searing kiss that nearly knocked the earth off its axis.

Or at least that was how Poppy felt about it.

Harry swept her up in his arms and carried her to the bed. He lowered over her and smoothed the rich tumble of her hair. "I never want to be apart from you," he said. "I'm going to buy an island and take you there. A ship will come once a month with supplies. The rest of the time it will be just the two of us, wearing leaves and eating exotic fruit and making love on the beach . . ."

"You'd start a produce export business and organize a local economy within a month," she said flatly.

Harry groaned as he recognized the truth of it. "God. Why do you tolerate me?"

Poppy grinned and slid her arms around his neck. "I like the side benefits," she told him. "And really, it's only fair since you tolerate *me*."

"You're perfect," Harry said with heated earnestness. "Everything about you, everything you do or say. And even if you have a little flaw here or there . . ."

"Flaws?" she asked in mock indignation.

". . . I love those best of all."

Harry undressed her, his efforts hindered by the fact that Poppy was trying to undress him at the same time. They rolled and struggled with their clothing, and despite the intensity of their mutual need, a few gasps of laughter escaped as they found themselves in a hopeless tangle of fabric and limbs. Finally, they both emerged naked and panting.

Harry hooked a hand beneath her knee, widening the spread of her thighs, and he took possession of her in a forceful plunge. Poppy cried out, quivering in surprise at the power of his rhythm. His body was elegant and strong, claiming her in demanding thrusts. Her breasts were cupped in his hands, his mouth covering a taut peak, and he suckled her in time to the lunges of his hips.

A deep flush came over her, the hard slide of his flesh in hers offering exquisite relief and erotic torment. She moaned and struggled to match his rhythm as ripples of pleasure went through her, stronger and stronger until she couldn't move at all. And he drank in her sobs with his mouth, making love to her until she eventually quieted, her body replete with sensation.

Harry stared down at her intently, his face gleaming with perspiration, eyes tiger bright. Poppy wrapped her arms and legs around him, trying to absorb him, wanting him as close as physically possible. "I love you, Harry," she said. The words made him catch his breath, shudders resounding through his body. "I love you," she repeated, and he surged inside her, hard and deep, and found his release. She curled up against him afterward, while his hand played gently in her hair. They slept together, dreamed together, all barriers finally gone.

And the next day, Harry disappeared.

Chapter Twenty-six

For a man who revered schedules as much as Harry, being late was not only unusual, it was akin to atrocity. Therefore, when he didn't return to the hotel from an afternoon visit to his fencing club, Poppy was more than a little concerned. When three hours had passed and her husband still wasn't back, she rang for Jake Valentine.

The assistant came at once, his expression perturbed, his brown hair in disarray as if he'd been tugging on it distractedly.

"Mr. Valentine," Poppy said with a frown, "do you know anything about Mr. Rutledge's whereabouts at present?"

"No, ma'am. The driver just returned without him."

"What?" she asked, bewildered.

"The driver waited at the usual time and place, and when Mr. Rutledge didn't appear after an hour, he went inside the club to make inquiries. A search was done. Apparently Mr. Rutledge was nowhere to be found on the premises. The master of the fencing club asked various members if they had seen Mr. Rutledge go off with someone, perhaps enter a carriage, or even mention his plans, but no one had seen or heard anything after Mr. Rutledge finished his practice." Valentine paused and drew the side of his fist over his mouth, a nervous gesture Poppy had never seen him make before. "He seems to have vanished."

"Has this ever happened before?" she asked.

Valentine shook his head.

They stared at each other in the mutual recognition that something was very wrong.

"I'll go back to the club and search again," Valentine said. "Someone had to have seen something."

Poppy steeled herself to wait. Perhaps it was nothing, she told herself. Perhaps Harry had gone somewhere with an acquaintance, and he would return any moment. But she knew instinctively that something had happened to him. It seemed her blood had turned to ice water . . . she was shaky, numb, terrified. She paced around the apartments, and then she went downstairs to the front office, where the receptionist and concierge were similarly distracted.

Evening had settled deeply over London by the time Valentine finally returned. "Not a trace of him anywhere," he said.

Poppy felt a chill of fear. "We must notify the police."

He nodded. "I already have. I once received instructions from Mr. Rutledge in case something like this ever occurred. I've notified a Special Constable who works from the Bow Street office, and also a South London cracksman named William Edgar."

"Cracksman? What is that?"

"Thief. And from time to time he does a bit of

smuggling. Mr. Edgar is familiar with every street and rookery in London."

"My husband instructed you to contact a constable and a criminal?"

Valentine looked a bit sheepish. "Yes, ma'am."

Poppy put her fingertips to her temples, trying to calm her racing thoughts. A painful sob rose in her throat before she could swallow it back down. She dragged a sleeve across her wet eyes. "If he's not found by morning," she said, taking the handkerchief he handed to her, "I want to post a reward for any information that leads to his safe return." She blew her nose indelicately. "Five thousand—no, ten thousand pounds."

"Yes, ma'am."

"And we should give a list to the police."

Valentine looked at her blankly. "A list of what?"

"Of all the people who might wish to do him harm."

"That won't be easy," Valentine muttered. "Most of the time I can't tell the difference between his friends and his enemies. Some of his friends would love to kill him, and one or two of his enemies have actually named their children after him."

"I think Mr. Bayning should be considered a suspect," Poppy said.

"I had thought of that," Valentine admitted. "In light of the recent threats he's made."

"And the meeting at the War Office yesterday— Harry said they were displeased with him, and he—" Her breath stopped. "He said something about Mr. Kinloch, that he wanted to lock Harry away somewhere."

"I'll go tell the Special Constable immediately," Valentine said. Seeing the way Poppy's eyes flooded and her mouth contorted, he added hastily, "We'll find him. I promise. And remember that whatever Mr. Rutledge is dealing with, he knows how to take care of himself."

Unable to reply, Poppy nodded and pressed the wadded-up handkerchief to her nose.

As soon as Valentine had departed, she spoke to the concierge in a tear-clotted voice. "Mr. Lufton, may I write a note at your desk?"

"Oh, certainly, ma'am!" He arranged paper, ink, and a pen with a steel nib on the desk, and stood back respectfully as she began to write.

"Mr. Lufton, I want this taken to my brother, Lord Ramsay, immediately. He is going to help me search for Mr. Rutledge."

"Yes, ma'am, but . . . do you think that wise at this hour? I'm sure Mr. Rutledge would not want you to compromise your safety by going out at night."

"I'm sure he wouldn't, Mr. Lufton. But I can't wait here without doing something. I'll go mad."

To Poppy's vast relief, Leo came at once, his cravat askew and his waistcoat unbuttoned, as if he'd dressed hastily. "What's going on?" he asked shortly. "And what did you mean, 'Harry's gone missing?'"

Poppy described the situation as quickly as possible, and curled her fingers into his sleeve. "Leo, I need you to take me somewhere."

She saw from her brother's face that he understood immediately. "Yes, I know." He let out a taut sigh. "I had better start praying that Harry won't be found for a good long while. Because when he learns that I took you to see Michael Bayning, my life won't be worth a tin of oysters."

After questioning Michael's manservant as to his whereabouts, Leo and Poppy went to Marlow's, a club so exclusive that one could only belong if his grandfather and father had been counted among its former members. The ennobled crowd at Marlow's looked down on the rest of the populace—including less-privileged bluebloods—with undiluted disdain. Having always been curious to see the inside of the place, Leo was more than pleased to go there in search of Michael Bayning.

"You won't be allowed past the door," Poppy said. "You're precisely the kind of person they want to keep out."

"I'll merely tell them that Bayning is a suspect in a kidnapping plot, and if they don't let me look for him, I'll see that they're charged as accessories."

Poppy watched through the carriage window as Leo went up to the Marlow's classical white stone and stucco façade. After a minute or two of conversation with the doorman, Leo went into the club.

Folding her arms tightly, Poppy tried to warm herself. She felt cold from the inside out, ill with panic. Harry was somewhere in London, perhaps injured, and she couldn't reach him. She couldn't do anything for him. Remembering what Catherine had told her about Harry's childhood, that he had been locked in a room for two days with no one giving a thought to him, she nearly burst into tears.

"I'll find you," she whispered, rocking a little in her seat. "I'll be there soon. Just a little longer, Harry."

The carriage door was wrenched open with startling suddenness.

Leo stood there with Michael Bayning, who was shockingly ravaged by his recent habits of excess. His fine clothes and meticulously tied cravat only served to accentuate the bloat of his jaw and the ruddy web of broken capillaries on his cheeks.

Poppy stared at him blankly. "Michael?"

"He's halfway pickled," Leo told her, "but coherent."

"Mrs. Rutledge," Michael said, his lip curling in a sneer. As he spoke, the scent of strong spirits wafted into the carriage. "Your husband's gone missing, has he? It seems I'm supposed to spout some kind of information about it. Problem is . . ." He averted his face and suppressed a quiet belch. "I haven't got any."

Poppy's eyes narrowed. "I don't believe you. I think you had something to do with his disappearance."

He gave her a distorted smile. "I've been here for the past four hours, and before that I was at my home. I'm sorry to say I haven't arranged any underhanded plot to harm him."

"You've made no secret of your animosity," Leo pointed out. "You've made threats against him. You even came to the hotel with a revolver. You're the most likely person to have been involved in his disappearance."

"Much as I'd like to claim responsibility," Michael said, "I can't. The satisfaction of killing him isn't worth being hanged for it." His bloodshot eyes focused on Poppy. "How do you know he hasn't decided to spend the evening with some lightskirt? He's probably tired of you now. Go home, Mrs. Rutledge, and pray that he doesn't come back. You're better off without the bastard."

Poppy blinked as if she'd been slapped.

Leo interceded coolly. "You'll be answering scores of questions about Harry Rutledge in the next day or two, Bayning. Everyone, including your friends, will be pointing fingers in your direction. By tomorrow morning, half of London will be looking for him. You could spare yourself a great deal of trouble by helping us resolve the matter now."

"I've told you, I had nothing to do with it," Michael snapped. "But I hope to hell that he's found soon—facedown in the Thames."

"Enough," Poppy cried in outrage. Both men glanced at her in surprise. "That is beneath you, Michael! Harry wronged both of us, it's true, but he has apologized and tried to make reparations."

"Not to me, by God!"

Poppy gave him an incredulous glance. "You want an apology from him?"

"No." He glared at her, and then a hoarse note of pleading entered his voice. "I want you."

She flushed with fury. "That will never be possible. And it never was. Your father wouldn't have consented to have me as his daughter-in-law, because he considered me beneath him. And the truth is that you did, too, or you would have managed everything far differently than you did."

"I'm not a snob, Poppy. I'm conventional. There's a difference."

She shook her head impatiently—it was an argument she didn't want to waste precious time on. "It doesn't matter. I've come to love my husband. I will never leave him. So for your sake as well as mine, stop making a spectacle and a nuisance of yourself, and go on with your life. You were meant for better things than this."

"Well said," Leo muttered, climbing into the carriage. "Let's go, Poppy. We'll get nothing else out of him."

Michael grabbed the edge of the door before Leo

could close it. "Wait," he said to Poppy. "If it turns out that something has happened to your husband . . . will you come to me?"

She looked into his pleading face and shook her head, unable to believe he would ask such a thing. "No, Michael," she said quietly. "I'm afraid you're too conventional to suit me."

And Leo closed the door in Michael Bayning's astonished face.

Poppy stared at her brother desperately. "Do you think Michael had anything to do with Harry's disappearance?"

"No." Leo reached up to signal the driver. "He's not in a condition to plot anything other than where he's going to find his next drink. I think he's essentially a decent lad, drowning in self-pity." Seeing her distraught expression, he took her hand and squeezed it comfortingly. "Let's go back to the hotel. Perhaps there'll be some word about Harry."

She was silent and bleak, her thoughts taking the shape of nightmares.

As the carriage jounced along the street, Leo sought for a remark to distract her. "The interior of Marlow's wasn't nearly as pleasant as I'd expected. Oh, there was quite bit of mahogany paneling and nice carpeting, but the air was difficult to breathe."

"Why?" Poppy asked glumly. "Was it filled with cigar smoke?"

"No," he said. "Smugness."

By morning, half of London was indeed looking for Harry. Poppy had spent a sleepless night waiting for news of her husband, while Leo and Jake Valentine had been out searching gentlemen's clubs, taverns, and gaming halls. Although Poppy was frustrated by her own enforced inactivity, she knew that everything possible was being done. The cracksman, Mr. Edgar, had promised to use his network of thieves to find any possible scrap of information about Harry's disappearance.

Special Constable Hembrey, for his part, had been exceedingly busy. Sir Gerald at the War Office had confirmed that Edward Kinloch had threatened Harry during their meeting. Subsequently, Hembrey had procured a search warrant from one of the Bow Street magistrates, and had questioned Kinloch early in the morning. However, a thorough search of Kinloch's residence had revealed no trace of Harry.

The Home Secretary, who was the acting head of the Metropolitan Police Force, had directed his Criminal Investigation Unit—comprised of two inspectors and four sergeants—to apply their skills to the case. They were all engaged in questioning various individuals, including employees at the fencing club and some of Edward Kinloch's servants.

"It's as if he's disappeared into thin air," Jake Valentine said wearily, lowering himself into a chair in the Rutledge apartment, taking a cup of tea from Poppy. He gave her a haggard glance. "Are there any problems with the hotel? I haven't seen the managers' reports—"

"I went over them this morning," Poppy said scratchily, understanding that Harry would want his business to continue as usual. "It gave me something to do. There are no problems with the hotel." She rubbed her face with both hands. "No problems," she repeated bleakly, "except that Harry is missing."

"He'll be found," Valentine said. "Soon. There's no way he can *not* be found."

Their conversation was interrupted as Leo entered the apartment. "Don't get comfortable, Valentine," he said. "Bow Street has just sent word that they have at least three men claiming to be Harry Rutledge, along with their 'rescuers.' It's assumed they're all impostors, but I thought we'd go have a look at them in any case. Perhaps we'll find a chance to talk with Special Constable Hembrey, if he's there."

"I'm going, too," Poppy said.

Leo gave her a dark look. "You wouldn't ask to go if you knew what kind of riffraff parades through that office every day."

"I'm not asking," Poppy said. "I'm telling you that you're not going without me."

Leo contemplated her for a moment, and sighed. "Fetch your cloak."

The Bow Street court was universally regarded as the foremost London magistrates' court, where the most publicized criminal cases were investigated and prosecuted. The Metropolitan Police Act had been passed more than twenty years earlier, resulting in the formation of what was still called the "New Police."

However, there still remained a few law enforcement establishments outside the Home Secretary's direct control, and Bow Street was one of them. Its mounted patrol and half-dozen Runners were answerable only to the Bow Street magistrates. Oddly, the Bow Street enforcement office had never been given a statutory basis for its authority. But that didn't seem to matter to anyone. When results were needed, one went to Bow Street.

The two buildings that comprised the court and

office, nos. 3 and 4, were plain and unassuming, giving little hint as to the power that was wielded inside.

Poppy approached Bow Street with Leo and Valentine, her eyes widening as she saw throngs of people milling around the building and along the street. "Don't speak to anyone," Leo told her, "don't stand close to anyone, and if you hear, smell, or see something offensive, don't say you weren't warned."

As they entered no. 3, they were surrounded by the mingled smells of bodies, sweat, brass polish, and plaster. A narrow hallway led to various holding rooms, charge rooms, and offices. Every inch of the hallway was occupied with jostling bodies, the air thick with exclamations and complaints.

"Hembrey," Jake Valentine called out, and a lean man with close-cropped gray hair turned toward him. The man possessed a long, narrow face and intelligent dark eyes. "He's the Special Constable," Valentine told Poppy as the man made his way toward them.

"Mr. Valentine," Hembrey said, "I've just arrived to discover this lunatic gathering."

"What's happening?" Leo asked.

Hembrey's attention switched to him. "My lord, Mr. Rutledge's disappearance was reported in the *Times* this morning, along with the promise of reward money. And his physical description was given. With the result that every tall, dark-haired swindler in London will appear at Bow Street today. The same thing is occurring at Scotland Yard."

Poppy's jaw dropped as she glanced at the gathering in the hallway and realized that at least half of them were men who vaguely resembled her husband. "They're . . . they're all claiming to be Harry?" she asked dazedly.

"It would seem so," Leo said. "Accompanied by their heroic rescuers, who have their hands out for the reward money."

"Come to my office," Special Constable Hembrey urged, leading them along the hallway. "We'll have more privacy there, and I'll apprise you of my latest information. Leads have been pouring in . . . people claiming to have seen Rutledge drugged and put aboard a ship to China, or robbed at some brothel, things of that nature . . ."

Poppy and Valentine followed Leo and Hembrey. "This is abominable," she told Valentine in a low tone, glancing at the line of imposters. "All of them posturing and lying, hoping to profit from someone else's misfortune."

They were forced to pause as Hembrey tried to clear a path to the doorway of his office.

One of the black-haired men nearest Poppy bowed theatrically. "Harry Rutledge, at your service. And who might you be, my fair creature?"

Poppy glared at him. "Mrs. Rutledge," she said curtly.

Immediately another man exclaimed, "Darling!" He held his arms out to Poppy, who shrank away and gave him an appalled glance.

"Idiots," Hembrey muttered, and raised his voice. "Clerk! Find some place to put all these damned Rutledges so they don't crowd the hallway."

"Yes, sir!"

They entered the office, and Hembrey closed the door firmly. "A pleasure to make your acquaintance, Mrs. Rutledge. I assure you, we're doing everything possible to locate your husband."

"My brother, Lord Ramsay," she said, and Hembrey bowed respectfully.

"What is the latest information?" Leo asked.

Hembrey went to pull out a chair for Poppy, speaking all the while. "A stable boy in the mews behind the fencing club said that around the time of Mr. Rutledge's disappearance, he saw two men carrying a body through the alley out to a waiting carriage."

Poppy sat hard in the chair. "A body?" she whispered, cold sweat breaking out on her face, nausea rising.

"I'm sure he was only unconscious," Valentine told her hastily.

"The stableboy had a glimpse of the carriage," Hembrey continued, returning to his side of the desk. "He described it to us as black lacquer with a small pattern of rosemaled scrollwork across the boot. The description matches a brougham in the mews of Mr. Kinloch's Mayfair residence."

"What next?" Leo asked, his blue eyes hard.

"I intend to bring him here for questioning. And we'll proceed by taking inventory of Mr. Kinloch's other properties—his arms manufactory, realty he may own in town—and obtain warrants to search them methodically."

"How do you know for certain that Rutledge isn't being held in the Mayfair house?" Leo asked.

"I went over every inch of it personally. I can assure you that he is not there."

"Is the warrant still applicable?" Leo persisted.

"Yes, my lord."

"Then you can return to Kinloch's house for another search? Right now?"

The Special Constable looked perplexed. "Yes, but why?"

"I'd like to have a go at it, if I may."

A flicker of annoyance appeared in Hembrey's

dark eyes. Clearly he regarded Leo's request as nothing more than a bit of self-important showmanship. "My lord, our previous search of the house and grounds was comprehensive."

"I have no doubt of that," Leo replied. "But I trained as an architect several years ago, and I'll be able to look at the place from a draftsman's perspective."

Jake Valentine spoke then. "You think there's a hidden room, my lord?"

"If there is," Leo said steadily, "I'll find it. And if not, at least we'll annoy the devil out of Kinloch, which should have some entertainment value."

Poppy held her breath as they waited for the Special Constable's reply.

"Very well," Hembrey finally said. "I can send you in with a constable while I bring Mr. Kinloch in for questioning. However, I will insist that you abide by our codes of practice during the execution of the search—and the constable will make certain you are aware of those rules."

"Oh, have no fear," Leo replied gravely. "I always follow the rules."

The Special Constable seemed rather unconvinced by the claim. "If you'll wait but a moment," he said, "I will confer with one of the magistrates, and he will assign the constable to escort you."

As soon as he left the office, Poppy leapt up from her chair. "Leo," she said, "I'm—"

"Yes, I know. You're going, too."

The Kinloch home was large and fashionably gloomy, the interiors done in dark crimson and green, the walls oak paneled. The cavernous entrance hall was paved with uncovered stone slabs that caused their footsteps to echo repeatedly.

What Poppy found most distinctive and unnerving about Edward Kinloch's house, however, was that instead of adorning the rooms and hallways with traditional artwork, he had filled the place with an astonishingly vast array of game trophies. They were everywhere, dozens of pairs of glass eyes staring down at Poppy, Leo, Jake Valentine, and the constable assigned to accompany them. In the entrance hall alone there were heads from a ram, a rhino, two lions, a tiger, as well as a stag, elk, caribou, leopard, and zebra, and other species that were entirely unfamiliar to her.

Poppy hugged her arms around her middle as she turned a slow circle. "I'm glad Beatrix can't see this."

She felt Leo's hand settle comfortingly on her back.

"Apparently Mr. Kinloch enjoys sport hunting," Valentine commented, gazing at the ghastly assortment.

"Large game hunting isn't a sport," Leo said. "It's only a sport when both sides are equally armed."

Poppy felt cold prickles of unease as she stared at the tiger's frozen snarl. "Harry is here," she said.

Leo glanced at her. "Why are you so certain?"

"Mr. Kinloch likes to display his power. To dominate. And this house is where he brings all his trophies." She shot her brother a glance of barely suppressed panic. Her voice was very quiet. "Find him, Leo."

He gave her a short nod. "I'm going to walk around the outside perimeter of the house."

Jake Valentine touched Poppy's elbow and said, "We'll go through the rooms on this floor and inspect the molding and paneling to see if there are discrepancies that would indicate a concealed door. And we'll also look behind the larger pieces of furniture, such as bookcases or wardrobes."

"And fireplaces," Poppy said, remembering the one at the hotel.

Valentine smiled briefly. "Yes." After conferring with the constable, he accompanied Poppy to the parlor.

They spent a half hour investigating every minute crack, edge, and surface elevation, running their hands over the walls, getting on their hands and knees, lifting edges of carpet.

"May I ask," came Valentine's muffled voice as he looked behind a settee, "did Lord Ramsay really study architecture, or was he more of a . . ."

"Dilettante?" Poppy supplied, moving every object on the fireplace mantel. "No, he's quite accomplished, actually. He attended the *Académie des Beaux-Arts* in Paris for two years, and worked as a draftsman for Rowland Temple. My brother loves to play the part of featherbed aristocrat, but he's far more clever than he lets on."

Eventually Leo came back inside. He went from room to room, pacing the distance from one wall to another, pausing to make notes. Poppy and Valentine continued to search diligently, progressing from the parlor to the entrance hall stairwell. With every minute that passed, Poppy's anxiety sharpened. From time to time a housemaid or footman passed, glancing at them curiously but remaining silent.

Surely one of them had to know something, Poppy thought in frustration. Why weren't they helping to find Harry? Did their misplaced loyalty to their master preclude any sense of human decency?

As a young housemaid wandered by with an armload of folded linens, Poppy lost her patience. "Where is it?" she exploded, glaring at the girl.

The maid dropped the linens in surprise. Her eyes went as round as saucers. "Wh-where is what, ma'am?" she asked in a squeaky voice.

"A hidden door. A secret room. There is a man being kept against his will somewhere in this house, *and I want to know where he is!*"

"I don't know noffing, ma'am," the housemaid quavered, and burst into tears. Scooping up the fallen linens, she fled up the stairs.

Valentine spoke quietly, his brown eyes filled with understanding. "The servants have already been questioned," he said. "Either they don't know, or they don't dare betray their employer."

"Why would they keep their silence about something like this?"

"There's little hope for a servant who is dismissed without references to find a job nowadays. It could mean devastation. Starvation."

"I'm sorry," Poppy said, gritting her teeth. "But at the moment I don't care about anyone or anything save my husband's welfare. And I know he's here somewhere, and I'm not leaving until he's found! I'll tear the house apart if I must—"

"That won't be necessary," came Leo's voice as he strode into the entrance hall. He jerked his head purposefully in the direction of a hallway that branched off the main entrance. "Come to the library. Both of you."

Galvanized, they hurried after him, while the constable followed as well.

The library was a rectangular room filled with heavy mahogany furniture. Three of the walls were fitted with shelved alcoves and bookcases, all topped by a cornice that was continuous with the wall joinery. The area of oak flooring uncovered by carpet was scarred and mellow with age.

"This house," Leo said, going straight to the draped windows, "is a classical Georgian, which means that every design feature in this half of the house is a perfect reflection of the other half. Any deviation is felt as a deep flaw. And according to the form of strict symmetrical arrangement, this room should have three windows on that wall, to match the corresponding room on the other side of the house. But obviously there are only two in here." Deftly he tied back the drapes to admit as much daylight as possible.

Waving impatiently at a cloud of dust motes in the air, Leo went to the second window, fastening those drapes as well. "So I went outside and noticed that the brickwork pointing is different on the section of the wall where a third window should be. And if you pace out this room and the one beside it—and compare the measurements with the exterior dimensions of the house—it appears there's an eight- to ten-foot space between these rooms with no apparent access."

Poppy flew to the wall of bookcases, examining them desperately. "Is there a door here? How do we find it?"

Leo joined her, lowering to his haunches and staring at the floor. "Look for fresh scuff marks. The floorboards are never level in these older houses. Or look for fibers caught in the seams between the cases. Or—"

"Harry!" Poppy shouted, using her fist to bang on a bookcase frame. *"Harry!"*

They were all still, listening intently for a response.

Nothing.

"Here," the constable said, pointing to a small white crescent scuff on the floor. "This is a new mark. And if the bookcase swung out, it would correspond."

All four of them gathered around the bookcase. Leo pried, pushed, and pounded on the edge of the frame, but the unit remained firmly in place. He scowled. "I know how to find the room, but I'll be damned if I know how to get inside."

Jake Valentine began to pull books from the shelves and toss them heedlessly to the floor. "The concealed doors we have at the hotel," he said, "are locked according to a pulley-and-dowel mechanism, with a wire running to a nearby object. When you tilt the object, the wire lifts the dowel and frees a doorstop wedge, and the door opens."

Poppy grabbed books and tossed them aside as well. One of the volumes she found was stuck in place. "This one," she said breathlessly.

Valentine slid his hand over the top of the book, found the wire, and pulled gently.

The entire bookcase swung open with stunning ease, revealing a locked door.

Leo pounded on the door with a heavy thump of his fist. *"Rutledge?"*

They were all electrified by a distant, nearly inaudible reply, and the quiet vibration of the door being pounded from the other side.

A few openmouthed servants gathered at the library doorway, watching the proceedings.

"He's in there," Poppy said, her heart thundering. "Can you open the door, Leo?"

"Not without a bloody key."

"Excuse me," Valentine said, shouldering his way to the door and pulling a small rolled cloth from his coat pocket. He extracted two thin metal implements, knelt beside the door, and set to work on the lock. Within thirty seconds, they heard a distinct *clack* as the tumblers shifted.

The door opened.

Poppy sobbed in relief as Harry emerged, dressed in fencing whites that were gray with dust. Her husband was pale and dirt smudged, but remarkably composed considering the circumstances. Poppy launched herself at him, and he caught her and said her name hoarsely.

Squinting in the brightness of the room, Harry kept Poppy against him as he reached out to shake the other men's hands in turn. "Thank you. I didn't think you'd be able to find me." His voice was ragged and rough, as if he'd been shouting for some time. "The room is insulated with slag wool to muffle sound. Where's Kinloch?"

The constable replied. "He's at the Bow Street Office, sir, being questioned. What do you say to accompanying us there and making a report, so we can detain him indefinitely?"

"It would be my pleasure," Harry said feelingly.

Ducking behind him, Leo ventured into the dark room.

"Quite professional," the constable told Valentine, as he replaced the lock picks in his pocket. "I don't know whether to commend you or arrest you. Where did you learn to do that?"

Valentine sent a grin in Harry's direction. "My employer."

Leo emerged from the concealed room. "Little more than a desk, a chair, and a blanket," he said grimly. "Commissioned you to do a bit of mechanical engineering, did he?"

Harry nodded ruefully, reaching up to touch a tender spot on his skull. "The last thing I was aware of was something crashing down on my skull at the fencing club. I awoke here with Kinloch standing over me, ranting. I gathered the plan was to keep me locked away until I had developed a set of drawings that would result in a workable gun prototype."

"And after that," Valentine said darkly, "when you were no longer useful . . . what did he intend to do with you then?"

Harry smoothed his hand over Poppy's back as he felt her tremble. "We didn't discuss that part."

"Have you any idea whom his accomplices were?" the constable asked.

Harry shook his head. "I didn't see anyone else."

"I promise you, sir," the constable vowed, "we'll have Kinloch in the Bow Street strong room within the hour, and we'll obtain the names of everyone involved in this wretched business."

"Thank you."

"Are you hurt?" Poppy asked anxiously, lifting her head from Harry's chest. "Are you well enough to go to Bow Street? Because if not—"

"I'm fine, love," he murmured, smoothing a stray wisp of hair back from her face. "Just thirsty . . . and I wouldn't mind having some dinner when we return to the hotel."

"I was afraid for you," Poppy said, and her voice
broke.

Harry pulled her close with a comforting murmur, tucking her body into his, clasping her head
against his shoulder.

In tacit agreement, the other men drew away to
allow them a moment of privacy.

There was much to be said between them—too
much—so Harry simply held her against him. There
would be time later to disclose what was in their
hearts.

A lifetime, if he had his way.

Harry lowered his mouth to Poppy's flushed ear.
"The princess rescues the villain," he whispered.
"It's a nice variation on the story."

After what seemed an interminable time at Bow
Street, Harry was finally allowed to return to the
Rutledge. As he and Poppy left the police office,
they were told that Edward Kinloch and two of his
servants were already being held in the strong room,
with Runners in pursuit of another, yet unnamed
suspect. And every last one of the charlatans trying
to claim Harry's identity had been banished from
the building.

"If there's one thing that today has made clear,"
Special Constable Hembrey quipped, "it's that the
world needs only one Harry Rutledge."

The hotel employees were overjoyed at Harry's
return, crowding around him before he could go
upstairs to his apartments. They displayed a level of
affectionate familiarity that they once wouldn't have
dared, shaking Harry's hand, patting his back and
shoulders, exclaiming their relief over his safe return.

Harry seemed a bit bemused by the demonstrations, but he tolerated it all quite willingly. It was Poppy who finally put a stop to the happy uproar, saying firmly, "Mr. Rutledge needs food and rest."

"I'll have a tray sent up at once," Mrs. Pennywhistle declared, dispersing the employees efficiently.

The Rutledges went to their private apartments, where Harry took a shower bath, shaved, and donned a dressing robe. He wolfed down a meal without even seeming to taste it, drained a glass of wine, and sat back in his chair looking exhausted but content.

"Bloody hell," he said, "I love being home."

Poppy went to sit on his lap, curling her arms around his neck. "Is that how you think of the hotel now?"

"Not the hotel. Just wherever you are." He kissed her, his lips gentle at first, but heat rose swiftly between them. He became more demanding, almost savaging her mouth, and she responded with an ardent sweetness that set fire to his blood. His head lifted, his breathing uncontrolled, and his arms cradled her tightly against him. Beneath her hips, she felt the insistent pressure of his arousal.

"Harry," she said breathlessly, "you need sleep far more than this."

"I never need sleep more than this." He kissed her head, nuzzling into the glowing locks of her hair. His voice softened, deepened. "I thought I'd go mad if I had to spend another minute in that blasted room. I was worried about you. I sat there thinking that all I want in life is to spend as much time with you as possible. And then it occurred to me that you had visited this hotel for three seasons in a row— *three*—and I'd never met you. All that time I wasted, when we could have been together."

"But Harry . . . even if we had met and married three years ago, you'd still say it wasn't enough time."

"You're right. I can't think of a single day of my life that wouldn't have been improved with you in it."

"Darling," she whispered, her fingertips coming up to stroke his jaw, "that's lovely. Even more romantic than comparing me to watch parts."

Harry nipped at her finger. "Are you mocking me?"

"Not at all," Poppy said, smiling. "I know how you feel about gears and mechanisms."

Lifting her easily, Harry brought her into the bedroom. "And you know what I like to do with them," he said softly. "Take them apart . . . and put them back together again. Shall I show you, love?"

"Yes . . . yes . . ."

And they put off sleep just a little longer.

Because people in love know that time should never be wasted.

Epilogue

THREE DAYS LATER

"I'm late," Poppy said thoughtfully, tying the sash of her white dressing gown as she approached the breakfast table.

Harry stood and held a chair for her, stealing a kiss when she was seated. "I wasn't aware you had an appointment this morning. There's nothing on the schedule."

"No, not that kind of late. The other kind of late." Seeing his incomprehension, Poppy smiled. "I'm referring to a certain monthly occurrence . . ."

"Oh." Harry stared at her fixedly, his expression unfathomable.

Poppy poured her tea and dropped a lump of sugar in it. "It's only two or three days past the usual time," she said, her voice deliberately casual, "but I've never been late before." She lightened her tea with milk and sipped it cautiously. Glancing at her husband over the rim of the china cup, she tried to gauge his reaction to the information.

Harry swallowed and blinked, and stared at her.

His color had heightened, making his eyes look unusually green. "Poppy . . ." He was forced to stop by
the necessity of taking an extra breath. "Do you
think you could be expecting?"

She smiled, her excitement tempered with a flutter of nervousness. "Yes, I think it's possible. We
won't know for certain until a bit more time has
passed." Her smile turned uncertain as Harry remained silent. Perhaps it was too soon . . . perhaps
he wasn't entirely receptive to the idea. "Of course,"
she said, trying to sound prosaic, "it may take some
time for you to become accustomed to the idea, and
that's only natural—"

"I don't need time."

"You don't?" Poppy gasped as she was snatched
off the chair and hauled into his lap. His arms went
fast around her. "You want a baby, then?" she asked.
"You wouldn't mind?"

"Mind?" Harry pressed his face against her chest,
feverishly kissing her exposed skin, her shoulder, her
throat. "Poppy, there are no words to describe how
much I want it." His head lifted, the depth of emotion
in his eyes making her breath catch. "For most of my
life, I thought I'd always be alone. And now to have
you . . . and a baby . . ."

"It's not entirely certain yet," Poppy said, smiling
as he scattered kisses over her face.

"I'll make certain, then." Still holding her, Harry
stood from the chair and began to carry her back
into the bedroom.

"What about the morning schedule?" she protested.

And Harry Rutledge uttered three words he had
never said in his life. "Damn the schedule."

At that moment the door reverberated with a brisk

knock. "Mr. Rutledge?" came Jake Valentine's voice. "I have the managers' reports—"

"Later, Valentine," Harry replied, not pausing as he took Poppy to the bedroom. "I'm occupied."

The assistant's voice was muffled by the door. "Yes, sir."

Crimson from head to toe, Poppy said, "Harry, *really!* Do you know what he must be thinking at this moment?"

Lowering her to the bed, he tugged her dressing robe open. "No, tell me."

Poppy squirmed in protest, a helpless giggle escaping her as he began to kiss his way down her body. "You are the most *wicked* man . . ."

"Yes," Harry murmured in satisfaction.

They both knew she wouldn't have him any other way.

LATER THAT DAY . . .

Leo's unexpected return to Hampshire had set Ramsay House into happy turmoil, maids hurrying to ready his usual room, a footman setting another place at the table. The family welcomed him warmly. Merripen poured glasses of excellent wine as they gathered in the parlor for a few minutes of conversation before dinner was served.

"What about the commission for the conservatory?" Amelia asked. "Did you change your mind?"

Leo shook his head. "The project is so small, I sketched something on the spot. They seemed pleased with it. I'll work out the details here, and send the final plans back to London. But never mind that. I have some news I think you'll find of interest . . ." He proceeded to regale the family with the story of Harry's abduction and rescue, and Edward Kinloch's subsequent arrest. They reacted with expressions of amazement and concern, and praised Leo for his part in the affair.

"How is Poppy?" Amelia asked. "So far this has certainly not been the calm, serene life she was hoping for."

"Happier than I've ever seen her," Leo replied. "I think Poppy has reconciled herself to the idea that one can't avoid the storms and calamities of life, but one can at least find the right partner to face them with."

Cam smiled at that, holding his dark-haired son against his chest. "Well said, *phral*."

Leo stood and set aside his wineglass. "I'll go wash before the meal is served." Glancing around the room, he affected an expression of mild surprise. "I don't see Marks. I hope she'll come down to supper—I have need of a good argument."

"The last time I saw her," Beatrix replied, "she was looking all around the house for her garters. Dodger stole every last one of them out of her dresser."

"Bea," Win murmured, "it's better not to mention the word 'garters' in mixed company."

"All right. But I don't understand why. Everyone knows we wear them—why do we have to pretend it's a secret?"

As Win tried to explain tactfully, Leo grinned and went upstairs. Instead of heading to his own room, however, he went to the end of the hallway, turned to the right, and tapped on the door. Without waiting for an answer, he pushed his way in.

Catherine Marks whirled to face him, gasping. "How dare you come into my room without . . ." her voice faded as Leo closed the door and approached her. Dampening her lips with the tip of her tongue, she backed away until she had come up against the edge of a small dressing table. Her hair fell in pale silk streamers over her shoulders, her eyes darkening to the blue gray of a turbulent ocean. As she stared at him, a flush rose in her cheeks.

"Why did you come back?" she asked weakly.

"You know why." Slowly Leo braced his hands on the table, on either side of her. She shrank backward until no further movement was possible. The scent of her skin, mingled with bath soap and fresh garden blossoms, rose to his nostrils. The memory of sensation hovered around them, between them. As Leo saw the shiver that went through her, he felt a rush of unwanted heat, his blood turning to liquid fire.

Struggling for self-discipline, Leo took a deep, steadying breath.

"Cat . . . we have to talk about what happened."